Kingston's Project

Carrie Beckort

For Jason and Julia -
you are my life, my light

CHAPTER 1

Two years. It seemed like enough time to overcome a tragic incident that changed one's life forever. If not overcome, then at least enough time to feel like you could start moving on again. Everyone was telling her she needed to move on.

"Sarah, sweetheart, you can't just sit in that house all day surrounded by memories and expect to be able to move on. You need a change of environment. Come home."

"I'll think about it."

"You said that six months ago." The growing frustration was evident in her mom's voice.

"It's a big move, and it's not like I can up and leave my job. I have a lot of responsibility, and I owe it to Andy to complete my projects. It will take him time to find someone to replace me."

"I thought Andy was your friend as well as your boss."

"He is, but what does that have to do with my leaving?"

"If he's your friend, then he'll be understanding and help you make the transition."

"Of course he'd help, but that doesn't change the fact that he has commitments to our clients—projects have to be done." There was a long pause on the other end of the line.

"You told me Andy has been working with you for awhile to pass your accounts to the other project managers at the firm."

Sarah had forgotten she told her mom about the transition of her work over the past three months. The gentle reminder meant her excuses weren't working.

"Well, it still takes time. Besides, there's the house to consider—it's not a good time to sell."

"Just leave it, or rent it. You can always put it up for sale later when the market turns up." Despite the nagging, she smiled fondly at her mom's insistence.

"You're right. I'll give it some consideration."

"Not that I don't trust you, but I'll come down there and get you myself in three months if you haven't made any inclination toward making a change on your own. I mean it." Her mom was certainly stubborn enough to follow through on her threat.

Sarah redirected her to more preferable topics, and twenty minutes later they said good-bye with a promise to talk the following week. She had always felt close with her mom, but they were never the type to spend hours on the phone. In the past her mom had called once or twice a month, and they spent an hour catching up. During Sarah's most difficult days the calls came daily, but then the routine settled into once or twice a week.

Sarah had become somewhat dependent on the frequent calls from home. She didn't have many people to talk to any more. Most of her friends had been the female half of 'coupled friends' she and Nick had made over the years. Now that Nick was gone, it was too awkward for her to participate in the gatherings on her own. However, she did have Maggie who had been her best friend for ten years. Maggie had her own family to keep her busy, but their twice-a-month Saturday brunch was cherished time they both made a priority.

Sarah thought about her mom's insistence at making a change. She knew her mom was right—it was painful to remain. And the reminders she encountered weren't contained by the walls of the house. Everywhere she went people were still asking her how she was doing. She wasn't so much bothered by the question itself—she knew it was asked with good intention. What irritated her most was the way people asked. It was always addressed to 'honey' and was accompanied by a shake of the head and a pat on the arm. And then there was the look from everyone not bold enough to ask. The look that said, 'you poor thing, thank God it wasn't my family.' She hated those looks more than she hated the honey-shake-pat routine.

Her thoughts were interrupted when she heard a sound in the direction of the family room, and she was overcome with an inability to move. She watched and waited for Nick to come in carrying Danny as they prepared for dinner. She knew they wouldn't come. The sound had just been the house settling. But still she waited for them to emerge and tell her it had all been a very bad dream. The tears fell as she acknowledged her new reality was not a dream at all. She wiped away the tears and looked at the clock. It was time for her evening run. Dinner time was still a part of the day she avoided. Family dinner was the one thing she and Nick had decided was going to be a firm tradition in their home. They both grew up with busy working parents and siblings always running to and from some sort of event. Despite all the activity, in both households family dinner was mandatory almost every night. At times, this resulted in very early or late meals, but it was worth it for the moments spent sharing with the family. The one exception Sarah and Nick granted was the weekly Wednesday Boys' Night—not only was she excused from those dinners but she was encouraged not to attend.

Now, sitting down to dinner was too painful a reminder that she would never again share those moments with Nick and Danny. As a surrogate she started running, discovering that the pain in her lungs and legs was a successful block for the pain in her heart. It was a welcome block, even if it was only temporary.

She grabbed a quick snack and headed to her bedroom to change. Moments later she was out the door, lost in the rhythm of her music and running.

Fresh from her run, a shower, and a quick frozen meal, Sarah sat down in her favorite chair and clicked on the TV. After a half-hearted search through the guide, she turned it off. She picked up her book to start reading, but the house was too quiet for her to concentrate on the words. There was a time when Sarah and Nick had cherished the quiet moments of the evening after Danny was in bed. Sometimes they talked all night, and other times they sat in the quiet of the family room enjoying a glass of wine and the companionable silence. It was like a warm blanket that cocooned them together each night and refreshed them for the next day.

Now the silence of the evening was a strong reminder of her painful loss. She closed her eyes and tried to hear the evening sounds she missed so much—Danny's soft breathing through the baby monitor, the tapping of fingers on keys as Nick worked on his computer next to her, Nick's laughter over something funny on TV. She sat for a long time, trying to hear the sounds she missed so much. Finally, she opened her eyes and picked up the family photo from the table next to her. She traced her finger first around Danny and then Nick. At only two, it was already clear that Danny would have been a carbon copy of Nick. They both had smooth blonde hair and light blue eyes.

She and Nick had been so excited when Danny joined their family. After years of putting off having children to focus on careers, they were nervous about what their life would be like with a child. Danny had expanded the joy and love in their life in a way they could never have imagined. He was an easy child with a loving personality.

She felt the familiar tightening in her chest and set the photo back down.

Maybe Mom is right. I need a change of environment.

Deciding to go to bed early, she turned out the lights and headed up the stairs.

The first door she approached was Danny's. The door remained closed. She could only allow herself to go in on his birthday and certain holidays—Halloween and Christmas. On those days she would spend most of the day curled up on his toddler bed or on the floor hugging Max, his favorite stuffed dog. The first few weeks after Danny was gone she spent her days and nights in his room, unable to leave except to go to the bathroom. She barely ate and cried more than she thought humanly possible. Being in the room was not a comfort to her, quite the opposite in fact. But she couldn't find the strength to leave.

After a month of living in a catatonic state in Danny's room, Sarah's mom took drastic action before she lost her daughter forever—she dragged Sarah out of the room. Literally. She deposited Sarah in the guest bedroom and planted herself in front of the door to keep her from leaving. It was the first time in her adult life Sarah had hit her mom. Sarah had tried desperately to remove her mom from the doorway, but the lack of proper nutrition for a month made her no match for her mom's strength and determination. Sarah stopped fighting at the sound of a knock and her mom's sudden movement.

Sarah tore out of the room, barely registering her dad, and went frantically down the hall toward Danny's room only to discover it was locked. It was as if everything around her was suddenly sucked away—walls, sound, light, air. Nothing existed except her and Danny's locked door.

"What did you do?" Her voice was so soft she barely heard herself. "Your father added a dead-bolt. You're not going back in that room, Sarah. We love you too much." At the sound of her mom's voice the space around her came back into focus.

She resigned to the fact that she wouldn't be getting back into Danny's room until her mom allowed her to do so. She sank to the floor and rested her tear-stained cheek against the door. She wrapped her arms tightly around her legs, staying there until her dad picked her up sometime later to deposit her on the guest bed. When she awoke twelve hours later, she discovered that without the suffocating sights and smells of Danny's room surrounding her, she was able to exist for longer periods of time away from the door. Eventually, she came to peace with stopping at the closed door on her way to bed—except for the three times a year she allowed herself to go in the room.

Now, she stopped at the closed door and leaned her forehead against the cool wood. She closed her eyes and started with the same lullaby as she did every night. "You are my sunshine, my only sunshine. You make me happy, when skies are gray. You'll never know dear, how much I love you. Please don't take my sunshine away." The last verse came out as a whisper and sounded more like a desperate plea. Then she talked to Danny. Some of it was the same as every other night, like how much she missed him and how proud she was to be his mommy. The rest was made up from whatever was in her heart at the moment. Finally, she told him good night and peeled herself away from the door.

The next door was the bedroom she'd shared with Nick. It too remained closed. Unlike Danny's room, she was never able to go back into her old bedroom. Her mom had moved Sarah's things into the upstairs guest bedroom and that's where she'd remained. In those first few weeks it was as if she didn't know how to grieve for both Danny and Nick at the same time. She poured all her soul into mourning Danny—Nick was added into that mix rather than given his separate moments. When she did allow herself to feel the loss of

Nick, her grief took the form of her wishing he was there to help her through the loss of their only child. She wanted him there holding her, assuring her it would be all right. She needed him to put the pieces of her life back together.

The pain she felt for missed moments—past, current, and future—centered on Danny. Remembering his first steps, his first words, his laughter. Knowing she would never know what sport he would have played, never see his first day of school, never cry at his wedding. In those soul shattering images she could feel the emptiness where Nick should have been at her side, but the pain was all for Danny. She held such strong guilt for not grieving Nick properly, and as each day passed she didn't know how to close the gap. Nick was always the one to help her let go of the guilt.

She paused and leaned her forehead against the door. Her words were the same as every other night. "I miss you. I love you. I'm so sorry."

CHAPTER 2

I slow the car in keeping with the traffic around me. I'm frustrated because I want to join my boys at the restaurant, but I'm stuck in traffic. I hear sirens, and as an ambulance speeds past I'm gripped by fear. I'm moving again, and I see the accident. At first I don't see anything but a truck I don't recognize. Then I see him—Max. He's on the ground near another badly mangled car. I recognize it as Nick's car. I'm floating toward Max. I scream for Nick and Danny. I search for them, but all I see is broken glass and metal scattered on the ground. Someone grabs me and turns me away before I can see them. I scream again.

Sarah sat up with a start. She looked around at her surroundings and realized it was a nightmare. Then she remembered it wasn't just a nightmare—it was her reality. She'd tried for two years to forget everything she saw that night. To erase the images of the accident that shattered all her happiness. She had finally succeeded in keeping them from popping up during the day, but at night she was unprotected.

She took a deep breath and went to the bathroom to start her morning routine. After a quick shower, she stood in front of the mirror and took extra care applying her make-up to cover the dark circles under her eyes. Twenty minutes later, she passed through the kitchen and grabbed a granola bar on her way out the door.

Her SUV stood tragically alone in the now too large three car garage. She had taken to parking in the middle of the two-car bay hoping it would lessen the impact, but the emptiness still hit her every morning. Shaking off the pain, she climbed in and drove to work.

She entered the lobby of her office and heard the firm's receptionist, Annie, pick up the phone. "Jacobs Management Firm, can you hold please?" She was waving Sarah over throughout her auto-pilot greeting. "Good morning, Sarah. Andy wants to see you in his office first thing."

"Did he say what it was about?" A call to Andy's office before she even reached her desk was something she'd learned to approach with caution.

"Nope, just that he wanted to see you first thing. Good luck." She playfully sang the last statement with a wink and a smile.

Sarah returned her smile and headed to her desk. She figured she could at least drop off her bags and grab coffee before seeing Andy. She turned to leave the kitchenette, but the entrance was engulfed by the large form of Janet, an analyst at the firm.

"Oh, Sarah. How ya' doin', honey? You look tired." Sarah stared at the hand planted on her upper arm.

A squeeze instead of a pat this time. That's different.

"I'm fine, Janet. No more tired than usual. If you'll excuse me, I need to meet with Andy."

"Sure thing, sweetie. You really should get more rest—" Sarah left the kitchenette before Janet could finish her sentence and slowly climbed the stairs to Andy's office.

"Andy Jacobs' office." Andy's assistant answered an incoming call as Sarah approached, but she waved her in.

"Sarah. Have a seat." She sat in the open chair across from Andy, setting her coffee on his desk.

"Good morning, Andy. Everything okay?" She was always one to choose the path of directness rather than prolong any awkward and unnecessary conversation.

Luckily, Andy also preferred to get right to the point. "Elijah Kingston was here earlier this week. He's looking for someone to manage a special project starting immediately. The position would be based out of their home office in Denver, and he requested to talk to you."

She couldn't hide the astonishment from her face. "Did he specifically request to speak to me or did you suggest me to him?"

"Does it matter?"

"It does to me or I wouldn't have asked."

He hesitated, no doubt deciding if he should tell her the truth. "A bit of both actually. Mr. Kingston asked how you were getting along these days, and I told him I thought you needed a change. That's when he told me he had this assignment and requested to meet with you."

"What's the project? How long will it last?"

"He didn't say, only that it was personal and needed to start immediately."

"When does he want to meet?"

"He has you booked on a flight Sunday night."

"*This* Sunday? He's already booked me a flight? What if I'm not interested? What if I have plans? It's a bit arrogant of him to assume I'll drop everything and fly across the country just because he requested it." She could feel her face getting flushed from her sudden anger at having her life dictated by a man she didn't know, especially one who in the past had given every indication he didn't like her.

"Sarah, relax. First of all, you know as well as I do that you do *not* have plans this weekend. Don't look at me like that. I'm not trying to upset you, but it doesn't do either of us any good to pretend you have a life outside of work. Second, you don't have to go if you don't want to. But if you want my advice, as your *friend*, I think you should at least go and check it out. Worst case you get a free vacation."

"I'm not sure I see the point in going. You told me yourself he had previously asked that I not be assigned to his account. And besides, I'm not sure I want to work with him." She crossed her arms over her chest and realized she looked and sounded like a spoiled child.

He let out a frustrated sigh as he sat back in his chair. After a short pause he continued in a softer tone. "Sarah, you know I only want what's best for you. You've been talking about making a change, and I think it's a good idea. The fundraising event you had been managing was last weekend, and your other accounts have been reassigned. I don't have anything new in the queue, so what are you going to do if you don't go? You said you don't want to go back to your parents' house, so what are your other options? Please, think about it."

"Alright, fine. I'll think about it." She grabbed her coffee and stood to leave.

"Here, take this. If you decide to go, you'll need it." She took the travel packet from his hand and left his office without another word.

Later that evening, after a run and a quick bite to eat, Sarah sat down at her computer. She pulled up her search engine and typed in Kingston Enterprises. Even though they were a client, her knowledge was limited since she had never been assigned to the account. It was a successful private family business, established over sixty years ago, and was led by Elijah Kingston. His daughter, Leanne Troupe, became a full partner in the company five years ago. They worked with small franchise companies by developing and executing their expansion strategies. A few years ago, they started to use regional firms such as Jacobs for the management of project timelines and deliverables, thus allowing them to focus on the more specialized aspects of their clients' start-up needs. The franchises they represented had a high rate of success in not only sustaining their business but also in growing their business over time.

Satisfied with her knowledge of the business side of Kingston Enterprises, she switched her search to Elijah. To her disappointment, she found little information. What she could find told her he was sixty-five years old and had two children, Marcus and Leanne. She was able to find articles on Leanne, but all were related to her role in the company. There was no information on Marcus other than the couple of articles that mentioned the whole Kingston family. She discovered Elijah's wife, Marlena, died suddenly about twenty years ago. She also found a link to a dance foundation started by Marlena that was still heavily supported by the Kingston family. That was the extent of the information she could find.

She closed her computer in frustration and stared at her travel packet. She decided to make a list of reasons both for and against going to Denver. She started with all the reasons she should go.

1. She had always wanted to go to Denver
2. She had no current projects to manage
3. Kingston projects were always demanding—good distraction
4. It would make her mom happy
5. It would make Andy happy
6. No one there would give her 'the look'
7. She needed a change

She was surprised she'd been able to come up with seven reasons. Sitting in Andy's office earlier, she couldn't even think of one.

She focused on the list of reasons she shouldn't go.

1. Mr. Kingston would most certainly be difficult to work with
2. She was scared

It took her over fifteen minutes to come up with the second list. Logic told her she would be on a flight to Denver in less than forty-eight hours, but her heart told her she would need to talk to Maggie first—they were meeting for brunch the next day. Lost in frustration she went to bed, stopping at each closed door before reaching her room.

It was a beautiful fall day, so Sarah requested a table on the patio. She was five minutes early which meant she had about twenty minutes until Maggie showed up in a hurried rush of apologies and explanations. Maggie was intensely different from Sarah in many ways and she was often amazed at how they were able to maintain such a strong bond over the years. Sarah was extremely organized and focused in everything from the mundane tasks of her personal life to the complex timelines she managed at work. The level of organization she possessed would cause one to assume she would become frustrated with Maggie's inescapable tardiness and haphazard approach to life.

Sarah's thoughts were interrupted by a sudden embrace from behind. "Sarah, honey. How ya' doin'?"

"You know, the 'honey' usually comes at the end of the question. And thank God no one but you or my mom gives me a hug when asking." Sarah couldn't keep the smile out of her reaction to her friend's jest.

Maggie sat down with an exaggerated flourish. "I'm so sorry I'm late. Every time I tell myself I'm going to be early or at least on time. Instead I think I just end up being later than usual." Even in her rushed state, Maggie looked as beautiful as ever. Her long, straight blond hair was pulled back in a high ponytail setting off her strong cheek bones. Her eyes were an undiscerning color of brown, which played to her advantage. She could practically stare into your soul without you even knowing she was looking at you. She wasn't very tall, only about five feet three inches, but she carried such confidence she was perceived to be much taller. Her weight was perfectly proportioned to her body—no doubt a credit to her endless chasing of two small children. The overall package resulted in a woman everyone was drawn to, like butterflies to a flower.

"Actually, it is only twelve minutes after eleven. By your standards, you're three minutes early."

"Very funny." Maggie set her utterly oversized handbag on the chair next to her. When she finally looked at Sarah, her tone sobered. "Joking aside, is everything okay? You look more distraught than usual."

"My 'usual' is distraught? How flattering." Sarah's cheeky grin faded when she realized there was no distracting Maggie from the subject. She was given a couple minutes to collect her thoughts as the waitress showed up to take their order.

"My mom is pushing me to move back home. She thinks I need a change of environment."

"You do need a change of environment. However, I'm not sure your parents' house is the right answer. What else are you considering?"

Sarah stared at the napkin she was torturing and took a deep breath. "Andy called me into his office yesterday morning to tell me Mr. Kingston—you know, our top client who's also extremely high maintenance—well, it appears Mr. Kingston has requested me for a personal project he's starting out in Denver. He's already booked me on a flight for tomorrow night."

"He booked you on a flight before you confirmed your interest? I'm sure you took that well." The arch in Maggie's brow as she replied suggested she was being both sarcastic and serious at the same time.

"No, I didn't take it well at all. In fact, I'm quite certain I looked like a spoiled teenager who had gotten her car keys taken away for no good reason."

"It's a good thing Andy is so patient with you."

"It's a wonder Andy never tells you any of this at home." Maggie and Andy had been happily married for fifteen years. Sarah was introduced to Maggie at her first office Christmas party and there was an instant connection. At first Andy was reluctant at the idea of them becoming such close friends, fearing there would be a conflict of interest. Andy put out some ground rules, and as a result there had never been any issues.

"An agreement of any kind is sacred to Andy. Even though our marriage license implies he should confide in me on everything, the deal we all struck ten years ago is considered the most current addendum. Don't ask, don't tell." Maggie paused to take a drink. "However, he did tell me that he had a proposal you would probably want to discuss. It's one of the reasons I'm late. Jaime woke up with a fever this morning and wanted me to stay home with her. Andy was so insistent I not cancel with you I knew something was up, so he had to divulge some sort of information to get me here."

"What did he have to promise Jaime to get her to let you go?" Their adorable nine year old was much more like Andy than Maggie, so Sarah knew there had to be some sort of payment rendered.

"He agreed to a movie marathon. And he actually has to watch and discuss—not just sit with her and work on the computer while she watches the movies."

"Wow. He must really want me to go to Denver tomorrow." Sarah looked at her friend in mock horror.

"Knowing my husband the way I do... yes, I would guess he probably does." The concerned look in Maggie's eyes was almost more than she could handle. "So, give me your list of reasons why you should or shouldn't go. I know you made one already."

Sarah ticked off her fingers as she recited her list of reasons she should go.

"That seems like a good list. What is on your list for why you shouldn't go?"

"The most obvious reason is I'm not sure I want to work for Mr. Kingston. He's so arrogant, and I have a feeling I would want to throttle him more than once during the course of the assignment."

"True, but you've been able to manage difficult clients before. Why should he be any different?" Maggie gave her an impatient look.

"Because it *is* different. It's personal this time. Up until now the Mighty Mr. Kingston made a special point to *not* have me on his account. Now, all of a sudden, he does an about-face and specifically asks for me to lead not just any project but a personal one. I mean, what the hell is that about?" Sarah's voice became involuntarily more animated as she spoke.

"I don't know, and you will never know if you don't go and ask him. Did you list any other reasons why you shouldn't go?"

"Just one." Sarah had to pause to check the tears that threatened to flow without control. When she finally felt like she could continue, it was barely more than a whisper. "I'm scared."

Maggie gave her a compassionate look. "It's okay to be scared. At least scared is an emotion other than pain. Emotions are what remind us we're still alive. That's your goal in all of this, isn't it? To feel alive? It's okay to live your life again. You know it's what Nick would have wanted."

"I know." Sarah absently stared again at her hands working over her napkin.

Maggie sat forward in her chair with new found determination. "Here's what you're going to do. You're going to Denver tomorrow with the intention of accepting, regardless of the circumstances. You should still get your answers, but decide now you will accept."

The confidence Maggie threw at her was infectious and for the first time she felt a twinge of excitement at the idea of going to Denver. "Okay, I'll go. I can't believe it, but I'm actually going to go. Oh—" Sarah realized there was a big obstacle to their plan. "What will I do about my house? My understanding is I would need to stay and start right away. I don't know how long it will last, and I don't like the idea of the house sitting empty for an extended period of time."

Maggie looked at her with a twinkle in her eyes. "I think Andy and I can help you with that one. Do you remember us ever mentioning Andy's college roommate, Travis? Well, anyway, he's moving to town in a couple weeks to work at the firm. He recently got a divorce and is also looking for a fresh start, so Andy's helping him out. He would probably be willing to rent your place while you're gone."

Sarah cringed. "I don't know, Maggie. I'm not sure I like the idea of someone I don't know living in my house."

"I get that, and I would agree if it was a complete stranger. But he's a good friend of Andy's, and he's a really great guy. You can let him know the upstairs rooms are off limits if that makes you feel better."

"It would. Well, I guess there's nothing holding me back then." The waitress appeared at their table with their food.

She smiled at Maggie and then Sarah. "Can I get you ladies anything else?"

"Um, can I get a new napkin?"

What the hell did I do to this one?

Between the three of them, Maggie was the only one who understood the fate of Sarah's napkin.

Sarah parked in the garage and met Maggie in the driveway. "How's Jaime feeling?"

"About the same. She still has a low fever and her throat is sore. But the movie marathon is a big hit. They're almost through the second movie, and I'm pretty sure she still has about four more to go. I won't be missed for hours."

"Thanks for helping me do this." She linked her arm through Maggie's and stared at the house. She and Nick had bought it five years ago after deciding they were ready to start thinking about a family. After searching for nearly a year, they finally came across the house of their dreams. It was a four bedroom new construction home that had two stories and a walk-out basement. The most perfect aspect was the back yard—a half acre that led down to a lake. At first she had reservations about having a house on a lake with small children, but Nick had assured her it would be fine. He had completely baby-proofed the house and yard, and they had enrolled Danny in swim lessons as soon as he was old enough to start.

"Ready?" Maggie gave her arm a gentle tug and they entered the house, setting their purses down in the kitchen. "I'll clear the fridge of any food that can go bad. You go do what you need to do, and I'll check on you if I don't see you for awhile." Sarah nodded and walked out of the kitchen only to stop in the living room to look around. She was suddenly overcome with anxiety.

This is crazy. I can't up and leave tomorrow not knowing when I'll be back. What about my mail? What if I forget something or leave something on? It's not enough time. I'm not ready.

She was about to turn and say she'd changed her mind when she felt Maggie's hands on her shoulders.

"It's going to be all right. Trust me." Sarah leaned back on Maggie allowing her words to calm her. "If you forget anything, I'll be here to make it right. And if Travis rents this place I'm sure he'd be more than willing to send you anything you need or take care of anything that needs to be done. He's a great guy, and it will all be okay. Besides, even though you may not know when you'll be back, you *will* be back. It's not forever, unless you want it to be."

Sarah nodded in agreement but was still unable to speak. She slowly climbed the stairs, and once she reached Danny's door she stood there for an indeterminate amount of time with one hand on the handle.

I can do this.

She turned the handle and looked at the room she and Nick had created for Danny. They'd hired an artist to paint a larger than life setting that included trains on the upper half of the walls. The bottoms were covered in a variety of surfaces allowing Danny to become his own artist through chalk, paint, crayons, magnets or stickers. His toddler bed was made to resemble a train's open box car. Stuffed animals and toys were neatly stored in pint-sized toy cabinets flanking the bay window at the back of the room. The window area itself became a secret hideaway by drawing the curtains closed.

She walked in and sat down on the floor, leaning against his bed, and automatically grabbed Max. As she looked around the room, she realized accepting the project meant she wouldn't be there for Halloween and possibly not for Christmas either. The realization caused sobs to come in a choking force, and she curled up into a ball on the floor. When her sobs finally diminished to quiet tears she rolled onto her back, still clutching Max. She started to speak what was in her heart, her voice sounding strange and far away.

"I'm leaving tomorrow. I don't know when I'll be back and won't be able to visit for awhile. I'm going to Denver, Colorado. Daddy and I wanted to take you there for a family vacation. They have lots of really big mountains with snow on top. I wish you and Daddy could go with me." She closed her eyes and let her mind wander through her memories.

"Everything all right in here?" Maggie's voice brought her back to the present.

"What time is it?"

"Four o'clock. Do you need more time?"

Sarah remained silent for a moment. "Should I take Max?"

She watched as Maggie hesitated before sitting down in the doorway. Over the years, she had not wanted anyone else in the room—not even Maggie or her mom.

"Are you asking because you think you need to take a piece of Danny with you to be happy or because you think by taking Max you won't feel guilty for leaving Danny behind?"

"Have I ever told you that you would make a good shrink?"

"Yes, but it's much more fun to pretend I know what I am talking about. Speaking of shrinks, when was the last time you saw yours?"

Sarah had been to every therapist in town, but she wasn't able to click with any of them. "About six months ago. She was as useless as the rest of them. I'd much rather not pay you and get better advice."

"I'm flattered. Now, stop avoiding the question."

"I can't help but feel like I will be leaving him behind. I'm afraid I'll start to forget without all the reminders around me."

Maggie studied Sarah. "You will feel like you're forgetting. I think the pain helps keep memories more acute. But just because memories fade and seem less vibrant doesn't mean you'll forget what's important. When you hold Max, does it bring you happy memories of Danny or does it cause you pain at the reminder that he will never again walk into a room dragging it behind him? Answer that truthfully and you'll know what to do."

With what felt like great difficulty, Sarah lifted herself off the floor. She looked down at Max and closed her eyes and truly reflected on what she was feeling. On her way out of the room, she hesitantly placed Max back on Danny's bed. She paused for one more look about the room and then closed the door. She turned to Maggie and accepted the hug that was waiting for her.

"Do you want to go into your old bedroom?"

"No, I'm still not ready. I guess once I do go in there you'll know I have finally been able to let go." She felt a migraine forming so she told Maggie good night and climbed into bed.

Sarah settled into the comfort of first class and reflected back on the whirlwind day. When she'd first woke up that morning, she had felt a surge of panic when she thought about all she still had to do before leaving. She had quickly dressed and went downstairs where she was surprised to find Maggie had not only stayed, but she had worked late into the night to get Sarah ready for her trip. Based on Maggie's usual chaotic approach to life, she was quite surprised at the level of organization used to manage the process. The only tasks she had left were confirming the logistics of her trip and packing her clothes.

She looked over the travel packet Andy handed her on Friday. She was more pleased than annoyed to find a personal driver and hotel had been booked along with her flight. Looking closer at the information, she found that none of the reservations had return dates. That little detail reminded her she had no idea when she would be returning home. She was still apprehensive, but Maggie had been right. Deciding to accept before she left had allowed her to relax and think of all the questions she needed to ask.

She placed the travel packet in her carry-on and pulled out the file she'd made from her research and project overviews from the Kingston account. Once she felt confident she was prepared for her meeting with Elijah, she closed her eyes until she heard the captain announce their descent into Denver. Her heart rate quickened, feeling her life was about to change forever. She hoped it was for the better. She hoped she was ready.

CHAPTER 3

It was late on Monday morning when Sarah pulled herself out of a deep sleep, feeling surprisingly refreshed. The rush of everything over the last couple of days, topped off by a long flight, was enough to deplete her of any energy she may have been holding on to. As a result, she had slept better than she had in a very long time. She still had plenty of time before her meeting, so she decided to go for a walk around the hotel. She changed, grabbed an apple from the hotel's breakfast bar, and walked outside. As soon as she exited the hotel, she was struck by all that was around her.

When she first stepped outside she couldn't do much of anything except sit on a bench and take in the magnitude of the landscape. She was overcome at the sight of the ground reaching for the sky in the rugged peaks of the mountains. It was so dark the night before she couldn't see the mountains at all. She knew they were there of course, but had expected them to be more of a vision on the distant horizon. These mountains were up close, demanding her attention. The power of the terrain made her feel so small, yet somehow stronger—as if the mountains themselves were transmitting energy.

The backdrop of the crystal blue sky made the view of the mountains even more striking. The sky reminded her of an ocean she would expect to find near some tropical paradise, and its brightness made everything around her pop with life. The trees were greener, the flowers were brilliant shades of the rainbow, and the occasional cloud was like a giant-sized cotton ball. She almost felt like she was Dorothy in a real life version of Oz—going to sleep in black and white and waking up to amazing color she'd never before experienced.

The sharp ring of her phone forced her attention away from her surroundings. Maggie. "Checking up on me already?"

"Yep, just making sure you're in Denver. I may require you to send me proof."

"I'll send you a picture of this amazing place. I'm actually about an hour northwest of Denver, which I don't yet understand since the company's home office is in the city. Regardless, it's breathtaking. I'm outside right now enjoying my new environment."

Sarah heard Maggie's muffled voice directed at one of her children. "Sorry. When's your meeting with Kingston?"

"Not for a couple hours. Don't worry, I still plan to go and accept as we discussed."

"Good. I'll be looking for a complete report tonight or at the latest tomorrow morning." Sarah heard a loud banging sound coming through the phone. "Crap! Gotta go. I mean it—full report. Bye." Sarah was left with silence.

She snapped a picture and sent it off to Maggie with a quick text.

Not sure what the banging was, but I bet you wish you were here with me looking at this.

She got up from the bench and set off for a short walk before heading back to her room to get ready for the meeting.

Sarah walked out of the hotel at exactly eleven to find her driver waiting for her. His greeting was formal as he opened her door. "Good morning, Mrs. Mitchell."

"Good morning, Mr. Thompson. Thank you." She climbed in the back of the car and waited for Thompson to get settled in the front. As he drove, she watched the picturesque view from her window. They drove for several minutes out to a more remote part of the area, and then finally the car turned onto a gated drive. "Excuse me, Mr. Thompson? Where are we going?"

"To Mr. Kingston's home."

She was confused. She knew Elijah wanted to talk to her about a personal project, but meeting at his home was very unprofessional. Apprehension started to take hold, and a knot formed in her stomach.

The feeling was displaced momentarily when the house at the end of the long drive came into view. She simply had no words to describe the magnitude and elegance of the home. The house was enormous and surrounded by a massive amount of land. She would have thought having a house in such a location would be wrong. That it would be an unwanted and ugly piece of lint that marred the natural beauty of the land. She couldn't have been more wrong. The house was a part of the landscape, proudly protected by the mountains like a precious child.

Thompson stopped the car and hurried around to open her door. "This way, Mrs. Mitchell."

He led her up the front steps and through the door. The inside of the home was as impressive as the outside. The entryway was grand and elegant. To the right, there was a short hallway and a staircase leading up to the second level. Thompson led her into a vast room that was clearly made for entertaining. The flooring was covered with stone tiling in muted shades of brown. The right side of the room was dominated by a floor to ceiling stone fireplace and the left opened to a formal dining area. There were clusters of seating all around the perimeter of the room, leaving the center open. However, the feature that made this room magical was the back wall. It was made up entirely of floor-to-ceiling glass and opened to a stone patio. Just beyond the patio was a meticulously manicured garden that appeared to extend all the way to the mountains in the distance. She was so enraptured by the view she didn't hear Thompson leave or Elijah enter.

"Mrs. Mitchell, it's nice to see you again. Welcome." She jumped slightly at the sound of his voice. She turned and was taken aback at the sight of him in the grand room. Somehow she had forgotten how handsome he was. Maybe it was seeing him in his home wearing relaxed jeans and a T-shirt rather than in a stuffy office and wearing a suit. He looked much younger than his sixty-five years, and it was obvious he kept himself in good health. His hair was dark brown with small streaks of gray fighting to take hold. He was taller than she remembered, just over six feet.

Luckily she was able to regain her composure before her hesitated response became awkward. "Thank you, Mr. Kingston. You have a lovely home, and I was just admiring the view."

"Yes, it's spectacular isn't it? I thought we could conduct our meeting out on the patio." He led her outside, and she noticed a dining area to the left and a seating area next to an outdoor fireplace to the right. She sat down in one of the patio chairs across from Elijah.

"Can I get you anything to drink?"

"Yes, water would be great."

"I'll be right back." She watched as he disappeared into the house and then glanced at the mountains in the distance.

I need to get a grip. I can't let him or the grandeur of this place put me off my game. I need the upper hand if I am going to make this work.

She pulled her notes out of her bag and scanned through them. Her nerves settled and by the time Elijah returned she felt confident in her ability to carry an intelligent conversation.

"Thank you." She took a sip of the cool water and set it down on the table next to her.

"How has your trip been so far?" He sat across from her and didn't try to hide the fact that he was looking her over.

She felt her face flush warm at the blatant way he had checked her out. "While I've only been here for less than twenty-four hours, it's great so far. It's gorgeous here." She paused to take another drink of her water. "Isn't the home office located in downtown Denver? I was surprised we were meeting here and not there." She had to somehow gain control over the meeting.

He stared at her for a moment, his brown eyes twinkling. It was easy to see how he usually got what he wanted. "Yes, the home office is in Denver. Andy told you I asked you out here for a personal project? Well, no one at the office knows about it and I'd like to keep it that way for as long as possible. The best place to have a completely confidential conversation is here."

He gave her the perfect lead for getting right to the point of why she was there. "What can you tell me about this assignment? Is it similar to the others our firm has managed for Kingston Enterprises?"

"No... It's quite different in fact. I'll get to the details later. First, I'd like to ask you some questions. I know I've already interviewed you once before, but that was a long time ago. And even though I requested you specifically, I'd still like to ask you some questions.

After that, you can ask me anything you like." He paused to take a drink of his own water. "There's only one condition—you have to answer truthfully to every question I ask. Even if the question may seem like it's irrelevant. Deal?"

She rolled his request around in her head. She couldn't imagine what he could possibly ask about her job she wouldn't be willing to answer.

"Okay, deal."

She waited while he studied her for a moment. "First, let me start by saying I'm aware of the tragic incident a couple years ago that took your husband and son from you. I know there's nothing I can say you haven't already heard or that would provide you with any comfort. Some of the questions I ask may be perceived as insensitive given all you've been through. I want to assure you it's not my intention, and I have my reasons for every question I ask."

He paused as if waiting for her to respond. The mention of the accident caught her so off guard, all she could manage was a nod of her head indicating she understood and he could continue.

"In reviewing your work history I noticed, on average, you managed approximately six projects per year. Is that accurate?"

"Yes, that's accurate. I was typically assigned to the larger, more complex accounts in our firm. Except for Kingston Enterprises, of course." She couldn't help sliding in the not-so-subtle jab and continued before he could form a reaction. "On average I managed between two or three at a time, depending on the size and timeline. Overall, about six per year. More than any of the other managers at my firm."

"Since the accident, how many projects have you managed?"

"Well, for the first six months after the accident I didn't work at all. Over the last eighteen months, I've led two." For some reason saying it out loud was more difficult than she had imagined.

"So, you went from managing two or three at one time while balancing a family to only two over eighteen months and no family life to balance. Did you pick up any other hobbies? Volunteer work? Anything?"

She felt her anger start deep and slowly expand through her body. She found it difficult to focus on formulating an answer. Not that she didn't know the answer. She did, all too well. She was in mourning and found it difficult to do anything. Andy was the one who had forced her back to work and take on those two projects. They were probably the easiest accounts at the firm, the kind they give to the new hires. No, she didn't take up any other hobbies. No volunteer work. Nothing. But could she admit to that? She wasn't even sure she realized how pathetic her life had become until that moment. Sure it was implied in the 'you need to move on' comments but those had become such a constant mantra in her life they were easy to ignore. No one had asked her point blank what she did, or did not do, with her time. She didn't like the way her answer made her feel. Completely and utterly pathetic.

She wasn't sure how long she stared at him before she spoke. When she did, it was strained by the effort to check her tears and her anger. "Mr. Kingston, I do not see how what I choose to do in my life outside of work has any relevance to this project. And truly, I do not need to be reminded I no longer have a family life to manage. I am painfully aware of that every time I take a breath."

He looked at her with those penetrating brown eyes, his facial features not betraying any emotion. "I warned you some of my questions may seem insensitive. A deal is a deal. I'll ask again, what else have you been doing besides work? Outline a typical day for me if that helps."

She looked down at her hands, mindlessly playing with her pen, when she felt the first tear fall.

Great. Just great. I've never cried in front of a client before. I would have to pick the Mighty Mr. Kingston as witness to my debut into this humiliating reality.

"I go to work. I go home. I run five miles. I eat a frozen meal and then I usually go to bed. Twice a week I talk to my mom. On the weekends I shop for groceries and clean the house. Twice a month I have brunch with a friend. Between all of that—a lot of crying and wondering what the hell I'm going to do with my life." She looked at him through her tears. "Based on the look you're giving me I would venture to say you already guessed this would be my response. So why the hell make me say it? I wouldn't have thought you the type to get cheap thrills off making women cry." It was so hard for her to maintain a professional filter when she was angry.

"Believe me I take no pleasure in making you or any woman cry. Yes, I had a strong inclination that was the response I would receive.

I wanted you to say it out loud because it feels different to say it yourself rather than hear someone else say it for you. You can't ignore it when you say it out loud."

She searched her purse for the packet of tissues she always kept on hand. She wiped her eyes and nose and glanced at Elijah to find him studying her.

"This project is very important to me personally, and it will be more difficult than any you have previously led. I need to be sure you can be committed. I know I will be taking a chance with you, and I want to feel confident I'm making the right choice." She didn't think it was possible, but she felt her anger rise several more notches.

"Mr. Kingston, I can assure you I'm *committed* to every project I lead regardless of how many I'm leading or my personal circumstances at the time." She couldn't help but saturate the word committed with a significant amount of emphasis. "As for my being a risk, we have plenty of competent managers at our firm so why select me?"

He gave her a smirking look. It was as if there was an invisible string attached to the left corner of his mouth to the center of his left brow and someone pulled up on it sharply.

Oh good. He must find this to be amusing. Glad someone is enjoying this meeting.

"I wasn't aware I had finished asking all my questions. If you don't mind, I would like to ask you a few more before answering any of yours."

You've already decided to accept. You've already decided to accept...

Keeping this mantra on repeat in her head was the only thing that stopped her from getting up, walking out the door, and booking a flight back to Indiana.

"Would you be able to move out here for an indeterminate amount of time?"

Since he seemed to enjoy her feisty attitude she decided to stick with it. "I would not have come all the way out here on such short notice if I wasn't willing to do whatever was required."

"You will not be able to return back home, or go anywhere else, for the duration of the project. Will that be an issue?"

"Do you have an estimate for how long it might last?" She could tell he was debating with himself.

He's no doubt trying to determine if it was acceptable I asked a question out of turn.

She was about to tell him that if they were to work together there would need to be better collaboration when he finally responded.

"I don't expect it to last longer than a year. There is the slight possibility it would be between one and two years. More likely it will be less than one."

"If it lasts for one year or less, I'll agree to remain here. If it goes longer, I want two weeks' vacation. We would agree on the timing of the trip of course."

"I wasn't aware this was a negotiation."

It was her turn to smirk, and he gave her a genuine smile.

"If it goes longer than a year, I will agree to *consider* you being able to take a leave. I cannot agree up front as it may be during the most critical part of the project which would make it impossible. And one week—not two."

While not completely satisfied, she understood this was the most she was going to get. Truthfully, it was more than she'd expected. Her research of the other Kingston projects her firm had managed showed he never conceded on anything. Since she had already decided to accept regardless of the conditions, she reminded herself it didn't really matter.

"Fine."

"I have one more question." He paused to take another sip of his water. "Why did you decide to accept this meeting?"

At this point of the meeting she realized there was no reason to not tell the truth. She kept her gaze on her hands as she spoke. "As you forced me to admit earlier, I currently have no life. I need a change, and there was no good reason for me to not consider this as an option." She was debating if she should tell him she had already decided to accept when his phone rang.

"Kingston. Yes, that's fine. Thank you." He stood and placed the phone in his pocket. "I had lunch prepared for us. We can continue inside and you can ask me your questions while we eat."

She followed him into the dining room. She didn't realize how hungry she was until she smelled the delicious aroma of Chinese food. She loved Chinese but couldn't remember the last time she'd had it. She and Nick would often get take-out from a small Chinese place not far from their home. As she approached the table, she noticed one of the options was Nick's favorite—Mu Shu Pork. She felt the hole grow in her heart and the tears threaten as her mind quickly cycled through memories of the two of them sitting around their coffee table, fighting over the fortune cookies.

She was suddenly overcome with emotion. It was the first time she had felt the loss of just Nick—Danny wasn't a part of the Chinese dinner tradition. It was something they did before he was born and then on date nights after. Her chest tightened, her breath coming in short spasms. Her legs turned into quicksand, trying to pull the rest of her body down into them. She clutched the back of a chair trying desperately to maintain her ground as her surroundings started to dim. Suddenly Elijah was next to her, and she felt the faint touch of his hand on her back. It was possible he'd said something but she wasn't entirely sure. She closed her eyes and focused on her breathing the way one of her past therapists had taught her. Really, it was the only useful thing she'd learned in all those sessions.

"Air. Please."

Elijah scooped her up and carried her out to the patio to one of the lounge chairs. She was in no condition to protest or even react. *Breathe, damn it. Breathe...*

"Do you need me to call for a doctor?" He looked genuinely concerned. She shook her head, continuing to focus on her breathing.

Finally the spasms eased and the grip on her chest released its hold. "Can I have a moment, please?" Her voice was still a whisper.

"Sure. Just lay back and rest as long as you need. We can continue when you're ready. Would you like me to stay?"

"No, thank you. I'll be fine. You go and eat. I'll join you in a moment." Really, she had no intention of going back in that room but she would deal with how to handle that particular issue later. As Elijah walked back inside, she closed her eyes and tried desperately to block the painful memories from her mind.

Sarah opened her eyes and forgot for a moment where she was. She focused on the mountains in the distance and it all came back. She closed her eyes again and put her arm over them as if she could block out the experience.

Shit, shit, shit. How am I going to face Mr. Kingston after breaking down over Chinese food AND him carrying me?

Reluctantly she opened her eyes again and sat up. She pulled out the band that was no longer doing its job and finger combed her hair back into a ponytail.

Time to face the consequences. Maybe I can still catch a flight back to Indiana tonight.

"Feeling better?"

Sarah jumped at the sound of Elijah's voice. She looked over and saw him sitting at the table working on a computer. "Did I fall asleep?"

He closed his notebook and crossed the patio to sit across from her. He leaned forward resting his elbows on his thighs. "For about three hours. I thought it best to let you sleep it off. You didn't answer my question. How are you feeling?"

"Better, thanks. I'm sorry for falling asleep. For the whole incident, actually. I understand if you want to retract your offer. I apologize for wasting your time and your money on this trip. I'm sure Andy would be happy to reimburse you for any expenses. If the car is still here—"

"I haven't changed my mind. I'd still like you to stay." He pinned her with a concentrated glare.

"Oh... I'm not sure I understand, Mr. Kingston. You made it quite clear you needed someone who can be engaged in the process at all times. I just had a panic attack over Chinese food! Maybe you haven't changed your mind, but I think maybe I have. I'm not sure I'm ready for this." She stood and started to walk over to where she had left her things.

"Don't you even want to know what the project is first?" His statement made her stop. "I won't force you to stay, and if you go I'll make sure Andy knows we came to the decision mutually. I understand this is hard for you, and I'll support you no matter what."

Remember, you already decided to accept. No matter what.

Maggie's voice in her head was as intrusive as it was in real life. Yes, she had already decided to accept, but the 'no matter what' she didn't expect was an injured pride. Sarah turned and noticed Elijah staring at her while she danced through her internal conflict. She slowly walked back to the lounge chair and sat back down.

"Alright. I suppose if you're willing to forget this... embarrassing episode, then I can try as well."

"I never said I would forget about it. I said it wouldn't keep me from hiring you."

She flushed and looked off to the mountains. They were even more striking in the late afternoon sun. She glanced at the table next to her and noticed he had brought her a fresh glass of water. She took a long, somewhat un-lady like drink and focused her mind back to the questions she'd organized on the flight. Trying to get back in her comfort zone, she went for her most natural approach—direct and to the point.

"I understand from Andy that up until now you specifically requested I *not* be assigned to the Kingston account. What was the issue? And what's different now for you to have such a drastic change in your opinion of me?" It was his turn to look uncomfortable.

"I'll start by saying my opinion of you has not changed. It's your circumstances that have changed. There are two main reasons I didn't want you on my account in the past. I remember the first time I met you. We had just started using Jacobs, and I was there to interview all the project managers. You were seven months pregnant at the time, and you came into the meeting room like a breath of fresh air. Your happiness was so infectious, and I remember thinking, 'This is who I need on my team.' I already knew you were the top rated manager at your firm. However, as the meeting progressed I began to realize I couldn't hire you. As you now know, Kingston projects are very demanding, and a home life for my managers is often nonexistent. I could tell by the way you talked about your husband and soon to be baby that they were your life, your light. I didn't want to take you away from them. It would have dimmed the very thing that drew me to you—your happiness."

She sat stunned at his unexpected response. "But shouldn't that have been my responsibility—to determine what would or would not make me happy?"

He sat back in his chair and his voice took on a much more serious tone, almost nostalgic. "Probably. But it was the second reason that kept me from being able to think objectively. You have a remarkable resemblance to my late wife, Lena. Not physically, but I saw it in your mannerisms, the way you viewed life, the way you laughed, even in the playful mischief that danced in your eyes as you answered my questions. I suddenly felt very protective of you and couldn't bring myself to risk your happiness."

She wasn't sure she was processing everything correctly. She stared back out over the mountains to gather her thoughts however Elijah kept talking, not really allowing her the chance to form a conclusion.

"This urge to protect you is one of the reasons I asked for you now. I understand the hole created when you lose your partner, the one you love most in the world." He paused for the briefest of moments and pulled in a breath. "I understand the depth of that hole must expand considerably when you lose a child as well. You probably don't realize it, but based on the information Andy has shared with me you appear to be approaching a pivotal point in your grief. You can remain in the grasp of the black hole, letting it become larger and larger until the darkness swallows you whole. Or you can break free. You can live again with happiness in your life. I want to help you choose, and accept, the latter."

She didn't even try to wipe the tears falling silently down her face. "Is there even a project? Or am I the project here, like some pathetic charity case?"

"Yes, there's a real project. You are not a charity case and you are certainly not pathetic. Consider my help in your recovery as a signing bonus."

"And you think I need your help to escape this, what did you call it? Oh, yes—this black hole. All because of what you have heard from someone who's not me?"

"I'm under the impression Andy is not only your boss, but also a close friend. And I know he's not inclined to exaggerate. So, yes, I can be confident of my conclusions based on his feedback. But if you need more, there's the information you provided earlier today confirming you're not working at the same level you were before, and you don't have a life outside of work." He paused and waited for her to look back at him. "Finally, there's your appearance. Have you really looked at yourself lately, Sarah?"

She was starting to feel like she wouldn't be able to contain herself much longer. She stood up and walked on shaky legs to the edge of the patio. She crossed her arms tightly over her chest as if she could literally hold herself together.

This is not what I came here for. What the hell is going on? She looked up toward the sky as if the answer might come to her through some sort of divine transference. Elijah's voice was almost too soft to hear. "Before the accident, you always looked so professional. Every time I saw you in the office on my visits I couldn't help but notice you. Your long brown hair was always neatly styled—usually down with the natural waves framing your face. A few times, when I saw you on your way to your vehicle, I would be mesmerized by the way the sun glistened off your hair. Your eyes, a curious mixture of brown and green, were always so full of life. Your smile lit up your entire face. Your physique showed you kept yourself in good health, even after the baby. You carried yourself with such confidence you commanded attention. Put simply, you were beautiful."

She stood very still and concentrated on her breathing. She wasn't aware Elijah had taken such a detailed notice of her during his frequent visits to the firm. She was thankful she still had her back to him so she wouldn't have to face him while hearing what she knew was coming next.

"And what do you see now?"

"Your hair has become dull and is either in a clip or a sloppy ponytail. Your eyes no longer sparkle and are constantly supported by those deep circles under them. You do well in trying to cover them up, but they're still noticeable. You're extremely thin—an unhealthy thin—as if you haven't eaten a proper meal in two years. The best way I can describe it is you're a very dim version of your former self."

On impulse she ran her hand down her ponytail. She knew it was all true. Maybe not so much his assessment of her prior to the accident—she's not sure she would have gone so far as to describe herself as beautiful. However, she was aware his description of her after the accident was accurate. Her mom, in all her lack of subtlety, told her several times over the past year she looked 'simply awful.' It was one of the reasons she stopped visiting her parents and inviting them to visit her. Maggie was much more tactful. On occasion she would surprise her by skipping their brunch and going to a day spa for pampering. Maggie gave her the works—hair, manicure, pedicure, facial, massage. Maggie came out looking fantastic for weeks where she only looked presentable for about five hours. Even though the results were fleeting, like a true friend Maggie never stopped trying. However, Maggie and her mom were supposed to tell her these things—they were family. Hearing it from a near stranger left it impossible to ignore.

She finally turned to look at Elijah. "With all due respect, Mr. Kingston, I have seen every possible therapist in the drivable vicinity of my home with no acceptable progress. What makes you think you will be able to alter the course of my life so dramatically?" She knew the man possessed an unnaturally high regard for himself, but even he would have to admit she was damaged beyond his repair.

He caught her gaze and held it. "Because I have lived it. As impossible as it seemed at the time, I found a way to live my life again, but I did it too late and in a way that cost me my relationship with my children. I can help you."

"And you think this can be done while I am leading what you described as the most difficult project I have ever led?"

"Yes."

"What exactly will it entail?"

He hesitated a moment before joining her at the edge of the patio. He tucked his hands in his pockets and looked out over the mountains. "I'm hiring you to be my personal assistant and companion. During this time you will manage my appointments and other critical tasks that will become more apparent over time. You will also be required to join me for all social functions I need to attend. Basically, I need you by my side at all times."

There was something in his tone of voice that kept her from being offended at his response. Instead, she felt chills creep over her body and her heart rate quicken.

"I don't understand. Why would you need an experienced project manager to act as your personal assistant and companion?"

"Because the things in my life are about to become very complicated, and I need someone I can trust to manage every detail."

"But why?"

He turned to look her right in the eyes. "Because I'm dying."

CHAPTER 4

Sarah sat on the balcony of her hotel room looking out over the mountains. It was possible she was still in shock from her meeting with Elijah. She had been stunned into silence after he had revealed the reason for the project. Recognizing she was incapable of continuing the meeting, he called for the car to take her back to the hotel. He handed her a packet of information and told her he would meet with her again the following day after lunch. She responded with the only thought she could formulate in her mind.

"I don't think I can do this."

Now she was back at the hotel, trying to determine what to do. Sitting on the table next to the packet of information was her tablet. She picked it up and opened her photo slideshow app. The first was of Sarah and Nick when they first started dating. They both looked so young and happy. She'd been a junior in high school, and he was a senior. It was a magical year, and she felt like she was on top of the world. Then Nick graduated and decided, for the both of them, it would be best to break up when he left for college. She was devastated and barely made it through her senior year. Her grades had slipped, and she wasn't accepted into the same university as Nick—but for her there was no other choice. She'd attended the local community college to get her grades back up and was able to successfully transfer in her second year.

She hadn't told Nick she would be attending the same university. Instead, she decided she would leave it up to fate to determine if they should be together again. She got her answer the first weekend she was there. She and some friends had attended a fraternity party and not an hour in she was approached by someone asking her to dance. She turned to find Nick smiling down at her. They were inseparable from that moment onward.

The photos continued to roll, reminding her of their wedding and vacations in those early years of marriage. Then there was Danny. His pudgy baby photos with those big blue eyes staring back at her. She watched the photos flash, wishing with the faith of a child they could be there with her. She closed her eyes and tried to hear Nick's voice. He always knew what to do. Her head reminded her, as it had tried to several times in the past, that he would have wanted her to be happy. This time she forced her heart to listen.

The sound of her cell phone interrupted her thoughts. Maggie. Again. It was the fourth time Maggie had called since she'd returned to the hotel. Just as she did the other three times, she sent the call straight to voice mail. She wasn't ready to face the logic Maggie would pour into the situation. Besides, she wouldn't be able to share any details with her. Elijah had made it clear the information he had shared with her was confidential. She was going to have to figure this one out on her own.

Accept no matter what.

Apparently, she didn't need to answer the phone to hear Maggie's advice. She took a deep breath, set her tablet down and picked up the packet of information. The first page was a letter addressed to her from Elijah.

Sarah,

Enclosed in this packet you will find details of my illness and the requirements of the project. As discussed in our meeting, this information is completely confidential. There's a lot of detail in this packet, but I expect you will have further questions when we meet again. What the following pages will not make clear is my history behind this illness. You will come to learn that Creutzfeldt-Jakob Disease (CJD) is a rare fatal disease—meaning there is no treatment and no cure. It's a rapidly progressive disease that will ultimately claim both my mind and my body.

I inherited the disease from my father who died at the age of 63 from familial CJD. The incidence of CJD is one case per million population, and the familial form represents 5-15 percent of all cases. Shortly after my father's death, I tested positive for the mutated gene and could possibly suffer the same fate.

It's been a difficult road. I've spent the last twenty some years scrutinizing every flaw my body or brain produced, looking for evidence that I too would someday die at the mercy of CJD.

Unfortunately, I've begun to show early signs of the disease. They are so subtle at this point that if I wasn't looking for them I probably wouldn't have noticed anything was different. As you read through the information, it should become clear why I will need you to be with me at all times. It's my wish to keep my condition quiet for as long as possible. In order to do that, I need someone with me to cover in situations where the symptoms might make my behavior seem odd. Please do not make any decisions until we have a chance to talk again.

Respectfully,
Elijah Kingston

She didn't fully understand CJD, but she had a feeling by the time she went to bed she would know more than she ever could have imagined. She got her notebook and pen out of her bag and turned the page.

Sarah finished getting ready and the sudden rumble in her stomach reminded her she hadn't eaten since the apple she had for breakfast the day before. She grabbed her bag and headed down to the hotel restaurant. It was another beautiful day, and she requested a table outside. She ordered a light lunch and dug in her bag for her notes. As she searched, she caught sight of her phone and remembered she had shut it off. She turned it on and saw Maggie had called four more times. She groaned inwardly, listening to the messages. There was no ignoring the higher level of urgency in the most recent messages. She still wasn't ready to talk to Maggie, but if she didn't contact her soon there was no doubt Maggie would call the local authorities. She decided on a quick text.

Sorry I haven't called. Still working through details with Kingston. Project is more complicated than expected. Will call tonight.

The replying text was almost instantaneous.

Thank God. You're lucky I'm not there to strangle you. Tonight.

Sarah chuckled and settled in with her notes from the night before. After eating she felt invigorated and believed she would be able to handle the meeting with Elijah much better than she did the day prior. The car arrived at precisely one o'clock. She took a deep breath and walked over to the door being held open for her.

"Good afternoon, Mr. Thompson. Thank you."

"Good afternoon, Mrs. Mitchell." His curt nod was stiff and professional. She remained quiet on the drive to Elijah's house, enjoying the view out the window. When they arrived, Thompson escorted her directly to the patio.

As she waited to be joined by Elijah, she walked down to the edge of the garden. A butterfly fluttered lightly out of one plant and on to the next. She watched the butterfly and remembered one of her favorite days when she and Nick had taken Danny to the park. After eating a picnic lunch Nick had packed with all of Danny's favorite foods, they played in the grass and watched Danny discover new things. He was inspecting a dandelion, and very likely thinking about trying to eat it, when he suddenly saw a butterfly dance across their picnic area. He dropped his prized 'flower' and, squealing with delight, took off after it. He chased it around until it flew out of sight which caused a sudden rush of tears. Nick quickly scooped him up and made his world right again with an always enjoyable shoulder ride. Sarah had sat on the picnic blanket and laughed at the sight of her boys being so playful.

"There you are." The sound of Elijah's voice brought her back to the present. She wiped away the tears that had fallen and turned, noticing he was standing at the edge of the patio watching her. "I wasn't sure you would be coming back today."

"I admit I wasn't sure either. I guess my curiosity won out." She joined him in the seating area they occupied the day before.

"I trust you're feeling better? At least you look better than you did when you left here yesterday afternoon." He sat down in the seat across from her stretching one arm over the back of the chair and an ankle over a knee.

"Yes, thank you. I'm feeling much better."

"Did you get in touch with Maggie?" He couldn't restrain the laughter in his voice or the playful sparkle in his eyes.

It took her a moment before she realized. "Ah, Andy must have called you. Yes, I sent her a text. I should be fine until later tonight."

"Good. Can I get you anything?"

"No thank you."

He nodded in acknowledgement. "So, how can I satisfy your curiosity?"

She paused and studied him. She knew from the packet of information he gave her, one of the first signs of CJD was often a decrease in muscular coordination. He seemed to move with such ease, and she was curious if she would notice anything unusual now that she knew what to look for.

"Mr. Kingston, I was—"

"Please. You are the only person outside of my doctor and my lawyer that knows of my condition. I would say that's grounds for putting us on a first name basis. Elijah will be fine."

"Okay... Elijah, I've been giving your proposal a lot of consideration. If I decide to accept, I will certainly have questions around the logistics of everything. But the main thing for me right now is I still don't understand how you think it will be beneficial for me to do this project. I will be spending every moment of every day with you, possibly over the next year. It's reasonable to assume during that time we will form some sort of... friendship. Then I have to watch you die. How will that help me recover from my loss?"

He studied and picked at a seemingly invisible, yet unmovable, piece of lint on his pant leg. "Yes, I would imagine we would likely form some sort of friendship over time. When I die it might affect you to some extent. My only hope is that what I can give you in return prior to that day will be worth whatever pain my passing may cause you."

"You really believe this will help me?" She hated how vulnerable her voice sounded.

He looked up and held her gaze. There was no hesitation in his response. "Yes, I do. As long as you trust me. It will not be easy but I truly believe you will be able to be happy again." He paused for a moment. "Let me ask you something. In the twenty-four or so hours you've been here so far, how many times have you suffered from the pain of not having Nick and Danny with you? More or less than when you're at home? I don't expect you to give me an answer. I just want you to think about it. If it's less, then you can use that as evidence it's already starting to work. For example, I noticed you were crying when I came out. I assume that was a result of a memory. When I addressed you, you were able to pull yourself from the moment and function in the current environment. That's normal. Yesterday's episode in the dining room was not normal or healthy."

She studied him and searched deep in her heart, in her soul. He was right. Not only were the episodes less frequent and severe here as they were at home, but she had also slept better the last two nights than she had in a long time. The logic was there, but she wasn't sure her heart was ready to embrace it. This was going to have to be a gut decision. She started to feel a trace amount of warmth radiate from her core.

Yes, it's worth any risk to stay and try. Really, could I be any worse when this is as all said and done?

She reached into her bag and pulled out the notes she made the night before. "When you say you don't want anyone to know about your illness, who exactly does that include?"

"Anyone. Everyone. The public, my employees, your boss and coworkers, your friends and family. And my children."

"Wait, you don't want your children to know?" The look he gave her indicated he had already made that clear. "For how long? They will have to know something at some point and don't you think they should know before the general public?"

"As I mentioned yesterday, my relationship with my children suffered after Lena died. I currently have a functioning relationship with Leanne, but that's mostly due to her role in the company. Marcus and I hardly ever speak, and when we do it's usually restricted to polite conversation at social events."

"But isn't that precisely the reason to let them know? To have time to mend the relationships before it's too late?"

"Not in this case. Look, Sarah, I appreciate your concern, but mending my relationships with my children is not part of your responsibility."

He obviously doesn't know me very well.

She never left any aspect of a project untouched and it was clear this would be a critical, and very difficult, requirement. For now, however, she would let it go.

"What am I supposed to tell people about what I do? Project manager isn't appropriate in social settings, and I can't tell Andy my role is to be your personal assistant and companion."

"We won't tell Andy anything. I've already told him it's confidential and you wouldn't be able to share any details. For social events, we won't give an explanation. Let people make their own conclusions."

"What if people assume we're, you know... together?" She couldn't stop the blush from creeping over her face.

He looked amused at her question. "Would that be so bad? It's not like you have to see any of these people again after I'm gone."

It stunned her how casually he talked about his impending death. "Right. I guess that's one we'll have to deal with as it comes up." She looked back down at her notes. "What about compensation? We already agreed to no vacation time during the first year."

"Your contract will outline that you will receive twice your annual salary for the first year, paid upfront when you start. If it goes into the second year, you will get a seven percent increase."

She was more than a little surprised at his response. She lived a very comfortable life financially. Certainly not as comfortable as Elijah, but she didn't lack for anything. She came from a family of money that went as far back as her great-grandfather, who had started a successful architectural firm in Chicago. Her grandfather took over the firm and then her father and then her eldest brother after that. Before he retired, her father took out a sizeable portion of the fortune and established a trust for her and her siblings. Smart investments over the years grew the comfortable trust to a sizeable fortune, allowing her the option to select any career she liked with no concern over how she would pay the bills. It was one of the reasons she was able to take such a big step back on her work load over the last couple years with no fear of losing her home.

"That's quite generous of you, Mr. King—Elijah. It's more than necessary. My regular salary would be fine. And seven percent in the next year is too much—"

"I insist. With the challenges you will have to face it's only fair." His authoritative tone told her their discussion on salary was over.

Even though she was sure she knew the answer to the next question, she had to ask anyway. "Since I will need to be by your side at all times, where should I expect to live?"

"You will occupy the guest bedroom closest to me. Come, I'll show you." She followed him back into the house, through the great room and up the stairs. "You can expect to have complete access to the house while you're here. I want you to make yourself at home." At the top of the stairs he stopped and pointed to the two rooms down the hall. "Those are additional guest bedrooms." He walked a short distance down the hall to the left and he stopped at an open door. "On the end is the master suite and this will be your room."

The room was huge—large enough for a king-size bed, a writing desk and a sitting area in front of a fireplace. The walls were a serene shade of light blue and were complimented by cream accents. She made her way over to the bed on the right side of the room and ran her hand along the top of the brocade duvet. It looked to be hand-sewn, and the details were so intricate she would be afraid to use it as a cover in the night. There was a set of doors to the left flanking the fireplace. One opened to a private bathroom, and the other opened to a large walk-in closet. The back wall had a set of double glass doors that led to a private balcony. The balcony was large enough for two lounge chairs and an accent table. She stepped out and looked around. The view was simply stunning. If this is what the guest room looked like, she was intrigued to see the master suite. She turned back to find Elijah watching her.

"I don't know. I'm not sure I'll have enough room for all my stuff in here." She was pleased to hear him chuckle.

Maybe we'll get along after all.

"Let me show you the rest of the house." He turned to leave the room.

As expected, the master suite was exquisite. The layout was exactly like the room she would occupy, except in reverse and much, much bigger. The main difference was the decor. Instead of blues and creams, the room was decorated in tones of gray, black and silver—giving the room a very masculine feel. As if reading her mind, he offered her some explanation on the room. "I had it redone a few years after Lena died. The room you will occupy was actually how this room used to look. I couldn't come in here after she died. The hole I felt without her in this room was so vast, yet suffocating at the same time. I couldn't let go completely, so I had the guest room redone at the same time I had this one done."

"Wouldn't it have been easier, and cheaper, to have moved into that room?"

He chuckled again. "Yes, probably. But... you have not yet seen the master bathroom. That may convince you it was worth the extra work and cost."

Taking his hint, she walked into the master bathroom and true to his word it did not disappoint. It was like a private spa. On the left there was a jet tub that looked like it might fit three people. Above it, the wall was completely made of glass and offered a similar view as the balconies. To the right was a large tiled shower surrounded by glass walls. There were more showerheads than she could count, including one in the ceiling.

"So if I don't know where to find you during the day I should look here first?"

"Yes, it's a possibility. But you should knock before coming in. The room wasn't necessarily designed for privacy." She was pretty sure she blushed at his response.

Damn, why do I keep blushing?

He led her out of the room and back downstairs. She had already seen the great room and the dining room, although she didn't spend much time in the latter due to her episode the day before. The main level was rounded out with a large kitchen, office, family room and a laundry room. He led her down another set of stairs off the kitchen. The basement was incredible. It had a fully equipped workout room, media room, full-size bar, a fireplace and a small dance studio. It was in this last room where he paused for a moment as he ran his hand along the dancer bars.

"Lena was a dancer." That was it and it was all the explanation she needed. He turned and leaned against the bars. "So?"

This is it.

"So... I assume I start now?"

He smiled. "Yes, you start now. Let's head back up and you can sign the contract."

Back at the hotel to pack her things, Sarah decided it was time to call Maggie. It was better to do it in private than at the house with Elijah lurking somewhere in the nearby vicinity. Not surprising, she picked up on the first ring.

"What the hell happened to you? I was starting to worry Mr. Arrogant had you locked up in his basement by now." After seeing the basement, Sarah wasn't so sure it would constitute as punishment.

"I know, I know. Sorry. Can I blame the altitude? I seemed to have lost all sense of time out here."

"Well, I suppose I'll take that excuse just this once. Crap, hold on a minute." She could hear Maggie's muffled voice in the background and then the sound of a children's program on the TV. "Okay, that should keep them off my back for awhile. Now, out with it. I want details. What's the project, are you staying, is he as arrogant as you remember... tell me everything."

"Unfortunately, I can't tell you much. It's highly confidential, and I can't share any details. I had to sign a non-disclosure agreement. Not even Andy gets the details."

"Okay, fine. Tell me the rest that doesn't violate the NDA."

She had been struggling with this the whole ride back from Elijah's—what to tell Maggie. Without understanding the details of the project, most of the aspects of her visit with Elijah would sound strange. Maggie wasn't the type to accept vague answers to her questions. She wanted specific details and then she wanted to analyze those details in a thousand different ways. Sarah hoped she could provide enough distractions to keep her from digging too deep.

"Mostly the meeting went well. Part of the reason I didn't call yesterday was because I had a panic attack... over lunch... he had Chinese and there was Mu Shu Pork... He took me out to the patio for some air, and I ended up falling asleep. He was actually pretty cool about the whole thing."

No need to tell her he actually carried me outside. I'd really like to forget that part ever happened.

Maggie was silent for longer than expected. Sarah thought maybe they had gotten disconnected when she finally responded. "I'm sorry I wasn't there when it happened. I know it must have been difficult for you."

"Yes, it was. I mean, obviously I miss Nick every second of every day and it hurts constantly. But I've only really allowed myself to grieve for Danny. I haven't allowed myself to feel the loss of just Nick and how it felt to be in love with him. This was the first time and it took me down." She stopped for a moment, squeezing the bridge of her nose with her finger and thumb. "Anyway, I thought for sure he would personally take me to the airport after that but he surprised me."

"Did you ask him why he never requested you before?"

"Yes I did. Look, Maggie, as much as I really want to talk to you about his explanation, I can't. I think it would reveal too much about the project and that goes against the contract I accepted. I can only say his reasons were unexpected, yet acceptable."

"Come on, you have to give me—wait, did you say you accepted?"

"Yes, I accepted. I start now. I'm still not sure how long I will be here though. Elijah thought it might last a year or less, but it could carry over to a second year."

"It's Elijah now? Boy, he sure did bring you around." She could hear the surprise in Maggie's voice.

"Yes, well. I'll be required to work with him closely and it seemed best to go with less formality. By the way, I need you to send me some stuff. I don't need much, but I didn't bring enough to last me a year." She paused a moment to consider how she should phrase the next part. "I don't really trust the hotel to deliver things properly, so Elijah said I could have my things sent to his house and he would get them to me. He said I could also forward my mail to his house. I'll email you the address and a list of things I need." She hated lying to Maggie and a knot formed in the pit of her stomach.

"You want your stuff delivered to his house and not the hotel or to the Kingston main office?" She noticed the curiosity growing in Maggie's tone. She needed to redirect her again.

"I know it's all somewhat unorthodox. Really, it's because of the confidentiality requirements. By the way, is everything still a go with Andy's friend? What was his name?"

"Travis. Yes, he's still planning to rent your house. I'll make sure he has your information in case he needs anything, but Andy will take care of everything for you."

"Great, thanks. I appreciate it. Look, I need to run but I'll call you again later this week. And hey, thanks. I probably wouldn't have come out here if you hadn't pushed me. I really think it will help. At least I hope it will."

She could practically hear Maggie smile through the phone. "Any time. I'll talk to you later."

CHAPTER 5

Sarah spent the rest of the week getting organized. Since Elijah's current symptoms were subtle, she wasn't required to be at his side every waking moment. He spent a lot of time at the office working with his leadership team on transitioning his responsibilities to his daughter, Leanne. He'd announced a few months ago he had decided on early retirement to begin a personal project. He said Leanne was ready and eager to take on her new role at Kingston Enterprises. Everyone was curious about his mysterious personal project, but every time someone asked questions he was able to expertly redirect them to his retirement plans. She noted the excitement in his voice when he told her all this, like he was proud to have been able to cause such chaos in the lives of his employees.

While Elijah was having fun throwing everything into havoc at his office, she spent her time settling into his home. She made note of what she wanted Maggie to send as she unpacked. She had to be thoughtful since she should be staying in a hotel and couldn't ask for a lot of things without causing suspicion. She tried to keep it to the basics—clothes, shoes, a few favorite photo frames and the box from under her bed. The box had been found in the trunk of Nick's car after the accident, wrapped and addressed to Sarah. It remained wrapped. Even though she couldn't bring herself to open the box, she liked knowing it was under her bed.

Once she got herself settled in, she focused on her timeline and list of deliverables. It took her a long time to get started. Everything was completely outside her realm of understanding, and she was nervous she would miss something critical. She tried to talk to Elijah about it one evening when he got home from work, and he asked her how things were going.

"You don't need to be so stressed out about the details. It's not like my life depends on it. Nothing you do, or don't do, will make me die any faster or slower."

She wasn't sure she would ever get used to him talking so casually about his death.

"True, but from what I've read the most important thing I can do is make you comfortable when things get bad. I want you to suffer as little as possible. And, what if something gets overlooked? It will be too late after you're gone."

He had walked over to Sarah and put his hands on her shoulders, giving her a serious but compassionate look. "Sarah, relax. I can guarantee I will be the most prepared man on his death bed. Most people have no idea when they're going to die, and they don't plan for it when they're healthy. It will be all right. I just need you to focus on how to mask my symptoms and make sure no one knows about it until there is no other option but to tell them. If you also want to find ways to make it more comfortable for me along the way, I would be grateful."

Now she sat in front of her computer, staring at the blank project tracker. She felt if she could identify one task then it would put her at ease. She checked back over her notes and finally found her answer in one of the case studies—she would interview and hire a private nurse. Elijah could certainly afford one and it would help with quick response and comfort management. It would also provide a back-up for when she had to run an errand. She suddenly had several tasks outlined in her tracker, and she felt more confident in her assignment.

Sarah was startled awake by the sound of her phone ringing. "Hello?"

"Sarah? Are you sleeping? You never sleep past six o'clock on a work day. Are you sick?"

"Mom, hi. Yeah, I mean no..."

Damn.

She hadn't yet told her mom about the assignment. She tried to rub the sleep out of her eyes. "Sorry, yes, I'm still sleeping. No, I'm not sick. I'm in Colorado actually. I'm now an hour behind you."

She knew the silence on the other end of the phone wasn't a good thing. "What do you mean you're in Colorado?"

"Well, you've been telling me for quite some time I needed a change of environment and an opportunity came up suddenly at work. I came out last Sunday to interview and long story short—here I am." She reached over and turned on the bedside light. She could hear her mom's breathing change slightly, and she closed her eyes waiting for the direct hit of her response.

"There are so many things I could say right now and be every bit justified as your mother. However, the only thing I *will* say is I'm glad you've decided to take a chance on something new. How long will you be out there?"

Well, that was easier than expected.

"I'm not sure yet. It could be up to a year or maybe a bit more."

Her mom hesitated again, letting out a short sigh. She could practically see her mother's pinched face on the other end of the call. "I'd like to hear all about it and how it's going. But I understand it's early out there, so it can wait. I'm sorry to call at this time, but you didn't call last week, and I thought I might try to catch you before work. I'm busy every night this week. How about I give you a call on Saturday?"

"That would be great. I'll talk to you then." She said good-bye to her mom and plopped back on her pillows. It was twenty minutes after five and it didn't appear she would be able to fall back to sleep so she got out of bed. She hadn't been running the entire time she had been in Colorado and decided it was a good day to start. She went to the bathroom, changed her clothes, and grabbed her shoes and music player before stepping out into the hall.

"Good morning. You're up early today." The unexpected sound of Elijah's voice caused her to jump. She turned to find him leaning on the frame of his bedroom doorway.

"Elijah. You startled me." She pressed her hand to her chest, trying to slow the too rapid beat. "My mom called. I'd forgotten to call her last week and tell her about the assignment. I wasn't able to fall back to sleep, so I thought I would run on the treadmill. How about you?"

He pushed off the doorway and stepped toward her. "I'm always up at five. My internal clock won't shut off." He paused and looked her up and down. "No running for you this morning. Today we start our work on you, and phase one is your health. No more running until we can get you back to your normal weight."

She stared at him in shock. After a few beats, she realized her mouth was hanging open and snapped it shut before she could look any more ridiculous.

"I beg your pardon? I thought I was here to manage your health, not the other way around."

"I said I was going to help you move past the pain you're holding on to. If you want to do that successfully, then you need to be healthy. Your heart can't heal if the rest of your body is fighting to hold on as well. Come in here for a moment please." He turned and started walking back to his bedroom. When he realized she wasn't following him, he turned and gave her an impatient look. "You said you would trust me."

She reluctantly moved her feet to follow. He led her through his bedroom and into his bathroom. He opened the closet, pulled out a scale and set it down in front of her. "You're what, about five-nine?"

"Yes."

"That's what I thought. I did some research of my own. At your height and build you should weigh somewhere between 140 and 160 pounds. Based on the look on your face right now, my guess is you haven't been on a scale in a long time. Do you even know how much you currently weigh?"

She looked down at her toe lightly kicking the side of the scale. "No."

"Just step on when you're ready." He leaned back against the counter and waited, watching her.

She could feel beads of sweat break out on her forehead.

This is ridiculous. It's just a scale.

But deep down she knew why she was afraid. She knew Elijah was right and she was very underweight. She wasn't sure she was ready to validate it. Stepping on the scale would mean she could no longer hide behind denial. Aside from pain and loneliness, denial had been her closest companion these last two years. Putting down her shoes and music player, she took a deep breath and closed her eyes as she stepped on the scale. She could hear Elijah walk toward her. She hesitantly opened her eyes and looked down at the scale. 113. She couldn't contain the sob that erupted from deep within. She flinched when he pulled her into a hug, but he tightened his grip. She quickly relented and let him hold her close until her sobs subsided.

He stepped back and looked down at her. "Come on. I'll make breakfast. From now on you will eat three full meals a day. Do you like French toast?"

She nodded, wiping the tears from her face, and accepted the tissue he handed her. She followed him out of his room and to the stairs. He paused and looked down the hall before descending. She looked past his shoulder and followed his gaze.

Oh, please. Not now. I'm not ready for that.

To her relief, he turned and went down the stairs. In the kitchen he waved toward the counter stools.

"You sit, and I'll cook. Coffee?"

She pulled herself up on one of the stools. "Yes, please. Just sugar." She watched him put on the coffee and pull out mugs, plates, pans and bowls. She was trying to register where he kept everything. If she was to make herself feel at home, she needed to be able to make a cup of coffee.

As he worked she studied his movements, trying to figure out if she noticed any of the early onset symptoms of CJD. He caught her staring when he turned to hand her the coffee and raised an eyebrow at her.

"See something you like?" His flirtatious attitude continued to create waves of embarrassment. She wondered if he was like this with everyone outside of work. Based on his reputation she never would have guessed.

"Actually, I was trying to see if I could notice any of the early onset symptoms you said you were experiencing." Before putting the bread on the skillet, he turned back to her and motioned for her to hand him her coffee mug.

"See if you can tell the difference." He held the mug in his left hand for a few seconds. Then he transferred the mug to his right hand. As he held it, she noticed the slightest bit of a tremble. She really only noticed it due to the small ripple it created in the liquid coffee.

"Do you have any of the other symptoms?" He put the coffee mug down and turned back to the oven.

"Random coordination issues. Sometimes I feel like I'm forgetting things, but it's hard to tell if that's a result of CJD or just old age. I was afraid of making a critical error at work, so I knew it was time to retire and start preparing for things to get worse."

They settled into a comfortable silence as he finished making breakfast. She was suddenly struck by how much more she could tolerate silence when she wasn't alone. It bothered her so much at home when she was by herself, reminding her of all that was missing. Now she felt content, lost in her thoughts while Elijah moved about the kitchen. The more she analyzed the situation the more she became annoyed.

Shouldn't I be able to be more comfortable with myself than I am with a near stranger? Am I too dependent on others to be happy?

One of her many therapists once told her that she needed to learn how to be alone and create her own happiness. At the time she dismissed it, just as she did everything else they'd said.

"Syrup or fruit topping?" Elijah set a hefty plate of French toast and bacon down in front of her.

Normally, she wouldn't eat any of it. It smelled delicious, but it was so much food. Much more than her usual granola bar she grabbed in the mornings on her way out the door.

You need to eat. 113, Sarah. 113...

"I'll take both." He sat down next to her as she took her first bite. "This is really good."

"Thanks. Cooking is one of my hidden talents. I had to learn after Lena died. Pizza and takeout got old quickly." They continued to eat in their newly formed comfortable silence.

Her plate still contained a slice of French toast and a couple pieces of bacon when she decided she couldn't eat another bite. She glanced at Elijah and noticed he had finished his plate and was watching her.

"I'd like for you to hire a nutritionist to help you get back to a healthy weight; one that can help you with fitness as well. While I don't think you should go back to running yet, you should probably keep up some sort of activity."

She put her fork down and shifted on her stool to face him. "I'd like to hire a private nurse as well. I think it will help to have one on call for when your symptoms get worse. I would conduct the interviews at the hotel I stayed at and not mention you're the client.

Once you approve the final selection, we can have him or her sign a confidentiality agreement. We can ask your doctor for a recommendation, if that's all right with you."

"That's a great idea. I knew you were perfect for this job. I'll give Dr. Holden a call now. That means you get to clean up." He gave her a playful wink as he got up and walked away.

Sarah sat outside on the patio working on a list of tasks. It was another cool but beautiful day, and she couldn't get enough of being outdoors. Prior to the accident, she and Nick had spent a lot of time outside by the lake or playing in the yard with Danny. After the accident she couldn't find the same solace. Sitting outdoors alone had brought back too many painful memories. However, out here she continued to feel the same surge of strength when looking at the mountains as she had the first time she saw them. Even her mom and Maggie noticed an improvement in her mood.

She reluctantly pulled her eyes away from the mountains and resumed her concentration on her task list. A short while later she got the feeling someone was watching her, and she turned to find Elijah looking over her shoulder.

"What are you working on?"

"My project. Remember, you hired me to do a job?" She looked back to her list and started to write down another line before she stopped again. He hadn't moved. "Did you need something?"

Finally he stepped away and sat down at the table next to her. "Oh, no. Sorry, I didn't mean to interrupt you. What kind of list are you creating?"

"I'm making note of the various symptoms of CJD, so I can brainstorm ideas on how I might be able to help you mask them when needed." She finished adding the new line and stopped again. She looked back—he was still staring at her. She raised her eyebrows to him in question.

"You make a lot of lists."

"Yes... I'm a project manager, and a good one at that. Lists are the best way for me to get organized and make sure I remember to do everything." She looked back to her list, but before she even wrote one letter she stopped. Sighing she put down her pen. "What's up?"

He sat back in his chair, looking embarrassed. "I just—it's nothing. I don't want to bother you." He started to get up from his chair.

She let out another sigh and sat back in her own chair. "Elijah. For all of this to work you need to be able to talk to me and trust me. Isn't that what you told me earlier this week? How can I help you through this if you won't talk to me?"

He settled back into his chair. "I don't know what to do. I led Kingston Enterprises for nearly thirty years. It wasn't only my life, it defined who I was. Prior to that, I worked closely under my father's lead. This is the first time in my life I don't have anything to do." He paused and looked down at his hands. "I don't know what to do now, and it feels very strange."

That simple statement made her feel more connected to him than anything else. "Why don't you watch TV?"

He waived his hand in front of his face as if she'd said something foul. "I lost interest in that a long time ago."

She pursed her lips trying to think of something he could do to occupy his time. The last few days they had been busy reviewing resumes of prospective nurses and nutritionists. Together they narrowed down the list to four candidates she would interview the following week. Elijah had taken the lead on drafting out the interview questions, but there was nothing else to do until after the interviews.

"Do you have any letters to write? Books to read? Anything you want to do before, you know, it gets too late?"

He stopped fidgeting and looked at her. She noticed new determination in his eyes. He rapped the table with his knuckles and stood up. "Yes, that's what I need to do. I need to make my own list." And without further explanation he walked into the house.

As usual Elijah had presented Sarah with an enormous amount of food. Her plate was filled with chicken covered with some sort of red sauce and a side of sautéed vegetables. It was all very delicious, but there was just too much food. Although she had agreed instantly to the nutritionist, internally she wasn't excited about the idea of having someone dictate what she could and could not eat. However, now it was starting to sound more appealing. Elijah's method of trying to get her back to a healthy weight was to stuff her full of food. And she missed running. It had become her release, a way for her to recharge her batteries. She couldn't ignore the fact that her pain had lessened since she'd started the assignment, but it was still there. Sitting outside looking at the mountains helped her relax, but it didn't give her the release she needed.

She was pulled out of her thoughts at the sound of Elijah's voice. "How's your list coming along? Do I get to help you brainstorm ideas for how to mask my symptoms?"

She finished her bite of food. "Yes, your help would be great. Right now I am focused on your current symptom, assuming it will become most noticeable first. I've been observing you while you do things. For example, eating—you hold your fork in your right hand and cut with your left. Then you place the bite of food in your mouth with your fork still in your right hand. Not that I would have given this much consideration before, but that seems to be normal for someone who is left handed."

He stared at his hands holding the fork and knife suspended above his plate. "You're thinking as the tremor gets worse it will be noticeable when I eat?"

"Yes. Even now I occasionally notice a bit of a shake as the fork makes its way to your mouth. However, I don't think it would be any better for you to try and cut your food with your right hand. That might be disastrous. You can't avoid eating food at social events, and I can't cut your food for you. So, I was thinking maybe it would be better for you to cut all your food into bite sized pieces all at once, and then you can eat with your fork in your left hand while placing your right hand in your lap."

He was still staring at his hands. He looked up at her and she was taken aback by the look of vulnerability in his eyes. He talked so casually about his condition and inevitable death she assumed he was ready for anything. She realized in that moment he was more scared than he let her believe.

"I never would have thought of that. Thank you."

"You're welcome." She looked at her own hands and thought about her recommendation. "It might be hard to remember. You know, old habits die hard and all. Maybe we should both try to eat that way. It might help us remind each other, and if we start now we should be in good shape before we have to eat a meal with others. That reminds me, when is the first time you will have to attend a social event? Or have family or friends over?"

He was taking his time cutting up the rest of the food on his plate. "Social events? Not until December. My children are my only family and as you know those relationships are strained. However, we do make an attempt at normality once a year on Christmas. In a couple of weeks there's a board meeting at Kingston, and I will want you to go with me. You can sit on my right and pretend to take notes. I'll try to remember to keep my right arm in my lap, but you can tap me or something if you notice I've forgotten. Hopefully, no other symptoms are noticeable until after the holidays."

She watched as he paused to eat. The first couple of bites he forgot to switch the fork to his left hand and then on the third bite he halted his fork mid flight and stared at the fork, which was making small sudden jerks back and forth. He slowly placed his fork in his left hand and finished the bite. She ate as much as she could before pushing her plate to the side.

"So, how about your list? Are you going to tell me what it's about?"

She was happy to see a genuine smile lighten his face. "I made a list of things I would like to do before I'm rendered incompetent to do anything."

She scrutinized his face to see if he was being serious. "You made a bucket list?"

He laughed a full, deep laugh. "Yes, I did. Why do you look so surprised? It's the most obvious list I could have made."

"What's on it?"

"Well, seeing as you need to accompany me everywhere I go, you will find out soon enough."

She sat back and folded her arms across her chest. "I'm not jumping out of a plane or off a bridge." She tried to settle her facial features so he knew she was serious. The amused look he continued to give her told her it wasn't working.

He sat back and crossed his own arms, fingers stroking his chin. "Those are some good ideas. I might have to add them to the list. But first, we'll embark on something much less dangerous. How are you at dancing?"

"I beg your pardon?"

He laughed again. "Dancing. You know, moving to music?" He did a little sway back and forth with his hands as he talked. "How well do you dance, specifically ballroom?"

She settled her hands in her lap and played nervously with her napkin. She watched her fingers absentmindedly as they continuously folded and unfolded the piece of cloth. She knew he had to be asking for a specific reason and she didn't like the possibility of where this might lead.

"My ballroom dancing skills are nonexistent."

"Well, I guess we'd better get started on your lessons next week." He got up and cleared the table.

She followed, helping to carry dishes back to the kitchen. "Aren't you going to tell me why I need dance lessons? You know I'm going to ask."

He set the dishes he was carrying in the sink and leaned against the kitchen island. "When you asked about social events coming up, I reserved telling you about the most important one. Every December we have a gala in honor of Lena. She actually founded the event ten years before she died to raise money for her charity, the Marlena Throsen Dance Foundation." He crossed his arms over his chest and looked down at his feet. Before he looked down, she saw the longing that he was trying to hide. "The first event was organized to celebrate her thirtieth birthday. She had been thinking about starting a dance foundation to benefit local kids for a few years and decided it was finally time to do something about it. I've continued to host the event since her death."

She stayed silent to allow him time to reflect on his memories. She set the dishes she was holding on the counter and pulled herself up on a stool.

"It sounds like a wonderful event. I understand since the gala is for a dance foundation there will be a lot of dancing, but I'm not sure why I need to learn how to dance. No one will know me, and therefore no one will think anything of me being a very quiet wallflower."

"You need to learn to dance because you will be anything but a wallflower at this event. There's always a lead-out dance after dinner. When Lena was alive, she and I performed our wedding dance. A beautiful Viennese waltz Lena had choreographed herself. After she died, I couldn't do the dance. Instead, Leanne joined me, and we did a different dance each year. However, this year's gala is extra special. First, as you know, this will be my last chance to attend. Second, it falls on Lena's birthday. I want to do our dance this year—with you."

The fork she was holding dropped back onto the dirty plate with a loud clank. She looked down, startled, not even realizing she had picked it up. She looked back to Elijah and tried to steady her thoughts.

"Why would you not have Leanne dance it with you?"

He took in a deep breath and held it for a few seconds. "I'm afraid my symptoms will be more pronounced by then. If so, Leanne would certainly notice and would ask questions. While you and I practice, we can find acceptable adjustments to keep it from being an issue." He crossed over to the counter across from her and reached out to squeeze her hand. "And, as I've mentioned before, you remind me a lot of Lena. It would mean more to me than I can express to be able to recreate the sensation of dancing with Lena as best as I possibly can in my last dance."

She gave his hand a slight squeeze in return and let go of the tears she was holding back. "Okay then. We'll start practicing next week."

CHAPTER 6

Sarah put the shopping bags away and joined Elijah in the office as requested. The door was open and she could hear him talking to another gentleman. She knocked on the open door before entering to let them know she was there.

Elijah stopped talking and walked over to Sarah. "Thanks for joining us. I'd like you to meet my lawyer, Miles Morgan."

Miles extended his hand in greeting and gave her a warm smile. "Mrs. Mitchell. It is nice to meet you. Elijah has told me a lot about you."

She shook his hand in return. Elijah had mentioned Miles several times since she'd been there. He was younger than she'd expected, probably in his mid to late forties. He was tall like Elijah, but had a smaller build. His dark blond hair was cut short and neatly styled. His dark blue eyes conveyed compassion and genuine interest when he looked at her. It was also clear they didn't miss much. She wouldn't exactly describe him as handsome, but he presented himself with such strong confidence and authority that she formed an instant admiration for him.

"Mr. Morgan. It's nice to meet you as well."

"Miles is here to drop off the contract for Ms. Reynolds." Sarah had conducted the interviews last week and was thrilled to hit the jackpot with Lisa Reynolds, who was a registered nurse as well as a nutritionist. After reviewing her interview notes with Elijah, he had agreed she was perfect.

She looked from Elijah to Miles. "Oh, great. We are looking forward to her starting next week."

Elijah turned toward the door. "Since Miles is here, I thought I would give the two of you a chance to talk."

She stared at the closed door in confusion. Remembering her manners she turned back to Miles. His chuckle put her back at ease.

"I'm sure you've learned by now Elijah has a certain way about him that leaves everyone else in his wake, struggling to determine which way is up. It was actually my suggestion you and I talk. Please, have a seat."

As she sat down, the ring of a phone sounded somewhere within his jacket. He pulled it out and looked at the display. "I'm sorry, would you excuse me for a moment?"

As he walked over to the other side of the room, talking quietly, she looked around the office. She had seen the room when Elijah gave her a tour of the home, but she hadn't spent any time there. Similar to the great room and dining room, the back wall was made up of floor to ceiling windows. A conference table large enough to seat eight was positioned in front of the windows. The opposite wall housed built-in cabinets and bookshelves in a rich, dark mocha color. Elijah's desk sat before it in the same color and she noticed everything was neatly organized. Next to the doorway was a stone fireplace. Based on its position in the room, she knew it was the backside of the fireplace in the great room. In front of the fireplace was a sitting area with two plush leather armchairs, and she occupied one of them. It was a luxurious room, just like the rest of the home.

"Sorry about that, it was my wife." Miles sat down in the armchair adjacent to her.

"No problem." She waited a moment, not sure who was to speak first. When it didn't appear he would initiate the conversation, she jumped right in. "So, have you been working with Elijah for long?"

"For about the last ten years. I manage his legal requirements both personally and professionally." He paused a moment and considered her. "I must confess Elijah has told me about your past. When he told me he was bringing you out to discuss the project, I expressed my concern. No offense, of course. It's just Elijah's a friend as well as a client, and I wasn't sure if you would be in the right frame of mind to help him through this difficult time."

She smiled. She could have been offended at his comment, but she knew firsthand how important it was to have a good friend that looked out for your best interests. "So you thought we should talk so you could determine for yourself if I was fit to continue on this project?"

He laughed in response. "Elijah said you were direct. I like that. It will be good for him to be challenged. Too many people just kiss his ass. I have a feeling there will be some difficult moments to come, and he needs someone who won't put up with his bullshit. How are the two of you getting along so far?"

"Well, I must admit Elijah is not quite what I had anticipated. He's certainly bossy and arrogant, which I did expect. But, I've also learned he has a surprising sense of humor and he's very compassionate. We actually seem to be getting along perfectly." She looked down and smiled at the thought of some of their moments together so far. As an additional surprise, Elijah had turned out to be a very patient dance instructor. His poor toes were certainly tired of her many failed attempts this past week, but his patience never wavered.

"That's good to hear. And how have you been feeling since you arrived?" She looked up to find Miles studying her closely.

She shifted uncomfortably in her chair, tucking her feet up under her. "I'm doing okay, I think. I still have difficult moments, but I'm finding the distractions to be helpful. Halloween is in a few days, and that will be difficult for me." She looked at her hands as they played with the end of her scarf.

"I didn't know Elijah when Marlena died, but he has told me stories of how he dealt with his grief. I know he can help you if you let him."

She nodded, more in trying to convince herself he was right rather than because she already believed it to be true. "Can I ask you a question? Do you understand what happened between Elijah and his children? I'm finding it difficult to support his wishes in not telling them about his condition."

He let out a sigh. "It's complicated. As you have no doubt learned, Elijah is a very proud man. He didn't handle Marlena's death well, and it was at a time when his children really needed him. Marcus rebelled and blamed Elijah for how things turned out. Leanne tried to take on the role left vacant when Marlena died. She was young, and practically overnight she had to assume the responsibilities of a grown woman. I'm sure you can imagine it changed her completely. By the time

Elijah tried to bring them back together as a family, it was too late. The damage had been done. If you would like to know more than that, you will have to hear it from Elijah."

"Thank you for that. It helps me put some things into perspective. Speaking of his decision to not tell anyone he's sick, I understand I cannot disclose his condition to anyone. All Elijah will say is he doesn't want people to know until there's no other choice but to tell them. Who determines when that is?"

"Elijah has stipulated only he or I can inform anyone else of his condition. If you find yourself in a situation where you're getting questions you can't avoid, you can direct them to me." He reached in his pocket and pulled out a card. "Here are my numbers. Call anytime should you need something."

"Thanks. Hopefully it will be awhile until I need to call you."

He remained silent and studied her for several seconds before speaking again. "It's a shame Elijah couldn't have found someone like you years ago. He never really allowed himself to get close to a woman after Marlena died. Not that it would have changed his fate, unfortunately, but he could have been a hell of a lot happier these last few years than he has been."

She knew he meant it as a compliment. That he was trying to tell her Elijah has been happier since she started working with him. The flush taking over her face betrayed the fact it only made her uncomfortable. She diverted her gaze to the fire.

"I'm sorry. I didn't mean to make you uncomfortable. I'm not trying to suggest your relationship with Elijah is more than it is. I've just noticed your companionship has made him smile a lot more lately. Given the circumstances, I'm happy for it. As you have probably learned, CJD is a very difficult disease. For someone with as much pride as Elijah has, it will make it even that much more difficult for him. He deserves some peace in these next few months before his life becomes a living hell."

She looked back to Miles. His eyes portrayed the depth of caring he had for his friend. Looking into those eyes, so full of pain, she felt suffocated by the desire to release him from his internal torment. The fact that his anguish would deepen as Elijah's condition got worse was almost unbearable. And she had just met the man. She couldn't imagine how it must feel for Elijah to look into his friend's eyes and see his own fear and pain reflected back to him. She suddenly understood why he thought it best not to tell his children. Based on what Miles had told her, he had already caused his children an unwarranted amount of pain over the years for which he was unable to make amends. No parent would want to compound that pain by telling them they were dying. The realization didn't dampen her resolve to see if there was a way to bring them closer together, but she could understand better why he didn't want them to know.

She gave Miles a warm smile. She wanted him to know he hadn't overstepped, and she appreciated what he had to say. "Thank you. I can tell you've been a great friend to Elijah. He's lucky to have you in his life."

He stood and extended his hand. "It's been nice meeting you, Sarah. Do you mind if I call you Sarah?"

She stood and grasped his hand in return. "No, not at all. I've enjoyed meeting you as well Mr.—"

"Miles. Please, call me Miles." He placed his left hand over hers, giving it a warm hug.

"Miles. I hope when we next get the chance to talk it will be for an uneventful occasion."

"Yes, I have the same hope. Would you mind letting Elijah know I'd like to have a quick chat with him before I leave?"

"Certainly." She left Miles in the office and went in search of Elijah. Along the way, she reflected on their short but enlightening conversation and was finally able to confirm she was right where she needed to be. Regardless of how this would turn out in the end, she knew she would be a better person for having met Elijah.

Sarah snuggled herself a little deeper in the blanket. Elijah sat in the chair opposite her, looking over the contracts Miles dropped off the day before. It was a cold evening and she was enjoying the fire, but she was still cold. Her thoughts wandered to the place they could not escape—back to Nick and Danny. The next day was Halloween and Danny would have been four. During her trip to the store she'd tried to ignore the Halloween section. However, somehow she had found herself in the aisle, not even realizing it had happened until she was staring at all the costumes.

She'd stood wondering what Danny would have wanted to become on that magical night. He was too young to enjoy Halloween for the candy—no, it was all about the costumes. He'd loved playing dress-up. At the store she had ran her hand down the Batman costume. Deep in her core she knew he would have loved it.

"Are you cold or are you trying to disappear?"

She looked up over the rim of the cocoon she had created and pulled the blanket down to respond. "My nose is cold."

Elijah smiled and walked over to the fireplace. He put on another log and stoked it a few times. "Hopefully that will help. Can I get you another blanket? Or perhaps a scarf? I know—a ski mask would do the trick. Ah, there's a smile." He walked back over to his chair and sat down. "Everything okay?"

"Yeah, I was just thinking." She continued to stare at the fire. She didn't need to look at Elijah to know he was waiting for her to go on. It had been so long since she'd talked about her feelings with anyone. Outside of Maggie and her mom, the last time was during a therapy session. Finally, she decided to open up. It was time to start trusting his process.

"I was thinking about Danny. More specifically, I was thinking about what he might have been for Halloween. At the store there was this Batman costume. I think he would have picked that one." She paused for a moment, considering if she could keep going. She wasn't sure if it was the newly invigorated fire or the emotion of talking about Danny, but she felt warmer, so she pulled her arms out from under the blanket. Instinctively, her fingers found their way to where her wedding ring used to be. She was no longer able to wear it, but her fingers twisted back and forth around her finger just the same. The motion gave her a small amount of strength.

"For Danny, capes were more exciting than ice cream. It all started one Saturday morning, just after he had turned two. I was looking through the TV channels and decided to check out a show he hadn't watched before. He loved it. His favorite character wore a cape, and suddenly he wanted one too, so I improvised with a blanket and a rubber band. He wore it every day for two weeks straight, and when I tried to take it away he'd cry. Nick saved the day, as he usually did, by coming home from work one day with a real cape. Nick told him it was a magic cape that only worked at home." She paused and smiled at the memory of Danny's excitement when he opened the gift. "He was too young to really understand what he was agreeing to, but all that mattered was it was a *real* cape and Daddy knew how to make the magic in it work. No more tears, no more fights. And, no more blanket-made-cape costumes at restaurants." She swiped at the loose tear that fell down her cheek.

"How did you handle the situation at the store, when you saw those costumes? You seemed okay when you got home." She looked at him and noticed genuine concern in his eyes. In any other conversation she would have reacted to his use of the word home, implying it was her home as well.

"From my perspective, I think I did all right. For a long time it was as if my feet were glued to the floor. Then, I couldn't flee fast enough when I saw a little boy and his excitement over what he wanted to be for Halloween. I composed myself in the bathroom. Overall, I think I did all right." She noticed the last line was a repeat of her first.

Are you trying to convince him or yourself?

"Have you been around any children since Danny's death?"

She darted a glance down at her hands and then looked back to the fire. "Not really. Maggie has brought her daughter Jaime by the house a few times. She's older though, and a girl so I had never really compared her to Danny." She paused, feeling her heart beat a little faster. She knew she needed to finally admit the next part—needed to say it out loud. It was something she was sure Maggie understood, but they never talked about it. "Maggie has a son, Nathan, who was born the year before Danny. They used to play together a lot while Maggie and I visited. I can't even look at Nathan now, and I never go to their house any more. Although I know Maggie understands, I think it hurts her that I can't bring myself to interact with him even on a basic level. She doesn't mention him at all, and I don't ask."

He took a long time considering her response. "Would you like to tell me more about Danny?"

She looked up to the ceiling and let out a deep sigh. A part of her wanted desperately to talk about Danny. However, the more dominate side wanted to hold it in. There was a fear in letting it out. Talking about Danny somehow made her feel like she would lose a piece of him each time. That telling someone even the slightest detail would take that particular memory and throw it out into the air, never to be caught again. In her extended hesitation she heard Elijah begin to speak.

"As you know, Lena was a dancer. She started taking dance classes when she was three years old—her mother always said she was born with music in her bones, and they were meant to move. When she was young she trained in every form of dance, but eventually she gravitated to study only ballet. After high school, she went on to study at the Colorado Ballet Academy. The love she had for dancing radiated from her and infected everyone who watched her." He got up and walked over to a table at the far end of the room. He picked up a picture frame and stared at it for several moments before handing it to her. It was a photo of Marlena dressed in a classic white ballet outfit on stage. The picture was in profile so she couldn't make out her features, but Elijah was right. There was a beauty that emanated from her.

"She's beautiful. How did the two of you meet?" She handed the photo back. He sat back down in his chair, setting the photo on the table next to him.

"My parents loved to go to the ballet. I enjoyed it as well but never really made time to go. One year for my mother's birthday my father purchased tickets for us to go as a family. I remember the first moment I saw Lena. It was about ten minutes into the performance, and she came out in a group with five other dancers. My breathing literally stopped, and my entire body felt electrified. I couldn't take my eyes off her the entire time she was on stage. In that moment, I knew I would marry her someday. Of course the logical part of my brain thought I was crazy. I didn't know anything about her, but none of it mattered. I was going to make it happen; I knew it had to happen." He looked at the photo again, running his thumb over the image of Marlena.

"The awkward part was my girlfriend of four years, Caroline, was sitting next to me the entire time. I dropped her off at home and broke up with her on impulse. She was shocked and kept asking me why. I didn't want to tell her, I didn't want to hurt her, but I wasn't thinking rationally. Finally, I told her it was because I had fallen in love with someone else. Caroline looked at me with this dumbstruck look and asked when it had happened. I said, 'Four hours ago.' She thought I was crazy or lying, or likely both, and kicked me out." He let out a small chuckle at the memory. "The next day I asked my father to pull in a favor and get me a meeting with Lena. I went to the performance and was admitted backstage afterwards. I introduced myself and asked her out on a date. Luckily it didn't take much convincing to get her to agree."

She studied his face as he looked at the photo, lost in his memories. The love he still held for his late wife was evident. Although he was the one sharing his memories, she herself felt exposed. The depth of feeling in his voice brought forth her feelings of love for Nick and Danny. For so long the only thing she had felt was pain and loneliness. She had forgotten what it felt like to love them, how it made her feel warm and alive. She wanted to hear more of Elijah and Marlena's story, to use his words to keep these born again feelings prominent.

"Did she dance professionally?"

"No. She was on track to join their company of dancers and she performed in several productions as a student. However, life set her on a different path. We married only eight months after our first date, and almost exactly a year later Marcus was born. Performing would have been difficult after that, so instead she decided to become a ballet teacher, turning her focus to children. She opened a dance studio and stayed there until she died."

There was one question she really wanted to ask, but she couldn't form the words. In a manner that was very unlike her, she decided to avoid the direct approach and go in another direction. "Did Leanne take to dancing as well?"

Instead of answering, he got up and walked over to the kitchen. "Let me get us some wine."

She waited quietly as he poured two glasses of red wine. She studied his movements as he poured and walked back in her direction. She wasn't sure she could prove it if asked, but she thought she noticed the slightest change in his walk. It wasn't as smooth as when she'd first arrived, but subtle enough that no one else would notice. He handed her a glass and she took a hesitant sip. She didn't drink much and she knew the next day would be hard enough without a hangover.

"Thanks."

He settled back in his chair. He glanced at Marlena's photo again as he set down his own glass of wine. "Leanne danced when she was young, and as she got older she held an appreciation for it, but it wasn't an important part of her life. Marcus was the surprise. He was Lena's little apprentice, participating in every one of her dance classes. He stopped when he got older and his need to fit in at school got stronger. He was too proud to talk about it, but Lena and I both knew he missed dancing. That's when we built the studio downstairs. It took time, but eventually he made the space his own. He once told me he could listen to the music and feel the movement before he danced a single step. I watched him a few times, discreetly from behind the studio door. Watching him was like seeing Lena on stage all over again. He was magnificent. Unfortunately, he stopped dancing after Lena died."

Even if the relationships were strained, the way he talked about his children make it clear he loved them deeply. "How did she die?" She finally got the question out of her head.

He picked up his glass of wine and swirled it around, watching the liquid move around the glass in a hypnotic motion. "It was just a normal day. I went to work and Lena was working from home, preparing a dance routine for one of her classes. I got home late, knowing she would be at the studio. I went to the kitchen to find the dinner she usually left for me in the fridge. She always took care of me that way." He took another sip of his wine. If she felt like splitting hairs, it was more like a small gulp than a sip. He set down the glass and picked up the picture of Marlena, holding it with both hands in his lap.

"Before my dinner had finished heating in the microwave, the phone rang. It was one of the dance instructors at the studio. She was talking hysterically, and I was having difficulty understanding what she was saying. I finally got her to calm down enough for me to learn Lena had collapsed at the studio. She was already gone by time the ambulance arrived."

Hearing him talk about what happened to Marlena triggered her own reaction, bringing forth the images in her mind she'd tried hard to erase the last two years—the broken car, the ground sparkling with shattered glass, Max... They appeared in her mind like a negative strip from an old 35mm film camera. She blinked back her tears and took a large sip of her own wine, trying to settle her thoughts.

"The doctors said she died of fatal heart arrhythmia. When Lena was younger, in the height of her dancing, she suffered from severe anorexia. As you can expect, it did damage to her body, although it was difficult to determine how much. She was told she had a higher risk for heart failure in the future. We focused on ways to keep her healthy, and our hope transitioned into belief as the years went by. We were happy and enjoyed life. Then, years later, I tested positive for the mutated CJD gene, and we were reminded all over again how fragile and unpredictable life could be. We started to focus on my illness and how we would handle it if the time came. We'd finally accepted the situation and found a way to be happy in the years we had left. Even though it wasn't guaranteed I would develop the CJD illness, deep down I think I always knew it was my fate. She wasn't the one who was supposed to die first."

Yes, life was fragile and unpredictable. She knew first hand all about that.

So why would I want to expose myself to the risk of loss and heartbreak all over again? It's safer to be alone. He stayed alone, and he seems normal enough now. Just his work and a few friends to keep his attentions after she died. I wonder why he said he did it wrong. Sounds like it worked out okay to me.

"What happened after? You said you didn't handle it well and lost your relationship with your children."

Setting Marlena's photo down, he got up and took their glasses back to the kitchen for a refill. She hadn't noticed hers was empty. Her head was swimming slightly and she was warm all over, enough that she kicked off the blanket.

I should probably stop drinking.

As logical as that thought was, the conversation was too heavy for her to approach without a little liquid courage. She took a sip as soon as he handed the glass back to her.

"People often talk about finding their soul mate, like it's the most divine type of love one can experience. Lena and I were so much more than that. It's hard to explain." He paused to consider his words. "When I was with Lena I didn't just feel alive, I felt *everything*. She opened up a part of me I never knew existed. It's hard to lose that kind of love, to lose the power source that keeps you alive. At first I didn't think I would be able to survive. I didn't want to. I threw myself into work, and when I wasn't at work I was no better than someone in a coma. It was three years after Lena died when I finally opened my eyes. I had come home from work and gone straight to the office as I did almost every night. I was sitting there, staring at the empty fireplace when I heard Leanne's hysterical crying.

"I found her sobbing uncontrollably on the kitchen floor, surrounded by what was supposed to be a cake. Between sobs she said, 'I'm so sorry Daddy. I've tried to make us a family, but I'm not as good as Mom.' She was eighteen. She should have been off to college, but instead she was still at home, trying to make it work. Marcus was in college and excelled academically, but he got into all sorts of trouble outside of school. Almost every night it was the same thing—drinking, fighting, a different girl. As I looked at Leanne broken on the kitchen floor, something in my head finally popped into place. I hadn't even remembered it was Marcus' birthday. I made every effort to move on after that, but it was too late."

So that's it. That's how he failed them. Fixing this will be more difficult than I thought. Oh boy, I think I'm getting drunk. But, it still doesn't help me understand why I have to move on if he didn't have to. I think he just likes to tell me what—

"I know you better by now, Sarah. Based on the look I see on your face, the one where your eyebrows pinch together in the center, you're thinking about something. You want to know why it was okay for me to not move on but it's not okay for you. Is that right?"

How the hell did he do that?

She put her fingers to her forehead, trying to push her eyebrows apart. "Yes, that sounds about right."

"Because you still have a life to live. I suspected my days were numbered—that I had about twenty years left, maybe even less. I couldn't bring myself to let someone else into my life just to have them go through this pain." He got up and walked over to the windows, looking out over the dark of the night.

"With my children, by the time I realized they needed me, they were already gone and didn't want me. All I had left was work." He turned back to face her. "I know for a fact, from experience, my way was the wrong way. You have a lot of life left in your future, Sarah. Sure, you don't know what will happen tomorrow, but believe me— twenty years from now you don't want to wake up and look back on your life only to wish you hadn't been so afraid of tomorrow. It never goes away—the unknown of tomorrow. You need to live as much life today as you would in a lifetime."

She drank down the rest of her wine.

The man makes a hell of a lot of sense. I just wish I knew how to do it...

"Come. I think you've hit your limit. It's time for me to put you to bed." He helped her out of the chair. "I need to remember in the future your drinking threshold is only one glass. Who knew you were such a lightweight?"

"I barely weigh more than your pinky, remember? Not much to hold a tolerance." She walked with him up to her room. She wasn't stumbling, but she wasn't exactly steady either. He escorted her to her bed and tucked her in. "Elijah? Thanks for sharing with me tonight. I'm sorry I wasn't able to do the same."

"Next time it will be your turn." He started toward the door and then looked back at her before turning out the light. "So, tomorrow is Halloween. What should I expect?"

She put her hand over her eyes. "Nothing. You should expect me to be able to do absolutely nothing. I'm sorry."

"I'll check on you a few times throughout the day if that's okay. Otherwise, I suppose I'll see you the day after Halloween. Good night, Sarah."

CHAPTER 7

Sarah opened her eyes and couldn't see anything in the darkness. She had no idea what time it was, but she knew what day it was. She got up, used the bathroom, changed into her pajamas, and crawled back under the covers. Despite her efforts to do otherwise, her mind produced images of Danny. The four year old Danny of her imagination was running around in the Batman costume, his hands holding the cape out wide behind him. Suddenly, she saw Nick chasing after Danny, both falling into fits of laughter as Nick caught up with him. She smiled at the thought, silent tears leaking from the corners of her eyes, before finally drifting back to sleep.

Sarah heard the faint sound of movement coming from Elijah's room. She rolled to her back and looked up to the ceiling. This time her mind presented her with images of Danny on his last Halloween before the accident. He wore a Thomas the Train costume and walked around most of the night making choo-choo sounds. They had spent the evening at the Jacobs' house for dinner. Every time the doorbell rang Danny rushed to the door, squealing with delight, trying to see all the costumes. He tired out before the end of the night and crashed on the floor. When it was time to leave, Nick picked him up to carry him to the car. As Danny snuggled into Nick's shoulder, he had said the cutest thing—

Wait, what did he say?

She sat up, pressing on the sides of her head with the palms of her hands.

What did he say? Oh God, why can't I remember?

She searched every corner of her brain but it wasn't there. She turned over and buried her face in the pillows.

What did he say? Please, God, please let me remember. I can't lose this too.

Her pain came in an extreme force, crushing her chest so tightly she thought her ribs might physically crack. She gripped the sheets, letting out a cry of agony. She was encased in her pain, struggling to catch her breath between sobs, when she suddenly felt two hands on her shoulders.

Nick?

She turned in confusion only to find Elijah reaching for her. She tried to pull away, but he held her tighter, whispering soothing words.

"I can't remember. I can't remember what he said." She finally stopped trying to pull away and gripped his arms.

"Shh, it's okay. It's all going to be okay." Elijah continued to hold her until she calmed down and fell back into sleep.

What the hell was that?!

Sarah bolted up. Whatever the sound was, it was followed by a sharp cry of pain.

Elijah!

She jumped out of bed and threw open the door.

"Elijah?" She heard another cry, followed by profanity, coming from his room. She hurried to the door and opened it without bothering to knock. "Elijah? Elijah, are you okay?"

"Shit! Sarah, I need help." His voice, laced with pain, came from the direction of his bathroom.

Panic gripped her as she ran to the bathroom. She found him in a heap on the floor, holding his head. She hurried over and dropped down on the ground, trying to pry his hand from his head. Once she got it away she noticed the blood.

"Oh, my God, Elijah! What happened?" She looked around frantically for a towel or something to press to his forehead.

"I hit my head on the counter. I'm sure it looks worse than it feels, but I can't get my balance to get up." He tried to grab for the counter and missed by about two inches.

"Here, let me help you." She stood and suddenly realized the full details of his state. "Holy shit, you're naked!" She turned her back to him and froze, not knowing what to do next.

How the hell did I not notice he was naked?

"Well, yes. I was in the bath and my towel was too far away. I fell when reaching for it. Do you mind handing it to me?" She didn't move. "Sarah, I'm bleeding here."

That snapped her back into action and she located his towel on the counter. She tossed it back to him without turning around. "Are you able to wrap it around you yourself?"

"Not all the way since I can't get up. But I've covered the offensive parts, so you can turn around now and help me up." She tried to keep her eyes locked on the back of his head. She wasn't strong enough to pull him to his feet and he felt her difficulty. "Can you help me reach the counter?" She placed his hand, the one that wasn't holding the towel to his private parts, on the counter and pushed him closer to help him get leverage. Finally, he was able to get to his feet and he wrapped the towel the rest of the way around his waist. He was unsteady on his feet, so she helped him get to the toilet so he could sit. He looked up at her, and she noticed the irritation and embarrassment in his eyes. "Thank you."

"Do you have anything I can use to clean your cut?" Without waiting for an answer she started opening drawers.

"In the closet, second shelf from the top." She opened the closet and located the box with the first aid supplies and a clean wash cloth. She turned back to find him holding toilet paper to his head. In the wrong spot. With the coordination issues he was experiencing he missed the cut completely and blood was trickling down the side of his face. She wet the wash cloth in the sink with warm water and crouched next to him.

"Here, let me." She moved his hand and placed the warm wash cloth to the cut. She lightened the pressure when he winced. "Sorry."

"It's fine. How bad is it?"

She wiped away the blood on his face. "You were right, it looks bad. You'll probably have a bump for awhile, but I don't think it needs stitches." She concentrated on cleaning and bandaging the cut.

"Thanks." He got up to look at his forehead in the mirror. He had regained some control over his movement, but he still wasn't very steady on his feet. He held the towel around his waist with his right hand and used his left to hold onto the counter for balance. His arms were well toned and she watched the muscles on his back flex as he leaned closer to the mirror to get a better look. He had a small amount of hair on his chest. Her eyes traveled down to his well formed abs just above the towel.

Man, he's in good shape for a 65 year old.

With sudden horror that she was checking out her boss she quickly turned away.

"Um, are you okay to get dressed by yourself?"

"If I sit down on the toilet again I think I can manage. However, you'll have to bring me something to put on. My boxers are in the top drawer, the small one, in the closet. Left side. You can get me a pair of pajama pants from the drawer just below that. Any T-shirt you see hanging will be fine." He sat back down and looked dazed.

She hurried out of the room and into Elijah's closet. She leaned against a cabinet and covered her face in her hands.

What the hell is wrong with me? It's not like I'm attracted to him or anything.

She let out an involuntary groan.

"Sarah, you okay?"

"Yeah, just... stubbed my toe."

Great, he's the one bleeding from the head and he's worried about me. Get a grip Mitchell.

She completed her task of finding clothes and hurried back to the bathroom. "Will this work?"

"Perfect. Thanks." He started to pull on his boxers and then looked at her with a curious gaze.

She blinked her eyes a few times before realizing she was staring at him. "Right, I'll be out here if you need help."

She turned and quickly went into his bedroom. She was feeling very awkward about the whole situation and decided to wait for him in a chair by the fireplace. She massaged her temples, thinking about all that had happened. It had turned out to be a wretched day.

What else could I have expected on Halloween?

She suddenly froze.

It's still Halloween and I was able to get out of bed.

"Sarah?" The sound of Elijah's voice came from the bathroom. His tone indicated it wasn't the first time he had said her name. "Are you okay?"

"Yeah, sorry. Just lost in a thought. Do you need help?"

"Yes, I think so. I'm better, but I think it would be a good idea for you to walk me to the chair." He leaned against the door of the bathroom while he waited for her. He put his arm around her shoulders and they made their way back to the sitting area.

"Can I get you anything else?"

"No, thank you." He rested his head on the back of the chair and stretched his legs out before him. He closed his eyes and let out a sigh. "Will you sit with me for awhile?"

She looked at the chair she had been sitting in a few moments ago and hesitated a moment before sitting back down, wrapping a blanket around her legs. "Of course."

He opened his eyes a crack and looked at her. He closed them again and put his hand to his head. "I'm sorry I interrupted your day of mourning. Please don't feel obligated to stay. I'm sure I'll be fine."

She let out a shaky breath. "Aren't I supposed to keep you awake for the next two hours or something? Isn't that what they say you should do after a head injury?"

He laughed while putting his hand down and shifting in his chair. "I think that's more of an old wives tale than actual medical advice. Even if it were true, I'm not sure my bump would qualify as a serious enough injury. But I'll still take you up on the offer. How do you plan to keep me awake?"

"Talking, I guess. It is my turn right? But first, I want to understand what happened in the bathroom. Was it a random incident or is this the start of another symptom?"

"Unfortunately, I think it's another symptom. I wasn't feeling well today. My arms, my legs—everything just felt heavy. Similar to what it feels like with the flu. I thought soaking in the bath would help."

The unwanted image of Elijah sitting on the toilet, holding toilet paper in the wrong spot on his head, came up in her mind. It was contrary to the 'Mighty Mr. Kingston' image she had assigned to him prior to the assignment. She shook her head and pulled her focus back to the present.

"Okay, so I'll give you fifteen questions. Anything you want to ask, I'll answer."

He shifted in his chair to face her directly. "Fifteen questions? Isn't twenty questions the standard game?"

"I'm feeling unconventional at the moment."

"Okay, fifteen it is. I guess I had better make these good." He thought for a moment and then the corners of his mouth curved in a playful smile. "Why do you get so embarrassed when I make flirtatious comments?"

Seriously? That's the first question he wants to ask me?

To her dismay, her face showed the apparent tell-tale sign of her embarrassment. "I started dating Nick when I was sixteen. I had been with him for nearly half my life—not counting the two years we were separated." She paused to collect her thoughts again.

You got yourself into this mess. You said you would answer any question.

"I'm not used to it I guess. I don't know how I'm supposed to respond without giving the wrong impression. I also didn't expect you to be so... playful. Your reputation implies you would have a much more serious nature than what you've shown me so far."

"I suppose that makes sense. However, you're going to have to find a way to be more comfortable around me. I intend to keep my personality intact for as long as I can. Also, given the circumstances of just a few moments ago, there will likely be additional moments when you will be required to help me when I'm less than fully dressed. Or even help me get dressed or undressed." She noted the embarrassment in his voice. No adult would want to require someone to help them with their basic needs, especially someone as proud as Elijah.

"That's why we've hired Ms. Reynolds. She will be able to assist you in any situations where your unmentionables might be exposed."

"Sure, but she won't be living here. At least not initially. Believe me, I'm hoping you don't find me in a naked heap on my bathroom floor again but you have to accept it's a possibility and it would be good if you weren't so... distracted next time."

She was sure her face was a full ten shades darker. "I wasn't distracted. I was caught off guard. And don't forget, I was practically in a coma when it happened."

At least her response earned a laugh. "Fair enough, you were simply caught off guard. Now that you know it's a possibility it should be easier next time." He looked her over with an assessing gaze. "Speaking of being in a coma, what happened earlier today when you had your breakdown?"

"I was thinking about one of my favorite moments with Danny. It was the last Halloween before the accident. We were over at the Jacobs' house and Danny had so much fun running to the door, trying to look at all the costumes. He tired out before the end of the night and fell asleep on the floor. When Nick picked him up to carry him to the car, he'd stirred and said something adorable. It was a day I had gone over in my mind hundreds of times, both before and after the accident. This time I couldn't remember what he'd said. It's gone. I don't want to forget. I'm afraid of forgetting."

He was quiet for a few moments, absorbing her response. "I hope you realize that part of this fifteen questions deal is I get to give you advice." He paused to ensure she wasn't going to complain. When she remained silent he continued. "I had a hard time when I first realized I was forgetting details about Lena." She could see pain flash across his eyes, and she knew it was more from long ago memories than the bump on his head.

"It got better when I realized I didn't have to hold on to every detail to retain the feeling of the moment. My guess is if Danny had not said whatever it was he said, that day would have still been one of your favorite memories. The joy at remembering his excitement of the day cannot be forgotten. And you will always remember the big details—the costume he wore, that he ran to the door each time the bell rang, that you were happy and enjoyed the night with close friends. Sure the smaller details are special, but they're not necessary to keep the moment alive." He stopped a moment to think, tapping his hand on the arm of the chair.

"Consider two televisions, side-by-side, showing the same football game. One is in high-definition and the other is not. The high-definition is really cool and gives you an amazing experience with very sharp, crisp images. You're able to see every detail, down to the individual blades of grass on the field. But on both televisions the game is the same. Over time the things you would remember about the game would be the same regardless of how you watched it. You don't have to hold on so tight. Don't worry about the details; just relive the emotions of the memory."

Tears fell silently down her cheeks. She wiped them away and rubbed at her eyes. Just hearing the words seemed to lift a heavy weight off her shoulders.

"Thank you." It came out as a soft whisper, but she knew that he had heard.

"What's your favorite color?"

"Aquamarine. It was the color of my grandmother's birthstone. I was very close with her when I was a child."

"How did you and Nick meet?"

She rubbed her eyes and thought for a moment about what she wanted to tell him. "I was a junior in high school, and he was a senior. He was a starter on the soccer team. I knew who he was, but I had no interest because I just thought he was an arrogant jock. My friend was infatuated with him and at a dance one day I went up to him and said, 'my friend over there likes you and wants to know if you'll ask her to dance.' He gave me this amused look and said 'no, but I'd like to ask you to dance.' I was so stunned I didn't think to stop him as he pulled me out on the dance floor. It turned out he was really sweet, and we were together from that moment on. Of course no matter how much I tried to explain it to my friend she never talked to me again."

"You mentioned the two of you broke up for a couple years. When was that and how did it happen?"

"To be clear, that counts as two questions."

"No, I don't think so. The two have to go together to get the full understanding."

"My game, my rules. It counts as two. We broke up when Nick left for college. The way it happened—he decided for the both of us long distance relationships were too hard."

He raised his eyebrow at her and then winced. The motion must have irritated the cut on his forehead. "That's all I get?"

"I said I would answer your questions. I didn't say how much detail I would go into. You want more? Ask another question. You have nine left."

"You've got your bite back. That's good." She refused to return his smile, but inside she was pleased with herself. "Okay, *question seven*—how did you two get back together?"

"I was a mess. When he broke up with me, it was as if he'd ripped out my heart, taking it with him and leaving the rest of me behind as a worthless shell. I struggled with my classes, and my grades slipped. He came home over summer break, and I saw him at a bakery we often went to together. I watched him through the window where he couldn't see me. I remember the way he had stared at the fruit pastry in the display case—it was what I always ordered. He always had the quiche. I could see his hesitation when the server asked for his order. He pointed to the fruit pastry, and I knew he still held feelings for me. It was all I needed to pull myself back together. I knew I had to go to the same university to have a chance to be with him again. My grades suffered from checking out all senior year, so I had to spend a year at the community college to pull the credits for a transfer. My determination didn't stop once I got there and not long after school started we were back together."

"What do you think would have happened if you didn't see him that day, or if he would have ordered the quiche without a moment's hesitation?"

She had never considered the possibility. Things had worked out, there was no need to look back into the past and consider the alternative. "I guess I would have eventually found a way to move on and would have met someone else."

The gravity of what she'd said sank in while she watched Elijah study her.

I would have eventually moved on. There would have been a life for me outside of Nick.

Whether that life would have been better, the same, or worse was unknown. The whole point was that she still would have had a life.

"How many brothers and sisters do you have?"

"I have three older brothers, Tom, James and Peter. No sisters."

She got up to look over his cut when he put his hand to his head and closed his eyes.

"Maybe you should rest."

He grabbed her hand and gave it a squeeze. She tried to ignore the fact that he missed her hand the first time. "Not a chance. I intend to take every advantage of my fifteen questions." He cleared his throat and sat up straighter. "On your first day out here we established you don't have any hobbies now, but what kind of hobbies were you into before the accident?"

She gave him an impatient look then resumed her position in the chair across from him. She tucked her feet under her and the blanket around her legs. She wasn't cold any more, but the added weight of the blanket gave her a sense of security.

"For some reason I was one of those people who never really had a hobby. I had looked into taking a photography class about a year after Danny was born, but I never found the time. After the accident... everything lost its beauty. If you can't see the beauty in something, why capture it indefinitely through the eye of a camera?"

Everything lost its beauty... until I came out here. I'm starting to see the beauty in things again. But what happens when I leave? Will the loss of Elijah and going home set me back again?

"What are you thinking right now?"

The sound of Elijah's voice brought her out of her internal thoughts. It was almost unsettling how in tune he was to all her little nuances. "I was thinking my statement, about everything losing its beauty, was true until I came here. The first day when I stepped out of the hotel I remember thinking everything looked so much more vibrant than at home. It was invigorating. I should be excited about the progress I've made, but thinking about it only made me sad and I was wondering why."

"And what have you discovered?"

She took in a deep breath and held it. She let it out slowly and tried to settle her hands that were suddenly playing with the end of the blanket. "I think I'm afraid it will go away when I get back home. That this place has become a form of sanctuary for me, and once I leave the magic will be lost with it. If I can only be happy in one place, far away from my home, have I really made any progress at all?"

"That's bullshit."

She felt an instant anger creep up her neck. "Excuse me?"

He sat forward and pinned her with a hard look. "You heard me. That's bullshit. I'm not trying to hurt your feelings or diminish your concerns, but I'm going to call it as I see it. Your penchant for self-deprecation has got to stop. You know you've made progress. Allowing yourself to even think otherwise is just a way for you to hide behind your fears of the unknown. By belittling your progress you're setting yourself up to achieve the one thing you're most comfortable with—going back to the way things were. You've made significant progress, and you're afraid of *that*. I think you know it, but you won't admit it to me or yourself. Living a fulfilling life without Nick and Danny is what scares you the most."

She sat completely still, staring at him, as she felt a multitude of emotions surge through her. She wasn't sure if she wanted to throttle him or run back to her bed and hide under the covers. He continued to stare at her, waiting for her to parrot back what she didn't want to acknowledge. She decided she needed to get out of the room.

"I'm hungry." She got up and walked out the door without waiting for his response.

About thirty minutes later Sarah returned back to Elijah's bedroom, carrying a half-eaten sandwich and two bottled waters. She placed one of the waters next to Elijah and sat back down in her chair, proceeding to finish her sandwich. She knew Elijah well enough by now to know he wouldn't ask another question until she said what he wanted to hear.

He can wait.

While in the kitchen she had been able to diffuse her anger by slamming a few cabinet doors. With nothing left to slam, she'd rested her hands on the counter and hung her head.

He's wrong, I'm not afraid of living. I'm afraid of losing again and the soul shattering pain that comes with it.

She allowed herself to consider Elijah's words. She thought of her time here, how she was handling things. She had made improvement, but she had also held on to certain patterns that had become the background fabric of her life over the last two years. Today was a perfect example. She didn't even allow herself to consider the possibility that she could spend Halloween outside of bed, protected by the familiar feeling of surrendering to her pain. And while she was wallowing in her self-induced coma, Elijah had needed her.

I didn't need to be in bed to survive Halloween. I needed to be in bed so I could ensure the day centered on Danny. It's because I won't let go. I won't allow myself to live without him or Nick.

The acknowledgement came easily and without shock, as if it had been waiting for a long time to make its way forward in her mind. She waited for the sobs to begin but to her surprise there were none. In its place she felt relief.

Now it was time. Her sandwich was gone and Elijah was waiting patiently.

"You're right, I'm afraid of living. At least living happily. It feels as if I would be discounting my love for them. You said so yourself, on my first day here. My family was my light, my happiness. If they were my life, how do I live without them? I'm not just afraid of living. I'm afraid of allowing myself to hope again, to dream of a future only for it to fall short. I don't know if I want to become dependent on another person for happiness. Life has shown me nothing is protected. Why would I want to risk losing everything again?"

"If you had decided all those years ago when Nick broke up with you that it was too risky to pursue him again, then you would have missed out on several years of a great marriage and the joy of being Danny's mother. You are who you are today because of your experiences with them. Sure, you could fall in love again and that person could leave your life in any number of ways. It would be painful and devastating but it would be worth the risk to love someone and have them love you back. Not taking the risk only assures you will live a very sad and lonely life. And we're not just talking about you falling in love with someone else. What about your general love for life itself? Like you mentioned earlier, the ability to see the beauty in the things around you? Nothing can take that away from you unless you let it."

She let his words penetrate past her defenses and stir up hope. She didn't speak but she nodded to let him know she accepted his argument.

"So, how many more questions do I have? I know you're keeping track."

"Of course I'm keeping track. You have three left."

"Hum, only three... okay, what's your favorite food?"

"Pizza."

He tilted his head to the side and gave her a curious look. "I wouldn't have pegged you for a pizza girl."

Just thinking about pizza made her stomach rumble. "Oh, yes. But not just any pizza. I mean, I'll eat any pizza you put in front of me and I'll enjoy it. However my favorite above all other is Chicago style deep dish. Growing up we would head into the city almost every weekend in search of the best pizza. Everyone in the family had a different opinion, but the purpose wasn't to form a consensus. It was to have an excuse to go and eat pizza. My favorite was this little place on Michigan Ave. Not only was their pizza my favorite, but the restaurant itself was so much fun."

"I've never been there. I'll have to go the next time I'm in Chicago." He stopped abruptly. It was the first time he'd forgotten there will likely not be a next time for many things. He shook his head slightly and continued his interrogation.

"Who's Max?" There was a sudden pressure in her head and she felt her ears throb with every beat of her heart. She didn't talk about Max with anyone but her parents and Maggie. His question threw her off balance. "You were asleep earlier today when I went in your room to check on you. You stirred and called out the name Max."

She took a deep breath before responding. "Max is a big brown stuffed dog Danny took with him everywhere. We gave it to him his last Christmas and there was an instant attachment. Max was the first thing I saw at the accident site. It's how I knew the tragic events unfolding around me were *my* tragic events." She had to stop and wait until the images faded from her mind. The tightening was returning to her chest, and she was finding it difficult to breathe. She squeezed her eyes closed and put her face in her hands. After a few moments she was able to go on.

"Now Max sits on Danny's bed. When I need to be close to Danny, like on Halloween, I hold on to Max. I decided not to bring him on this trip. I... I don't know if Max is healthy for me."

After a few moments of silence she looked back over to Elijah. He was staring at the empty fireplace. "I can understand the need to hold on to something that reminds you of him. Something he cherished. I also think it was wise of you to evaluate the dependence you've formed on Max. It will take some time, but you will no doubt come to terms with a healthy attachment to the memory of Danny's love for Max." He looked back to her and she saw the slightest hint of moisture in his eyes. She had to look away before she lost control over her own emotions again. She needed her strength for the final question she knew was coming.

"So, my final question." His voice was soft and she kept her eyes locked on the fireplace. "Since you have come to stay here, I've noticed every morning the doors to both guest bedrooms are closed. At first I thought it was the cleaning service, but quickly realized that wasn't the case. So, my assumption is you're the one closing the doors—although I'm not sure why. Why do you close the doors Sarah?"

This was the question she had been expecting. When she continued her nighttime ritual at Elijah's house, she didn't stop to think whether he would notice or what his response would be. It wasn't until the morning when he had taken her into his bathroom to determine her weight that she realized he'd found it strange. On their way downstairs he had hesitated and looked down the hall to the closed doors. Since then, she knew this question was coming and had contemplated her answer. Now that the time was here, her prepared answer seemed too superficial, so she explained to him how she had reacted after the accident and how that turned into her saying good night to Nick and Danny each night.

"My first night here, I was having difficulty falling asleep. I eventually went down to the kitchen to get something to drink. On my way back to my room I looked down the hall and it was like I was on autopilot. I closed each door and started my routine. It's my way of talking to them. Some people like to visit a grave site, but I prefer something more familiar."

"After Lena died, I used to talk to her for hours in the dance studio. When I finally began to move on, I realized I needed to find a way to talk to her anywhere. By talking to her only in the studio I was keeping myself securely seated in two separate worlds. One where I had to function without her and one where I could relive the memory of her. Merging my two worlds enabled me to feel like I always had her with me and my reality became better."

She looked at him with amazement. "How did you do it? How did you know what to do? Did you have a great therapist or something? I've been to *eight* different therapists and none of them helped. No, that's not fair. One did teach me how to overcome my panic attacks, and a few have echoed some of your words. But none were able to actually help me move past the pain."

"No, I didn't see a therapist though I probably should have. I simply had to get through it, had to figure it out. Don't forget, it took me three years to get to the point of even trying. Once I finally realized I had my children to consider, I found a new purpose and it propelled me forward. I also had about twenty years of trial and error. I made a lot of mistakes, and I'm hoping to be able to pass along my lessons learned to you." He paused to take a drink of his water. The way he took his time, focusing on the bottle and moving his hand slowly to ensure he connected with his target made her catch her breath. She knew the symptoms of CJD could escalate rapidly, but she wasn't ready. He set the bottle back down and closed his eyes before looking back to her.

"I also believe you didn't *want* to make the change. The reason I feel so strongly that you being here, working on this project, will help is because you're forced to face reality. You've been removed from the major stimulants of your environment, and you're able to acknowledge a change is needed. When you return home, I recommend you reach back out to a therapist and continue to heal."

"Did I just hear you admit you won't be able to fix me completely? Certainly the Mighty Mr. Kingston doesn't need anyone else to finish his job." After the heaviness of their conversation she felt it would do them both a world of good to end on a lighter note.

"Mighty Mr. Kingston?" There was no hiding the amused tone in his voice.

"Yes, well, you earned the distinction fully. Now, your questions are all used up and I think it's time for you to rest." She got up and put the blanket back where she found it. When she returned she did a quick check of Elijah's forehead. It looked like he would have a nasty bump for a few days. "Do you need help making it to the bed?"

He gave off a frustrated sigh. "I hope not." He got up on shaky legs and stood for a moment gaining his balance. He took a few hesitant steps and once he was assured he wouldn't fall he picked up a more normal pace. Sarah turned to leave and paused at the door.

"If you agree, I'll leave our doors open tonight in case you have any more problems. That way I can hear you better if you call for help."

"Sure, that's fine." He climbed into bed and turned on the bedside light. "Thanks for sitting with me and answering my questions. I know some were difficult for you, but you did a good job. It was enlightening for me, and I hope it was for you as well."

"I have to admit the experience was surprisingly easy. And yes, I found it enlightening too. Also, thank you for helping me escape today. Although, I hope next time you pick a slightly less dramatic way of doing it." She turned out the main light and heard his soft chuckle. "Good night, Elijah."

When she got back to her room she sat on the bed, thinking about her conversation with Elijah. It had felt more like a therapy session than a chat with her boss.

I suppose that was the point.

It was early evening and she wasn't tired based on all the sleeping she had done earlier in the day. To top it off, the impromptu therapy session did its job because she no longer felt the need to hide out under the covers. She sat down at the writing desk to make note of Elijah's incident and brainstorm ways to cover for it. A few hours passed before she was satisfied with her list and subsequent questions she wanted to review with the nurse the following week. She sat back in her chair to think about what she could do next.

She thought back over her conversation with Elijah and on impulse tore a sheet of paper from her notebook to start a new list. This one was more difficult and kept her up late into the night. It was a list of ways she was holding on too tight to her pain. It wasn't a very long list, but what it lacked in length it made up for it in impact.

CHAPTER 8

"There you are. You look really nice today." Elijah took a sip of his coffee and set down his newspaper as Sarah entered the kitchen. She noticed there was a plate of food sitting in front of the empty chair next to him. He got up and carried his plate to the sink then refilled his coffee. "Sit. Eat."

She stared at him in disbelief. "Don't we need to leave? Besides, my stomach is in knots."

He shook his head and pointed at the chair. "We leave after you've eaten something. They can't start without me anyway. It's my last board meeting, and I'm central to the topics of discussion. Eat."

"Yes sir." She gave him a mock salute and sat down in the chair, knowing there would be no point of arguing with him further. She was grateful it was just a bagel, fruit and yogurt. She wasn't sure her stomach could handle much more than that.

"Thank you. I need to grab some things from the office. I'll be right back." By the time he returned, she was done with her breakfast and putting the dishes in the sink. "Ready?"

"Yes." She followed him out the front door where they were greeted by Thompson. The two men shook hands and chuckled over something before Elijah got in and slid across to the other side of the backseat. "Good morning, Mr. Thompson." She gave him a warm smile before sliding into the car next to Elijah.

"Mrs. Mitchell." His reaction to her was always the same, stiff and professional.

"Is your stomach still in knots?"

"Yes, unfortunately." She kept her eyes locked on the landscape that passed outside her window.

"There is nothing to be nervous about you know."

She shifted in her seat. "I know." The next twenty minutes passed in silence. She was lost in thought when she felt Elijah squeeze her hands, stilling their fidgeting.

"Tell me what has you so nervous. It's just a board meeting for a few hours."

"This is the first time we will be out in public, and I'm concerned I might... miss something." She lowered her voice on her last words glancing over to Thompson in the front of the car.

Elijah's gaze followed her own to the front of the car. He nodded in understanding. "It will be fine. Trust me."

She wished she could believe him. After finding him on his bathroom floor, unable to get up, she wasn't sure of anything. The only certainty of his disease was that the symptoms would continue to escalate rapidly until the point when he took his final breath. They had been practicing ways they could cover up his symptoms, but this would be the first time they would be surrounded by the very people he didn't want to know about his illness. What if he fell on his way into the boardroom? What if his memory chose this meeting to start escaping him? There were so many ways this could go wrong and she couldn't plan or anticipate all of them. She wasn't used to feeling so unprepared. He had been better yesterday, and so far this morning he seemed to be functioning normally. She was hopeful the bathroom episode had been a solitary event.

She was lost in her thoughts when the car entered the stop and go traffic of the city. Her nerves intensified as the car made its way downtown, growing in proportion to the size of the buildings. Thompson stopped in front of a large high-rise.

"Thanks, Thompson. We'll let ourselves out. The meeting should be over at noon. See you then." Before Thompson had a chance to respond Elijah was out of the car and on his way to open her door. He ushered her through the revolving doors and over to the elevators. As the elevator doors closed her breathing became more strained, and around the thirteenth floor her stomach cramped. She felt a hand on the small of her back and she jumped in response. "Relax." Although whispered for her ears only, it was a command with enough force her stomach actually started to comply.

"If I can visit the ladies' room prior to the meeting I should be fine."

At least I hope so.

He nodded as the doors opened on the twenty-fourth floor, and he led her into the lobby of Kingston Enterprises.

The boardroom contained a table that ran the length of the room, large enough to seat at least twenty people, and a coffee area to the left stocked with refreshments. The wall opposite the door overlooked the city. Given the time of day and direction of the sun, the blinds were half closed to block out as much of the glare as possible. Several people milled about the room, chatting over coffee or checking things on their computers. As soon as Elijah entered the room, the individual groups dispersed and greetings began. Sarah instantly felt like an outsider. As if sensing her unease, Elijah promptly led her to the vacant coffee bar.

"You doing okay?" He stirred in sugar and handed her the cup. He poured another cup for himself and she looked back about the room, noticing two men staring in their direction. One lifted his coffee cup and nodded at it with a furrow in his brow as he commented quietly to the man standing next to him. The other man looked from her to Elijah and chuckled. She could imagine what the comment might have been.

"Since when does Elijah get coffee for the assistant?"

The two men chuckled again looking over in their direction.

Assholes.

"Yes, I'm fine." She was surprised to find it was true. The arrogance of the two men laughing at her and Elijah stirred up her confidence. There wasn't much she hated more than a show of disrespect. It was time to turn on her professional persona and let these people understand that while she may not belong at their meeting, she certainly deserved to be treated with respect while she was there.

"Good." Elijah must have noticed the change in her confidence because he suddenly seemed more relaxed as well. He led her over to the conference table where they took their seats, making sure she was located on his right.

Elijah sat, giving the others the cue to take their seats. She retrieved her notebook and pen and positioned her chair so it was slightly angled toward Elijah's. Just then a stir of voices came through the door and she looked up to see three women enter. She was sure the one on the left was Leanne. She held a strong physical resemblance to Elijah, with the exception of her petite stature. Leanne's dark hair was cut short with several layers framing her face in a flattering way. Her eyes, exact replicas of Elijah's, scanned the room and ultimately settled on Sarah. She looked from Sarah to Elijah and then back to Sarah. She didn't try to hide the irritation in her face at the sight of Sarah in the room. She set her things down in the place directly across from Elijah.

"Elijah. Can I speak with you a moment before we start?"

Elijah?

Their relationship certainly was strained. Elijah gave her a playful wink before following Leanne to the back of the room. Sarah tried to watch them but didn't want to appear obvious. She was able to discern Leanne was irritated about something, probably Sarah's presence. She also saw Leanne make a swiping motion with her finger across her forehead, causing Elijah to reach up to the bump on his own head. The bump had taken on a nasty bruising color. Leanne shook her head a few times before returning to the conference table. As she and Elijah sat down, the murmurs around the table faded into whispers.

"Good morning, everyone. I hope you all have your coffee and have made your last minute calls or checks to emails. Sorry for the delay." Leanne paused and looked at Sarah.

Great, she automatically assumes I'm the reason we were late and delaying the meeting. Of course, she's right, but still.

"First, Elijah, would you like to introduce your guest?" Leanne's eyes never left Sarah even though her question was directed at Elijah.

Elijah leaned forward in his chair and introduced Sarah to the group. Several people extended her a warm welcome and the gentleman sitting to her right leaned over to extend his hand in greeting. She didn't miss the way his gaze traveled down her legs, and she was grateful she had changed into the pantsuit.

"Welcome, Mrs. Mitchell. I'm sure Elijah has explained that the topics we will discuss today are confidential and—"

"Yes, Mrs. Mitchell is aware." Elijah gave Leanne a warning look.

"Good. Then let's get started." Leanne launched into the first topic on the agenda and Sarah settled back in her chair under the ruse of taking notes. She sent frequent glances to Elijah's right arm to ensue he had it in his lap under the table. The tremor was still slight, but when resting on a table it could be obvious he was making small, involuntary movements. The first part of the meeting went smoothly, and she was starting to believe they would get through it without incident. Elijah kept his hand in his lap and there were no other major surprises. He'd hesitated a few times on his thoughts or words, but nothing stood out as unusual.

The only discomfort she had experienced was the way the gentleman on her right kept inching his chair closer to hers. She had learned his name was Mark Tanger and he was head of their marketing department. He was engaged in the meeting, but she was uncomfortably aware he was also paying very close attention to her. She had to admit Mark was good looking. He had short dark hair styled with some sort of product, giving it a look just shy of stiff and wet. He had light blue eyes and dimples when he smiled. However, his good looks were significantly diminished by something she couldn't quite put her finger on. There was something about him that just made her uncomfortable. She was grateful when the group broke for a twenty minute break.

"Mrs. Mitchell, will you join me in my office for a few minutes?" She followed Elijah out of the room, trying not to be bothered by the cold look Leanne was giving her. Elijah led her down the hall to a private office. She could tell by the decor that it was a temporary space allocated to him during his transition into retirement. He closed the door behind them before taking a seat behind the desk. "Well, so far so good, don't you think?"

She sat in the chair across from him. "Yes, I agree. The first half of the meeting seemed to go well. You're doing a good job of keeping your right hand under the table, and I haven't noticed any coordination issues. You hesitated a few times with your words, but I don't think it was considered to be unusual to anyone else."

"Yes, I noticed the same thing." He put his ankle on his knee. The invisible lint must have returned because he started picking at his pant leg. "I'm sorry about Leanne. There's no point in pretending she's fine with you being at this meeting."

"It's fine. I understand. Besides, we knew beforehand she wouldn't like my being here. It's nothing I didn't expect." She did think Leanne was being unnecessarily cold, but she wasn't going to make such a comment to Elijah. They may not have the best relationship, but she was still his daughter, and she knew he cared a great deal about her.

He nodded and continued to play with his pant leg. Suddenly he dropped his leg and sat forward. "So, I think people seem to be accepting the excuse we gave them for why you're here. Do you agree?"

"I think so." She hesitated and looked down uncomfortably.

"What are you not saying?" She forgot he could read her clearly.

"It's nothing. Just... I don't know." She shook her head. The more she stumbled over it, the bigger deal Elijah would make out of it. "I just think the guy next to me, Mark, he seems to be very interested in what I'm doing. I guess I'm afraid he might notice I'm paying close attention to you. And he makes me uncomfortable. Although, I'm sure I'm just misreading the situation."

He was clearly annoyed. "Mark. No, he's a worm. Very good at his job and he never crosses any lines at the office, but your instincts are probably correct on this one. I'll take care of it."

"No, I don't want to cause a scene—"

"Don't worry. I'll take care of the situation without being obvious."

Why did I have to say anything?

She closed her eyes and tried to dismiss her guilt at calling out Mark. "By the way, when you and Leanne were talking at the back of the room I noticed she must have asked about the bump on your head. What did you tell her? I want to be sure I have the same story in case it comes up again later."

Instinctively his hand went to the bump on his forehead. "I told her a version of the truth—that I slipped in the bathroom and hit my head. I just left out all the parts about your assistance and my not being able to get up. She probably won't bring it up again." He looked at his watch. "Have you been able to capture good notes? Just in case Leanne decides she needs to do a quality check or something before we leave. I probably should have warned you prior to the meeting not to make any notes about my symptoms."

As odd as the statement was, after having met Leanne she figured it was a distinct possibility. "I had thought about recording the moments when you stumbled on your words, but Mark's watchful eye over my shoulder kept me from doing so. I'll make sure I keep appropriate notes." Leanne's comments about the confidentiality ran back through her mind.

"Good, the next couple of hours should go by quickly—" He was interrupted by a sharp knock on the door. "Come in." The door opened and Leanne stepped inside, looking from Elijah to Sarah. An awkward silence fell over them.

"So, Mrs. Mitchell, how have you enjoyed your time here so far?" It was a friendly enough question, but somehow the friendliness had escaped her tone.

"It's been great."

"Based on my father's glowing praise earlier in the meeting I'm surprised you've never worked a Kingston project before."

"Yes, well, that was somewhat outside of my control." Sarah sent a playful look Elijah's way and he winked in return. It was clear Leanne didn't appreciate their silent interaction.

"Isn't it hard on your family for you to be out here for so long?"

Sarah felt the blood drain away from her face. Elijah immediately recognized her discomfort and tried to come to her rescue. "Leanne, I don't see how that's any of your—"

Sarah found her voice before he could finish the sentence. "No, it's okay, really." Leanne was now looking back and forth between her and Elijah with confusion and annoyance. Sarah took in a deep breath, letting it out slowly before she spoke. "I lost my husband and son almost two and a half years ago in a car accident. There's no longer a family to miss me." She wiped away the single tear that fell, grateful it was only one.

"I'm sorry. I didn't realize..."

"It's fine, really. There's no way you could have known." Another awkward silence hung around them.

Leanne looked at her watch then at Elijah. "Can I talk to you for a moment?"

"Sure." When he didn't make a motion to leave Leanne looked at

Sarah with another annoyed look. Really, it was probably the same annoyed look as Sarah was certain it had not yet left her face since she had met her. Elijah understood her unspoken question. "Whatever we have to discuss we can do so in front of Mrs. Mitchell. She will be a part of all my business requirements going forward, so she should probably be here to listen anyway."

"This is personal. I'd like to speak to you alone if it's not too much to ask."

Elijah looked to Sarah with exasperation. Given she wanted to escape the tension in the room and he was having a good morning, she didn't see a risk in leaving them alone.

"Actually, I need to use the restroom. I remember where it is so I'll meet you back in the boardroom." She left the office and closed the door behind her. Checking her watch she saw she still had about ten minutes until the meeting would resume.

Sarah got back to the boardroom with a minute to spare. Elijah and Leanne were still out, but Mark was back and he seemed excited to see her. Instead of going back to her seat, she went to the coffee bar to get two bottles of water. She turned around and came face-to-face with Mark. She was so surprised she nearly dropped the waters.

"Sorry, I didn't mean to startle you." He laughed and put a hand on her shoulder. It was innocent enough, but certainly improper given she had just met him a few hours ago. She tried to pull away, but she was backed against the coffee bar. His hand lingered on her shoulder too long before he finally removed it, only to reach behind her to grab a bottle of water for himself.

What the hell is wrong with this guy? Hasn't he ever heard of personal space?

He was close enough that she could smell the mint on his breath. She practically knocked over the trash can trying to put space between them.

"So, where are you staying while you're in town?"

"Mark." The sound of Elijah's voice was the most welcome thing she had heard in a long time. Mark immediately stepped back and took a swig of his water.

"Elijah. So, how's retirement treating you so far? You're not overworking Mrs. Mitchell are you? Hopefully you allow her some personal time to go out and have fun." He looked over her with his eyes and she felt like she might vomit in her mouth.

She saw Elijah's jaw tense in response. "So, how's Claire? You guys have been married for what, fifteen years now?"

Mark shifted on his feet and she noticed a hint of color rise above his shirt collar. "Actually, I'm not sure. My *ex*-wife tries not to talk to me much these days."

"Ah, right. I forgot you were going through a divorce. It must be finalized then? My condolences. Or are congratulations more appropriate? I never know what to say when someone gets divorced." She could see the enjoyment Elijah was having at causing Mark discomfort. "If you'll excuse us, Mark, I have a few things I'd like to cover with Mrs. Mitchell before we get started."

She was fighting hard to hide the smile that wanted to plaster itself across her face. She really enjoyed watching Elijah put Mark in his place. Normally she would have put him there herself, but she was an outsider and didn't feel comfortable taking a stand against him. She followed Elijah back to the table, and he made a show of looking at something in her notes. She looked across the table and noticed Leanne watching her. This time, as opposed to ignoring it, Sarah gave her a small smile in acknowledgement. Leanne pursed her lips and looked down at her notes.

"Let's get started again." Leanne's tone cased those that remained standing to take their seats. Mark pulled his chair close to Sarah's and leaned over to whisper.

"So, you never did tell me where you were staying while in town."

"No, I didn't." She turned away from him, but not before she saw the look of annoyance on his face.

Before Leanne could resume the meeting there was a knock on the door followed by someone entering. She walked over to Leanne and whispered in her ear.

"Thank you." Leanne looked at Mark. "Mark, it appears there's an issue that needs your attention."

Sarah glanced at Mark, who looked even more irritated, and watched him pick up his stuff to leave. She glanced back at Elijah, and he gave her the quickest of winks. An involuntary chuckle escaped her and she quickly covered it with a cough, reaching for her water.

It was about twenty minutes later when things took a turn for the worse. Materials were being passed out and when Elijah took his copies he forgot to put his right hand back in his lap. She didn't react immediately, hoping it wouldn't be an issue or that he would soon remember on his own. He was holding the papers in his right hand while he took notes with his left. Holding the papers up above the table accentuated the tremor in his hand as the papers shook. She looked about the room. No one was looking in their direction so she decided to tap his arm, giving him a gentle reminder to put his hand in his lap. Before she had a chance to connect with his arm, his hand suddenly jerked forward, knocking over his uncapped bottle of water. She quickly jumped up to grab the bottle of water.

"Oh, my gosh, I'm so sorry." She rushed back to grab some napkins from the coffee bar. When she returned Elijah was staring at her with a confused look. "I dropped my pen, and when I reached down to get it I must have bumped your arm, causing you to spill the water." The look she gave Elijah was pleading him to catch up. Finally, his confusion broke away and he started to play along with her cover-up.

"Don't worry about it. It's just water. I assume we have more copies of these documents?" Sarah cleaned up the water and walked to throw away the napkins. When she got back to her seat, she noticed any headway she had made with Leanne was gone and the scowl was back on her face. Elijah was passed new documents and the meeting resumed. His right hand was back in his lap so she settled in her chair and tried to relax. She had made a spectacle of herself, but she had kept the focus off Elijah which was the goal.

Over the course of the next hour, he kept his right hand in his lap but started to have more memory lapses. He paused on a word or he would get a name wrong. Near the end of the meeting he started to say something and then completely stopped, forgetting what he was going to say. Just one or two of these in isolation wouldn't have been considered unusual. However several in the span of one meeting were noticeable. As Elijah's silence grew longer, she noticed those around the table studying him. She quickly filtered through possible solutions. She certainly couldn't claim responsibility for his memory lapses the way she did for his spilling the water.

"Dad? Is everything okay?" Sarah looked over at Leanne and saw real concern on her face.

"Mr. Kingston? Is your head hurting you again?" Elijah looked at Sarah and put his hand to his forehead, as she knew he would. Since it had happened, every time the bump was mentioned his hand automatically went to his forehead.

She watched as comprehension crossed his face. "Yes, actually it is hurting."

She looked over to Leanne. "Mrs. Troupe, do you have anything he could take for the pain? I forgot to bring a bottle with me. Ever since he bumped his head he's been getting random headaches. I've noticed when he gets them he seems to lose his focus."

Elijah nodded. "Yes, thank you. I do think that will help. I was feeling better this morning and didn't take any medicine before I left."

"I think we might have some." Leanne looked over to her assistant who immediately got up and left the room. She looked back to Elijah. "Have you seen a doctor? It doesn't seem right that you should be getting such bad headaches."

Elijah rubbed at his temples. "No, really they've been getting better. I think I'm just starting to feel the effects of a long morning."

"How did you get that bump Kingston? Looks pretty nasty." This came from someone at the end of the table whose name Sarah couldn't remember.

"Oh, you know me. Bar fight." The responding laughter took away most of the tension in the room. Leanne was the only one who wasn't laughing. She was still looking at Elijah with concern. Leanne's assistant returned with a bottle of ibuprofen and handed it to Elijah. "Thanks, Marjorie." He swallowed down two pills and checked his watch. "So, where were we?"

"I think you were giving us an excuse to end this meeting early." This came from one of the assholes. After observing the two men throughout the entire meeting, Sarah was able to maintain her original assessment of them as accurate.

Leanne rolled her eyes at the comment and checked her watch. "Given we're due to end in about fifteen minutes anyway, I'd say we can call an end to it. Elijah and I can connect offline to close out this last item." With that, people immediately got up and collected their things. "Mrs. Mitchell, please work with Marjorie to set up a time for Elijah and I to go over the open items from today's meeting."

"If you will follow me, Mrs. Mitchell, we can compare schedules." Sarah looked to Elijah to confirm he was okay with her leaving him alone and he nodded in approval. With that, she followed Marjorie out the door.

"Sorry!" They were in the dance studio and Sarah had stepped on Elijah's toes for the sixth time that evening.

He shook out the injured foot. "Stop apologizing."

"I can't help it. Maybe you actually fell the other day because my bad dancing has caused you to lose the feeling in your feet." He looked at her with an amused look. "What?"

"I think that's the first time you've cracked a joke about my illness. That's very good progress on your part."

"Yeah, well, we can debate another day if it's good progress or bad." She crossed her arms over her chest. "Really, Elijah, I'm never going to get this. We only have seven weeks left and I can't even stop stepping on your toes. This will be awful. And in front of over five hundred people?! You didn't tell me there were going to be that many people when you conned me into doing this."

"So now I conned you into this?" The amused look on his face told her he wasn't offended.

"You made it sound like it was one of your dying requests. How could I have said no?"

He let out a deep, genuine laugh. "*Very* good. That's two now. I'll bring you over to the dark side yet." Once his laughter subsided he placed his arms on her shoulders. "You're doing great, trust me. Your main problem is you won't let me lead. You need to trust me, and let me guide you. I can tell you know the steps, and you're responding to the music well—you just have to let me lead you."

She studied him, trying to read his thoughts. "Why is this starting to feel like a therapy session, hidden under the guise of a dance lesson?"

He shrugged his shoulders. "I guess in a way it is. Part of the reason you can't move on is because you don't want to trust anyone to have a hand in your happiness, not even yourself. You have to learn to trust again, in life and in dancing. Let someone lead you for a change, show you the way to go." He walked over to the music player. "Let's try it again."

They had already been practicing for a couple hours. "Are you sure you don't need to rest?" He had taken a nap when they'd returned from the board meeting and it had rejuvenated him, but she still didn't want to push him too hard.

"I'm fine. Besides, if we don't get this down soon I'm afraid I might forget the steps."

She gave him a scolding look. "Okay, I think I've had enough CJD jokes for the day. I may have made progress, but I'm not yet on the same end of the comfort scale as you are."

"Fine, one more time through and then we can stop. Besides, we should get some rest—we have a big day ahead of us tomorrow."

"Oh? What are we doing?"

He hit play on the music player and walked toward her. "It's time to cross something off my bucket list."

CHAPTER 9

"Rise and shine!" Sarah bolted up at the sound of Elijah's voice.

What the hell?

"Come on sleepy head, time to get up."

"What time is it? And why are you in my room, I do have an alarm you know." She flopped back on her pillows and looked at the clock.

Five in the morning. On a Saturday. Really?

"I didn't trust you to not hit the snooze twenty times. Remember, today we get to cross something off my list. I'm excited, so let's go." He sounded like a kid on Christmas morning.

"What could possibly be on your list that's required to be done at such an unholy hour?" She threw a pillow over her eyes as he turned on her bathroom light. He then turned on the faucet.

"Have you ever had a cold water wake-up call?"

That got her to sit up. "You wouldn't."

"Oh, but I would..."

"Fine. I'm up. Out! I'd like to at least get dressed and attend to my morning needs in private."

He walked out with the glass of water, taking a sip along the way. He closed the door smiling. She stuck her tongue out at the closed door. It was childish, but at the moment it felt required. She got up and went into the bathroom, taking her time. Another childish move, but she supposed she was just in that kind of mood. She stood looking around her closet and groaned before pulling on her robe and peeking into the hall.

"Elijah?" No response. "Elijah?" She called a bit louder hoping he would hear.

He must be downstairs already.

She pulled back into her room, struggling internally a few moments before looking down at her robe. She was fully covered. She opened the door and stepped out into the hall, clutching her robe tightly. She walked over to the stairs and leaned her head down to call out for Elijah again, louder this time.

"Yes?"

She screamed and jumped, almost falling down a step. But she maintained a hold on her robe. She turned to find him smiling at her from his bedroom door.

"Why didn't you answer me?" She quickly retreated to her own room and hid in the doorway.

"I was in the bathroom and didn't see the need to yell. I wasn't aware it was an emergency, so I figured I would finish my business and then see what you needed." It was apparent he found the situation humorous.

"You didn't tell me where we're going."

He shook his head. "No... I wanted it to be a surprise."

She gave him a look that in any culture could easily be translated to express her exasperation.

"What?"

"I don't know what to wear..." She drew out the last word, indicating she thought it was completely unnecessary she actually had to point it out.

"Ah, right. That would probably help. You should wear something comfortable, layers would be good as there will be temperature fluctuations, and hiking boots. Happy?"

She gave him a sarcastic smile. "Yep, I'm all sunshine and roses." She closed the door and leaned against it.

Why do I have the feeling this is going to be a difficult day?

Sarah found Elijah in the kitchen, surrounded by a large mess. She scanned the items on the countertops and realized he was making sack lunches. As she sat down at the counter, she watched him put water bottles into a backpack.

"You like peanut butter and jelly sandwiches, right?"

"Who doesn't?"

Anyone over the age of twelve perhaps...

She kept her sarcastic comment to herself. She was feeling cranky but didn't want to spoil his mood. This was the first item they were going to cross off his list, and she wanted it to be special for him. She looked around the kitchen again and marveled at the amount of stuff he had on the counters.

"How long have you been up?"

"Awhile. I couldn't sleep. I'm just excited I guess." She knew insomnia was another symptom of CJD. She reminded herself again that this was a special day for him, so she didn't question his reasoning. However, something she saw in his eyes told her he was thinking the same thing.

"You know, I have never seen you giddy before. It might cause me to question your tough guy persona."

His movements came to a halt, and he looked at her with mock astonishment. "I am *not* giddy. I don't get *giddy*. I am simply excited. It's a beautiful day, we're going to a beautiful location, and I will be accompanied by a beautiful woman. What's there not to be excited about?"

She shifted in her seat at the unexpected compliment. "Okay, I believe you. Your image will not be tarnished due to this unusual display of excitement."

"Thank you." He smiled as he poured trail mix into snack bags.

"What can I do to help?"

"You can make the coffee." She was happy to oblige and quickly made two cups, handing one to Elijah before she sat back down.

"So, I'm hoping this hike isn't too rugged because I didn't pack any hiking boots. In fact, I don't own any hiking boots."

He gave her a huge grin. "Wait here." He walked off in the direction of the garage and came back holding a large shoe box. She raised her eyebrows in question. He shrugged his shoulders in return and went back to packing the backpacks. "When I knew I wanted to go on this hike I figured I would need to get you some boots, assuming you didn't bring any appropriate footwear for the occasion." She saw the faint appearance of a blush creep up his face.

Recovering from the surprise of his reaction, she took the boots out of the box and put them on. She was impressed they were the right size. "They fit perfectly."

He gave off another shrug.

He's actually embarrassed.

"I snuck a peak at the shoes in your closet one day when you went to the store."

She felt her crankiness subside a little. "Thank you, this was very thoughtful. And they are very comfortable. Although, I'm not sure I like the thought of you poking around in my closet."

"Why not? You've been in mine."

It was her turn to blush at the reminder of finding him naked on his bathroom floor. "Yeah, well..." She sat back down and tried to ignore his amused grin. "When did you get a chance to buy these anyway? You never leave the house without me."

"There's this new technology called the Internet. Have you heard of it? It's amazing. You can buy anything online and they will deliver it right to your door. Crazy, right?"

She couldn't help but laugh. His good mood really was infectious. "Well, again, thank you." She quietly sipped her coffee while he finished packing the backpacks. He paused to pull his phone out of his pocket when it alerted him of a text. He clicked off a response and put the phone back in his pocket.

"Ready?"

She followed him to the garage where he put the backpacks in the trunk of his car. He turned to look at her.

"Okay, what's on your mind?"

"I don't think you should be driving." She was aware her tone came out sounding apologetic.

He shoved his hands in his pockets and looked down at his feet. "I agree. You should drive."

"But I don't know where we're going."

"I'll direct you." He cocked his head to the side and looked at her through narrowed eyes. "Come on, Sarah, just say what you're thinking."

"What if you forget? Can't you plug the location in to the GPS, just for insurance? I know you want it to be a surprise, but I've never been anywhere around here so putting in the location won't give anything away. This will be my first hike in the mountains, assuming it's somewhere in the mountains since we're surrounded by them, so everything will be new to me and a surprise. It's not like—"

"Sarah, you're rambling. And... you're right, I will plug it into the GPS." He paused to consider her. "What else? I can tell there's still something on your mind."

"What if you have coordination issues on the hike? Or fall? I couldn't even get you off your bathroom floor, how can I get you off a mountain?"

"That one I have thought of and I have it covered." She gave him a curious look. "Nope, I have to at least keep one surprise on this trip." With that he tossed her the keys, which she missed, and climbed in the passenger side.

Sarah looked at Elijah when he let out a big yawn. He stretched his hands above his head, sliding them toward the back of the car along the roof before settling them back on his legs.

"So, if the hike is only forty minutes away, why did we have to leave so early?" Even though she had tried to delay by taking her time getting ready, they had been out the door around six-thirty.

"This particular hike can be very popular. Given the time of year it usually isn't too busy. However, we've had unusually warm weather, and there's a possibility people will want to get one last chance at the hike before the snow falls."

They discussed the things he needed to complete as a result of the board meeting the previous day and she reminded him of his upcoming meeting.

"We'll have to get everything done this week. I set up your teleconference with Leanne for Friday. It was made clear I shouldn't be at the meeting, so I figured over the phone was safer than meeting with her alone in person. Based on the reaction I got from her assistant on the suggestion, Leanne might not be happy."

"No, she won't, but I can handle it. I'll come up with some acceptable excuse for why." He paused and she glanced at him out of the corner of her eye. He was watching her. "So, you seem to have a pretty good read on Leanne after one meeting."

Although it was a statement, she knew there was a question in there.

I wish he wouldn't bring this up right now.

She needed to concentrate on the unfamiliar roads, with their occasional sharp turns, and couldn't focus on the right words to say. Leanne was his daughter and she had to tread carefully.

"Well, I've observed she's a lot like you. Given I've been able to get a better understanding of you that would translate to a pretty good understanding of her."

"Is that a good thing or a bad thing?" Although not looking at him, she could hear the smile in his voice. She returned his smile.

"For business, it's a great thing. Your personality and business tactics have made you very successful. I can see she will be able to keep Kingston Enterprises going in a positive direction for a long time. And the people at the office really seem to respect her."

"And for non-business?"

"That's harder for me to judge. I've learned you're very different outside the office than in. If I assume the same is true for Leanne, then I don't know."

"What do you think? I know you always have an initial opinion formed."

He's just not going to give this up.

She waited until she followed the instructions from the GPS. When it was finally silent, she knew she couldn't delay any longer. "I think she doesn't like me very much."

"Why do you think she doesn't like you?"

She glanced over and noticed his genuine look of confusion. "It's a chick thing. We have this ability to know when another woman doesn't like us. Her 'I don't trust you or like you' vibe was very strong."

"It's just because she was mad at me for inviting you. You probably noticed the formality that exists at Kingston. We don't often let outsiders join our meetings."

"Yes, that was part of it. But it was more than that." She bit down on her bottom lip, willing herself to stop talking. But now that she started, it was like she couldn't turn it off. "I could tell she didn't like the way you and I interacted with each other. As much as we tried to tone it down, I think she noticed our interaction was friendlier than a typical boss-employee relationship."

"What does our being friends have to do with it? She likes Miles."

"Last I checked Miles wasn't a woman."

"How does that matter?"

She sighed in frustration. "I think I read she's the same age as me. Thirty-five, right?" She glanced in his direction and he nodded. "Admit it, when an older man and a younger woman appear to be more than general acquaintances it's assumed they're intimate. While there's nothing wrong with that, most daughters are not okay with their dad being involved with a woman their own age. On the flip side it's possible she thinks I'm trying to take her place in your life. Your relationship with her is mostly professional, and she might be jealous. In either case, she can't hate you so she hates me."

He was quiet, contemplating what she had said. "I find it hard to believe she would think either of those things. For one, I haven't had a serious relationship with anyone since Lena died, so I don't know why she would assume I was having one now. As far as her being jealous because she thinks I'm transferring my fatherly feelings toward you rather than her, that's just ridiculous. She's never been concerned about what I thought. It was Lena's approval she always wanted."

She looked at him with shock. "Are you kidding me? I've known her all of five minutes, and I can see that's a load of shit. I don't disagree she wanted her mom's approval, but it's yours she strives for. She took over your business, Elijah. She molded herself after your footsteps. No child would do that if they didn't need their parent's acceptance. I come from a history rich with family business remember? I know the dynamics very well. And besides, I can tell by the way she looks at you."

She found it hard to believe he had never realized Leanne wanted his acceptance and approval. Not just wanted, *needed*.

"Mark my words, next time you meet with her, *alone*, she will grill you with questions. She will try to find out the context of our relationship and she will start dropping hints that you should be cautious of my untrustworthy nature."

"That sounds like a challenge. I accept. If, on Friday, she starts asking me questions about our relationship I will make you a special dinner on Thanksgiving. If she doesn't, then you get to cook."

It wasn't much of a bet, really. He did all the cooking anyway. But the idea of a little competition was intriguing. "You're on."

"This is for you. Don't think I didn't notice you skipped breakfast this morning." Sarah looked at the apple Elijah was holding out and took it without a fight. She then took one of the backpacks from him and slung it over her shoulders.

"It's about time you two showed up."

She looked around to find Miles walking toward their car and couldn't resist smiling. "You must be my insurance." She was expecting a handshake and was surprised when he leaned forward for a hug.

He walked over to Elijah, and they did the stiff man-hug she'd seen Nick do with Andy many times. He looked back to her with an amused grin. "Insurance?"

"Sarah was concerned I would fall, and she wanted to know how she'd be able to get me off the mountain. I told her I had it covered."

Miles let out a deep laugh. "I've been carrying your ass for the last ten years. That should make it pretty easy to carry you a few miles down the mountain if needed."

"Let's hope no one will have to carry anyone." Sarah turned at the sound of a woman's voice. She was tall with blonde hair pulled into a ponytail behind a baseball cap. Even through her layers of clothing Sarah could tell she had a very athletic body. The woman walked right up to Sarah and gave her a hug. She stepped back and held Sarah at arm's length, looking her up and down. "You're even more beautiful than Miles said."

Sarah felt the blush return to her face. She was certain she had blushed more in the few weeks she had been there than she had in all the other years of her life.

"Sarah, this is my wife, Tina. She's been anxious to meet you."

"Of course I have. All these years of having to hang out with you two grown boys, I was ecstatic to learn I would finally have another woman to share in my torment." She looked at Sarah and winked. "I think you and I are going to become very good friends."

Sarah liked her instantly. She reminded her of Maggie and she missed her friend a great deal. Tina linked her arm through hers and started toward the trail head.

"Are we ready? There aren't many people out right now so we should take advantage and get going."

Elijah waved his hand forward. "Lead the way."

The trail began in a wooded area, surrounded by tall trees, and

Sarah looked around marveling at the serenity of it all. The sun was coming out from behind clouds, and the rays filtering through the trees gave her a surge of energy.

"So, Sarah, have you ever been hiking before?"

"No, this is my first time. I ran outside everyday at home, but it's nothing near what you can find here. I think I've become very dependent on this landscape in the short time I've been here."

Tina nodded and smiled. "The outside living is one of the main reasons I love living here. There are so many opportunities to hike, mountain bike, rock climb, you name it we've got it."

"You do all of that?"

"Every chance I get. However, our schedules don't often allow for too many long excursions. We usually have to settle for day trips on the weekends."

They walked in silence for a moment, enjoying the peace of the trail. "So, I know Miles is a lawyer. What do you do?"

"I manage a few small to medium sized charitable organizations, including Marlena's. I took it over a few years ago when the previous executive director retired."

"It sounds like very rewarding work."

Tina nodded at the comment. "It is, and I enjoy it very much. How about you? I admit, Elijah's told me what it is you do but I don't think I fully understand it."

"I'm kind of like a consultant for hire. I'm assigned to clients who pay me to do the tasks they don't want to do. I thrive on organization so putting those skills to use seemed like the logical thing to do. I also like the closure I get at the completion of a project. Being able to see something through from a plan on a piece of paper to final implementation is very rewarding. Another perk is the variety that comes with the job. Every project is something different than the last—it can range from managing a fundraising event to helping a firm open a satellite office."

"Well, from what I've heard of your performance through Elijah, if you ever want to apply your skills in a different direction let me know. I'd love to have you on my team."

Sarah smiled. "Thank you, I'm flattered. However, this is the first time I've worked with Elijah so you might not want to put too much stock into what he says this early in the game."

She felt a playful poke at the back of her shoulder above her backpack. "Watch it. Besides, your comment carries no weight here. Tina and Miles know I can spend five minutes with someone and come out with a very accurate assessment of their skills and personality."

Tina laughed. "It's true. I would have hired you without even meeting you based solely on Elijah's recommendation."

"Well, your husband wasn't so convinced. Our first meeting was so he could decide if he should tell Elijah to send me packing or not."

She heard Miles and Elijah laugh behind her. "Touché, Sarah. But that I can blame on being a lawyer. We don't trust anyone but ourselves." Tina cleared her throat. "And our spouses of course." Miles grabbed Tina from behind and planted a kiss on her cheek. She ran away from him playfully and he chased after her. Sarah smiled in their direction and looked to Elijah as he walked up next to her.

"Looks like you and Tina are hitting it off well."

"Yeah, she seems great. I can tell you're all really good friends. I'm happy to get a chance to know them better." She looked at the couple ahead of them.

They continued to walk in silence, enjoying their surroundings. The trail led them out of the wooded area and into a meadow. A few minutes later, Elijah tapped her on the shoulder and pointed. A lake was set back from the trail, but there was something wonderful about the way it appeared to be hidden behind the trees. Almost like it was being protected and only those who were taking the time to pay attention could catch a glimpse of it. She was taken in by her surroundings and remained silent for most of the hike, enjoying everything around her. At one point they saw a small waterfall meandering its way down the mountain. She stopped for a moment, watching the waterfall as the others made their way ahead of her across a small bridge cut out of a log. She was lost in the moment, not thinking of anything but just feeling the peace surrounding her. It had been such a long time since she had felt so content.

"Sarah, you coming? We're almost there." The sound of Elijah's voice drifted over to her and she quickly caught up with the others.

They reached the end of the trail and what she saw simply took her breath away. A large lake was before them, surrounded by snow topped mountain peaks. The sun was shining down, causing the surface of the lake to shimmer. She followed the group over to an area where Elijah sat down on a rock near the edge of the lake. She stood a few yards behind him, taking in everything she was seeing and feeling.

"Beautiful, isn't it?" She turned to see Miles standing next to her, looking out over the lake.

"I've never seen anything like it. It's amazing." She looked over at Elijah and noticed the ease he portrayed sitting back on the boulder. She then looked over to Tina who walked into areas as if she had done so hundreds of times. "Do you guys come here a lot?"

"At least once a year." He pointed in a direction of the peaks behind the lake. "Over in that direction is a glacier. The trail becomes more difficult at that point. Elijah has decided not to attempt it given... anyway, Tina would like to take the trail forward. If you would like to see the glacier as well, you could go with Tina and I'll stay behind with Elijah."

If the glacier was anything like the view of the lake, she knew she would enjoy it immensely. However, something about the way Elijah was sitting and staring over the lake told her this was a time she should remain with him. "I think I'd like to stay here."

He smiled and gave her shoulder a pat. "We'll be back in a bit." He walked off in the direction of Tina where they talked for a moment and then waved. She waved back and they turned to continue up the trail.

Elijah looked back at her and scooted over on the rock, allowing room for her to sit next to him. She dropped her backpack next to his and sat down. She wanted to ask him why they were there, what the significance of the location was, but she knew he would tell her when he was ready. Instead, she sat quietly next to him and looked at the beauty surrounding her.

Nick would have loved it here.

Even though the idea made her sad because she would never be able to share it with Nick, the tranquility of her surroundings kept her from breaking down.

Her thoughts were interrupted when Elijah cleared his throat. "This is where I asked Lena to marry me. We considered it our special place and came back each year. I stopped coming after she died until I met Miles. I had mentioned this place to him, and why it was important to me. He convinced me to come back with them, and we've been coming every year since."

She remained silent, not really knowing what to say. She decided it was best to wait and let him continue. It didn't take long.

"God she was so beautiful that day. I mean, she was always beautiful, but that day... It was like she knew it was going to be a special day, and happiness radiated out from within her. It was—" He suddenly stopped, and she looked over at him. He rubbed at his temples and pulled his hands through his hair. She saw a pained expression on his face. "I don't actually remember when it was, but it was a great time of year for hiking. I wanted everything to be a surprise." He stopped and let out a soft laugh. "However, much like I did this morning, I forgot women need details. I picked her up early in the morning, and she came to the door wearing a dress and high heels. I had to tell her we were going on a hike so she would change. I'd been on this trail before and I wanted to share it with her. I wanted the most important day of our lives, up until that moment at least, to be united with the magnitude of this place."

His explanation shed a lot of light on his behavior that morning. His excitement, the surprises he had planned for her—it all fit neatly into his memory of how this day was for him with Marlena.

"So, tell me about the day Nick proposed to you."

She pulled in a sharp breath. "It was after Nick had graduated from college. I think he knew it was a difficult time for me since the last time he'd graduated he broke up with me. He had gotten a job several hours away and it was getting close to the time when he had to leave. I was a wreck." She paused, contemplating. She had never before voiced out loud what was going through her mind. But this was Elijah, and in the time she had been there she had told him more about some things than she had told Maggie. They had a connection she couldn't explain, and the more she was with him the more she wanted to share.

"For awhile I was convinced even he didn't know what was going to happen—that he wanted to spend the summer figuring it out. I was so stressed out. Every date we went on I wondered if my life was about to change. He would either ask me to marry him, or we would break up. About a week before he was due to move he showed up at my house, unannounced. He took me to this park that was lit up year round with Christmas style lights in the trees. He took me to a bench, sat me down and then dropped to one knee. I think the amount of relief I felt in that moment surpassed my happiness."

They fell into a long silence before Elijah spoke again.

"So, you were pretty quiet on the hike up here. Several times I tried to point something out, but you were lost in your thoughts. Anything you want to talk about?"

She played with the cap on her water bottle, twisting it off and then back on, over and over again. "Mostly I was enjoying the hike. It's like the atmosphere here energizes me. When I woke up this morning, I was a bit cranky." She glanced at him and saw his smirk. "But your good mood, tied with all this beauty, has made me feel at peace for the first time in a long time."

"I'm glad you're enjoying it here. As for your crankiness, it's entirely possible you just need more food. An apple isn't enough." He reached into his backpack for water and trail mix.

"You two are still sitting here?" Sarah turned to see Miles and Tina, returning from their extended hike.

"If it's okay with everyone, I'd like to sit here a bit longer. Then we can head back down, eat lunch, and possibly take on another trail." Given this would be the last time Elijah would make this trip, no one was going to turn down his request. They would have pitched tents and spent the night if that's what he wanted.

Sarah got up and stretched her arms above her head. "I'm going to walk around. Don't leave without me."

"Not a chance, you're stuck with me for the next few months." Elijah winked up at her and then turned to Tina. "Tina, why don't you walk Sarah around the lake? That way I can relax knowing she won't fall in."

"I'm not the one with the coordination issues here. You just stay put on that rock." The innocent jabs at his symptoms were becoming easier. She turned to Tina. "Regardless, I'd enjoy your company if you're still up for more walking. If you want to rest that's fine, I promise not to get too adventurous."

"This little hike is nothing compared to some of the rocks I've climbed. I'd love to walk with you." Tina dropped her backpack by the others and led Sarah around to various parts of the lake, pointing out different things along the way. Each angle brought something new, yet just as beautiful as the last. Sarah could understand why this hike was so popular. They stopped at one spot where there were no other hikers and sat down to rest and enjoy the view.

"So, Sarah, Miles told me about your loss." Tina paused and Sarah looked over to see her staring out over the lake. "I know there's nothing I can say. 'Sorry' always seems so inappropriate. I guess what I feel like saying is that I hold the deepest respect for you being able to recover from such an unimaginable nightmare."

Well, that's a first.

Sarah had heard just about every possible comment in regard to her loss. Most were the same, but there were still a few unexpected ones. "Thank you. However, I'm not so sure I would agree I've recovered very well."

"You're still breathing aren't you? Getting up and out of bed each day? You may not have reached your final point of recovery, but you've recovered. And you're here, trying to make more progress. I respect that."

Sarah looked back out over the lake. "I guess I never thought of it that way."

"I think you already know this, but when Elijah first told Miles about you and that he wanted you to manage his... project, we were concerned. Actually, I was concerned, Miles was furious. Not knowing *you* but knowing your *situation,* we were afraid you would be too fragile to help Elijah through what would be the most difficult days of his life. But Elijah was adamant it was the right thing to do. After seeing the impact you've had on him, I'll say it was probably the only time we were grateful Elijah was so stubborn. Miles and I understand he has been helping you recover from your loss and we're very happy about that. It's the least you deserve for what you have given him. But we're concerned about how you will be affected when he dies."

As Sarah felt the growing urge to talk to this woman she had met only hours ago, she realized how far she had come in such a short time. She'd arrived wanting to keep everything to herself, hidden and locked away for only her to know about. In a few weeks Elijah had chipped away at that wall, allowing her to feel more comfortable in sharing her feelings.

"To be honest, I'm scared. I've come to consider him a friend and I can't think about what it's going to be like when he's gone." Sarah closed her eyes, focusing on her words and controlling her emotions. "Even though I know it's going to happen, I still can't quite believe it. Every time one of his symptoms pop up it's like a punch to the gut. Just when I start to forget why I'm really here something happens, and it knocks the wind right out of me. I'm scared I won't be ready before he dies. I'm scared I'll have a setback once he's gone. I'm scared I'll mess up, and somehow someone will find out about his illness before he's ready."

Sarah felt anger rise, anger she didn't even know was hiding behind the fear. She stood up and took a few steps closer to the lake, crossing her arms. "But more than any of that, I'm *pissed*. I'm pissed Elijah has to suffer with such a painful and humiliating illness. I'm pissed there's no cure. I'm pissed he won't tell his children. And I'm pissed because the one person in my life right now who really gets me will be ripped unwillingly from my life."

Sarah turned and looked at Tina who was wiping her own tears from her face. Sarah looked away and noticed hikers a few yards to the right who were staring at her with a look that could have either been pity for her plight or disgust for her outburst. Given her experience over the last two years she figured it was probably pity. She wiped her nose on her sleeve and then rubbed at her eyes, trying to take the sting out.

"But, I'm going to try my best to learn the tools I need to pull through all that fear and anger before Elijah dies. I'm going to listen to everything he says and truly take it all to heart. Opening up to you, right now... that's all due to Elijah. I wouldn't have been able to do this just a few weeks ago. Hell, I probably wouldn't have been able to do it four days ago. That's the first thing I've learned. I have to start trusting in myself and others around me. If I can do that, I know I'll eventually be okay. I want to live the life Elijah is teaching me to embrace."

Tina got up and walked over to Sarah, giving her a long hug. When there are no appropriate words, a hug can say it all.

Sarah put on her pajamas and then decided to throw on a sweatshirt. She put on her warm, fuzzy socks and grabbed the duvet off the bed before stepping out on the balcony. Elijah had already gone to bed, the hike taking a lot out of him. She was worried about his comment from earlier that morning indicating he hadn't slept much.

Another symptom showing its ugly head. I'm concerned things are going to start escalating quickly. I hope not, I'm not ready.

As much as Elijah liked to portray the opposite, she knew he wasn't ready either. He needed to be able to go to the gala which was still over a month away. She wondered if things got too bad if he would still consider going even if it meant people would know something was wrong with him. Her mind wandered back to the hike from earlier. Elijah had stumbled a few times on their way down the trail so they'd decided to end their hiking for the day.

She was happy to have met Tina. She hadn't realized how much she needed someone to confide in until Tina told her she could call anytime. Sure there was Elijah, but she may need to talk to someone *about* Elijah. She had felt a strong connection with Miles and Tina from the start. They all shared a concern for their friend who would soon be facing a nightmare they would help him through, but would never be able to fully understand.

She smiled to herself at the conversation they had at the cars before departing ways. Apparently, Miles and Tina would be joining them over Thanksgiving. When she asked Elijah about it on the drive home, he'd told her that Miles and Tina didn't have any children and so they had decided long ago to be each other's family on that particular holiday. Miles had indicated he was excited for Sarah to cook for them, his comment revealing Elijah had told him of their bet. They filled in Tina and she immediately sided with Sarah.

When she had woken up that morning her mood made her believe the day would be full of challenges. She couldn't have been more wrong. Her day was not only enjoyable, but she felt more at peace than she had since before the accident. In the four weeks she had been here, Elijah had been able to help her make more progress than she had in two years. Every day she felt stronger and she wanted to capitalize on this newfound strength. She got up and went back in her room, deciding it was time to do something. She went over to her writing desk and pulled out her list of all the ways she held on too tight to her pain. Every time Elijah crossed something off his list, she would do the same. Her eyes scanned the list, settling on one.

Stop nighttime ritual of talking at doors

She took in a deep breath and walked to one of the closed doors. She closed her eyes and opened it. When she opened her eyes she expected some sort of cliff event, but there was nothing. All she saw was an elegantly decorated guest bedroom. She quickly went and opened the second door before returning to her room. She thought back to Elijah's advice on how she needed to find a way to talk to them anywhere. On impulse she took out a fresh notebook and started writing. She wasn't sure why, but putting her words down on paper rather than speaking them to an empty room behind a closed door made her feel better. The words were the same—those she had spoken out loud every night for nearly two years were now written down on paper. Looking at them, she could see the imbalance and couldn't ignore it. Three full pages for Danny. Three short sentences for Nick. She focused on the last sentence.

I'm so sorry.

When she spoke those words each night at her bedroom door they came without thought or consideration. Now, looking at them, she found herself wondering what she was sorry for. She knew she held guilt for the lack of mourning she had shown for Nick in comparison to Danny, but was that all? The box sitting under her bed came to mind, but she pushed it away. She wasn't ready to analyze it yet, maybe tomorrow night.

Or maybe the next.

CHAPTER 10

Sarah had set her alarm to wake up early and prepare for their meeting with Lisa. She woke up feeling sluggish so she took a long, hot shower before sitting down at her computer. She verified she had all of Elijah's current symptoms logged in the tracker and then reviewed her notes. Once that was completed, she checked her email for the first time since Friday. There was the typical spam to get rid of, a note from her mom letting her know she planned to call later in the day, and one from an address she didn't recognize. She opened the email and scanned down the message. It was from Andy's friend Travis.

She was happy to get a message from the guy renting her house. While she trusted Andy's judgment, it was still strange for her to think about someone she didn't know living in her home. His email gave her a glimpse of the person he was—recently divorced with two young children, polite, and a decent sense of humor.

Overall, it was a friendly email. He mentioned he liked living in her house and was happy to take care of any required maintenance. Apparently the water softener needed salt. In the email he also requested to use her SUV and for some reason she became irritated by the request.

He certainly seems to be making himself at home.

Nick had always taken care of things around the house, and then Andy did it for her. In the years since Nick's death she'd realized there were so many things she took for granted, things she never worried about because Nick took care of them. Even though she and Nick viewed their marriage as a partnership, there was still separation in their roles. She did not do water softeners. Or grills... that was a disaster she was still trying to block out of her memory.

Looks like I'll need to make a new list before I get home. One that outlines all the things I still need to learn to be self sufficient.

She focused her attention back to the email and typed a quick reply to Travis, letting him know she would think about it. She read back over her response. It seemed curt and snippy, but she found she didn't really care. Just as she clicked send her phone rang. Her mom's name stared back at her from the display.

"Hi, Mom."

"Hi, Sarah. How are you doing out there in the mountains?"

"I'm fine. A bit tired today, but overall I'm doing well. I went for a hike on Saturday."

"A hike sounds nice."

"It was very peaceful. How was your week?" She listened patiently as her mom went into the details of her week. She asked about her dad and smiled at her mom's frustration with his idle lifestyle. Winter was always a trying time for her mom. Her dad was an avid golfer and in his retirement it had became his life's mission. Since he couldn't play in the winter, he talked about it. Constantly. It got so bad last year, her mom sent him and a friend away for a week to a golf resort as his Christmas present. The amount of irritation she heard in her mom's voice at the moment told her the same gift was likely to be under the tree again this year.

"So, Sarah, the reason I'm calling is because we need to settle our holiday plans. It's only a few weeks to Thanksgiving. Since I hadn't heard anything from you, I assume you're planning to come home for Christmas. However, James plans to be home for Christmas this year. I know he'd want to see you, but I won't force you to come." There was an awkward pause, and Sarah sat down on her bed. She put her head in her hand and felt the tears threaten. She let them fall, too tired of fighting.

"I'm sorry, Sarah. I figured James being here on Christmas would keep you away, so I thought we should plan to get together over Thanksgiving instead. Your dad and I talked about it, and we think it would be fun to come out there and see you. I wouldn't mind having Thanksgiving dinner at the hotel restaurant. The meal is not a big deal; we just want to see you. It's been a long time since we've been to

Denver, and it would keep you from having to interrupt your assignment."

Oh, this can't be happening. This really can't be happening.

Sarah cleared her throat. "Do you mind if I think about it for a day or two? I'd, um... love to have you and Dad visit, but, um... well the project is really busy right now. We might work through some of Thanksgiving so, um... just give me a day or two, okay?" She was struggling to hold it together.

In the soft sigh flowing through the phone Sarah recognized her mom understood her struggle. "That's fine. Just give me a call when you're ready. It's okay to take a break you know. I can tell this assignment has been good for you, but don't trade in one vice for another. Working yourself into the ground and using it as a distraction won't make your progress effective long term. What will you do once the assignment is over? You don't want a relapse."

"I know, Mom. Thanks. I need to go, okay? I love you." She hung up and turned her face into her pillows, letting the sobs take over.

"Elijah?" The house was eerily quiet. Sarah suddenly heard the patio doors open, and she turned to see Elijah walk in. "What are you doing outside? It's cold."

He smiled at her as he entered, carrying his newspaper and coffee. "I needed some fresh air. I wasn't out there long." He stopped when he got close enough to see her face. "What's wrong?"

"I'm just having a bad morning." She wasn't ready to discuss it with him. She knew she would eventually, but she needed coffee first. The coffee finished brewing and she slowly stirred in the sugar, letting the rhythmic movement hypnotize her and block out her mind. The clank of Elijah's coffee cup on the counter brought her back to the present. She turned, expecting him to be watching her but was grateful to find him reading the paper. She walked to the fridge and retrieved a yogurt. He wouldn't be happy with such a paltry breakfast, but she didn't care. She stood at the counter, eating her yogurt in silence. Once she was done, she took her cup of coffee and walked over to look out the windows of the family room. She took in a deep breath, held it for a few seconds and let it out slowly.

"So, I got an email from the guy renting my house. You know, Andy's friend? Anyway, he was wondering if he could drive my SUV while I was away. Something about helping each other out since it's not good for the car to sit for an extended period of time."

"And that upset you to the point of crying?"

She shook her head and turned to face him. "No... that was something else." She paused and took a sip of her coffee. "Anyway, I wanted to get your advice since I don't know much about cars. It seemed like an odd request, but maybe it's a good idea. What do you think?"

He put down his paper and walked into the room. He sat down in one of the chairs by the fireplace, crossing his ankle over his knee. "Well, it is better for the vehicle to be driven rather than sit idle for a long period of time." He continued to rattle off all the reasons it was a good idea.

"Okay, thanks. I'll send Travis a message letting him know to work out the details with Andy." She finished her coffee and walked to the kitchen to set the empty cup in the sink before returning to the family room to sit across from Elijah.

"Do you want to talk about whatever made you upset this morning?"

She pulled her feet up on the chair and hugged her legs, resting her chin on her knees. "My mom called. I don't know... I've been feeling cranky, and I probably overreacted." She rested her head on the back of the chair and closed her eyes, waiting until she felt like she could tell him about the conversation.

"She called because she wanted to finalize plans for the holidays. Usually I go to their house on either Thanksgiving or Christmas. It's the only times I have visited them since the accident. With Thanksgiving just around the corner, she assumed I was planning to visit for Christmas. I guess I never told her I wouldn't be coming home while on this project. Anyway, Christmas isn't an option so she offered to come here for Thanksgiving."

"Why is Christmas not an option, assuming I allowed you to go?" He was picking at that invisible piece of lint again.

"Allowed?" It was only one word, but she managed to saturate it with a significant amount of irritation. She knew he didn't mean anything by his choice of words, but she wasn't in the mood for his overbearing nature.

"Sorry, poor choice of words. Assuming I *agreed* to you spending time at home over the holidays."

It must be obvious I'm in a bad mood. He gave up way too easily.

She rubbed her forehead. "Because my brother James is planning to be there. I haven't seen James since the funeral." She looked away as she felt the tears threaten again. She was so tired of crying all the time. "James lives in California with his wife and twin sons. They're about two years older than what Danny would have been. That night, when you asked me if I had been around other children... I didn't tell you the worst of it. I don't like to admit I can't face my own brother and nephews. James is hurt by it. Although we're separated in age by five years, we were always very close. I miss him so much, but I just can't..." She lost her voice in her sobs, burying her face in her hands until they ran their course.

After a few minutes she noticed a shadow cross over her. She looked up to find Elijah holding out a box of tissues. She tried to say thank you, but nothing would come out. He placed his hand on the side of her head, rubbing his fingers into her hair. She leaned into his hand for a second, closing her eyes, and then pulled back. He went and sat back down in the chair while she blew her nose and wiped at her eyes with the heels of her hands.

"Do you have any other nieces or nephews?"

"Tom, the eldest, has three children. They're all grown and are either in college or almost in college. They're not around much and when they are I'm usually okay. They're more like adults than children. Peter, the youngest of my three brothers, is a perpetual bachelor slash playboy with no children or prospects."

"So what made you so upset? The thought of not seeing your brother or the thought of seeing his children?"

She looked up to the ceiling and shook her head. "Both. Mostly I just miss James. I hate that my pain has ended our relationship and hurt him in the process. Immediately following the funeral he sent me emails every day. I never responded and eventually his emails came only once a week, then once a month, then not at all. I miss him. But I'm not ready to see the boys." She had expected Elijah to respond with words of wisdom. Instead he remained quiet. She wasn't sure how many minutes they sat there in silence.

"If you want your parents to come visit over Thanksgiving, I'm sure we could figure something out."

"Thank you, but no. They would never understand my living here. You don't want to experience the wrath my mother would lay down on you if she found out."

He raised his eyebrow at her and the faintest hint of a smile crossed his lips. "I would have expected your father to be the issue."

"Oh, he wouldn't like it either. But he's a teddy bear compared to momma bear."

"You could move into a hotel, just for the weekend."

"I can't leave you. You're falling down, forgetting things, not sleeping... We don't know what will be going on in three weeks. No, I'm not leaving you." Her tone told him there were to be no more arguments. "I'll figure out some excuse. She won't be happy, but she'll get over it. Eventually." Her mom was an expert at handing out guilt, which wasn't good given Sarah's propensity to horde it.

He looked back down at the invisible piece of lint. "I'm serious, Sarah. If you want them to visit, or if you need to go home at some point, I'm sure we can work something out. Ms. Reynolds is starting today and I'm sure I could pay her a hefty holiday bonus to stay—"

"Elijah. No." She actually startled him with the force of her response. "But thank you anyway." She ran her hands through her hair and let out a groan.

"You okay?"

She pulled her head forward and pressed her fingers to the bridge of her nose. "I'm fine. I'm just... irritated. By everything. I don't know what my problem is."

"Ah, so that's it. Do you need some chocolate?"

She glared at him. She was pretty sure her mouth was hanging open and her brows were touching each other. The look on his face told her he was completely serious. That just made her even angrier.

"It's what? And why would I need chocolate?"

He rolled his eyes. "Okay, I should have known you'd have a reaction. Like I said before, it's been a long time since I've lived with a woman, but I have lived with two before. And I lived with those two for a very long time. Usually when they were affected by this kind of mood..." He waved his hand at her. "...chocolate helped."

She continued to glare at him. At least she managed to close her mouth. "And what exactly is 'this kind of mood?'" Sarah waved her hand back at him.

"You know, the whole 'I'm cranky and don't know why' mood. My past experience tells me you're likely suffering from P.M.S."

"Why do men always blame a bad mood on P.M.S.?"

"Why do women always claim it's not P.M.S. when it clearly is? When are you due for your next menstrual cycle?"

I can't believe we are actually having this conversation. I can't believe he asked about my menstrual cycle without cracking a smile.

"It's not P.M.S. and I am NOT talking to you about this! *Why* are we even talking about this?"

He let out a frustrated sigh. "Sarah, it is common knowledge that all women between certain ages have a menstrual cycle once a month. Is it the fact that I'm calling it a menstrual cycle? Would it lighten the conversation if I referred to it as your period? Or being on the rag? How about your monthly visitor? Or my personal favorite Leanne used to use, Aunt Flow? Whatever you call it you shouldn't be so embarrassed to talk about it. And why are you so surprised at the suggestion?"

"Because I haven't had a period in eighteen months!" The elevated volume of her voice surprised even her. "You seem to know so much about it, so you should also know when the body goes through a significant amount of stress, or if you lose a significant amount of weight, it sometimes stops. I had both of those, so no surprise." She rubbed her eyes with her hands. "Can we just stop talking about this, please?"

His face softened. He put his hands on the arms of his chair and stood up. "Fine. The last thing I'll say is that your stress has shifted since you've been here and you've gained weight. Don't say I didn't warn you when Aunt Flow barges back in without knocking." With that he walked off in the direction of the office.

She continued to stare in his direction long after he was out of sight. The entire conversation was so ridiculous, and frustrating, she couldn't formulate a single thought for several minutes. She finally got up and stomped off toward the kitchen. She got out a glass and slammed the cabinet door shut. She filled it with water and took a huge gulp. She stood in the kitchen, leaning against the counter. Her mind was fighting to put a thought in her head but she refused to let it surface. Her mind finally won.

Damn it.

She walked to the closet, slipped on her shoes and grabbed her coat and purse.

"Going somewhere?" She hadn't seen Elijah enter the kitchen.

"Shut up." She slammed the door on his soft laugh behind her.

Sarah dropped her shopping bags on her bed and searched through them. Finding what she was looking for, she went in search of Elijah and was relieved to find him in the office. She had stormed off so quickly she forgot leaving him alone wasn't a good idea.

"Hey." He looked up at the sound of her voice.

"Hey yourself. Get what you needed from the store?" The playfulness was back in his eyes.

"Yeah. I won't interrupt. I just wanted to say I was sorry. And to make sure you weren't lying on the floor somewhere."

"I stayed right here in this chair to ensure no casualties occurred while you were gone. And I'm the one who should apologize. I've made it my life's mission to have fun tormenting you. I should have realized the circumstances and taken the day off."

"Well, at least your mission won't last long." She turned to leave and stopped.

What the hell is wrong with me?

She turned back to his office. "I'm sorry, that wasn't funny."

He was smiling. "Actually, it *was* funny." He got up and walked to the other side of his desk, leaning against it and crossing his arms. "Sarah, what have I been telling you? You're wound up too tight. You get embarrassed at compliments. You look like you want to crawl back into yourself when someone touches you. You can't talk about female 'issues' without being mortified. My jokes make you uncomfortable." He paused to make sure she was listening. It was a long list, but she looked him straight in the eye to make it clear she was following along just fine. "The old Sarah, the one I met years ago in a conference room at Jacobs, would have been comfortable with all of that. I want you to relax. We're trying to get you to enjoy life again."

"I don't know any woman who would enjoy casually talking about their female 'issues', including the old Sarah." She leaned against the door frame and looked down at her feet. "I'll concede to the others though." She looked at him through her eyelashes. "Since we're sharing, why are you so flippant about your illness?"

He took a moment to consider his words. When he spoke, his voice was quiet and full of sadness. "Because it's all I can do. Soon I will have to succumb to this wretched disease. I will have no more choices in life. I will lose control over every aspect of my being—both my body and my mind. I don't want to waste the last days of my coherent life feeling sorry for myself. Joking about it is the only way for me to function. It's the only way I can get out of bed in the morning. If I knew I could fight it, if I had even a one percent chance to beat it, then that would be enough to propel me forward. But CJD conquers everything. By not taking it seriously I don't let it take my good days too."

She held his gaze. She understood the power humor could have over fear. He was right. She needed to find a way to relax. She looked down at the bag in her hand, opened it, and tossed him one of the contents.

"What's this?"

"Chocolate. You were right about that too. In the past it made Aunt Flow happy, so I'm hoping if I eat a lot of it she won't be so hard on me during this visit. Maybe it will make CJD happy as well and he'll take it easy on you for awhile."

He smiled. "Then you'd better give me a few more."

"Ms. Reynolds, please, come in." Lisa was older than Sarah, somewhere in her mid to late forties. Her graying dark hair was pulled back in a neat bun at the base of her neck. She was average height and had a stocky build. She wasn't overweight; she was thick—strong. In light of the recent incident with Elijah in his bathroom, Sarah was grateful Lisa would be able to physically help him in the future. Sarah took her coat and noticed she was wearing plain blue scrubs and white nursing shoes. Sarah led her to the office where Elijah was waiting for them.

"Ms. Reynolds, it's good to have you here." Elijah extended his hand in greeting.

"Thank you, Mr. Kingston." Lisa shook his hand in return. Sarah noticed she instantly registered the bump on his forehead.

Elijah sat down at the table across from them and folded his hands on the table. "Sarah and I thought today we should focus on getting to know each other, talking about my current symptoms, what's to come, expectations... essentially the basics. Do you agree?"

Lisa pulled several things out of her bag, including a manila envelope that looked like the one Elijah had given Sarah on her first day. "Yes, I agree. I'd like to meet with the both of you together first, then each of you individually."

Elijah nodded. "The first thing I want to make clear is I don't want anyone to know about my condition. You coming by the house dressed as a medical professional would cause anyone who might see you to suspect something is wrong."

"Understood." Lisa's expression told Sarah she didn't fully agree with Elijah's request.

Maybe I can get her to help me convince him to tell his children.

The three of them spent the next three hours planning. They all agreed it would be best for Lisa to move in once Elijah needed to remain on the main level. When he reached that point of decreased physical capability he would need more assistance, which would fall to Lisa. They planned to convert his office into a bedroom. Elijah also made it clear he didn't want to die at home, but he also didn't want to be admitted to the hospital until the last possible moment. Deep down Sarah felt it was his way of trying to maintain as much control over his disease as possible.

They then moved on to discuss Elijah's current symptoms, starting with what caused the bump on his head. Sarah pulled out her tracker and showed Lisa all the incidents since she had been there. Lisa liked the tracker and decided they should continue in the same way. When it was time for a break, Sarah showed Lisa to the bathroom and then joined Elijah in the kitchen.

"I think things with Ms. Reynolds are going to work out well."

She took the glass of water he held out. "I think she's not going to let you get away with any crap. So, yeah, it's going to work out great." He responded with a mischievous smile over his glass. A few seconds later Lisa walked into the kitchen and thanked Elijah when he handed her a glass of water. She took a drink and looked from Elijah to Sarah.

"Mrs. Mitchell, how about you and I talk now?"

"Certainly." Sarah led the way back to the office and Lisa closed the door behind them.

"Mrs. Mitchell, I know you're in need of both a nutritional plan and an exercise plan. What we didn't discuss was why. When we first met I could tell you were underweight. You're still underweight, but you look as though you've gained a little. I hope you don't mind my saying you also look better."

Sarah smiled and settled in her chair. "No, I don't mind. I am better, but I know I still have a long way to go."

"What got you to this point?"

Sarah sighed and took a drink of her water, stalling for time. It was getting easier for her to explain her circumstances, but she still preferred not to. She continued to look at the glass of water in her hand, playing with condensation forming on the outside of the glass.

"A little over two years ago I lost my husband and two year old son in a car accident. In the process I lost myself. From a nutritional standpoint, I was used to eating with a family every night, and then suddenly they were gone. Eating never regained its priority in my life. I also took to running five miles every day. It was my way of releasing the pain, at least for those five miles. On some level I knew I was heading in the wrong direction physically, but I refused to acknowledge it. At least until Elijah made me face it." She was silent for several seconds after speaking. She finally looked up to meet Lisa's gaze. The hard look she associated with her had softened.

"It's a tragic loss, and I can understand how you lost yourself in the process." Lisa turned to her computer. "What was your weight when you arrived here, and how tall are you?"

Sarah cleared her throat. "I'm about five-nine, and I weighed 113 my first week here. That was about four weeks ago."

Lisa pursed her lips. "How much do you weigh now?"

Sarah shifted in her seat. "I don't know." Her response was soft, highlighting her embarrassment. The look she received from Lisa made it clear she wasn't pleased with Sarah's lack of attention to her own health.

Lisa rapidly clicked at the keys on her keyboard. "What have you done so far to make improvements?"

"Well, Elijah has refused to let me run until you and I have agreed to an appropriate plan. In addition, he has decided to help by feeding me vast amounts of food. I'd like to think there's a way to accomplish this without eating so much."

Lisa continued to type in her computer. "You're right, there are things we can do to focus more on what you eat rather than how much. Your first assignment is to start writing down everything you eat. We'll use it as our basis to create a meal plan you can be comfortable with. As for running, I agree with Mr. Kingston. I don't think it's good for you to do any excessive running yet. However, it's okay if you start back with a mile or a mile and half a day."

Sarah felt like a huge weight had been lifted off her shoulders. She was unaware how much tension she was holding from not being able to run.

"In addition to running, we need to establish a weight training routine. Given the situation you and Mr. Kingston outlined when he fell and hit his head, we need to make you stronger. I want you to get back on the scale tomorrow morning and weigh in once a week going forward. It's important to not be afraid of your weight, but I also don't want you to obsess over it. We'll see where you are now and establish a target weight gain for each week." The look Lisa was giving her left no room for argument. Resigning to her fate, Sarah nodded in response.

Lisa turned her computer around so Sarah could see what was on the screen. They talked through several nutritional facts and dietary plans. Sarah felt overwhelmed at all the information. She had never needed to consider what she ate and how her body responded to its nutritional value. She suddenly had a greater appreciation for anyone who had to eat for consideration of their weight.

Lisa pulled a small spiral notebook out of her bag and handed it to Sarah. "You can use this to log your meals. It's a food journal so it's all laid out for you. Just fill in the blanks." Sarah flipped through the pages and then set the journal in her lap.

Lisa pushed her computer off to the side and took a drink of her water. "Now, I would not be doing my job if I didn't talk to you about your emotional health. Given the tragic events you went through and the way you responded to them, I'm concerned about how you will be affected once Mr. Kingston dies. We'll need to work on healthy coping mechanisms you can use when the time comes. My goal will be for you to not have a relapse."

Sarah looked down at the table and nodded her head. "That's my goal as well."

"I can recommend a therapist."

Sarah contemplated her answer before shaking her head. "No, thank you. I've seen several therapists over the years, and I don't want to go through the process right now. I promise to go to one once I get home."

Lisa typed something into her computer. She glanced at Sarah but continued to type. "I must say I don't agree, Mrs. Mitchell. But I will respect your decision."

"Thank you." Sarah sat forward in her chair. She decided this was her moment to ask her question. "Speaking of not agreeing with someone's decision, what do you think of Elijah's request to not tell his children about his condition?"

Lisa stilled her fingers on the keyboard and looked over at Sarah. She cleared her throat and took a drink of her water before responding. "It doesn't really matter what I think. Just as it's your right to decide not to see a therapist, it is Mr. Kingston's right to decide to not tell his children. Neither of us should be trying to undermine that decision. He has enough to deal with right now, don't you think, Mrs. Mitchell?"

Sarah felt her face flush from embarrassment.

Great, not even one day with this woman and she already has me feeling guilty.

"Of course. You're absolutely right."

"Well, I think that's enough for today. We can go over additional items in regard to Mr. Kingston's care once I've had a chance to review my notes. I'm looking forward to working alongside you, Mrs. Mitchell."

"Yes, me too. I'll see you tomorrow."

Sarah left the room in search of Elijah. She decided to get in her first run while he met with Lisa. It was the first time she smiled all day.

It had taken all of Sarah's strength to turn off the treadmill and stop running. Those ten minutes had been the most invigorating since she'd been there. She walked across the great room, looking forward to a quick shower. As she passed the short hallway leading to the office, she heard voices through the open door. She climbed the first two steps and stopped, her attention caught by what she heard. She had no intention of eavesdropping, but she was frozen nonetheless.

"I don't understand why the nature of my relationship with Sarah is any of your concern."

"Mr. Kingston, I agree that in any other circumstance it would be none of my business. However, you are about to die. That poor woman has been through more heartache than any one person deserves. I was hired to look after not only your health, but hers as well. Given how she responded the last time she experienced loss, I need to understand the depth of your relationship so I know what I'm dealing with."

There was a pause in the conversation and all she could hear was her rapidly beating heart. She willed her feet to move but they refused. When she heard Elijah speak again, his voice was much softer. Unconsciously she leaned her head in the direction of the office to hear him better.

"I can assure you Sarah's feelings for me do not equal that of her husband and son. While my passing may cause her pain, it will not be near the same magnitude. If she can continue to make progress while she's here, I'm convinced she will be fine after I'm gone. Better even."

"How can you be sure? It won't take a significant loss to set her back over the edge. I'm not sure it's best for her to be here."

"Let me be clear. Sarah will remain here until the project for which she has been hired is complete. The only thing that will get her out of here is her own desire to go home. I expect you to assume and plan for the worst when it comes to helping Sarah at the end."

"Of course, Mr. Kingston."

Somehow she got her feet to move quickly, and quietly, up to her room. She leaned against the closed door for a few minutes trying to calm her heart rate and make sense of what she'd heard. She finally moved toward the bathroom and turned on the shower. Standing under the warm water she replayed their words over in her mind several times. One comment continued to overpower the others.

I'm not sure it's best for her to be here.

Everyone was concerned about how she was going to respond once Elijah died. It was like they were all waiting to catch her, fully expecting her to fall. Even her mom was afraid she would relapse at the end, just for different reasons since she didn't know what was really going on. She suddenly felt anger directed at herself.

How weak are you to cause everyone to have such little faith in your strength to overcome this? For the past two years you've not even tried to move on. Sure you needed time to grieve, but you could have tried to heal, to make progress. Now, all of a sudden you think you can give some half-hearted attempts and think you'll be fine? They're all right! You will fall down again if you don't stop feeling sorry for yourself! You need to stop being a victim and start being a survivor.

She sat down in the shower and let the water run over her downturned head. She thought about Elijah and all he had been through and all he still had to face. The loss he had experienced was no different than hers. He had lost his wife suddenly just as she had lost Nick. Sure his children were alive, but he had still lost them when Lena died. The fear he was facing over what will happen in the near future was much more than her fear of tomorrow. She feared living again, falling in love again, and losing it all. But at least she knew what to expect if it happened again. Elijah had no idea what to expect from his illness. He could read an infinite amount of research and use his own experience from when his dad went through it. But none of it would be able to properly prepare him for what it would really be like to live it. What it would feel like to lose complete control over every aspect of his body.

Yet he still wakes up each day with a smile on his face. He falls down in the most embarrassing of circumstances and gets right back up. He's reminded of that fall every time someone asks him how he got that bump, and every time he answers without missing a beat. He dedicates his final days to helping me, a near stranger, get back on my feet. He may not be able to survive CJD in the end but he will survive the humiliation of the disease. He is living like a survivor and not as a victim. He's living each day as if there's no tomorrow.

The thoughts danced in her mind, creating a flurry of emotions. As she pondered her next steps, Elijah's voice echoed in her mind.

The only thing that will get her out of here is her own desire to go home.

She didn't know what to do.

I need to decide what I think is best for me and my healing. Am I better here where I'm at risk of relapsing when Elijah dies or at home where I will once again be alone on this journey?

Her need for Nick was so strong in that moment. She needed him to tell her what to do. She always trusted in Nick without fear. Now he was gone.

She could feel the anxiety bubble within her as she struggled to sort through her emotions. Then she did something she hadn't done in a long time. She prayed. She buried her face in her hands, rocking back and forth. She pleaded for God to give her strength to do what she needed to do to overcome all she had been through and all that was to come. She asked for forgiveness for blaming Him in those darkest of days. Then she handed it all over. She let go of the control. She took the faith she wanted to give to Nick and gave it to God instead. She sat under the water until she felt her sorrow turn into numbness and then into determination. Finally, she reached up and turned off the water, watching her desperation wash down the drain.

CHAPTER 11

Sarah shifted the pizza boxes on her lap, her mind drifting to Elijah's meeting with Leanne. She couldn't shake her nervous feeling, so Tina had taken her gown shopping as a distraction. Leanne had insisted on meeting at the house, but luckily they were able to make an excuse for Miles to be there to cover for any of Elijah's odd behavior. Miles had sent messages periodically to let them know the meeting was going well and Elijah was doing fine. One of those messages confirmed he and Elijah would be making Thanksgiving Day dinner. The news thrilled Tina, but Sarah couldn't share in her excitement. Winning the bet meant Leanne was suspicious of her relationship with Elijah.

Sarah tried to settle her nerves by thinking about her gown. It was black and sleeveless with a neckline that came up high across her collar bones but dipping low in the back. Even though she normally wouldn't want to expose so much skin, the high neckline helped make it feel modest enough for her comfort. There was a narrow black satin sash around the waist and below it the gown fell in layers of chiffon she knew would float dramatically when dancing. The most stunning part of the gown was the tiny hand-sewn crystals covering the entire bodice above the sash. The crystals were a mixture of light aqua and clear colored beads. The fit was almost perfect and required only a few alterations.

Thompson parked in front of the house and quickly retrieved the shopping bags. Tina got out first and took the pizza boxes from Sarah before walking toward the house. Sarah followed until Tina suddenly stopped and turned to face her.

"Sarah, before we go inside I think there's something you should know." She couldn't explain it, but something in Tina's tone made her heart hammer in her chest. Before either could speak again, Elijah opened the front door.

"There you are. Come in, we're starving."

Sarah looked back to Tina but she just sighed and gave a slight shake of her head. Thompson walked past them with a quick nod before climbing back into the car. She followed Tina through the door where Elijah took the pizza boxes.

"I hear you found a dress. I can't wait to see it. Although, I wish you would have told me you were also going to shop for clothes."

"Why, so you could have forced payment on those as well? Sorry, but a whole new wardrobe wasn't part of the compensation agreement." The only downside to the shopping experience was Elijah had insisted on paying for everything.

"Fair enough." He walked to the kitchen with the pizzas. Sarah lowered her voice and asked Tina what she was going to tell her outside. Tina hesitated and stared in the direction of the kitchen.

"I'm sorry, Sarah. I told Elijah I didn't think this was a good idea." The hammering in her chest became deep and painful.

She didn't need to ask Tina to explain. She had her answer in the next moment. She immediately tried to reject the familiar sounds. Panic enveloped her with a sudden intensity and she dropped her coat as she gripped the wall for support. She vaguely felt Tina's hand on her arm, and she was aware Tina had said something, but she couldn't hear the words. Her eyes had found the source of the sounds, forcing her to accept what was going on. The next thing she saw was blackness.

Sarah opened her eyes and blinked. The events from moments before came rushing back to her with a sudden force, causing her stomach to roll. She stumbled awkwardly to the bathroom, faintly registering Tina sitting at the desk. She reached the toilet in time for it to catch the reappearance of her lunch. As her stomach clenched for the second time, she felt Tina's hands grip her hair.

Sarah spit into the toilet and reached for the toilet paper to blow her nose. She hated throwing up. She had done quite a lot of it after the accident. She wanted to go over to the sink to wash her face and mouth, but her stomach clenched again. She gripped the sides of the toilet and let out a loud groan.

"You knew about this didn't you? That's what you were going to tell me outside? You had all day... why..." She lost her voice in the eruption of her stomach. All the food had been purged from her system, and she was left with dry heaves. It was starting to hurt, but she welcomed the pain.

"Yes, I knew, and yes it's what I was about to tell you outside. Elijah told me not to say anything and you know how he is. But I made the choice. I knew there was no stopping him and so I chose not to tell you because I wanted you to enjoy the day. You deserved the break, and you really did need a gown." Sarah was startled by the cold cloth Tina pressed to the back of her neck.

Sarah felt her nausea transform into anger. She stood on weak legs and turned to look at Tina. Instead her eyes focused on Elijah standing in the bathroom doorway. Her anger was so intense she started to shake. "No. I'm not ready to talk to you right now. Out. Get OUT!" She saw pain flash through his eyes before he turned to leave. She knew later she would feel guilty for lashing out at him but in that moment she was glad for his pain. Tina reached out for her.

"Sarah, you should sit—"

She shook her head and walked away from Tina. "This isn't supposed to be happening. This isn't what I signed up for." She walked around the bathroom, not really aware of her surroundings. Her eyes finally focused on the shower floor and a sob broke free from her chest. "I sat right there. Right there. I gave it over. I gave Him my trust, and this is what I get in return? I thought... I thought when I handed it over God would make it clear. That it wouldn't hurt any more because He was leading the way. If I would have known this is what was waiting for me, I would have made my own choice. I would have gone home. At least there I would have known what to expect."

"Perhaps that's why He doesn't show us where the path leads until we're already there. Many times the path laid out for us by God isn't the easy one. It's why handing it all over is so difficult sometimes. We tend to follow the easy path. If you handed it over, then this is what's supposed to be happening right now. It doesn't mean it will be easy, just that it's the right path."

Sarah sank to the floor, feeling the weight of Tina's words. Going home would have been the easy path to take. She put her forehead on her knees and wrapped her arms around her legs. "I can't do this. I'm not ready."

"You'll never feel ready for something like this."

"So you believe in Elijah's therapy by immersion?"

"Not always. But I understand his reasons this time. For one, you would never choose to do this on your own, yet it's something you want to overcome. Also, Elijah wants to help you and he doesn't really have much time left. With limited time, immersion is often the only option."

Sarah lifted her head and looked at Tina. Neither said anything for a few moments. Finally, Tina walked over and sat down on the floor in front of her.

"You also have to understand, it's because he's running out of time that he needs this for himself too. This is the last time he will be able to spend the weekend with his grandson. He struggled for a long time over how he would be able to spend time with Oliver given your understandable aversion to children. He needs this as much as you do."

Oliver.

Hearing his name brought on fresh tears. "I didn't even know he had a grandson." Sarah looked to the ceiling and tried to shake away her selfishness. Tina was right. Elijah needed this time with his grandson, and he shouldn't have to sacrifice because she was too fragile for the situation.

"I knew the surprise of Oliver being here would be difficult for you, but your reaction was much more severe than I had anticipated. I know you haven't spent time with children since the accident, but you see them when you're out in public. Even earlier today at lunch, I saw you watching a mother and daughter. You had a sad, distant look in your eyes, but you didn't break down. Here... the moment you saw Oliver you passed out. Now this. Why was this so much more difficult?"

Sarah wiped her face. It was a pointless effort since the tears kept falling. "When I'm out, I'm prepared to see and hear children. Tonight, when I heard those sounds... his little feet running on the floor, his laughter... For more than two years, I've driven myself to near hysteria trying to hear those sounds again in my own home. I would sit on my couch for hours, just listening. Waiting for something I knew would never come. When I first heard those sounds tonight, it was like a culmination of those years finally finding me. And for the briefest of moments, when my eyes saw Oliver, my heart saw Danny."

"Oh, Sarah. I'm so sorry I didn't tell you." Tina looked away and wiped at her eyes. Finally she looked back to Sarah. "So, what do we do to get you through this?"

"I don't think I can be in this house with—" Sarah averted her eyes from Tina's. There was nothing but silence between the two of them. As the silence extended, Sarah's mind wandered back to the image of Oliver running around the corner, laughing, with Miles at his heels. She felt her breathing become more rapid. Tina must have recognized her struggle because the sound of her voice filled the empty space, distracting her thoughts.

"Miles and I waited to have children, both focused on establishing our careers first. When we decided it was time, nothing happened. We tried fertility treatments a few times, but it was too much for me emotionally and physically. We decided it was best for us to pursue a life without children. When we were going through it I buried myself away. It was too painful for me to hear my friends talk about their baby showers and nurseries. I thought I could protect myself through isolation. It was easier to be alone than face the pain of hearing about the one thing I couldn't have that came so easily for them. I was wrong, Sarah. Isolating myself from the world didn't protect me or take away the pain. It just made me have to face it alone."

Sarah heard the words, but they couldn't find a way to penetrate through the reconstructed wall around her heart. "I understand what you're saying, but I just don't think I can."

"Maybe Miles and I can stay for the weekend. We can take turns keeping an eye on Elijah and—"

"No." They both turned their attention quickly to the door at the unexpected sound of Elijah's voice. "Tina, do you mind if I talk with Sarah privately for a moment?"

Tina looked to Sarah for approval. Looking at Elijah she knew her anger was still there. She still saw him as an intrusive man who forced his way on everyone else. However, after her talk with Tina she could also see he was a dying man who wanted to spend time with his grandson and help a friend in the process. She gave Tina a short nod indicating she was okay to talk alone with him. Tina got up and quietly left the room. Elijah looked down at Sarah and held her gaze. His eyes contained pain, but not remorse.

"I'm sorry I hurt you, Sarah. I knew you would have a reaction, I just didn't think it would be this significant. I know this weekend will be hard for you, and I won't force you to interact with Ollie, but I want you to try. I want you in the house, but I won't allow you to use Miles and Tina as a crutch. I know you can do this."

She let out a harsh laugh. "Why is it you're the only one who actually thinks I can do these things? Everyone else is waiting for me to collapse. Including me. How can you have so much faith in my ability to do this?"

"Because I know you want to. That's all you need to succeed. It won't be easy, and I'll be here to help, but you *can* do it."

She bit on her lower lip, trying to hold back the tears. "Why are you doing this for me? I get that you want to see your grandson before it is too late. I get that, I do. But why do you care if I do this?"

He hesitated and looked down at his feet. "Because I know how much you want to see your brother and nephews, and I promised to help you. I want to give you as much of your life back before my life is gone. It's that simple."

She held his gaze while she dug deep for strength. "I'll try. But I only promise to remain in the house. I'll most likely stay in my room. I'd like to offer more, but I can't."

"It's a start and I'll take it." He checked his watch. "I need to get Ollie to bed."

"Um, before you go... you didn't carry me upstairs when I passed out did you?" The image of him stumbling and the both of them crashing to the floor caused her to cringe internally.

"No, Miles did." His slight smile told her he understood her reason for asking.

"Awesome."

How is it I've managed to have myself carried by both of these men in the short time I've been here?

Any strength she had felt she gained over the last week had officially been stripped away.

It was Saturday and somewhere in the house was a little boy.

Oliver.

Sarah hoped saying his name in her head would remind her he wasn't Danny, and eventually she would be able to confront him. She still wasn't sure how she didn't know Elijah had a grandson.

Two times Elijah asked me about being around other children. Those would have been perfect opportunities for me to ask if he had any grandchildren. But I was too caught up in my own feelings to consider his.

The realization of how deep her selfishness had grown as a result of her pain caused a fresh wave of guilt to settle in the pit of her stomach.

Oliver.

Based on what she observed in the few seconds she saw him before passing out, she thought he was probably around two years old. She pictured his full head of black ringlets and the dimple on his right cheek. The image of Oliver transformed into an image of Danny. She squeezed her eyes closed and rolled over, burying her face in the pillows. Her thoughts were interrupted by a soft knock on the door. She didn't respond, knowing Elijah wouldn't wait for one anyway.

"What can I bring you to eat?"

"I'm not hungry."

She heard him sigh. "You know how I feel about that. Again, what would you like me to bring you? Toast? Fruit?"

"Nothing."

"That wasn't an option." He went quiet and still she didn't respond. "Fine, I'll just bring you something. Sarah, I'd like for you to at least try. Sit up, read a book, answer emails, something. Just try to function. Staying in bed allows you to hide from reality and won't give you a chance for progress. Can you do that for me? Can you try to spend at least a few hours outside of your bed today?"

She wished she could do as he asked but didn't have the strength. "I only promised to stay in the house. Nothing more."

After a few seconds she felt a hesitant hand on her ankle. "You're stronger than you think, Sarah. Even if I am the only one who believes it, it's true. And I'm always right, remember?" She heard the soft click of the door and pulled the blankets up over her head to escape the truth in his words.

Sarah put on warm clothes and walked out on the balcony. It was cold and overcast, but she hoped she could receive strength from the surrounding mountains. She wrapped herself tightly in her blanket, trying not to think about what Elijah and Oliver were doing. As she sat looking at the rugged beauty surrounding her, she thought about the years she had missed in the lives of her nephews and Maggie's children. The official death toll of the accident was three. The driver of the truck hadn't survived either. However, the relationships she lost as a result of her reaction to the accident drove the unofficial death toll higher. She couldn't bring back Nick or Danny, but she could bring everyone else back into her life.

After an indeterminate amount of time she felt the effects of the cold and moved back into her room. Without thought, she went straight to the bathroom to take a warm shower. Later, she dressed and sat down at her desk to work on the tracker she was keeping for Elijah's symptoms, but her mind kept wandering.

I wonder what they're doing now?

She closed her eyes and listened carefully for any sounds from downstairs.

No. No, I have to stop.

The feeling was too close to the last two years of sitting on her couch listening for Nick and Danny.

Abandoning her attempt to focus on work, she clicked on her inbox. She looked down the list of emails, deciding where to start first. She bypassed the one from her mom, knowing it would be a bomb of guilt exploding all over her the moment she opened it. Instead she focused on the daily emails from Maggie. Some emails contained only three words—'I miss you' or 'thinking of you' and others contained three pages of mindless nonsense. She read through the emails and sent one in return, impressed with her ability to form a response that didn't give away any of her current pain. She filed away Maggie's emails, unable to delete any of them, and recognized an email from Travis.

Since the email he'd sent her requesting to use her SUV a week ago, they had corresponded a few times. They were all short messages—questions regarding various things about the house or vehicle. She clicked on his newest email and had to read it a second time to ensure she hadn't missed something. It was the first email

Travis had sent her without a purpose. It was the kind of email Maggie would send her. It also reminded her of the emails Nick had sent on the rare occasions he traveled for work.

Tears sprang to her eyes, and she slammed her computer shut. She jumped to her feet and paced the room. She stopped at the balcony doors and looked out over the mountains. She took a deep breath and tried to figure out what had made her so angry.

I'm angry because I'm tired of getting upset over basic life experiences.

She was missing Nick more and more every day. She was finally feeling the loss of Nick in her life rather than just missing his support in the loss of Danny. It was these little, everyday interactions that brought it forward. When she had been at home alone, none of this existed. There was no one to drink coffee with every morning. No one to tell her good night every evening. No one to send her random emails. Sure, Maggie's emails were often as random as they came, but those had been there before the accident.

She often wished she still had those emails from Nick. To have something of his voice when time was trying to take away her memories. It's the reason she started saving Maggie's emails. She turned and looked back at her computer. She wasn't sure how long she stood there, trying to find the courage to send a response to Travis. Unfortunately, it never came.

Sarah was soaking in the bath, trying her hardest to stay out of bed.

I wonder what they're doing now. I wonder if Oliver likes hot dogs, like Danny did. I wonder if he sleeps with a favorite blanket or stuffed animal.

The last thought brought Max into her mind. Today was the kind of day she wished she had Max.

She soaked in the tub until the water cooled and her feet and fingers felt like wrinkled prunes. After drying off and dressing, she went into her bedroom to find Elijah had left her a sandwich. There was a note propped up on the plate.

I'm proud of you.

She hadn't realized how much she needed those words until she read them. When the sandwich was gone, she sat with nervous energy, tapping her fingers on the arm of her chair. She looked over to the closed door and after a few minutes got up. Heart beating rapidly she reached for the handle but pulled back suddenly, as if the contact had sent a full voltage shock up her arm.

I can do this. I can do this.

She lurched forward and pulled the door open before she could change her mind.

She slowly walked toward the stairs and stopped at the top step, listening carefully. She heard Elijah's faint voice drifting up the steps but she couldn't make out what he was saying. She crept her way down to the second landing. Her heart was pounding fiercely, and she knew she couldn't go any further. She sat down and closed her eyes, listening to Elijah's voice reading Oliver a story. Silent tears fell down her cheeks. Although she was hearing Elijah's voice, her mind was showing her a memory of Danny sitting on Nick's lap. Her head started spinning and her breathing became rapid. She had reached her limit and quickly retreated back to her room. She went straight to bed and remained there until the next morning.

It was Sunday afternoon and Sarah was back sitting at the computer, where she found herself staring at a blank screen for nearly twenty minutes.

Why is this so hard?

She asked herself the question, but she already knew the answer. If she responded, it would be her first general conversation with a single man that wasn't a family member, a boss, or a friend. She took a deep breath and started typing before she chickened out again. She read over her response and closed her eyes as she clicked send. She felt nervous and invigorated at the same time. She really was amazed at how these little actions made her feel like her old self again.

Imagine how it would feel if you did something big, like go meet Oliver.

She looked at the closed door and knew she had to walk through it. Maybe she would only get to the second landing again, but she would try. She walked toward the stairs, listening for sounds. Nothing. She quietly crept down to the second landing, and although she still didn't hear anything, she smelled something burning.

She suddenly realized Elijah hadn't checked on her all day. Her heart beat rapidly as her concern grew. She got to the stove and found a smoking pot. She turned off the burner and turned on the vent to get rid of the smell.

She looked around. Oliver's toys were still in the family room, but they were neatly packed away in bags. She opened the basement door but all the lights were off. She turned to check upstairs and ran into Elijah as she rounded the corner.

"Sarah? What are you doing? I expected you would be in your room all day." The look on his face contained genuine confusion and she felt the hairs rise on the back of her neck. He sniffed and made a face. "Were you cooking something?" She was suddenly on alert. He walked over to the stove and turned off the vent, picking up the pot to examine the contents.

"No, you were. Elijah, where's Oliver?"

His movements froze. He turned to her and she could see he had paled about five shades. "How do you know about Ollie?"

"Elijah, listen to me. I need you to think. Where's Oliver? He's here for the weekend."

His eyebrows furrowed in confusion. Panic quickly settled into his eyes. "No, I don't remember. What are you talking about? It's Halloween. Leanne would never let him stay here on Halloween. They have some sort of big party with all their friends—"

"Elijah! It's not Halloween. That was a couple weeks ago. Leanne dropped Oliver off on Friday, while Tina and I were shopping. Miles was here and you met with Leanne about work stuff. Oliver is staying here until tomorrow. Think, Elijah, where's Oliver?" She jumped at the sound of the pot hitting the floor.

"I don't remember." His eyes were rimmed with tears and there was panic in his voice. He ran out of the kitchen, yelling for Oliver.

She ran after him and grabbed his arm. He tried to pull away so she pulled harder. "Elijah, you need to calm down. We'll find him. Yes, it's a big house, but he couldn't have gone far. Were you just in your office, before you came out here?"

He shook his head. "Yes, but I was alone."

"Okay, so he's not on the main floor and he can't be in the basement because the door was closed. Same with the house doors, so he must be upstairs."

They both ran, Elijah leading the way. She couldn't say it out loud, but she really hoped he hadn't walked away in the middle of giving Oliver a bath. A threatening lump formed at the back of her throat at the thought. They reached Elijah's bedroom, and he flipped on the overhead light. They both breathed a sigh of relief at the sight of Oliver sleeping on the air mattress.

"He's here. He's sleeping." She could hear the confusion in his voice. On some level he still hadn't believed Oliver was in the house and the sight of him cemented the fact he had forgotten about his grandson spending the weekend.

He sank into the nearest chair, dropping his head in his hands. She noticed the shaking start in his shoulders before it took over the rest of his body. The sight of him broken was the glue she needed to seal up her own cracks. Her pain was old—she had grieved for two years. Elijah's pain was fresh and it was about to get worse. He needed her, and she had to be strong to give him what he needed.

She remembered all the times he had comforted her in her grief without hesitation. She moved to the chair and put her hand on his shoulder. She knelt down before him, and he quickly rested his forehead on her shoulder. She put her arms around him and tried to soothe him by patting and rubbing his back. They stayed that way until his tears finally ran dry.

"How did I forget he was here? What if..." He didn't raise his head from her shoulder and his voice cracked when he spoke.

"It's okay. He's okay. He probably won't sleep tonight from such a long nap, but he's fine. It will all be fine." He pulled away and looked at her. His eyes were red, and she didn't recognize the vulnerable man sitting before her.

He nodded his head slightly. "You're right." His face crumbled again and fresh tears surfaced in his eyes. His voice was only a whisper. "Oh, God. I don't remember. It's my last weekend with him, and I don't remember any of it."

"You still have tonight. You have tomorrow morning. It's his memories that are important now. He's young, but he'll be able to have memories of his time with you and the fun you had. I'll take pictures of the two of you, and I'll make sure Leanne gets them after..." She stopped, searching his face for any clue she was saying the right things. She was. "He'll have memories. We'll make sure of it. That's what matters now."

Slowly he relaxed and he wiped the tears away from his face. "Okay. You're right. That's what's important."

"Why don't you wake up Oliver while I go start on a new dinner?" She stood when he nodded and then looked over to Oliver. The tightening in her chest returned and her heart was hammering so hard she thought it would escape from her body. She felt lightheaded and squeezed her eyes shut.

Please Lord. Please give me the strength to do this.

"Dinner's ready." Sarah caught the words after they were out. She had to make a run for the bathroom where she turned on the cold water and splashed it on her face.

Two years. I haven't said those words to anyone in two years.

She sat down on the closed toilet and hung her head between her knees, focusing on controlling her breathing.

Oh, my God, am I ever going to make it through this?

She pulled herself back up and looked in the mirror. She looked like crap. She redid her ponytail and tried to pinch some color into her cheeks. She walked to the dining room and took her seat next to Elijah. Normally she would have sat across from him, but that would have placed her too close to Oliver. A couple times during the meal she tried to look down the table at Oliver, but the view of him was obstructed by Elijah.

"Mohgehe. Mohgehe." It had been a long time since she had listened to 'toddler speak', but she was pretty sure Oliver was asking for more spaghetti.

"Would you like some more to eat, little buddy?" She looked up from her plate as Elijah took Oliver's bowl to the kitchen. Oliver was bouncing in his seat with spaghetti all over his face and in his hair. She couldn't take her eyes off him. Oliver stared back at her with a huge smile and waved. Her heart broke just a bit more but she forced herself to stay in her seat, looking at him. She slowly raised her hand and waved back.

Oliver bounced up and down a few more times and reached for his sippy cup. His hands were full of spaghetti sauce and the cup slipped out of his hands and onto the floor. He craned his head over the side of his chair, mesmerized by the disappearance of the object.

He then looked up to Sarah, patting his mouth with one hand and pointing to the fallen cup with the other. "Ink, ink."

She looked over her shoulder to see if Elijah was on his way back. He was still in the kitchen. She looked back to Oliver who was now struggling to escape his chair and groaning. "Ink, ink, ink."

She slowly got up and walked over to Oliver. She squatted down and picked up his cup and placed it on his tray. Oliver was quick and he reached for the cup, brushing her hand before she could fully retract it. She pulled back so fast she fell on her butt.

"Sarah, are you all right?" She looked over her shoulder to see Elijah enter the dining room.

"Yeah, fine. Oliver dropped his cup, and I stumbled on my way up." She could tell by the look on his face he knew she wasn't telling him the full truth. She sat back down and pushed her food around her plate. The spot on her hand where Oliver had touched her still burned. She felt like she could collapse at any minute, but she was fighting hard to stay in the present.

Sarah shut the door to her room and collapsed against it, sinking to the floor. She closed her eyes and rested her head in her hands. She was shaking again. Elijah was putting Oliver to bed and she took the opportunity to escape to her room. It was late, after eleven, but Oliver hadn't shown any signs of slowing down, and it took significant effort to get him to relax.

Now, back in her room, she wasn't sure what to do or how she was feeling. She had expected to be broken. She was visibly shaken but beyond that she was confused. The longer she had watched Elijah and Oliver the more she had wanted to be a part of it all. She longed to have Oliver climb up in her lap and cuddle close while she read him a book. She wanted to smell his baby soft skin, to look into those beautiful brown eyes. But she couldn't do it. She was afraid the contact would send her spiraling over a cliff where there was no bottom.

She needed to do something. She got up and went to her writing desk, taking out her journal. So far she had still mostly been writing to Danny, unsure of what to say to Nick. She decided she would start talking to Nick by explaining how she felt being around Oliver. She told him what a wonderful father he had been. She told him she was happy he was with Danny in Heaven so they wouldn't be alone. She poured everything she was feeling out onto the paper and when she was done she was surprised to find that she had written over five pages. It was the most she had said to Nick since he had been gone.

Sarah lay awake in bed for several hours, thinking about Oliver sleeping in the next room. She could feel a tingling sensation gradually take over every inch of her body and her breathing became more rapid. She flipped the covers off and walked slowly to the door. Taking a deep breath she stepped out in the hall and walked quietly to Elijah's room, her heart beating harder and faster with every step. She put her hand on the handle and slowly pushed the door open.

She could hear the rapid, steady breathing coming from where Oliver was sleeping. She took in a sharp breath, remembering how much she missed listening to the same sound every night over the baby monitor. She kneeled down next to him and let her tears fall, hoping each tear carried away one more ounce of her grief. She slowly extended her hand and reached her pinky finger down, touching Oliver slightly. Then, as if pulled by a magnet, the rest of her hand fell into place on his chest. Warmth radiated through her palm, up her arm and straight to her heart. It melted away the remaining protective layers she had wrapped around it. In that one touch she felt all the love she had been so afraid to remember. The tears turned into strong sobs and she felt hands settle on her shoulders. The sudden contact should have startled her, but she found she had been expecting it.

"Sarah. It's okay." Elijah's voice was whispered and she could barely hear him over the sound of her sobs and thundering heart. He pulled her hands away from Oliver and scooped her up in his arms.

"No, don't—" Her protests came out quietly between sobs.

"Hush. I'm just going to set you on the bed." He propped her up against the headboard before sitting down next to her, pulling her into his arms. She was grateful for the comfort and warmth his embrace provided and was amazed she had only known him five weeks. In the time she had been living in his house she had become as comfortable with him as someone she had known her entire life. She supposed pain and suffering did that for people. It gave them a common ground to connect on an intimate level in a short period of time.

It was a long time before her tears finally ran dry. She wiped at her eyes and nose with the sleeve of her shirt and rested her head on Elijah's shoulder. A part of her felt like she should move and put some respectable distance between them. But the greater part of her wanted to hang on to the comfort he provided for as long as he was willing to give it.

"So, I've been wondering this all night. Did I force this situation on you?"

"Yes. I guess you don't remember that when I first saw Oliver I passed out."

"Shit. I figured as much. Even though I don't remember, I know me and therefore I knew it was a strong possibility I forced this on you. I'm sorry. Did I say that already?"

"You apologized for hurting me but not for bringing him here. You knew your actions were right so you didn't apologize for those, just how deep the impact of those actions cut."

"And was it the right thing? To bring him here?" His voice was soft and uncertain. It was unlike Elijah to be uncertain about anything. The progression of his illness created small cracks in his confidence that were slowly growing wider and deeper with each passing day.

She thought about the weekend and the way she was feeling. "Yes, it was the right thing to do. I hope after today I will be able to spend time around my nephews and Nathan. This was the most difficult thing I've been through since the accident, but yes, it was the right thing to do." She shifted so her back was more leaning on Elijah's chest than on the pillow. "How are you feeling?"

She felt his arms around her, clasping his hands at her waist and resting his chin on the top of her head. She could hear him thinking and waited until he was ready to answer.

"I'm still shaken by the fact I forgot Ollie was here. That I thought it was a completely different day. I knew I would forget things. Hell, I've already been forgetting things for awhile. But I expected I would forget dates, conversations, names... I wasn't prepared for how it would feel to find myself living in a world apart from reality. And, worst of all, knowing Ollie could have been hurt in the process." She felt herself rise as his chest inflated with the deep breath he took in.

"Do you remember Halloween or the days that followed?" She was reluctant to ask. She was hoping he remembered. If he didn't, she wasn't sure if she should mention the hike or not. It had been so important to him, and she didn't want to cause him more pain if he didn't remember.

"I don't know. I remember stuff, like falling and hitting my head, our hike, the board meeting, teaching you to dance, but they're all jumbled up in my head. Like pieces of a puzzle I can't seem to fit together. I don't know which came first, or even what might be real or not real." The frustration was evident in his voice. To ease his mind, she started talking. If the memories were mixed up puzzle pieces, then she would provide the cover picture showing him how to put them together. When she finished they sat quietly for several minutes.

"So, I need to ask. Do you have any other grandchildren I should know about?"

"Unfortunately, no." He grew quiet again and she lost herself in the sound of Oliver's gentle breathing. She felt herself drifting toward sleep. Elijah pulled a blanket around them and said something, but she was losing her focus. Before she could counter the action, she fell into a deep sleep.

Sarah's eyes fluttered open and shut immediately to close out the recognition of morning. She felt movement beneath her and froze, confused. She opened her eyes again and looked down to find Elijah still had his hands clasped around her waist. She rubbed her eyes wondering what time it was. She relaxed into Elijah for a few minutes, contemplating the events of the weekend. Finally, she lifted her head to get out of bed and instantly snapped to attention as dread drained all the blood from her head and settled into her limbs like lead.

Oh shit.

CHAPTER 12

"What in the hell is going on here?"

"Elijah." Sarah's voice came out as a hoarse whisper. Elijah finally startled awake, looking at Sarah in confusion. He followed her gaze and cursed under his breath.

"Leanne, what are you doing here?" Elijah gently pushed Sarah off of him and got out of bed.

"What am I doing here? What the hell is SHE doing here? In your BED? Nothing going on my ass. I knew you were hiding something."

"Leanne, calm down. You'll wake up Ollie."

"He *should* be awake. It's after seven for Christ's sake! I told you to keep him on schedule. I guess you're too busy shacking up with your 'assistant' to take proper care of your grandson." The way she said assistant made it clear that she wanted to call Sarah something much more inappropriate. Leanne stomped off in the direction of Oliver who was stirring from all the noise.

"Knock it off, Leanne. Ollie had a rough night and it was late by the time he fell asleep. As for me and Sarah, well that's none of your business. Nothing inappropriate happened. End of story." He ran his hands through his hair in exasperation. "You never answered my question, what are you doing here? I thought I was bringing Ollie back later today." Sarah was grateful he'd remembered the details she'd told him the previous night.

"Why, so you could continue to hide your little tryst with Sarah?" Leanne finally turned her fiery gaze to Sarah. She burned a hole through her for a few seconds before turning back to Elijah. "He has a doctor's appointment that unexpectedly got bumped to today. I tried to call, but now I know why you didn't answer." She turned her attention back to Oliver who had settled back into sleep. "Hey, little man. Mommy's here. Time to wake up." She rubbed his back.

While Leanne was engaged with Oliver, Sarah took the opportunity to make her escape. Elijah reached out to grab her arm as she passed. She looked at him and understood the question in his raised eyebrows. "I'm going to let you two talk." She patted his hand and turned back toward the door. Just as she reached the doorway she heard Oliver's faint voice.

"Bye, bye." She hesitated and turned to look at him. He was waving at her over Leanne's shoulder. She took in a sharp breath and felt tears sting her eyes, but they didn't fall.

Thank you, little Oliver, for helping me find my way back. You'll never understand how much you saved me.

She offered him a small smile and waved before she turned and left the room.

Back in her room, she closed the door and leaned against it. She could hear the muffled sound of Elijah and Leanne arguing but couldn't make out what they were saying. She closed her eyes and thought of Oliver. She had avoided children for so long, fearing the contact would send her into a deep depression. But Elijah, in his overbearing way, had decided for her that she was going to face her fear. And he'd been right. She'd survived and now that it was over she was surprised to find she didn't feel the need to hide away for days.

Her thoughts were interrupted by the sound of Leanne's voice outside the door. "Quit lying. It was obvious to me from day one you two had something more than a professional relationship. The fact that you insist on hiding it and lying about it makes me believe it's something I wouldn't approve of." Although Leanne wasn't yelling, Sarah could clearly hear the anger in her voice. There was a pause in the conversation. "Is she living here?"

"Leanne—"

"Don't even THINK about lying to me again. She's staying in that room, isn't she?"

"We can continue this conversation downstairs."

"So that's a yes." Sarah heard Leanne give off a harsh laugh. "Unbelievable." The sound of their footsteps going down the stairs took the rest of their conversation outside of her hearing range.

She put her hands over her face and squeezed the bridge of her nose. She didn't like people thinking she was in an intimate relationship with Elijah. The current path they were on of letting everyone believe what they wanted and explaining nothing was like being on a train destined for derailment. She wasn't sure which was worse, playing into the misperceptions or continuing to deny them and cause even more conflict in his family. She needed to decide quickly which outcome she was most willing to live with.

By the time Sarah made her way downstairs, Leanne and Oliver had left. She found Elijah in the family room, quietly sipping his coffee and staring at the fire. She watched him for a moment before making her own coffee and sitting down next to him.

"So, I assume Leanne is still mad?"

"She'll get over it. Eventually."

She took a sip of her coffee and studied him over the rim of her cup. "She doesn't seem like the type to get over things quickly."

He shook his head and gave a half smile. "No, she isn't."

"I've come to terms with the fact that it doesn't matter if Leanne likes me or not. As you've pointed out, more than once, I won't have to see anyone I meet here after I return home. However, I don't think it's good for her to be mad at you with what you're about to go through."

"Sarah, as I've said before—"

"I'm not saying you should tell her about your illness. As much as I don't agree with you, I know I can't change your mind. All I'm saying is there might be more damage done if she's actually mad at you about all of this. I can't help but think Leanne will regret these moments once you're gone and she realizes they were among the last she had with you. That she spent her time arguing with you over a misunderstanding, rather than sharing special moments. I think it would be good if you could try to at least maintain the relationship you do have with her, and Marcus, rather than make it worse."

"Sarah, you don't seem to understand. This *is* our normal relationship. If she weren't mad at me over you or how I let Ollie sleep in past schedule—which I do every time he spends the night by the way and each time she yells at me—then she would be mad at me for something else. I worked too much or I wasn't engaged enough in certain aspects of the business. She's constantly upset with me over the state of my relationship with Marcus. Our normal is saturated with agitation. If I started bending to her every wish, she wouldn't be happy and she'd probably commit me to a mental institution."

She was trying to understand. She really was. Except her mind kept circling back to how she had wished she knew that her time with Nick and Danny would be so short.

If I had known our days were limited I might have said or done things differently. Maybe I would have worked less, gone to the park more, played more, yelled less—

Elijah's voice interrupted her thoughts. "I can tell you're thinking about this too hard. Sure, I could 'play nice' and try to have a different relationship with my children in my final days. But it wouldn't be real. In my opinion, to treat someone differently because I'm dying would be like saying all along our relationship was false, and I didn't care enough to do something about it until right before I died. I've known this moment was coming for thirty years. If I'd thought something needed to be changed in my relationship with my children, don't you think I would've addressed it a long time ago?"

"What about the old adage that it's never too late?"

"Let me try to explain it a different way. What's your relationship like with your father?"

She could feel her eyebrows knit together. "What's that got to do with anything? I love my dad."

"That's not what I asked. I asked about your relationship with him. Since you've been here, you've often mentioned you talked to your mother. What about your father? Do you talk to him on the phone? Does he ever call you or is it always your mother?"

Her mind tried to retrace the calls she had received from her parents. She had never really thought about it before.

When was the last time I talked to my dad on the phone?

Usually it was her mom who called. The only times she talked to her dad was when he answered the phone because her mom wasn't nearby. And those conversations were usually only a few minutes long until her mom got on the line.

"I've never really thought about it before. I guess I usually talk to my mom. I consider my relationship with my dad to be close so how can it be I can't recall having conversations with him outside of when we visit in person? I'm not sure there are very many of those either."

"It's probably never occurred to you because your mother is the link between the two of you. It sounds like she's the active parent in your life and by default you're connected to your father in the same way. It's not because your father doesn't love you or doesn't care. It's just the way it is. Lena was the active parent—she was the one who got them to and from school each day, took them to birthday parties and kissed their scraped knees. She was the one they confided in and went to when they needed a shoulder to cry on. I was the shotgun parent and the disciplinarian. I was there for dinner and family game night and dance recitals, but I wasn't the one they relied on for their everyday needs. Instead, I was the one responsible to take down the threats and barriers in their lives. I was the one who handed out punishments when rules were broken." He paused and ran a hand through his hair.

"When Lena died no one knew how to fill the gap. My children lost their parent who got them through everyday circumstances. They tried to rely on me, but I was lost in my own grief. As I've told you before, by the time I realized there was a problem my children had moved on. I didn't know how to suddenly play a role I had never done before, at least not with grown children. Perhaps if I had tried when they were younger it would have been more natural for all of us, but that's not the way it turned out. So, might Leanne regret some of these moments after I'm gone? Sure. But I can't fix all the missed or botched moments of our lives. There will always be something she will regret. It's just the way it is."

She understood how his words applied to her own life. Her mom was the filter between her and her dad. The difference was she didn't fight with her dad the way Elijah fought with his children. She looked back to Elijah when he started speaking again.

"I'm an only child and I was always close with my father. Growing up my mother always said she felt like a cheerleader, standing on the sidelines watching her two men tackle the world. When he got sick, I took it as a personal mission to figure out what was wrong and fix it. At first the doctors had no answers. Then they predicted he was having early onset dementia, and I worked with my mother on long-term care. We were completely unprepared for the rapid progression of the disease and ultimate death that followed a few months later. After several additional tests and multiple doctors we found out it was CJD, only two weeks before he died. His death deeply affected me. He was my mentor as well as my father. And I *still* had regrets. There were still things I wished I had said or done differently while he was alive." He looked over and locked his gaze with hers.

"The bottom line is no relationship is perfect. There will always be some sort of regret. Some larger than others, but regret nonetheless. I love my children and my hope is that they know it. Beyond that, my plan is to keep things as normal as possible."

"Fine, I understand. Your normal is abnormal. But I won't stop reminding you to be nice to your children." There might always be regrets but she hoped to avoid some of them by removing the misunderstandings.

"I wouldn't expect anything less." He checked his watch. "Last night you agreed it was the right thing to bring Ollie here. Do you still feel that way? You're out of your room so I assume you're doing okay."

"Wow, how sad is it my metric of well being is whether or not I'm cocooned up in my room?" The question was meant more for herself rather than Elijah so she quickly continued before he felt compelled to respond. "Yes, I'm doing fine actually. It was the most difficult weekend I've had in a long time; however, I not only made it through but I feel stronger as a result. It was a risky move you made, but it paid off. I don't understand how you can have so much faith in me all the time." Sarah looked down at her fingers that were twisting her invisible wedding ring.

"I can't understand why you don't." The simplicity of his statement surprised her. "If you don't mind my asking, why don't you wear your wedding ring any more?"

She took a deep breath and slowly let it out. "It got too big when I lost weight, and I was afraid of losing it. I wore it on a chain around my neck for a long time. One day the clasp broke, and my mom suggested it was a sign that it was time I move on. So, I let her put the ring in my jewelry box in my room, which I haven't set foot in since the accident. On some level I think she was trying to use it as bait to get me to go in there. Apparently, the need to stay out of that room has been greater than the need to wear my ring."

He nodded his head in silent understanding. The doorbell rang, signaling the end of their conversation. "That would be Ms. Reynolds. I'll get it since she's here to spend the day torturing me. She's going to love hearing about how I forgot Ollie was here." She saw the pain flash through his eyes at the admission of his newest weakness. "What are you planning for today?"

"I'm not sure exactly, but... I think I'll start by calling my dad." She caught the small smile on his face as he walked away.

It had been three days since Leanne had found Sarah sleeping in Elijah's bed. Those three days had been full of activity but most were uneventful. Sarah had spent her time with Elijah at doctor appointments or shopping for things Lisa said they would need in the weeks to come. Most of the items she understood, such as an electric shaver for when he could no longer shave himself. Other items were not as obvious, such as the baby monitor. When she asked Lisa about it, her response was so simple Sarah had wondered why she never thought of it herself.

"As his CJD symptoms progress, his nights could become very intense. Not only will the insomnia get worse but it's also likely he'll start to have hallucinations. The monitor will allow us to hear what's going on at night so we can react quickly if needed. That is unless you're planning to start sleeping in his room on a regular basis." Sarah knew it had been a mistake to tell her about the incident with Leanne.

In those three days Elijah's symptoms had moved from random to regular. They were still fairly mild, but something happened every day. He forgot something that should have been obvious to him, he dropped things, or he tripped over his own feet. The most disturbing was the change in his personality. He had always been arrogant to the point of annoying, but he was usually respectful about it. Lately he seemed to enjoy pissing people off. The directness he usually delivered with a perfect balance of authority and respect was now thoughtless and almost hurtful.

By Thursday morning, Sarah had almost forgotten about the incident with Leanne. Then her phone rang and one look at the incoming number told her the bomb was about to drop. She closed her eyes and answered the phone.

"Hi, Andy, what's up?" She knew he would want to get right to the point, so there was no use trying to distract him with small talk.

"Is there something you want to tell me?"

She sat back in her desk chair. Dread settled into a knot deep in her stomach.

"Why don't you just tell me what this is about?"

"I just got off the phone with Leanne Troupe. I thought I would give you a chance to explain your side of the story. A chance to explain why our largest customer just told me that effective immediately all Kingston projects are to be pulled from our firm. A chance to explain why, when I asked her the reason for this decision, her response was that if you were a representation for how our project managers conducted business then she didn't want to have anything to do with our firm. Explain it, Sarah. Now." She had to hold the phone away from her ear by the end of his rant.

"I'm sorry, Andy. This is all just a misunderstanding between Elijah and Le—Mrs. Troupe. I never imagined she would do something like this as a result. I'll talk to Elijah."

"Sarah, I want to know what happened. Whatever it is, it impacts me and the rest of the firm, and I think I have a right to know what's going on."

"Nothing is going on. Like I said, it's all a misunderstanding. Apparently, Elijah's relationship with his daughter is strained. This was the state of their relationship well before I got here. They don't effectively communicate with each other, and I think you know well enough how stubborn they both are. Mrs. Troupe showed up at Elijah's house on Monday and misinterpreted a situation. As opposed to explaining it, Elijah elected to tell her it was none of her business and dismissed the conversation. I guess she didn't take it well. I've been living here during the project—"

"You're living there?" She pulled the phone away from her ear.

"Yes, but you have to believe me, Andy. Nothing inappropriate is going on—it's simply an overreaction to a misunderstanding. I'll have Elijah fix this."

There was a heavy pause on the other end of the line. "I'll give you the benefit of the doubt for now. But if you can't fix this, then I expect you on the next flight home."

"Andy, I can't abandon—"

"Sarah, it's not up for discussion! Losing the Kingston business would be a significant hit to our firm, but we'll survive. However, if this can't be fixed I don't want you there living in his house. I won't allow you to be subjected to that kind of personal censure, and if he won't stand up to his own daughter then you're not staying."

"I can't leave. Not before the project is complete."

"What part of 'this is not up for discussion' do you not understand? Fix it to my satisfaction or you're coming home! I'll come out there and get you myself if I have to."

She took a breath to calm down and select her words carefully.

"I appreciate your concern for my personal reputation. However, I knew the risks when I signed on. For reasons I won't go into right now, I'm committed to this project until completion no matter the personal costs. I will make it clear to Elijah that the impact Mrs. Troupe is trying to place on the firm is not a part of the package. He *will* fix this so my decision to stay is irrelevant."

Andy was silent, but she could hear his uneven breath fade in and out. She could picture him pacing back and forth in his office.

"Maggie tells me she thinks you're making significant progress. That's the only reason I'm going to give you another chance on this, Sarah. I'm going to trust you, but I want to be clear—I *don't* trust Kingston. If this ends badly for you... if I find out he's taking advantage of you when you're in a vulnerable state, then I don't want his business. Promise me you'll consider the situation objectively and make sure Kingston is being open with you on everything."

His concern touched her. He was a good friend and she knew he was trying to protect her. He felt it was his responsibility now that Nick was gone. But it was time for her to take over the responsibility for herself.

"I'm confident Elijah has been very open about everything in regard to this project. But, I will evaluate everything again if it will make you feel better about the situation."

"Yes, it would. Thank you." He hung up the phone without another word.

"Sarah. What's up?" Elijah glanced at Sarah before turning his attention back to the papers on his desk.

"Do you have a few minutes? We have a situation that needs your attention."

He looked up, but only for a brief moment. "Sure, come in."

"Elijah, this is serious. Have you talked to Leanne since the incident on Monday?"

He finally focused on her. "No. What's happened?"

"I got a call from Andy. Apparently, Leanne called to tell him that effective immediately all Kingston projects are being pulled from Jacobs Management."

She could see his jaw tense. "What was her reason?"

"She told Andy it was due to what she observed of my behavior and if that was an accurate representation of the firm then she didn't want Jacobs managing Kingston projects."

He closed his eyes and placed his palms flat on his desk. When he opened his eyes, she could see the anger he was fighting hard to contain. "What did you tell him?"

"I told him she was overreacting to a misunderstanding surrounded by my living here, but I didn't tell him any of the specifics. I also told him you would fix this."

"Damn it!" He ran his hand over his face. "Yes, I'll fix this." He punched the speaker button on his phone and started to dial a number. She quickly reached over and hung up the phone, causing him to look at her in confusion.

"Before you call we need to get something straight. You will fix this, Elijah. I don't care what comes down on me as a result of Leanne's misunderstanding and everything surrounding this project, but it is not acceptable for Andy and the firm to suffer anything. I need to know you will do whatever it takes to fix this. Even if it means telling Leanne everything."

He locked eyes with her for several seconds before hitting the speaker button again. "Yes, of course. But it won't come to that."

"Kingston Enterprises, Leanne Troupe's office."

"Marjorie, I need to speak with Leanne—"

"Mr. Kingston, I'm sorry but she's—"

"Now, Marjorie. I don't care what she's doing."

"Yes sir, hold one moment please." Soft music drifted through the line. It wasn't long before she was back on the line. "Mr. Kingston, I'll put you through now."

"Dad. I'm in the middle of an important meeting. Whatever the issue is I'm sure it can wait." Leanne's tone could only be described as condescending.

"Cut the shit, Leanne. You know why I'm calling. What the hell were you thinking pulling all the Kingston projects from Jacobs?"

"I think it's pretty clear. I have issues working with any firm that allows their employees to become intimately involved with clients. Since he refused to fire Mrs. Mitchell, my only other choice was to pull the projects. It's important our clients are represented by a respectable firm. There are other qualified companies in the area that would be able to manage our projects just as effectively and with more integrity."

Elijah hit the mute button. "Did Andy mention the other alternative was to fire you?" Sarah stared at the phone and shook her head. He clicked off the mute button. "Leanne, first of all I told you I don't have an intimate relationship with Sarah. Second, she's not even working on a company project so even if there was a relationship between us it has no reflection whatsoever on Kingston Enterprises. Finally, you know damn well Jacobs is the best firm in the area. They've managed our projects for several years with no incidents. Your actions are completely unfounded."

"Boardwick Management out of Illinois could certainly manage the projects in that region. We've looked into them before and—"

"And you discovered they were a distant second to Jacobs. You know firsthand the shortcomings Boardwick brings to the table and why Jacobs is the clear choice. Their employees have impeccable reputations and histories with their clients. Including Sarah." Sarah sent up a silent thank you to God for giving Elijah the capacity to remember all the facts that were helping him win the argument. This would not be a good time for his memory to fail.

"I can't believe this. She sure has you wrapped around her finger doesn't she? You don't lead Kingston Enterprises any more, I do. This is my call."

"Damn it, Leanne, don't be so obtuse! Yes, you lead the company now, but I certainly did not put you in that position for you to run the company into the ground by making snap decisions based on your emotions rather than sound business requirements. And you know I still have a primary say in how it *is* run. I will not stand by and watch you run our family business into the ground by making emotionally based decisions. Your emotions are what almost kept you from this role. Are you trying to prove I was wrong and shouldn't have stood my ground, insisting you were the right person for the job? Are you really willing to jeopardize your position over your personal objections of me and how I live my life?"

"You would seriously have me replaced over this? You would pick your latest fling over your daughter?"

"Yes, I would. And not because I'm picking Sarah over you but because if you can't see your error in this then you're not the right person for the job! Stop acting like a girl, and start acting like an executive. Call Mr. Jacobs back, *personally*, apologize for the misunderstanding, and reinstate the relationship. Do I make myself clear?"

"Perfectly."

"I will follow-up with Mr. Jacobs and if you don't fix this to my satisfaction I'll call an emergency board meeting by the end of the day to start the process for your replacement." There was a silent pause for a few seconds before the phone line went dead. Elijah hung up on his end and ran his hand through his hair. He got up and walked over to the windows where he stood for several minutes, quietly staring out over the mountains with his arms crossed over his chest. Finally, he turned back to face Sarah. "I'm sorry about all of this. I'll call Andy myself in a few minutes to make sure Leanne called him. There shouldn't be any more issues going forward."

She nodded and looked down at her hands. "Those things you said to Leanne, about being a girl and all..."

He let out a deep sigh. "I said those things to get Leanne to react. The thing she hates most is for people to think she can't do something because she's female. Leanne knew there were several board members with concerns about her ability to take my place. They were very vocal in saying they thought she, or any other woman, would ruin the company by allowing emotions and hormones to take control. I don't share the same beliefs, but I know it's Leanne's kill button."

"Kill button?"

He shrugged his shoulders. "My version of an Achilles' Heel. I have a strong ability to recognize weakness in people, or in a business, and I know when I need to exploit them." She was quickly reminded that he was still the Mighty Mr. Kingston. "What?"

She looked up to him in confusion and remembered he could read her with ease. He knew she had something on her mind. "I was just wondering what my kill button was and what might force you to use it."

He quickly looked away and walked back toward his desk. "Let's hope we never have to find out. Do you mind if I speak with Andy alone?"

She scrutinized his reaction. He appeared to be holding something back but she tucked the knowledge away. It wasn't the time to address his exploitations of her weaknesses. The most important thing was the situation with Andy.

"No, I don't mind." She turned toward the door but stopped before leaving. "Thank you, Elijah."

It was a Saturday afternoon, and Sarah was feeling claustrophobic. Elijah's house was starting to feel like a fortress, and she needed to escape. Lisa had planned to spend the day at the house with Elijah so Sarah drove to Boulder. It was another unseasonably warm day and she was outside a coffee shop in the downtown area, watching the people around her. It was a wonderful atmosphere with lots of activity. She thought she could spend all day exploring the shops and watching the random events unfold around her. She snapped a photo and sent it off to Maggie with a quick text letting her know she wished she could be there with her. Her phone rang just as she was finishing up her coffee. She smiled and looked at her phone, expecting to see Maggie's name and number on the display. Instead she saw a number she didn't recognize.

"Hello, this is Sarah."

"Sarah, hi. Um, this is Travis Dixon. You know, the guy renting your house? I hope you don't mind, I got your number from Andy... Am I catching you at a bad time?"

"Um, no, it's fine. Is everything okay?"

There was an awkward pause. "Oh, yeah, everything's fine. I just had a question Andy wasn't able to answer, so I thought I'd call instead of emailing this time."

Sarah waited for him to ask his question. When he didn't, she felt compelled to fill in the conversation gap. "Sure, no problem. What's your question?"

"Right. Well, my children are spending a few days here this week. I understand all the upstairs bedrooms are private, so I was wondering if you had an air mattress I could use. I didn't want to go nosing around in your closets and Andy wasn't sure if you had one. My kids are ten and eight, a girl and a boy so they won't want to share a room. Katie, my little girl, she could probably sleep on the couch but I thought it might be more comfortable for her if there was a mattress for her to use." Even though Sarah had never talked to him before, it was clear he was rambling out of nerves.

"Yes, I do have one. It's in the basement storage area on one of the shelves. There are sheets for it in the bag as well. It hasn't been used in a long time, but it should be in good shape."

"Excellent, thank you. That will be a big help." He breathed out a sigh that seemed to relax him. "So, you said in your emails you plan on staying out there over the holidays. Hopefully, Kingston gives you some time off to enjoy yourself. Although, the holidays can be lonely without family around, so working might be a better option." There was a note in his voice that forced Sarah to wonder if he was talking of her circumstances or his own.

"I should be able to have some time off. But you're right. The holidays can be lonely without family. And, contrary to popular belief, Mr. Kingston is not so bad. I actually have today off and am enjoying a day of normal tourist activities in downtown Boulder."

"Ah, I love that area! Is there a guy on stilts there?"

"Yes! I think I cringed about as much as I gasped in awe at what he was doing." They spent a few more minutes talking about the downtown area and he gave her some recommendations for shops and restaurants. Their conversation was flowing much more naturally and Sarah found that she was enjoying talking to him.

"Okay, so I have to ask, what did you do to put Andy in such a state of panic this week?"

Her mood turned instantly to caution. "What do you mean?"

"Well, I had a meeting with Andy earlier this week and in the middle of it he got interrupted with an urgent call. When the call ended, he told me we would have to continue our meeting later. On my way out of the office he yelled for your number. He was up in his office all day after that, but the next day he seemed fine again." There was a hint of humor behind his recollection of the events.

"So why would you assume it was something I did just because he asked for my number? Maybe it was Mr. Kingston, *or* maybe it was something else entirely and he simply needed to talk to me to get some information."

Travis laughed. "You're right, that wasn't fair of me to assume. It's just you're his favorite employee, as well as his friend, and the way he demanded your number was a clear indication of his frustration with you. You forget I have known Andy a long time. I've been on the receiving end of that tone many times."

"Yeah, alright. I'll give you that. Yes, he was upset with me but it was a misunderstanding. Sorry, you'll get no more details—it's between me and Andy. But it's been resolved and hopefully I will soon be back in the position of favorite employee."

"That's good. Speaking of things between you and Andy, I wanted to grill some steaks the other day. What happened to the grill? I asked Andy about it but he only laughed and said it was your story to tell."

She shivered at the memory of the grill incident. "Sorry, that's another one that will remain in the vault."

"I'll get it out of you someday." He laughed and they slipped back to another awkward pause. "Well, I should go. I promised the kids I'd take them to the movies. It's been nice talking to you. Thanks again for the use of the mattress."

"Sure, no problem. Enjoy the movies." After they said good-bye she stared at the phone. The conversation had been enjoyable and made her feel normal. However, after she hung up she was reminded of how much she missed having similar conversations with Nick. She felt an odd mixture of happiness and sadness at the same time. The feelings were all mixed up and neither overpowered the other. She was starting to recognize this feeling more and more these days. This odd concoction of opposing feelings she didn't yet have a name for.

Endurance.

She reflected on the term her subconscious brought forward.

Yes, endurance—finding happiness while enduring a certain amount of sadness. That's what will allow me to live a full life again while keeping Nick and Danny with me in a healthy way.

CHAPTER 13

"Happy turkey-day!" Miles leaned in and gave Sarah a peck on the cheek as he hurried past. "I'm going to run these bags upstairs." She turned back to the door in time to relieve Tina of a bag as she entered.

"Thank you. Miles won't tell me what they're planning to make for dinner, but based on all this crap he brought I'm not sure if I'm intrigued or scared." Tina talked as she walked to the kitchen where they dropped the bags on the counter. She then turned to Sarah and gave her a hug before pushing her out to arm's length. "You look good. I know we've talked since Oliver was here so I knew you survived the weekend, but when I left you were spilling your guts to the toilet."

Sarah smiled and patted Tina's hand. "Thank you. I feel good."

"Alright you two, out of the kitchen. We men have some serious cooking to do." Miles walked into the kitchen, rubbing his palms together. Elijah followed behind with a grin on his face.

"Don't forget, you guys have to clean up too. Although, I suppose packing boxes isn't exactly the spa." Tina looked at Elijah. "You ready for us to start working on the office?"

"Yeah, sure. Don't worry about the desk or filing cabinets. Miles and I will go through those later." He paused and looked from Tina to Sarah. "You know, you don't have to do this right now. You can go relax while watching a chick flick or something. By the time I have to move in there I don't think I will care if I have to sleep with a few dusty old books."

Tina narrowed her eyes at Elijah. "Tempting, but no thank you.

Even if you won't be in your right mind most of the time to enjoy your surroundings, we want to make it feel like an inviting space for you. Besides, we have orders from Ms. Reynolds and I certainly don't want to disobey. Shall we?" Tina held out her arm and Sarah took it with mock flourish.

Once in the office, Tina focused on the books while Sarah went through the closet. They talked casually while they worked and the morning passed quickly. By the time Miles arrived to announce lunch was ready, they had finished packing up the items assigned to them. *Smells like Italian.*

Sarah and Tina took their seats in the dining room and waited for the men to join them. Elijah and Miles entered carrying two plates each. The plates were topped with stainless steel plate covers so the food wasn't visible. Tina leaned over and whispered loudly in Sarah's ear.

"When Miles found these plate covers the other day, he got so excited and insisted we bring them today. I'd forgotten I even had them. In fact, I'm not sure they've ever been used before."

Miles set one of his plates down in front of Tina and winked at her before taking his seat. Elijah did the same for Sarah, including the wink. Sarah looked around the table, unsure of what to do next. Her own family just put all the food on a side table and everyone was eating before butts touched seats. Each of the faces around her had taken on a somber look as they stared down at their covered plates. It suddenly occurred to her it was the last Thanksgiving these friends would share. The reminder caused her heart to leap and she wished there was something she could do to make the day easier for them all. Finally, Elijah looked up and broke the silence by clearing his throat.

"Well, I believe it's my year to lead the round of thanks." He cleared his throat again and took a sip of his wine. "I..." His voice fell away and he cleared his throat again. He closed his eyes and gave his head a sharp shake. "I've known moments like this were coming for a long time, so I'm not sure why I'm so choked up." He took in a deep breath, held it and then let it out slowly. He opened his eyes, which were moist with the threat of tears, and continued. "Okay, so I need to keep this light. I can't function through sentimental today so I pick Thanks of Light. Sarah, for your benefit, that means we'll give thanks on things that are absurd, yet they bring us happiness anyway. We'll each give three. So, my first Thanks of Light is for my sturdy dance shoes. I never knew how protective they were until I started dancing with Sarah."

"Hey! I've not stepped on your toes for... a couple days now." Everyone laughed and it was clear from the look on Elijah's face he was happy to have the tension removed.

"My second Thanks of Light is for my sonic toothbrush. It's so damn efficient and effective. My third Thanks of Light is for modern technology. I love being able to get what I want, when I want it." Sarah watched as everyone picked up their wine glass and raised them in a toast. Miles set his glass down and clapped his hands together.

"Okay, my first Thanks of Light is for my sports app on my phone. I love being able to check scores during boring meetings while my clients think I'm looking up important information."

"Miles! You're so bad." Tina laughed, showing she found more humor than shock in her husband's admission.

"My second Thanks of Light is for my long working hours. It means I drive in and out of the city before and after most of the heavy traffic."

"You're lucky your reason for loving your long hours is because of its impact on your commute rather than its impact on your marriage." Tina tossed her napkin at him, which he caught and tossed right back at her.

"My third Thanks of Light is for these amazing plate covers. I mean seriously, how cool are these? They're fitting for the elaborate meal Elijah and I worked so hard on all morning." Elijah coughed into his napkin. Miles shot him a sideways glance as they raised their glasses in toast. Tina sat forward in her chair, ready for her turn.

"My first Thanks of Light is for my digital e-reader. It allows me to read steamy romance novels without anyone knowing."

"Really? Hum, I guess I should stop complaining about you reading in bed..." Miles wiggled his eyebrows at her.

"Yes, you should... My second Thanks of Light is for my candles that don't actually have a flame. They smell like real candles, yet I don't have to worry about Scat burning off his tail." She looked over at Sarah. "Scat is my cat."

Sarah laughed at the absurdity of the cat's name. "How does the poor thing know if you're calling him or telling him to get away?"

Tina shrugged her shoulders. "Maybe that's why he hisses at me all the time. Okay, my third Thanks of Light is for my new hydration pack that arrived this week. I can't wait to go for a ride and put it to good use!" They toasted Tina and then it was Sarah's turn.

"Okay, wow. I'm not prepared for this." It had been such a long time since she had felt thankful for anything at all—even the small absurd stuff.

"The point is to *not* think about it, although I know that alone will be a challenge for you. Just say 'My first Thanks of Light is for' and then say the first thing that pops into your mind."

"Okay, okay. My first Thanks of Light is for... Elijah's coffee maker. It's so damn fast and I really don't function until I have my coffee. Um, let's see... my second Thanks of Light is for... my cozy socks. They make my feet warm and happy."

"If only they didn't look so hideous." Elijah cringed and shuddered.

"What are you talking about, they're not hideous!"

"When you wear them, it looks like your feet have been stuffed into Persian cats that have been dipped in rainbow water. They *are* hideous."

"Well, hideous or not, I love them. Okay, my third Thanks of Light is for chocolate. I've recently rediscovered how much magic it can produce." Everyone raised their glasses in toast to Sarah.

"Okay, now, on the count of three everyone lift your covers. Remember, Elijah and I worked very hard on this meal. Even though he's a great cook, this is something neither of us has attempted—"

"Oh, let's just get on with it counselor." Miles nudged Elijah at his interruption but didn't stop him from stealing the spotlight. "One, two... three." They all lifted their covers in what could have been practiced synchronization. Sarah laughed at what lay beneath.

"Salad? You two worked all day to make us a salad?" Tina was looking back and forth from Miles to Elijah. "I know for a fact you have made a salad before so what's different about this one? The way you chopped the tomatoes?"

The fake look of wounded pride on both the men's faces was priceless and caused Sarah to laugh harder. Miles placed his hand over his heart. "I'm hurt you can't see how special this salad is and how much effort we put into it."

"There had better be something else in that kitchen. I can smell something that would appear to be more substantial than this rabbit food so I'm going to assume you're just trying to goad me." In the short time Sarah had known Tina she knew her eating habits were a stark contradiction to the way she looked. She looked as though she didn't eat anything that wasn't picked straight from a garden. The reality was almost the exact opposite.

"Alright, alright. In an effort to keep the peace, yes, there's more in the kitchen." Elijah looked at Miles. "Get the reaction you were looking for?"

Miles' face changed instantly from his mock hurt into a huge smile. "Yep, it was perfect." He looked over to his wife and blew her a kiss. "Love ya, babe."

"Yeah, yeah. Just remember that in payback I'm a bitch." They fell into animated conversation as they ate their salad. When they finished, Elijah and Miles quickly cleared the plates and disappeared into the kitchen. Elijah came back with a bottle of wine and refilled all the glasses, except for Sarah's. Instead he produced a bottle of water and placed it in front of her. Sarah tilted her head and looked at him through narrowed eyes.

"I may be forgetting a lot these days but I do remember your limit is one glass. I think my days of carrying you are over."

"Miles is here. Apparently, he's very capable of carrying my sorry ass upstairs." Sarah smiled sweetly at him. He considered her rebuttal for a moment before refilling her glass.

"Fine, since it's a holiday. But just one more." He disappeared back into the kitchen. Miles and Elijah returned to the dining room with their covered plates.

There was no opening argument this time in Miles' presentation of the food. "One... two... three!" They lifted their covers and Sarah's mouth dropped open.

"You made Chicago style deep dish pizza?" She looked up to Elijah.

"Now *this* is what I'm talkin' about!" Tina was clearly more pleased with the meal's second round than she had been with the first.

Elijah shrugged and Sarah noticed a blush creep up his neck. "Yeah, well, you said it was your favorite. Since this meal is the result of a bet you won, I figured it would be nice to make you something you really liked."

She cut off a sizeable piece and popped it into her mouth. "Oh, my God. This is wonderful. Are you sure you've never made this before?" She took another bite and closed her eyes, savoring the flavors.

"You boys have really outdone yourselves this time. Man, this is good." Tina was talking around the bite of pizza she had in her mouth. Miles and Elijah exchanged satisfied glances with each other.

As Sarah continued to savor each bite she was transported back in time. The smell and taste reminded her so much of the restaurant she enjoyed while growing up. "I would swear this tastes exactly like the pizza from my favorite restaurant when I was a kid. I can't believe you've never made this before—" She noticed the change in demeanor in both men sitting across from her. "Wait, you actually made this didn't you?"

Elijah pushed some food around on his plate and squirmed in his seat. "We made *a* pizza." His response was just above a mumble.

Sarah stifled a laugh. "But did you make *this* pizza?"

Now Miles was squirming as much as Elijah. He leaned over and whispered something in Elijah's ear. Elijah's only response was a shrug of his shoulders. Miles sat back in his seat and crossed his arms over his chest.

"Well, we tried to make *this* pizza the day you two went shopping. Leanne had actually left long before we told you she did. It didn't work out so well. It's why we asked you to bring pizza home that night so you wouldn't wonder why the house smelled like pizza. We wanted this to be a surprise after all."

"So, who made this pizza?" Tina was now drawn into the same curiosity as Sarah.

"Um... well... that little place in Chicago you love." Sarah was so shocked by the response she almost dropped her fork.

Tina was just as confused. "I find it hard to believe they would deliver a pizza across three states."

Miles scratched the side of his head. "Turns out they do, but, we didn't have a name. So, you remember that all-day meeting I had on Monday? Really I flew to Chicago and back with frozen pizzas..."

"You flew all the way to Chicago, and back in the same day, just to get pizza? And then you pretended to be in the kitchen all morning making it?" Sarah was about to burst with amusement.

"Yeah, that about sums it up..." Elijah rubbed the back of his neck.

"So what the hell did you two do in the kitchen all morning?" Sarah could tell Tina was also trying to hold it together.

"Made a salad?" Miles at least had the decency to sound guilty.

Sarah couldn't take it any longer. The laughter started as quiet giggles. When her mind presented her with an image of Miles trying to send pizza boxes through the security scanner at the airport, the gentle giggles exploded into hysterical laughter. She laughed so hard her sides hurt and tears leaked from her eyes. She accidentally snorted and it caused her and everyone else to laugh even harder. Tina reached out for her when she snorted again.

"Oh God, I have to pee!" Tina shot out of her chair and ran for the bathroom.

Sarah laid her head and arms on the table, trying to regain her composure. As her laughter settled, she realized it was the first time she had truly laughed since the accident. It made her feel so alive, so happy. The enormity of the emotions she was feeling caused her laughter to rapidly transform into sobs. Face in hands, she quickly slid from her seat and left the dining room in the direction of the bathroom. She stopped in the hall, remembering Tina was occupying the room she was in need of, and sank down along the wall. She was still crouched on the floor when Tina emerged from the bathroom.

"Oh, Sarah, you startled me. I can't remember the last time I laughed so hard. Those men—" Sarah heard her walk rapidly in her direction. "Sarah, what's wrong? You're crying... Why the dramatic change?"

"I... I... d-don't... kn-know." The words could only escape between sobs.

"Come on. Come with me before the men realize you've had a breakdown. We don't want them to think it was their crazy antics that brought this on. They worked so hard to deceive us after all." Tina helped Sarah to the bathroom and sat her down on the toilet.

"When will this stop happening?"

"The crying? I wish I knew. What happened?"

"I'm really not sure. I think all the emotions suddenly became too much for me. It felt *so good* to laugh again. I haven't laughed like that since before the accident, and I think the realization just... I don't know." Sarah grabbed some toilet paper and wiped her nose.

"I get it. Sometimes strong emotions, even the good ones, can be too much for us."

Sarah offered Tina a weak smile. "Thanks. I'll be all right. You can head back if you want. We don't want the guys to think we abandoned them."

Tina left and closed the door behind her. Sarah stood up and splashed some cold water on her face. Tina was right, what she was feeling was the enormity of her emotions. The knowledge made her feel better, like she was still on the right track. She took a final deep breath and went back out to the dining room.

It was Sunday afternoon and Sarah was sitting on her bed, looking at the box. It was beautifully wrapped in silver paper with a pink bow. There was a card on top with Sarah's name written in Nick's neat handwriting. She slowly ran her finger across her name.

The night before, they had gone to the ballet, crossing another thing off Elijah's bucket list. When they returned she'd pulled out her own list, having made a deal with herself that if Elijah crossed something off his list she would do the same. She scanned through the list, the clear choice standing out from the rest.

Open the box

She knew it was time. On impulse she walked out of the room to find Elijah. She quietly sat down next to him with the box in her lap. He looked up from his paper and put it aside. He was somehow able to gauge the seriousness of her mood and he sat there, waiting for her to explain what she needed. It was a few minutes before she found the strength to speak.

"So, this box was found in the trunk of Nick's car after the accident. I've never been able to open it. I'm not sure if you know this... well... you might know this... but anyway, the accident happened three days before my birthday. I know this was to be my birthday present that year." By the end her voice was hardly above a whisper. There was more she should say about the box and its significance for her, but she couldn't bring herself to say the words. Instead she cleared her throat. "I think it's time I open it. I didn't want to do it alone... if you don't mind."

"Of course."

She looked at the box and noticed she was gripping it so tightly her knuckles were white. She released her hold and flexed her fingers. She wasn't sure how long she sat there, staring at the box. A clock chimed somewhere in the house and brought her back to the present. She looked over at Elijah who was still watching her.

"Maybe we should go practice first?" She started to stand.

He shook his head and she slowly settled back into her seat. "I don't feel like it. Besides, you already know the dance perfectly."

"What are we going to do the day of the gala if you don't feel good? Or if something else is wrong? Why can't we talk about a contingency plan?"

"Sarah. All the distractions in the world won't take that box away from your lap. You said it's time, so open it." The look he gave her was compassionate, yet at the same time stern.

I need to learn how to master that look. It really is effective.

She took in a deep breath, held it and then let it out slowly. She pulled a folded piece of paper from the envelope with shaking hands. Nick never did like giving cards purchased from the store. He always jotted a note down on a piece of paper. It was simple, yet so much more thoughtful and beautiful than any professionally written greeting card. She closed her eyes and unfolded the paper. When she opened her eyes, the first thing she saw was a tear drop hit the paper and the resulting water mark, slowly expanding. Ironically, her tear hit the paper right on the word 'love' in his closing. She stared at it for a few seconds and then allowed her eyes to travel to the top of the paper.

Sarah (Mommy),

Although you claim to have stopped having birthdays 4 years ago, we still like to give you gifts. Personally, I find I love you more each year so I'm happy for another birthday to arrive. It means I get to look forward to loving you even more in the upcoming year! Our Little Man Dan can't yet express the full extent of his feelings but I know he feels the same. We hope you enjoy your gift, and that it will always help you love the world around you as much as we love you. Happy birthday, sweetheart.

Love always and forever,
Nick (and Danny)

More tears dropped to the paper. She clutched it to her chest and let herself cry. Reading Nick's words brought forth his voice in her head. She missed his voice so much. Her mind focused on one specific part of his message.

...that it will always help you love the world around you.

Somehow, before his death, he was able to give her the words she needed to hear.

That's what he wants from me. It's right there in his handwriting. He wants me to love life.

When she was able, she pulled at the wrapping paper, exposing a plain box giving her no indication of what was inside. That was another thing Nick liked to do. He would always remove everything from its original packaging, placing it in a plain box so the surprise could last as long as possible. She lifted the lid and unfolded the tissue paper, heart hammering loudly in her chest. She let out a gasp as her hands lifted a digital SLR camera. It was the one she had been researching when she'd looked into taking a photography class. Her vision blurred from tears, and she blinked rapidly trying to dispel them. She flipped the switch to turn it on, hoping the battery was still functional, and it instantly came to life. On impulse she pushed the button that would display the captured images.

When an image of Danny appeared on the screen she almost dropped the camera in surprise. Her eyes looked over every detail. It was a close up shot of his face and his blue eyes were sparkling with the glint of sunlight. The next image was of Danny again, but farther away. She let out a choked sob when the following image showed Nick and Danny together in a field. She could tell they were at the park near their house. She scrolled through image after image, pausing on each long enough to memorize every detail. The first image came back up and she went through them again. She heard a sound and looked up, startled, forgetting Elijah was in the room.

"It's a camera."

He smiled at her. "You've commented a few times you wished you had one. It appears you had one all along."

She looked back at the camera in her hands. "Yes, I suppose so. But the real gift is what's on it. There are over twenty pictures on here I didn't even know existed. It's like having new memories... I didn't think that was possible. To be able to experience something new about Nick and Danny... I don't even have the words."

"Are you glad you opened it?"

"Yes." Her voice was quiet. "A part of me wishes I would have opened it sooner, but I'm not sure I would have been able to appreciate it for its full value before now. You've gotten me to this point."

He smiled and looked down at his hands. "Not really, but I appreciate the gesture. I simply forced you to do it yourself." When he looked back up she could see he was tired. "If you're all right, I think I'll go up and lay down."

"Yeah, sure. I'm good. Go rest and I'll wake you for dinner." She was starting to worry about him. She knew it was getting difficult for him to ignore his illness. He didn't seem to have the same 'fight it till the end' attitude as when she'd first arrived.

She looked through the pictures one more time before placing everything back in the box. She picked up her phone and clicked on Maggie's number. There was an answer on the third ring.

"Hi, Maggie, is this a good time to talk?" Although it was quiet in the background she felt compelled to ask. Quiet in Maggie's life wasn't always a good thing.

"Perfect actually. Andy's getting the kids ready for bed. I needed the break." She could hear Maggie moving through the house. "So what's up? How was your Thanksgiving? Did you get any sort of break or did the tyrant work you all weekend?"

"Tyrant? Really, Maggie, he's not all bad. It was fine and yes, I got a break. How about you? It sounds like you're still recovering from having a house full of people." Maggie and Andy always hosted their family's Thanksgiving dinner which involved nothing short of three families of five spending the weekend at their house. Maggie spent the next twenty minutes ranting about her family and the antics of the weekend. Sarah played her typical supporting role, interjecting the appropriate words of encouragement in the brief moments Maggie took a breath.

"I'm sorry, I'm sure you didn't call to hear me complain."

"Nothing to be sorry about. You know I enjoy hearing about your crazy family. However, there is something I wanted to tell you. I opened the box today." She knew she wouldn't have to elaborate on what box she was talking about.

"Oh, Sarah! What prompted you to open it?"

"I figured it was time. I've been trying to let go of things I think are keeping me from fully overcoming my grief."

"And? Are you okay?"

"I am actually. Maggie, did you know what was in the box?" The long pause on the other end of the line gave her the answer. "It's okay. I just wondered who took the pictures."

"Yeah, it was me. I was never sure if I was doing the right thing by not telling you what was in the box. I knew having the pictures would mean so much to you but I didn't want to push you into something you weren't ready for."

"Thank you." For the next hour, Maggie told Sarah about that day in the park with Nick and Danny. Sarah cried through it all, but the tears were mixed with laughter as she imagined the events Maggie described. She welcomed this feeling, the feeling she now recognized as endurance, because it reinforced her confidence that she would again find happiness in her life.

CHAPTER 14

Relaxed from the spa where Tina had paid for a full make-over, Sarah climbed the stone steps. They were somewhere outside of Denver, on a private estate where the gala was held each year. When the estate came into view out her car window, her first thought was it was a castle that had somehow been teleported from eighteenth century England.

"Mrs. Mitchell, I presume?" She was met by a pretty young blonde. "Yes."

"Welcome. I'm Miss Hawthorne. Mrs. Morgan mentioned you would be arriving at this time. Your bags arrived earlier and I've already had them placed in your room. Will you follow me please?" She led Sarah up the grand staircase at the back of the entryway. "The guest rooms are located on the third floor and you will be in room two, right next to Mr. Kingston as instructed."

"Will many of the guests be staying overnight?"

"No, we only have a limited number of rooms. Besides you and Mr. Kingston, the other guests staying are the other Mr. Kingston, Mr. and Mrs. Troupe and Mr. and Mrs. Morgan." The large room was decorated in soft tones of yellow and the furnishings fit the eighteenth century feel of the estate. "Your bags have been placed in the armoire and I've had your gown steamed." She walked across the room and placed her hand on a closed door, a sly smile playing at the corners of her mouth. "This door leads to Mr. Kingston's room. I have been instructed to leave it unlocked. Here's the key to your room. As you know the gala begins at six, but it's my understanding Mr. Kingston would like you to meet him in the grand ballroom at five. There's a map of the estate on the desk. Can I get you anything before I leave?"

"No, thank you."

"Very well. Enjoy your evening, Mrs. Mitchell." Sarah had just enough time to review the gala agenda and estate map before she had to get ready to meet with Elijah. A silent auction was being held on the second level, and between dinner courses there would be short dance performances. The auction winners would be announced after dinner, and then Leanne would give a speech before her dance with Elijah. Reading through the itinerary caused her heart palpitations to return, so she switched her attention to getting dressed.

She looked in the mirror and couldn't believe the transformation. She was certain she'd never looked more elegant in her life. Maybe at her wedding, but she didn't want to think about that. She had gained weight, and her make-up hid what remained of the dark circles under her eyes. The lack of dark circles, combined with the way her eye make-up was done, brought out the green in her eyes making them look bright and alive. Her hair was swept into a side ponytail with a small twist at the base, leaving her soft curls to hang over her right shoulder. She had resisted the style at first, feeling she would have been more comfortable if her hair had fallen down her back and covered up her exposed skin. But the stylist had been insistent, and after seeing the final product she was happy she had relented. Taking a deep breath, she left the room in search of Elijah.

Elijah walked across the dance floor and stopped, staring at Sarah. Suddenly feeling exposed, she ran her left hand down her opposite arm. She watched as he held out his hand in a silent invitation for her to join him.

"Sarah... you look breathtaking." She felt like she had regressed back to when she first arrived, blushing at every compliment. She decided to battle it with humor.

"Thank you. Apparently I'm very good at spending your money." He closed the gap between them and placed his hands on her arms.

"Yes, I would say you are. You might have a hard time keeping me from giving you more money if this is the end result." He gave her a playful smile.

"You look very handsome." She reached out and adjusted his tie. "I like your tie. The color reminds me of my room at your house."

"You noticed. This was Lena's favorite color." He paused in reflection and put his hands in his pockets, looking down at his feet. "Anyway, I was thinking we should practice the dance. A dress rehearsal so to speak. Get the bugs worked out before anyone is watching." He held out his hand to her. "What do you say, will you dance with me?"

She thought it was a great idea to practice one more time, in her gown and shoes, before anyone would be watching. She placed her hand in his, silently accepting his request.

He walked her to the center of the dance floor, and they took their position. Just as she was about to ask what they would do for music the first chords of the song drifted softly through the room. She looked around in surprise and found a group of musicians off to the side of the room.

Elijah tugged her hand softly, bringing her attention back to him. For the first few steps she felt the need to look down, not used to the feel of her gown flowing while they moved. She quickly became comfortable, and they waltzed their way around the dance floor. Halfway through the dance Elijah closed his eyes and pulled her closer to him.

The dance ended, and the music faded, but Elijah didn't let go. She waited, unsure of what to do next. He opened his eyes, and she could see a faint hint of moisture threatening to turn into tears. He cleared his throat and turned to signal for the music to start again. This time he held her close from the start, close enough their cheeks were almost touching. She couldn't see his face, but she could feel his struggle with his emotions in the way he held her and guided her across the floor. He pulled her into a hug when their second dance ended.

"Thank you." His whispered voice tickled her ear, and her movements froze when he placed a soft kiss on her temple. She felt him wipe at his eyes before he pulled away. She searched his face and found only sadness.

"Elijah, are you okay?" She touched his cheek with her hand.

He grabbed her hand, planted a kiss on the inside of her wrist, and tucked it into his elbow. "Yes, I'm fine. I promise." He guided her through the tables to the door that led to the reception area. "You did wonderful by the way. You have no reason to be nervous later this evening."

"Thank you, but I fear the number of left feet I possess will grow exponentially with the number of eyes watching me. I'm bound to stumble, so you'll have to keep me standing upright." He glanced away from her quickly and rubbed at the back of his neck. She stopped walking, causing him to stop with her. "Are you sure you're okay?"

"I'm fine, really. It's been a long day, that's all."

She searched his face, looking for the truth. "Okay. I'm just worried about you. I'm not really sure how I'm supposed to help you tonight. I'm not even sure I'll be able to remain by your side the entire evening. What if something happens—"

"Sarah, please, relax. Everything will be fine."

"You know me better than that. You know I take my job seriously. I'm supposed to protect your secret and help you through events like this—"

"Sarah! It's not your—" He didn't yell, but his voice contained enough projection to startle her. He pulled his arm from her grip and ran his hand across his face. Whatever else he was about to say was lost in his frustration. "Please, I need you to relax tonight. Yes, you're very good at your job and that's why I hired you, but I've come to realize that tonight I need you to be here as my friend and not as my CJD watchdog. I'd like to try really hard to forget, for just one night, that I'm sick. If I fuck something up, who cares? I don't owe anyone an explanation for anything. I want to forget. That's how you can help me."

"Okay, I'll do my best to let it go tonight. But you can expect the bulldog back first thing tomorrow morning."

"Here you are my dear." Miles handed Sarah a glass of wine and led her over to one of the tables in the reception area. They had returned from walking around the estate, and in the time they were gone the room had filled with people. Tina, Elijah and Leanne were at the entrance greeting guests as they arrived. She stood next to Miles watching the guests mingle with one another. A few times, as she glanced about the room, she caught sight of Elijah and he smiled. Unfortunately, she also once caught sight of Leanne who laser-beamed a hole through her head with her death glare.

"So, Miles, do you know if Leanne knew before tonight I was attending the gala?"

"She did *not* know before this morning. She found out you were coming when Miss Hawthorne went over room assignments. At first she made some sort of smart-ass comment about not understanding why you would need your own room... Then later, when going over the events for the evening, she put two and two together and asked if you were the one Elijah would be dancing with and she kind of flew off the handle."

"Awesome." She took a big drink of her wine.

I knew tonight was going to be a disaster.

Miles pulled back quickly and produced a phone from his pocket. He looked at it and cursed under his breath.

"Problem?" She watched him tuck the phone back into his pocket.

"Not really. A client I need to talk to. But I promised Tina no work tonight."

"But she's working, isn't she?" She gave him a playful smile.

"True..." He craned his neck to catch a view of his wife.

"Go, make your call. She'll be busy for at least another twenty minutes and if she gets here before you're done I'll cover for you." He looked at her through narrowed eyes. "Go. I'll be fine. I can hold up this table just fine all by myself." He smiled and mouthed a thank you as he quickly weaved his way out of the room.

She stood watching the people around her. A waiter walked up and offered his tray of hors d'oeuvres but she declined, her stomach not yet settled enough for food. As she waited, her mind wandered back to the events with Elijah on the dance floor. His behavior had confused and worried her. She knew this night was special for him but at the same time difficult. There was a movement to her left, bringing her back out of her thoughts. She turned, expecting to see Miles, and dropped her smile as her eyes landed on the person standing next to her.

"Mrs. Mitchell, or can I call you Sarah? I see Kingston has allowed you time to play after all. I must say... you look ravishing." The last comment was made with a sweep of his eyes over her body.

"I'm sorry, have we met?" She knew who he was. She just didn't want to give him the satisfaction of knowing that she did.

"Mark Tanger, Vice President of Marketing at Kingston Enterprises? We met at the board meeting." He leaned his elbow on the table. She was satisfied at the annoyance she saw on his face at her lack of recognition.

"Ah, yes. I've met so many people since I've been here it's hard to remember all the names and faces." She tried to keep her voice cool and indifferent while maintaining a small amount of respectfulness. She hoped it would encourage him to go away. Unfortunately, he leaned in closer.

"Can I get you another drink?" He leaned back and looked around for a waiter.

"No, thank you. I'm fine." He signaled for a waiter anyway and asked for another glass of whiskey.

"So, will you reserve a dance for me later this evening?" He grazed his finger down her arm. She pulled away, only to bump into someone standing at the table behind her.

"Sorry." She gave a half hearted smile to the woman she bumped before looking in the direction Miles had gone, hoping to find him on his way back, but there was no sign of him. She felt Mark move closer and started to panic. She didn't want to make a scene, but she had to find a way to get away from the creep. She took a deep breath and turned so she was facing Mark and at the same time putting some distance back between them. "I'm sorry, Mr. Tanger—"

"I insist you call me Mark."

She continued on as if he had not spoken a word. "I'm not much for dancing. I'm sure there are better partners available this evening."

"Oh, I doubt that, Sarah." He reached out for her hand, and she pulled it back so quickly she almost knocked over her wine glass.

She backed away from the table as she responded. "If you'll excuse me, I need to—" Her movement stopped as she bumped into someone again. A hand settled on her back and moved slowly across her exposed skin to settle on her hip, pulling her into a protective grip. She felt like she'd been hit with a jolt of electricity at the touch. Her heart hammered loudly in her head as she turned to see who was holding her. The man she looked at caused her to catch her breath. He was absolutely beautiful, and he was staring down at her with the most enchanting blue eyes. He studied her face for a moment and then turned to look at Mark.

"Mark. I didn't think you'd show this year after the spectacle you made at last year's gala. I suggest you walk away before we have a repeat of that unfortunate situation." It took all her strength to pull her gaze away from his face to look at Mark. He was staring at the man with pure hatred. He darted his eyes to her once more and then walked away, grabbing his whiskey from the returning waiter in the process.

She looked back to the stranger. He was looking at her again.

I should say something. Or move. Or say something and move. He still has his arm around me. His hand is on me. His hand... oh God, why am I feeling this way? I have no idea who this is, and I should not want to be standing here with him like this.

"Are you all right?" His voice was soft on her ears and resonated down her spine. He slowly removed his arm from around her back and placed his hand on her arm. She looked down at her arm, now tingling from the contact.

Oh God, what's happening to me?

She looked back up into his eyes and felt a sudden lightheadedness from the heat taking over her body.

"Sarah?" The sound of her name sounded like it came from a tunnel. She turned to see Miles standing next to the stranger. She focused her eyes on Miles, trying to regain her composure. The stranger reluctantly stepped aside, allowing Miles to reach her. "Sarah, are you all right?"

"Yes, I'm okay. I... I think the wine went to my head a little too quickly." The look Miles gave her told her he didn't believe she was telling him the truth. She attempted another glance at the stranger. "Thank you." His response to her gratitude was a smile that stopped her heart for multiple beats before setting it into a rapid pace.

Oh, God. I think I'm attracted to this man. I haven't been attracted to anyone since Nick. This can't be happening.

The room started to spin. She tried to force her gaze back to Miles and gripped his arm. She felt like she was starting to cause a scene, which increased her anxiety. She tried to ask Miles to take her outside when she felt a hand on her other arm. It was Elijah.

"Sarah, what's wrong?" She focused on Elijah's face. She thought she had nodded, but he kept looking at her with concern before looking at Miles. "Miles, what happened?"

"I don't know, I came back and she looked like she was about to pass out."

She watched Elijah turn his gaze to the man standing next to Miles. "Marcus, do you know what happened?"

Marcus? Marcus?

She turned her head slowly to the man Elijah had just addressed as his son.

No, this isn't possible.

"I think I need some air."

Elijah quickly ushered her through the crowd of people and out to the back terrace. As soon as the door opened, the blast of cold air shocked her back to her senses. She closed her eyes and took in one more deep breath before turning around. Elijah held on to her elbows, searching her face. She looked past Elijah to see Miles standing next to Marcus by the door. Marcus' arms were folded across his chest and he was glaring at Elijah.

"Sarah, can you please tell me what happened?" She turned her attention back to Elijah.

"I... I'm not sure really. Like I told Miles, I think the wine went to my head too quickly—"

"That asshole Mark was pouncing on her. I could tell from across the room she was trying to get away, but as usual that man has no respect for boundaries. I stepped in and told him to leave." Everyone looked at Marcus.

"Where the hell were you?" Elijah turned his angry gaze to Miles.

"Elijah, it's fine. Miles had to step away for a moment. I don't need to be watched—"

"Apparently, you do. Mark is relentless and no matter your progress I don't think you're up for the likes of him." She looked at Elijah, stunned.

"Why the hell haven't you fired him by now?" The anger was apparent in Marcus' voice.

"It's not my job any more. You can take it up with your sister."

"You should have fired him after the incident last year!"

"Yeah, well, he kept it in his pants at work so what was I supposed to do? You punched him, I put him on notice, and I thought that was good enough. He's—"

"Stop! Mark's not the problem. Yes, the guy's an ass, and he should probably be fired based on his general lack of integrity and respect for others, but can you not argue about that right now?" Her outburst startled them all, including herself. "I'm fine, really. I probably shouldn't have anything else to drink tonight. I didn't have lunch today, and I should've known even one glass was too much." Her voice was shaky, but she had regained her control. Everyone continued to stare at her. Elijah finally looked away to Marcus.

"Well, it's obvious you two have already met but given the circumstances I suppose a more formal introduction is appropriate. Sarah, this is my son Marcus. Marcus, this is Sarah Mitchell." It didn't go unnoticed that he didn't explain his association with her in his introduction. Marcus looked at her for several seconds before speaking.

"The same Sarah that Leanne has mentioned?"

Oh, that's just great.

Her heart sank. She wasn't sure if it was from embarrassment or disappointment at what he most likely thought of her association with Elijah.

"She's the only Sarah I know, so I assume so."

Marcus continued to look at her and a slight frown formed at the corners of his mouth. His response was muttered and was not intended to be heard, but she could have sworn he'd said, "That's too bad." Her heart leapt once more as she watched him turn and walk back inside.

"Well, now that you've had the pleasure of meeting my son, you can see I wasn't exaggerating about the challenge of our relationship." He let out a harsh laugh and shook his head. "Let's go in. It's cold out here and dinner's about to start." Elijah took Sarah's hand and they followed Miles back inside.

Miles guided them through the reception area and into the grand ballroom to a center table. Miles engaged Leanne in conversation while a gentleman walked over and shook hands with Elijah.

"Brad, I'd like to introduce you to my friend Sarah. I've no doubt you've heard she's here helping me on a project." He shot an irritated glance in Leanne's direction and then took his eyes to Sarah. "Sarah, this is my son-in-law, Brad."

"It's nice to meet you." She accepted the hand he offered.

"You too. I've heard so much about you." He said this with a smile.

"I'm sure you have. However, I hope you've decided to wait to form your own opinion until you can assess the situation for yourself." His smile became wider.

"I have. And now I'm very glad that I did." He gave her a wink and walked over to Leanne who wasn't pleased at witnessing the friendly exchange. Everyone took their seats. As she reached for the glass in front of her, she felt someone lean down to whisper in her ear.

"I hope that's water." She tried to hide the hitch in her breath, but she wasn't sure if she'd been successful. She slowly turned her head to see Marcus pull away and walk to his seat. He pulled out the chair next to Elijah for a woman before taking his seat.

Sarah took another drink of her water and looked up to see Marcus watching her with a blank expression. He tore his gaze away when the woman to his right leaned over and whispered something in his ear.

"Everyone, I'd like you to meet my friend Heather." Marcus put his arm around the back of her chair and turned to look at Brad. "This is my brother-in-law, Brad, and that's my sister, Leanne. Next to her is Miles Morgan. Miles is my father's attorney as well as a friend of the family. His wife, Tina, is the director of the foundation and she'll join us shortly." He looked at Sarah and paused for a moment. "This next lovely lady I've just met tonight. Her name is Sarah Mitchell, and she's my father's... friend?" He tilted his head to the side and raised his eyebrow at her. In that look, there was no doubt he was Elijah's son. "And of course, last but never least is my father, Elijah."

Heather offered everyone a wide smile. "Hello, everyone." Sarah studied her out of curiosity. Marcus introduced her as nothing more than his friend, but she didn't look like the type of girl who would settle for being a friend. She was very pretty with short blonde hair and beautiful eyes in a color that was hard to discern, but they looked either blue or gray. Even though she was sitting, Sarah could tell she was very petite.

The lights in the room dimmed and the conversation dropped to whispers. Sarah looked up to the stage and smiled when she saw Tina walk to the podium. She looked stunning in a strapless white mermaid gown, covered in tiny hand-sewn pearls. Her hair was down and pinned at the sides behind her ears. As she took her place behind the podium to address the crowd, the lights went back up.

"So, what did Marcus say to you?" Sarah turned and gave Elijah a curious look as she leaned in to whisper back.

"He wanted to make sure I wasn't drinking any more wine."

"I think this might be the first time my son and I actually agree on something."

"Be nice, Elijah." He pulled back and gave her a mock look of shock. She pulled him back to whisper in his ear again. "If I can take a night off from hounding you on your symptoms, you can take the night off from fighting with your children." He pulled back again, and she offered him a sweet smile. He held her gaze in a challenging stare. Finally, he closed his eyes in defeat and mouthed the word 'fine' before turning his attention back to Tina.

Sarah turned her own attention to Tina and noticed Marcus in her line of sight. He was watching her. She locked her eyes with his, unable to pull her attention away. She felt her body start to react again, so she closed her eyes and took a deep breath.

It has to be the wine. And the nerves. I'm just oversensitive right now, that's all this is. I can't be attracted to someone. Especially not Elijah's son.

The thought of being attracted to someone other than Nick caused an errant tear to escape, and she quickly wiped it away.

Sarah forced her mind to focus on Tina's words. The soothing sound of her friend's voice anchored her and she forced her eyes open. She tried to look past Marcus, but she caught a glimpse of him before her eyes found Tina. The look she saw on his face was one of confusion. She was able to remain focused until Tina completed her speech.

Before taking her seat, Tina pulled Sarah to her feet. "Sarah, my God, you look stunning! I knew that gown would be perfect on you. Did you enjoy the spa?"

Although embarrassed at the attention, she couldn't help but smile at her friend. "Yes, thank you, it was very relaxing. I *love* your gown and your speech was wonderful." As they took their seats, the rest of the table echoed Sarah's compliments for Tina's speech.

Tina shook off the compliments. "Well, thank you. Really, it was nothing compared to what Leanne has prepared. Her speech is nothing short of touching and inspirational." It was the first time Sarah had seen Leanne smile. It softened her face so much she actually looked approachable and friendly. Tina looked over to Marcus' date and introduced herself before the first course of dinner was served.

"So, Sarah, I understand you're from Indiana. Is this your first time in this area?" Sarah looked at Brad and noticed the disapproving look from Leanne in the process.

"Yes, this is my first time here, and I'm really enjoying it. The scenery is so much different than back home. There's something so calming about the mountains. Don't get me wrong, Indiana has some very redeeming qualities but picturesque scenery is not one of them."

She felt Elijah's hand on her shoulder. "You'll have to put that present to use and take some pictures..." His words trailed off as he realized what he'd said. His look turned apologetic for reminding her of Nick's gift.

"You bought her a camera? What, early Christmas present or something?" Sarah was irritated by the accusation Leanne slipped into her comment.

"No, it wasn't a gift from Elijah. I—" Sarah wasn't sure what she should say. Leanne wasn't someone she felt comfortable sharing with and half the people at the table she had just met that night.

"Heather, tell us about you. How do you know Marcus?" Sarah looked at Tina and offered a smile of thanks for diverting the conversation. As she turned her eyes to Heather, she saw Marcus studying her again.

Why the hell is he still looking at me?

She automatically crossed her arms in front of her in a protective fold.

Heather looked at Marcus who finally took his eyes off Sarah to acknowledge his date. She smiled at him and he smiled back, shaking his head. "We met through mutual friends." The exchange made it obvious there was more to the story they weren't willing to share.

Sarah was frustrated with herself that she was irritated by their shared connection.

"What do you do, Heather?" Leanne's tone was more suspicious than curious. Sarah wondered if she was naturally resistant to any female associated with the men in her life.

"I'm a dance instructor."

Sounds like she's perfect for him. The way Elijah explained it, dancing is an important part of Marcus' life so why shouldn't he be with a dancer? And why do I even care? It has nothing to do with me. I only reacted to him because of the wine, and my nerves, and that jerk Mark. What the hell is wrong with me tonight?

The lights in the room dimmed again and conversation hushed as several children in ballet costumes shuffled to the dance floor. When they finished, the lights went back up and the second course was served. Leanne continued to ask Heather questions and Sarah took the opportunity to study Elijah. He was doing a good job of keeping his right hand in his lap and using only his left to eat.

"Are you dancing again, Marcus?" Elijah studied his food as he spoke. Marcus hesitated as if surprised his dad had asked him a question.

"No."

"Sarah, you must be a wonderful dancer." Marcus' eyes darted to Sarah with an assessing look at Leanne's comment.

"No, not really."

"Oh? I'm surprised given you'll be performing the spotlight dance with my father." Leanne's irritation was now bordering on anger.

Sarah's own anger was rising and she willed herself to remain respectful. "Yes, well, you're not alone in your surprise. Luckily I had a patient teacher."

"Patient? That must be the first time anyone has ever described my father as patient." Leanne's laugh was bitter.

Elijah sat forward in his seat and looked down the table at Leanne. Sarah could see his jaw tensing. "Leanne, can we please not do this tonight." She was impressed he was able to keep his voice calm.

"Leanne, this salmon is amazing. Everything so far has been wonderful." Sarah sighed and looked down at her plate. Her level of irritation was rising and she felt guilty Tina had to keep coming to the rescue. Tina and Miles successfully diverted the conversation throughout the rest of the meal. Once the plates were cleared and the second performance of the evening was complete, people started to mill about the room. There would be a brief break before dessert was served and the auction winners were announced.

Sarah needed a break from the tension building around the table so she excused herself. "If you will all excuse me, there's something I'd like to bid on before the window closes."

"Sarah, wait. I'll go with you."

She froze and cursed silently in her head. She closed her eyes and prayed for strength before turning around.

"That would be great." She watched as Leanne walked around the table to join her.

Sarah placed a bid on a golf and spa package she wanted to give her parents for Christmas before checking out the other bid items. She passed a table with intricate vases and froze as someone stepped in front of her. The hairs rising on her neck told her it was Marcus before she even looked up.

Seeing him now she found it hard to believe she didn't recognize him as Elijah's son the first time she laid eyes on him. They mirrored almost exactly in height and facial expressions. However, the characteristics of his face must have come from Marlena. Where Elijah was all angles and contrast, Marcus was fluid. Each of his features worked together in cohesion and the only thing that stood out, demanding attention, were his eyes. He had not smiled at her since she first thanked him for his help with Mark, but she remembered it vividly. It was a mesmerizing half smile that produced the faintest dimple in his cheek. Just the memory of it caused a flush to creep up her neck.

"So, you'll be dancing with my father later?"

"Yes. I hope it will actually be recognized as dancing though. Elijah assures me it will be fine, but I've never done anything like this before."

"My father's not one for passing out compliments, false or earned, so if he says you'll do fine I'm sure you will." He paused to take a drink. "I was curious about something, if you don't mind my asking. What—"

"Marcus, the item you wanted got another bid." She frowned as Heather pulled on his arm until he reluctantly walked away. Heather looked at her with a satisfied grin before following. She stared after them in confusion, left wondering what he was going to ask.

"Sarah, if you're done in here I'd like to talk privately for a moment." She looked to see Leanne standing a few feet away.

"Yes, I'm done."

Leanne led her to a private balcony down the hall. When they stepped outside, Sarah pulled her arms across her chest and rubbed her bare arms, trying to take out the instant chill.

"There's no hiding the fact that I'm no fan of yours. I'm only saying this once, and I'm only saying it because my husband asked me to. I'm sorry if I've put you in an uncomfortable situation tonight."

This is so, totally, not what I expected.

Sarah had been preparing an entirely different rebuttal and had to redirect at the unexpected apology. "Thank you, apology accepted." Leanne looked at her, expecting more. She took a deep breath, thinking quickly. "I'm also sorry if I've done anything to upset you. If I have, please believe it was unintentional."

Leanne gave her a measured look. "This doesn't mean we'll be friends. It also doesn't mean I trust you. I'll just refrain from voicing my comments in public for the rest of the night." She pushed off the railing and walked toward the door. She stopped before walking back inside and looked back over her shoulder. "Also, I might suggest that since you're with my father you should stop checking out my brother."

The last statement hit Sarah like a brick, momentarily knocking the breath right out of her. She was freezing, but after Leanne's comment she needed a few moments alone. It bothered her that Leanne recognized how her attention had been drawn to Marcus. She wondered if Elijah had noticed. Or Marcus.

Maybe that's why he keeps staring at me. He's wondering why his dad's girlfriend is ogling him. This night really is a disaster.

Sarah was still chilled from the cold. She hugged her arms, rubbing them with her hands. As the waiters delivered dessert, Elijah leaned over.

"What's wrong? Are you cold?" He reached over and touched her arm before she could respond. "Christ, Sarah, you're freezing. Were you outside?" He stood up, took off his jacket, and draped it over her shoulders.

"Not for very long. I needed some air." She pulled his jacket tight around her. She pushed away her dessert, deciding she couldn't eat anything else with the dance looming ahead.

"So, Sarah, what part of Indiana are you from?" She smiled at Brad, grateful for his continued efforts to be civil to her.

"I live in a small town not far from Indianapolis."

"Do you still have family there? It must be hard to be away from them during the holidays."

She felt the familiar pang of loneliness when asked about her family. "My parents and two of my brothers live near Chicago." She wasn't sure she had been successful at keeping the unsteadiness out of her voice.

"Well, after meeting you I'm certain you've left a trail of broken hearts behind." Brad said this with a friendly smile, and she knew he was trying to flatter her but she couldn't stop her shocked reaction. Leanne's eyes darted quickly to Brad who looked confused. "I'm sorry. I hope I haven't said something to offend you." He looked to his wife for support.

"That's all right, Brad. When it comes to Sarah, I can see Leanne has chosen to only share details that best paint her accusations as true." The warning in Elijah's voice was clear.

"I felt those details weren't relevant to the situation and were certainly too personal for me to share." Although Leanne squared her shoulders and lifted her chin in confidence, there was a note of uncertainty in her voice.

"Marcus, are you hoping to win one of the auction items?" Sarah closed her eyes and took a deep breath. Again, Tina had come to her rescue. She was tired of being made the object of discomfort around the table. She allowed her feelings of embarrassment to turn into anger and her thoughts to form arguments of defense.

"Sarah, how about you?" She looked up, uncertain who had asked the question and what she was supposed to be answering. They were all looking at her, some with pity and some with curiosity. Her irritation went up another notch. Suddenly, she remembered Tina had asked about auction items and she assumed it must be her turn to share.

"I bid on one item, a golf and spa package. I'm hoping to give it to my parents as a Christmas gift."

"You should have let Elijah bid on it for you. I noticed the items he bid on didn't have a single name after his." Heather seemed proud of herself for the observation.

"Yes, well, I supposed that would have been a strategy to use, but then he would have insisted on paying for it as well." Sarah looked over to Elijah and he smiled at her.

"You know me too well."

Heather giggled. "I just assumed he'd be paying for it anyway. From all the conversation I've gathered tonight you two are together, right? I mean, what's the point of having a super rich older boyfriend if he's not paying for everything?" Sarah couldn't tell, but she must have learned to adopt the Kingston look of death because Heather's giggles stopped abruptly.

"Marcus, I suggest you control your date."

"Well, Dad, in a way I have to commend Heather for having the capacity to state the obvious. You two say you're not together, but your actions speak otherwise. Why should she feel embarrassed about making light of your relationship with Sarah?" Reluctantly, Sarah had to allow Marcus a bit of respect for defending his date, as irritating as she was. Elijah started to respond, but she put her hand on his arm to stop him.

"I have something to say, and I *hope* this is the last of it." Sarah settled her gaze on Leanne and allowed the pause to hang long enough to make her uncomfortable before looking around to the others. "Two and a half years ago, I lost my husband and two year old son in a car accident. My world shattered into a billion unrecognizable pieces. When I was certain there was no way out of that darkness, someone reached out to me." She turned to look at Elijah. The look of caring in his eyes caused her to reach out and grab hold of his hand.

"Elijah has not taken advantage of me, nor I of him. He saw my pain and my struggle, and he offered me a lifeline. He has helped me emerge from that darkness and live my life again. Yes, I consider Elijah to be more than my boss. He's my friend. My catalyst. You say our actions contradict what we say, but do they really or are you only able to see what you want to see? What you should see are two people who care about each other. Two people who are helping each other not be afraid of their ghosts and make the most out of the life they have been given. So, if you don't mind, I would appreciate it if you would all keep your snide comments to yourself from now on."

No longer cold, she shrugged off Elijah's coat and handed it back to him. He stood to put it back on, chuckled, and leaned down to kiss the top of her head. She didn't want to, and she tried not to, but her eyes made their way to Marcus just the same. As expected, he was looking at her.

CHAPTER 15

Sarah stood off to the side of the room, cracking her knuckles and biting her lip. She couldn't remember ever feeling so nervous. Leanne had finished her dedication speech and she watched Elijah embrace her in a hug. It was the kind of father-daughter moment she had been waiting to witness, but she couldn't tell if it was genuine or just for show. Elijah moved to the podium to address the crowd before their dance.

He talked about the foundation and the accomplishments made over the years. She noticed he continually glanced at note cards he had set on the podium. She shifted her eyes about the room in hopes of distracting her mind from her growing anxiety. She watched Miles and Marcus as they walked to the back of the room. It was obvious Marcus was agitated and she was startled when he looked in her direction, holding her gaze. He turned back to Miles, ran his hand through his hair and pointed in the direction of the stage. She turned her attention back to Elijah, hoping she might understand what had caused Marcus to become so upset.

"—has given me great pleasure to watch my wife's dream continue to grow over the years. As Leanne already mentioned, this night holds a special significance for my family. If Lena were here tonight, we would have celebrated her sixtieth birthday. As many of you know, Lena and I always performed our wedding dance. After she passed, it didn't feel right for me to continue that tradition. This year, in honor of her memory, I had planned to perform our wedding dance with someone who has become a very close friend." He paused and looked over to Sarah.

He said 'had planned.' Why did he say 'had planned?' We are going to dance his wedding dance.

Sarah was thinking maybe she had misinterpreted his words, but the growing knot in her stomach contradicted her. His next statement cemented her anxiety.

"Unfortunately, I have to attend to urgent business. I do apologize, but you know it must be significant to pull me away from something so important to me. But don't worry, I have an alternative I know you will enjoy far more than watching me pretend I can dance the way I had when I was a young man. I'd like for you to welcome my son, Marcus, who will take my place dancing with the lovely Mrs. Sarah Mitchell." There was a round of applause. She should have been walking out to the dance floor, but she was too stunned to move. Before her mind could assimilate a single thought she felt a hand on her back, gently pushing her out toward the dance floor.

"Smile, Sarah, or people will assume you don't want to dance with me." Marcus' touch and whispered voice brought back the dizzying emotions from earlier. Elijah came down to meet them as they walked onto the dance floor. He first greeted Marcus and gave him a hug that, unlike the one he gave Leanne, she knew was just for show. "I can't believe you did this to me. A little warning would have been nice." Marcus' voice was only loud enough for the three of them and his irritation was clear.

"If I would have told you, I'm sure you would have found a way to get out of it." Elijah turned to Sarah and he at least had the decency to look guilty. "I'm sorry. We'll talk about it later. You'll do great." He gave her a quick hug and a kiss on the cheek before walking off the dance floor and out of the room with Miles. She turned to look at Marcus and felt the shakes start in her legs. He took her hand and led her to the center of the dance floor where he pulled her into position. He must have felt her trepidation because when he looked at her in the few seconds before the music began his face softened. He pulled her closer to him so he could whisper in her ear.

"Sarah, relax. You'll do fine, just follow my lead. I won't let you fall or even step on my toes."

The music began and so did their movement across the dance floor. She was in such a state of shock she didn't register he continued to hold her closer than required until a few seconds had passed.

Suddenly, everything came crashing down on her—the anxiety of the dance and everyone watching, the negative comments from earlier, Elijah backing out of the dance, and her continued reaction to Marcus. In the enormity of it all she felt herself falter, but Marcus tightened his grip to keep her steady. He pulled back enough to look in her eyes while he whispered encouraging words.

"Look at me, Sarah. Keep your eyes on me and we'll get each other through this."

She looked in those startling blue eyes and a surprising sense of calm surged through her. Elijah had not been exaggerating, Marcus was a wonderful dancer. When she had danced with Elijah, she was aware of each step she took and what her next step needed to be. With Marcus she felt like she was floating, tethered to the dance floor only through her contact with him. As the dance continued, she felt herself being drawn more and more into Marcus' trance. The dance ended, the music faded, but the feelings remained. He held on to her for several seconds after the music stopped, looking down at her. She felt the intensity of his eyes. She felt the rapid beating of his heart. She felt his soft breath on her cheek. She felt her knees go weak.

Marcus pulled her into a gentle hug. "Don't faint on me now. We're all done and you did great." He turned her to face the crowd keeping his arm around her and holding her to his side. As they weaved their way through the tables, several people reached out for Sarah's hand or clapped Marcus on the back and told them how much they enjoyed watching them dance. None of it registered with Sarah, but she was somehow able to smile and acknowledge the compliments. She wasn't able to absorb what was happening because she had to put all her energy into not passing out and deflecting the thoughts racing through her mind.

It's not the wine. Lord help me, but it's not the wine. I can't be attracted to him. This wasn't supposed to happen.

Sensing her struggle, Marcus led her out of the ballroom, through the reception area and toward the terrace. As they approached the doors, they could hear agitated voices coming from outside and Marcus paused their movement. He quickly redirected their course to the stairs and he led her to the second floor balcony where she had met with Leanne earlier. The cold air had the desired effect, and she regained her composure. She took a deep breath and closed her eyes.

Get a grip Mitchell. So what if you're attracted to him? You're human after all, and he's a very attractive man. Being attracted to someone isn't a crime. It's part of your journey to feeling alive and normal again.

Her thoughts didn't calm her, but they gave her the strength to control her emotions. She felt Marcus place his jacket over her shoulders and she pulled it close.

"Thank you." She walked across the balcony and leaned against the railing.

"Are you feeling better?"

"Yes, thank you. I'm sorry. You must think I'm a complete idiot." Her comment was met with a long silence. When he finally responded, it was soft and sincere.

"No, not at all." Although it was dark, there was enough light filtering through the windows to make out his features. She watched as a slow smile took over his face. "You know, as much as I hate to *ever* admit my father could be right about something, he was right in that you did a great job. He taught you well."

Her heart beat more rapidly than she thought possible. "Thanks. That means a lot coming from you."

He tilted his head to the side and raised one eyebrow. "More than coming from my father?"

"He gives me compliments all the time. I think he thinks it will help boost my confidence. Besides, when it comes to the assessment of dancing skills I'd be a fool not to place more value in your opinion. You're the dancer in the family after all."

"Not any more. Not for a long time."

Realization suddenly hit Sarah. "Oh... I'm so sorry. I was so caught up in my own anxiety I forgot to consider yours. Elijah mentioned you stopped dancing after your mom... and tonight at dinner when he asked you if you had started dancing again... I'm so sorry he put you in that situation."

He didn't respond right away and his head was down so she couldn't tell if she had upset him further. "Please, don't ever feel the need to apologize for my father's actions. I'm well aware by now how he goes about things. But thank you just the same."

"Have you danced at all since your mom passed?"

"No."

"Then I have to agree with Elijah on something as well. You really do have an extraordinary talent for dancing. To be able to remember all the steps of the dance after that length of time is beyond my understanding. And, while I'm no expert on the subject, I could tell by the way you led me through the dance... it was as though you still danced every day of your life."

He was quiet for a long time. When he did speak again there was a hesitation. "I... I wanted to say that I'm sorry about all the stuff said earlier."

"It's okay—"

"No, it's not. You were right, we were all reacting to assumptions and it wasn't fair to you. I can't speak for Leanne, but I'm sorry for what Heather said and I'm mostly sorry I defended her."

"You shouldn't be sorry for that. We all feel the need to defend the people we care about, even if we know their actions to be misguided." She couldn't help but relate the situation to Elijah not wanting to tell his children about his illness. She felt it was misguided, but if challenged she would defend his actions without a moment's hesitation.

She heard him let out a deep breath. "Will you dance with me again?" His words were rushed and uncertain, almost as if he wasn't sure he even wanted to ask. The question came as a surprise on the heels of his recent confession of not dancing for the last twenty years. If she were being honest with herself, there was nothing more she wanted than to dance with him again. It scared her so much she decided to deflect the question rather than give him an answer.

"I'm not sure Heather would approve." She crossed her arms and pulled his jacket tighter.

"I'm not sure why she should care, we're just friends." He put his hands in his pockets and shrugged his shoulders.

"Does she know that?"

"She's the one who set the boundaries in our relationship." He moved a few steps closer.

"So, it's one of those situations."

"One of what situations?" She could hear the genuine puzzlement in his voice. He moved a few steps closer, but still maintained a comfortable space between them.

"One where the girl is hopelessly in love with the guy and the guy either has no clue or doesn't care." He leaned up to the balcony next to her. He was still a few feet away, which was good. If he got any closer, she wasn't sure she would be able to form a coherent sentence. It was hard enough to ignore the smell of him on his jacket wrapped around her.

"I'm not sure I understand why you're under the impression it's that sort of situation."

"Any woman who needs to set boundaries in a relationship only does so to protect her heart." Seeing the confusion still on his face she tried to explain herself. "What's one of the boundaries?" There was a glint in his eyes. "No kissing."

Right, of course he would say that.

She felt the flush take over her face. She couldn't remember the last time she'd talked about kissing with a man other than Nick, let alone one she'd just met. She gave him an irritated look hoping he would give another example but he just raised his eyebrow and shrugged his shoulders.

"Okay, fine, no kissing. If she was truly okay with only being your friend and you tried to kiss her, she would either be able to easily reject you, or she would be able to kiss you knowing it meant nothing. However, because she *does* want to be more than friends and she knows you don't, she sets up the boundary to protect her heart. Because if she did kiss you, her heart would no longer be hers and it's likely it would be shattered into a million pieces." She hoped he didn't notice the change of inflection in her voice as she spoke.

"And you're able to come to this conclusion simply because she's set up boundaries in our relationship?"

"Also from my observations tonight. When you talk about her you sound very... noncommittal. It's clear you only see her as a friend. But I'd wager she'd like more from the relationship, and she's sticking around waiting for the moment when you want it too. I say this not only based on the way she has hung on your every word tonight, but also by the way she has tried to make it clear to me, more than once, that you're with her. It's like she's mistaken me for competition and wants to mark her turf. We women don't do that with guys we only want to be friends with."

She watched as realization crossed his face. He let out a resigned sigh while closing his eyes and hanging his head. "So... do you have any of these boundaries set up between you and my father?"

"No. As I've said before, it's not that kind of relationship. I don't feel the need for any boundaries with Elijah."

Why can't anyone let this go, and why do they even care so much about it? She couldn't help but be irritated by his question. He quickly looked up and had an apologetic look on his face.

"Sarah, I—"

"There you are." They both looked in the direction of Elijah's voice. Miles was right behind him and Sarah noticed he had a look of concern on his face. She immediately went to Elijah's side.

"Is everything all right?" She searched Elijah's face for any clues. He looked tired, but he smiled anyway.

"Everything's fine." She looked back to Marcus, realizing too late she had left him mid-conversation. There was a sudden awkward tension she was sure they all felt.

"I hear you two put on a wonderful performance." Miles guided easily into the role of peacemaker.

"Yes, I'm sorry to have missed it." Elijah was looking back and forth from Sarah to Marcus.

"Did your 'urgent business' get resolved?" The sarcasm in Marcus' comment was about as thick as the tension surrounding them.

"No. In fact, it will take up the rest of my evening. I just wanted to come and see how you two got along and let you know I plan to be in my room for the remainder of the night."

"Do you need my help?" She was concerned he wasn't feeling well. It was the only thing that would send him to bed so early.

"I'll be able to manage without you this evening, and I'll catch you up on the details tomorrow. Why don't you go back down with Marcus and Miles?" She turned to find Marcus staring in their direction with a hard look. She followed his gaze and it ended at the sight of her hand on Elijah's arm. She slowly pulled it back and tucked her arms inside Marcus' jacket.

Marcus pushed off the balcony and slowly walked toward them. He looked from Sarah to Elijah. "Actually, Sarah was politely reminding me that I've been ignoring my date. If you'll excuse me." He glanced at her one last time before heading back inside.

"Are you and Marcus getting along well?" The question was laced with curiosity.

"Considering you ambushed us with your disappearing act for the dance, I'd say we were bonding quite well over our shared frustration."

"Sarah, I'm sorry about—"

"How long had you planned this, Elijah?"

He looked at her and held her gaze. "For quite awhile. I was afraid I wouldn't feel well, and I don't, so I had to come up with a plan. And besides, I—" He gave a frustrated sigh and ran his hand through his hair. "Besides, I wanted to see Marcus dance one more time. I knew it was the only way I would be able to get him out there. He's the only other person who knows the dance, so he's the only one who could have filled in. He wouldn't have left you standing up there. It was my only chance to see him dance again."

She tried to stay mad, but the honesty of his confession stripped away all her frustration. She was about to ask how he knew Marcus wouldn't leave her stranded, but then remembered he was an expert at knowing people's weaknesses and how to exploit them. He'd called it a kill button.

"But you left the room. You didn't even get to see him dance."

"I slipped back in once the dance started. I knew no one would notice because once he was dancing no one would be able to look away. As expected, I went unnoticed in the back of the room."

"Why didn't you at least tell me?"

"You were nervous as it was. I was afraid if I told you that you would be dancing with Marcus, someone you had never met, you would've had a panic attack or something. I had changed my mind and was going to tell you but then that whole incident with Mark happened and you almost passed out... I didn't want to add to your stress."

She nodded her head in acceptance of his excuse. "Are you sure you don't need me tonight? Please, tell me what's going on."

"I just want to rest in my room. Really, I'll be fine. Go back downstairs and enjoy the rest of the evening. Tomorrow when we compare notes I'd like to hear that you danced at least a few more times." She searched his face and found only fatigue.

"Okay, but I'm going to check on you when I get back to my room."

"Deal. Now get back inside before you get yourself sick. I'm not sure why you keep insisting on exposing yourself to these frigid temperatures." He quickly pulled her inside and gave her another hug. "Good night, Sarah."

"I'm going to walk with Elijah to his room then I'll meet you downstairs. Tell Tina to be ready to dance when I get there." Miles flashed a smile and a wink before walking off with Elijah.

"Heather, for the last time, I don't want to dance."

"It didn't stop you from dancing with *her*."

"I told you, I didn't have a choice. It was a result of my father's usual lack of consideration for anyone but himself." They were sitting facing away from Sarah, and she felt guilty for eavesdropping on their conversation, but she couldn't make herself turn away.

"But you're *so good*. I mean, I knew you said you used to dance, but you never told me you were *that* good. I don't understand—it's such a waste of talent. Can't you imagine the two of us out on the dance floor? We'd make a spectacular couple." Sarah wondered if Marcus caught Heather's true meaning behind her statement.

"Heather! Please, I don't want to dance. You can sit here and keep me company or you can go back to your hotel." Sarah couldn't see his face but she could hear the agitation in his voice. He turned to face Heather and saw Sarah standing behind them.

"I hope I'm not interrupting, I wanted to return your jacket." He stood and walked over to accept his jacket.

"So I guess my father has left you alone for the rest of the evening after all."

"Yeah, well... you know your dad when it comes to business. But he promised me the night off so I guess I get to stay and enjoy myself." He was about to respond but was cut-off by a rather excited voice.

"Sarah! You're back." Tina pulled her into a tight embrace. "My God, you and Marcus on the dance floor, what a sight! You did a wonderful job. I swear I couldn't stop the tears for at least ten minutes after it was over. I'm so proud of you." Sarah couldn't help but laugh at Tina's over embellishment of her dancing. "Come with me, I need a drink."

"Are you sure? It seems you've already had quite a few."

"Nonsense. My job for the evening is done, I don't have to drive, and I'm not the lightweight you are. Maybe my husband can carry *me* up the stairs instead of you for a change."

"Fine, but I'm not drinking. Miles may be in fine shape for a man of his age, but I doubt he could carry us both upstairs."

"Marcus can carry you." She smiled and winked at Marcus as she pulled Sarah over to the bar. After Tina requested drinks, Sarah turned on her.

"Tina, what the hell was that about?"

"What?"

"Marcus can carry you." She did her best imitation of Tina's voice.

Tina took the drinks from the bartender and tried to hand one to Sarah. She held up her hands and shook her head but Tina pressed the glass closer to her face.

"Drink. Have some fun. The Kingstons have put you through enough shit tonight, and you deserve it more than anyone." Sarah stared at the glass Tina held before her. She wasn't sure what it was, but it looked fruity and inviting.

What could it hurt? Tina's right, I deserve to relax and have a bit of fun.

She took the drink from Tina and took a sip.

"Seriously though, what was that about with Marcus?"

Tina studied her over the rim of her glass and pulled her to a vacant space at the side of the room before responding. "Okay, so normally I'd hold my tongue but, again, I think you've dealt with enough shit from people tonight. It seemed to me there was an attraction between the two of you. I thought if I encouraged a bit of playfulness it might take everyone's focus off of your relationship with Elijah."

"Right, because nothing says whore better than someone who bounces from father to son. At the same event no less."

Tina winced. "Okay, I admit I didn't think it through very well. I'm sorry."

Sarah sighed. "No, it's fine. I'm just being oversensitive about the whole situation." She took another sip of her drink.

"Why?"

"It's just... I haven't been attracted to anyone since Nick. I've been—*had* been with Nick since I was in high school. In truth, I can't remember ever having a physical attraction to anyone other than Nick. Not only am I not used to this, but I feel guilty." Sarah looked down at her drink.

"Don't you see? This is a good thing! You're feeling things again. You're allowing yourself to have natural, human reactions to the things and people around you. That's good! It's progress. I understand you feel guilty, and that will probably last for awhile, but it's still a good thing. And if you're going to start having feelings of attraction again, Marcus is definitely the right place to start. I mean, *damn*, he's gorgeous." Sarah couldn't help but laugh.

"Careful, Miles might hear you."

"What might I hear?" Miles' timing was so impeccable it almost seemed staged.

"That I'm hot for Marcus." Tina smiled at her husband before taking another drink.

"Oh, that. I've known it for years. Good thing the line is long and he doesn't seem interested in working through it anytime soon." He looked at Sarah and she noticed a hesitation, as if he were about to say something else. Instead, he leaned down to kiss Tina chastely on the mouth.

Sarah smiled at them. The strength and ease of their relationship caused a familiar pang in her chest. "You two go dance." They looked at her in unison and she was certain they would protest. "Go! I'll take my drink and sit at the table with Marcus and Heather. That's all the entertainment I'll need for the evening." Tina kissed her on the cheek, handed over her drink, and pulled Miles out to the dance floor.

Sarah slowly walked back to the table and was relieved to find it empty. The dance floor was packed with couples. As she watched the couples dancing, she saw Miles and Tina drift past and smiled again at their obvious love for each other. The newly familiar feeling of anticipation rippled through her and she looked to see Marcus sit down next to her. She looked past him, expecting to find Heather.

"What happened to Heather?"

"She decided to find someone who was willing to dance with her." They sat without talking, and while it was comfortable between them, the silence amplified her growing attraction to him. That was something she wasn't comfortable with, so she attempted to create a normal conversation.

"Is this considered ballroom dancing?" She looked over to him and he nodded in agreement. "Is it all the same dance with some variation, or is everyone doing something different, making it up as they go along?"

"Right now, they're all doing various forms of the waltz." He proceeded to educate her on dancing. As the music played, and people danced, they sat watching and talking. He may not dance any more, but it was clear it was still his passion. The relaxed conversation was enjoyable and she found her nervous energy subsiding. After an undetermined amount of time, she saw Tina and Miles approach the table. Before she could even say hello in greeting, Miles was pulling her out of her seat.

"What are you doing?"

"We're going to dance." She pulled her arms away in protest and shook her head.

"No, I can't dance remember? Not like them at any rate." She waved an agitated hand across the crowded dance floor. Everyone laughed and she looked at each of them, annoyed. "What's so funny?"

"Sarah, you dance just fine. Besides, I promised Elijah I would make you dance at least one more time. I don't want to tell him I failed, do you?" Miles gave her a pleading look.

"But I only know the one dance."

"If you can do that one, the basic waltz will be a piece of cake. I'm sure Miles will go easy on you." Marcus gave her an encouraging smile which only succeeded in making her heart flutter and her limbs weaken. She supposed the smile worked as intended, because she was too flustered to refuse any further. Once Miles had her on the dance floor, she relaxed and had fun. He twirled her around for two songs and she smiled and laughed the entire time. At the end of the second dance he loosened his tie.

"Okay, I need a break. And a drink." She walked with him in the direction of the bar. "Want anything?"

"Just water." The drink Tina forced on her had helped her relax, but she knew when to cut it off. She stood off to the side of the bar to wait for Miles. When he finally joined her, Tina was with him.

"Here you go." He handed her the glass of water. "Sorry to dance and ditch, but apparently there's someone I need to meet."

"We shouldn't be long. We'll meet you back over by the table."

Sarah remained for a moment after they left, contemplating what to do. A strong part of her was ready to retire for the night. She was also worried about Elijah and wanted to check on him. She decided to stick around long enough for Tina and Miles to return so she could say good night. She turned in the direction of their table only to be stopped short.

"Hello, Sarah." His words were slightly slurred, indicating he'd had way too much to drink.

"Mr. Tanger."

"Didn't I mention you should call me Mark?" He looked at her for a few seconds then waived a hand as if he could shoo away the formality.

If only I could shoo him away like the gnat he is.

"Anyway, I was thinking... it's funny because I thought you said you didn't dance, yet you were just dancing with Miles and there was that dance you did with Marcus." He swayed slightly as he looked at her with a crooked grin.

"If I recall, what I said was I wasn't much for dancing. Meaning I don't dance very much, not that I don't dance at all. Now, if you'll excuse me." She stepped to walk past him, but he blocked her path.

"Now, now, now. Where're you off to in such a hurry?" He placed his free hand on her waist and she tried to push him away while taking a few steps back. "I was thinking it was time for that dance you promised *me.*"

"Mr. Tanger, I never promised you a dance, and I'm not sure what led you to believe that I did. Again, if you'll excuse me—"

"Sarah, come on, it's just one dance." He took another step toward her. Anger flashed through her core.

"Apparently I've been too subtle, so let me be clear. I'm not interested in dancing with you or even continuing this conversation." She stepped to the side and walked away, crying out in shock as she felt a sharp pain. She turned to find Mark's hand on her arm. She tried to pull away, but he squeezed harder.

"Now Sarah, what's the problem? Come, it's just one dance." He put down his drink and grabbed the water from her hand.

"Let go of me." She pulled again and winced as he dug his fingers deeper into her arm. Suddenly, her arm was free and she stumbled a few steps. Confused, she looked to see what happened to Mark and found him at the mercy of Marcus. Brad appeared quickly behind Marcus and separated the two men.

"Sarah, are you all right?" She stared at Leanne in mild shock. The last thing she had expected was a civil comment from her, regardless of the situation. Quickly regaining her wits, she nodded. "Yeah, I think so." She looked down at her arm. "But I think I might have a nasty bruise in the morning." Leanne gently took her arm and looked it over.

"Damn it. He must have had too much to drink." Marcus stepped up to them and also looked at Sarah's arm. Even the turbulent events that had just occurred couldn't keep the shiver away when he touched her. For distraction, she looked past Marcus to see what had happened to Mark. Brad and another gentleman she didn't know were walking him out of the ballroom. She looked at Marcus as he dropped her arm and took her hand in his, entwining their fingers. He was staring at his sister.

"Two years in a row. His ass had better be fired by Monday. Dad didn't have the balls to do it last year, so you'd better step up." He walked past Leanne without waiting for a response, gently pulling Sarah with him.

She was trying her best to keep up with his quick pace. "Where are we going?"

"To dance." Her feet froze, causing Marcus to come to a halt as well. He turned and looked at her in confusion. "What's wrong?" She desperately wanted to dance with him again, but it was also the last thing she wanted to do.

How do I get out of this?

"I don't want to dance."

"Sure you do." He turned and tried to move forward, but she stood her ground. He looked at her again. "Why aren't we moving?"

"I just got manhandled by some jackass who was insisting I dance with him even though I didn't want to, and now you're trying to do the same thing. Although, I admit your approach is much more gentlemanly. I said I don't want to dance." She could see the effects of her words settle into his expression.

"You're right, I'm sorry." He let out a quick breath and gently squeezed her hand. "Sarah, will you please dance with me?"

"No." She pulled her hand away and crossed her arms. He opened his mouth to respond, but nothing came out so he closed it again. He narrowed his eyes and looked at her, still confused. He reminded her of Elijah in that moment. Both men were obviously used to getting anything they wanted. It was as much adorable as it was annoying. She felt her resolve weaken, so she pushed forward to try and regain it back. "Look, I don't feel like dancing. Besides, I thought you said you didn't want to dance. Several times in fact."

"That was with Heather." He paused to let out another breath and ran his hand through the side of his hair. "Look, I can't fully explain it. It's just that seeing Mark harass you, *again*... it beyond pissed me off, and to calm down I want to dance. With you. It doesn't make any sense seeing as dancing is the one thing I've avoided the most over the last twenty years, but it's the way I feel. Besides, if you recall I already asked you to dance with me a second time when we were outside. You never answered my question, so I'm asking you again. Will you dance with me?" He held out his hand and with all her resolve officially gone, she hesitantly placed her hand back in his. He gave her a small, victorious smile and turned to continue their path to the dance floor.

A song was already in progress, but he swept her up and they moved smoothly in sync with the other couples. By the time the song ended she could feel he'd relaxed. She intended to pull away, but the music began again and so did their movement. He held her close and she had to resist the urge to lay her head on his shoulder. The longer she danced with him, the longer she was even around him, the more real it felt, and she couldn't allow that to happen. The second song ended, and she immediately pulled away, but he prevented her from leaving. She quickly began to consider arguments in her mind for why she needed to leave when the form of her reprieve came into view.

"Um, I hope the dancing calmed your mood."

"It did... why?"

"Because I think you might need to talk to Heather. She looks like she might be about to flip a table and it would be good if at least one of you were calm." He turned in the direction of Sarah's gaze and his shoulders dropped with a heavy sigh.

"Do you mind waiting for me at the table while I talk with her?"

"Actually, I'm going to retire for the evening." Her heart flipped at the disappointed look on his face.

"Are you sure? There's a lot more dancing left in the evening."

"I'm sure. I've well surpassed the amount of dancing I thought I would do tonight." They stood in awkward silence. It almost felt like she was a teenager again and was standing on her front porch after a first date, unsure of how to say good-bye. She couldn't allow herself to compare this to a date, so she quickly stuck out her hand. "Well, it was nice meeting you, Marcus. Thank you for the dancing, especially for bailing out your dad and not leaving me stranded. And for getting rid of Mark, twice..."

Wow, we really accomplished a lot in our first meeting.

He looked at her hand and back up, and the amusement was clear on his face. He took her hand, but instead of giving it a shake he gently pulled her toward him until his mouth connected with her ear.

"You're welcome. I look forward to the next time we meet." He pulled back, winked at her, and walked off in the direction of Heather.

As Sarah scrubbed the last remnants of make-up from her face she thought back over the events of the evening. Her mind was full of conflicting thoughts that made her feel as though she would never be able to sleep. She dropped the wash cloth and squeezed some toothpaste onto her toothbrush. Her thoughts wandered again as she scrubbed away the alcoholic bitterness in her mouth.

What was that with Marcus tonight? I mean, I've interacted with good looking men over the years, but none have caused even the slightest reaction in me. I'm not ready for this. It's a good thing I won't see him again. Wait, crap... I'm going to see him again in a little over a week when they all come over for Christmas. I wonder if I can somehow get out of being there. Maybe he won't come. Maybe—

"AHHH!!" The cry sent a terrifying ripple through her entire body. She dropped her toothbrush and ran to the door that led to Elijah's room. Somewhere along the way she unconsciously swallowed the toothpaste. "AHHH! Stop, stop!" She threw open the door between their rooms and rushed to Elijah's bed. He was thrashing about and she tried to place her hands on his shoulders without getting hit in the process.

"Elijah, wake up. Elijah!" She turned on the light next to the bed and his eyes opened, looking wildly about the room. In his confusion he pushed her away and she fell to the floor, hitting her already bruised arm on the side table. He sat up and ripped the blankets off, grabbing at his legs. She got up and went back to his side, keeping out of arms reach.

"Elijah, it's okay, it was just a dream." When he looked back at her she realized there was a chance he either didn't remember where he was or who she was, or possibly both. "Elijah, it's okay. You left the gala early to go to bed. We're staying the night here and will return to your house in the morning. You were having a really bad dream." Finally, some of the confusion left his face and his breathing slowed. He looked back down at his legs.

"It was eating my legs." His voice was shaky and so soft she had to strain to hear him.

The hallucinations are starting.

"See? It was just a dream. Your legs are still here. Everything's fine."

"But I could feel it. I could feel them—" His words were cut off in his throat. She slowly sat down on the edge of the bed. He jumped away and looked at her with renewed fear. She instinctively put her hands up to show she didn't mean him any harm.

"Will it make you feel better if I pull up your pant legs to verify it was a dream?" She had been told it was important to try and talk him out of the hallucination, but not deny what he was feeling. He looked at her with uncertainty. "You can trust me, Elijah. This is my job, to help you through this. I'm here to help you any way you need. Do you want me to check?" After a few moments of consideration he gave her a slight nod of his head. He watched her movements, and she saw the relief flood through him as his legs became visible. "See, it was all just a bad dream." They both sat in silence, not sure of what to do next.

"Are you thirsty? Can I get you some water?" When he nodded in response, she retrieved a glass of water from the bathroom and paused at the door to his room, overcome with a sensation that someone was listening. She was confident everyone was still downstairs, but she remained for a few seconds to make sure. When she returned to Elijah's side, she had to help him take a drink because his hands were still shaking from the terror he'd experienced.

"Thank you." He settled against the headboard with the blankets still off and his pant legs raised. She pulled the desk chair over next to the bed and sat down. "So, the gala was tonight?" Her heart sank at his question.

"Yes. Do you remember anything?" He was quiet for several seconds and then finally shook his head. "Do you want me to tell you?"

"If you don't mind."

She sat back in the chair, propped her feet up on the bed, and started telling him about the events of the evening. She elected to omit the stuff about Mark and the things said during dinner. It helped her to find a positive in his condition, and one of those was being able to censor his memories. The more she talked, the more relaxed he became. When she got to the part about the spotlight dance she hesitated, but she quickly decided to tell him the truth. He stopped her before she could move on.

"Wait, Marcus danced?" Her heart broke even more. He had so badly wanted to see Marcus dance one more time and now he didn't even remember it.

"He did."

"Did it go well?"

"Yes. You were right, Marcus is a wonderful dancer. And, I think you will be happy to know your underhanded scheming worked out once again. Marcus danced with me two more times later in the evening." The surprise on his face was clear. They remained in silence as he processed her words. She watched him, wondering what she should do. She noticed a slight shiver and realized he might be cold.

"Are you cold? Do you want to pull the blanket back up?" He looked down at his legs but didn't respond. When it was clear he didn't want to cover his legs, she offered another solution. "Maybe I could turn up the heat?" He looked at her with gratitude and nodded his head. "It might be good if you could try to rest again. I'm sorry I didn't think to bring any sleeping pills."

"It's okay. I'll talk to—" His brow wrinkled and she couldn't resist the urge to rescue him.

"Yes, good idea. We'll talk to Ms. Reynolds tomorrow and make sure we have some sleeping pills on hand." Her sorrow was growing. She had the feeling things might start to evolve quickly. "Do you think you might be able to fall back to sleep?"

He looked about the room with uncertainty. "Maybe you could sit with me? And leave the light on." She walked back to the chair and resumed her position.

As she watched him rest, she felt her own fear fighting to surface. She needed to make sure she was ready for what was apparently just around the corner. She had read several testimonials and research papers. She had also talked at length with Lisa and Dr. Holden. She knew what to expect. She knew hallucinations were a possibility and they could be really bad. But the reality was so much harder than her imagination could have ever dreamed.

It's terrible to think Elijah had to watch his dad go through this without any preparation at all. It must have been terrifying.

Thinking about Elijah's dad caused a chill to run through her body. She remembered from her research that with his familial CJD mutation, there was a fifty percent chance the disease would be passed on to his children.

If Elijah hasn't told them then they haven't been tested. What if Leanne has it? It may not have stopped her from having children, but she might have wanted to make a different choice. Once again, Elijah made the decision for everyone. She should have been able to make the choices for herself. And Marcus...

She shuddered. She didn't want to analyze the growing anxiety within her at the thought of Marcus going through this someday. Instead she studied Elijah's sleeping face. Her mind wandered long into the night, but eventually fatigue came and forced her to bed.

CHAPTER 16

Sarah wiped the sweat from her forehead and flung the towel back over the arm of the treadmill. Elijah was with Lisa at the doctor, and Sarah had taken the opportunity to work out her stress. In three days it would be Christmas. The pain of missing Nick and Danny at this time of year was always acute. On top of that, Miles and Tina were planning to come over the following day and then Elijah's family would be over on Christmas Eve.

Elijah's condition had continued to get worse since the gala and she wasn't sure they would be able to easily hide it from Marcus and Leanne. She tried to talk to Elijah about it but he blew her off, insisting it was only dinner and they would manage. His doctor had prescribed medication designed to help him stay calm and Elijah felt it would be enough to get through the dinner without incident. That same night, she tried to ask if Marcus and Leanne had ever been tested for familial CJD. Her question earned an explosive response in which Elijah threw a vase against the wall, shattering it to pieces. He never answered her question, and she never asked again.

She tried to shake the stressful thoughts from her mind. She ratcheted up the pace on the treadmill until she was lost in the rhythm of her breathing and music, finally bringing quiet to her mind. The digital display on the treadmill rolled six miles and she kept going. She finally forced herself to stop when it reached eight. As her pace and breathing slowed, she could feel the tension return to her shoulders. The stress was still there, but at least she'd achieved a few moments of a quiet mind. She hopped off the treadmill, turning toward the door.

"Shit!" She clutched a hand to her chest and pulled out her ear buds, staring at her intruder. "What the hell are you doing here? You scared the shit out of me!" She let out a jagged breath.

"Obviously." The amused look on his face was not appreciated.

"Seriously, what the hell are you doing here?"

"You need to work on your greeting skills. After last week, I had the impression you at least liked me enough to give me a friendly welcome when we met again." He was leaning on the door frame with his arms folded across his chest. He looked as good in jeans and a casual button down as he had in a tux. Better even. She needed to keep her defenses up if she had any hope of making it through the unexpected encounter.

"If you would have arrived on Monday, as *expected*, I would have given you a friendly greeting." The smile on his face, along with the sweep of his eyes over her body, made her feel suddenly exposed in her skimpy jogging shorts and sports bra. She had expected to be alone and had therefore chosen comfort over coverage. She used her hand towel to cover up as much exposed skin as possible, which seemed to only enhance his amusement.

He pushed off the door frame and closed the distance between them, stopping just inches away from her. He gently took her arm and ran his thumb over the faint bruise that remained of her encounter with Mark and she felt an instant flash of heat at his touch. His jaw tensed, but he didn't say anything. Instead, he let go of her arm and leaned over to look at the display on the treadmill.

"Impressive. You run like that all the time?"

Uncomfortable at his nearness, she walked to the space he had just vacated. "Not any more. My running kind of got out of control for awhile, and I've been backing off." He turned to face her. "Marcus, I don't mean to sound rude, really, but you never answered my question. What are you doing here?"

His lazy smile returned, and he leaned against the treadmill. "It's Christmas. Aren't families supposed to spend time together?"

"Most normal families, sure. However, the last thing I would call the Kingston family is normal."

"Are you always this suspicious?" Her only response was a raise of her eyebrows and he laughed in return. "Fine, you win. Leanne and I agreed we had been too harsh at the gala and so we thought, since it is

Christmas after all, we should spend more time getting to know each other. Leanne, Brad and Ollie will be here tomorrow and we're all staying until Christmas Eve."

"Does your dad know about this?"

"No, we thought we'd surprise him. Where is he anyway?"

"Have you ever known him to appreciate a surprise?" She elected to ignore his second question.

"No." His intoxicating eyes were filled with humor and mischief.

"So... your plan is to spend the weekend here to make amends with your dad over the way you all acted at the gala, yet he doesn't know you're staying which is something he won't appreciate. Am I the only one that recognizes this is a bad plan?"

He slowly shook his head. "I never said I was here to make amends with my father. Our plan is to get to know you better."

She buried her face in the corner of her towel that wasn't busy covering up her exposed skin.

We can't hide Elijah's condition for an entire weekend. They're bound to recognize something is wrong with him. What do I do?

She raised her head and jumped back a foot when she realized Marcus was standing right in front of her. She needed to escape and send a warning message to Elijah before he got home.

"If you'll excuse me, I need to take a shower. Since you let yourself in, I assume you can make yourself at home." She turned for the stairs but was stopped when Marcus gently grabbed her hand.

She turned to face him, poised for an argument, but he wasn't looking at her. All the humor from just a few seconds ago had left his face. She followed his line of sight and found he was looking at the dance studio. She relaxed, understanding his emotion at seeing the space where he spent so much time with his mom. Unconsciously, she squeezed his hand in comfort and the action brought his attention to her.

"Will you do something with me?" His words were soft, hesitant. She nodded in agreement even though she didn't know what he wanted. In that moment she probably would have given him anything he asked.

Pulling her with him, he walked in the direction of the dance studio. She watched as he looked into the darkened room for a few seconds before turning on the light. The raw emotion in his eyes told her he hadn't stepped foot in the room since his mom died. Gripping her hand tighter, he walked slowly inside. He held on to her hand until they reached the middle of the dance floor where he sat down, patting the floor next to him in an invitation to sit. She sat down across from him, feeling it was too intimate to sit next to him. They sat in silence for several minutes before he finally spoke.

"My mom often had to force me to sit down and take a break when I was dancing. She'd talk to me about her dance classes or about the time she danced in the academy. God, I wanted to be just like her and was intent on making dancing my career. After she died... I lost sight of everything, and I spent the next year rebelling. I'm sure my father has told you all about that phase of my life."

"Not really. He mentioned you had a hard time after she died and that you got into some trouble with fighting and other stuff, but that's about it. You said you hadn't danced since your mom died, so I assume you didn't go back to the academy?"

"No. To my father's dismay I enrolled at Colorado State University and eventually degreed in veterinary medicine." She couldn't resist the smile slowly spreading across her face.

"You're a veterinarian?" He smiled in return and nodded his head. "Why do you say to your father's dismay? I would think Elijah would be very proud of your career choice."

"Yes, most typical parents would be thrilled to have their child become a doctor. But, as you have so elegantly pointed out, we're not a typical family. My father only would have been proud if I had studied business in order to take over Kingston Enterprises. However, he felt dancing was a worthy substitute since it honored my mother. He can't relate to a vet—he's never even owned a pet."

"Just because he can't relate doesn't mean he's not proud of you."

He considered her words for a moment. "You give my father too much credit. To illustrate my point, don't you find it odd he told you about my dancing, something I haven't done for twenty years, but he never mentioned what I do now?" His observation was very astute. She didn't want to throw salt on his wounded pride by voicing her agreement, so she asked another question instead.

"Do you still live in the area?"

"I live north of Colorado Springs."

"Do you have your own veterinary practice there?"

"I do. It's a small clinic with one other doctor, but we do well." There was a pause in their conversation and he continued to stare at her. His focused attention caused her insides to turn to mush so she racked her brain for something else to ask.

"So, Elijah has never owned a pet? Not even a fish?" He smiled at her question.

"Not even a fish. When we were kids, Leanne and I used to beg him for a pet. He said animals belonged in the wild, not kept in homes for people to gawk at and use for their own pleasure. Given his natural ability to use anyone that comes across his path to serve his purpose, I never could understand why he extended this supposed courtesy to animals."

She chuckled. "So that's the issue. Elijah views your career choice as an extension of your rebellion. Not only have you chosen a profession he can't relate to, but it also strongly goes against his principles." He rewarded her with his heart stopping smile.

"You know, I never actually thought about it that way. You're probably right."

"Do you have any pets now?"

"Not at this particular moment. I take on rescued pets, nurse them back to health, and find them a permanent home. Given my line of profession, it seemed like the right thing to do."

"Do you ever keep any of the animals?"

"No. But if I ever had one I couldn't place, I'd keep it. I guess I've never found one that was meant for me." He leaned forward, resting his elbows on his crossed knees, and reached out with a finger to gently push on her shoe. Her heart surged, and she internally scolded herself to get a grip. "What about you? Do you have any pets?"

"No. Growing up we always had a pet of some sort—dog, cat, fish. One of my brothers even had a guinea pig for awhile. But... well, Nick was allergic to just about every animal imaginable so we never had pets." Thankfully she didn't need to explain who Nick was. His expression told her he figured it out in a matter of seconds.

"How many siblings do you have?"

"I have three older brothers, no sisters."

"Three older brothers, ouch. Nick must have had nerves of steel." Surprisingly, her heart warmed at how casually he was able to mention Nick.

"Yes, well, Nick and I started dating in high school, and he was good friends with my youngest brother, so he sort of had it easy. My oldest brother, though, loved to make him nervous. I always told Nick that Tom was just messing with him but still, every time, he got flustered and made a blubbering idiot of himself. It was quite adorable." She looked down and studied her fingers as they played with her music player. It felt good to talk about Nick. She had spent so much effort avoiding it in fear of the pain it would cause, and she had not expected to feel comforted sharing personal experiences with someone she barely knew.

Marcus snatched her music player from her hands. "Let's see what kind of music you have on this thing."

"Hey, don't you know looking at someone's playlist is equivalent to reading their diary?" She tried to snatch it out of his hands but he pulled away.

"There once was a time when everyone displayed their music on CD towers for all to admire. It was a point of pride to show people your music collection."

"Yes, but you still had the option to put the more embarrassing CDs in the closet for no one to see. I can't hide anything on my playlist."

"It doesn't look like you have anything here to be ashamed of. It's a pretty admirable collection, actually. Very eclectic." He continued to scroll, and then he broke out into a hearty laugh. "Okay, I spoke too soon. You should be ashamed of this one. It can't even be called music." He showed her the offending song and she smiled, not at all ashamed of owning it.

"Admit it, when you hear that particular song it makes you want to move. I like listening to it when I run, it keeps me motivated."

"Only because it makes you want to outrun the sound of it." His criticism came out as a mumble while he continued to scroll through her playlist. He suddenly looked up at her and she was taken aback by the intensity in his eyes. However, in a blink his eyes were alight with mischief, and she wondered if it had happened at all. "Now this is a song that makes you want to move."

He hopped up and walked over to plug the player into the speaker. He pressed play and she smiled when she recognized the song. It was one of her favorites, and impulsively her foot began to tap out the quick beat. It was a current song, but it had an old big band sound. Her smile quickly faded when he reached down and pulled up on her hands. She shook her head in protest, understanding what he was about to do, but he pulled her to her feet anyway. She tried to at least hold on to her towel, but he threw it to the side of the room. Before she could protest any further, he twirled her out and back in. She stumbled over his feet trying her best to keep up. She thought she had an escape when she accidentally kicked him in the shin and he let go to rub out the pain. She backed away, but he quickly recovered and pulled her back in. Halfway through the song he started to sing along, and Sarah couldn't contain her laughter. He may be a great dancer, but he was an abominable singer. Near the end of the song he pulled her in close, cheek to cheek, and she felt her knees weaken. The music ended, but he continued to hold her to his chest. She was near panic, fearful that he might try to kiss her, and even more fearful she would let him.

"Ahem." She jumped at the sound of Elijah's voice from the doorway. She turned and tried to step away but Marcus planted his arm around her waist and held her tightly. She looked back and forth between father and son. They were glaring at each other with the classic Kingston look of death. She felt like she had been caught in the middle of a pissing contest.

"Elijah, you're back." She tried again to step away which only caused Marcus to tighten his hold. She decided to stop before he ruptured her spleen.

"What the hell are you doing here?" Marcus let out a sarcastic laugh at Elijah's question. "What's so funny?"

"Those are pretty much the exact words Sarah used to greet me." Elijah's face softened a fraction, and only for a second.

"Sarah, if you don't mind I'd like a word alone with my son." Marcus still wouldn't allow her to move, causing Elijah to finally look at her. He crossed his arms and raised his eyebrow. She pulled on Marcus' arm and looked at him, pleading with her eyes for him to let her go before Elijah erupted. Marcus narrowed his eyes at her but he removed his arm. She walked to the door, pausing in front of Elijah. She mouthed 'are you okay' and he gave her a stiff nod. She then mouthed 'be nice' and waited until he rolled his eyes in response before she stepped away.

"I'm going to go grab that shower. You boys play nice..." She looked from father to son and felt an eerie sensation at how much alike they were in that moment.

What the hell have I gotten myself into?

With a silent prayer they wouldn't do bodily harm to each other, she left the room.

Sarah was worried about leaving Marcus and Elijah alone for too long. She took a quick shower and dressed, skipping her make-up and hair to save time. She also hoped her plain look would keep Marcus' attentions at bay.

Although he sure didn't seem to mind flirting with me when I was drenched in sweat after my run. I couldn't possibly look much worse than that.

"Sarah." Her foot had just left the last step when Elijah called out from the office. She looked around the room and was relieved to find him alone. He waited for her to close the door before continuing. "Get him out of here." He pointed to the closed door.

"Elijah, I know this is a disaster, but I'm not sure what you expect me to do." He paced the length of the room. The lack of a conference table gave him a lot of ground to cover. He had developed a slight limp in the last week, but he refused to use a cane.

"I expect you to get rid of him. And Leanne can't show up here tomorrow."

"Did you ask him to leave?" She tried to keep her patience. He was becoming more difficult, but she reminded herself it was the CJD speaking.

"Yes, and he refused."

"So what makes you think he will listen to me? Your children are as stubborn as you are, Elijah. I don't know how I could possibly get rid of him. Or stop Leanne from coming."

"Well figure it out! That's your job damn it!" She closed her eyes and took a breath. She knew she shouldn't say it, but she felt the words cross her lips just the same.

"You know, there is an alternative. If you would just tell them—"

"NO! And you're not going to tell them either. Remember you signed an agreement promising me you wouldn't tell anyone."

"Lower your voice, Elijah. He's in the house, remember? If you don't want him to know then keep it down." She saw some of the air deflate out of him. "Elijah, seriously, I don't know what to do. I'll talk with him, but it would probably be a better use of our time to come up with a plan for how we should approach the weekend."

"Why did you let him in?"

"I didn't! He's your son. I assume he has the house code." His brows furrowed and he reached in his pocket to pull out a small notebook. He flipped it open and wrote something down before placing it back in his pocket. She had seen him with that notebook for a few weeks, but he wouldn't let her see it. "Elijah—"

"I can't do this, Sarah. Go figure it out. If he won't leave, I'll spend the entire weekend in here or in my room." The look on his face and his tone of voice told her there would be no budging him. She let out a sigh in defeat. He sat down at his desk and turned away from her. She had been dismissed.

She left the office and found Marcus in the family room reading the newspaper. She hesitated a moment to study him. Looking at him caused her to think about their playful dancing downstairs and she smiled at the thought. He really could be a lot of fun and very charming. Marcus looked over at her and set down his newspaper. She turned away and walked to the coffee maker, not wanting to acknowledge she had been observing him. It was mid-morning, and she usually didn't drink coffee so late, but she needed a jolt. She finished making her coffee and walked over to lean on the counter separating the kitchen from the family room.

"You can sit next to me. I promise to behave."

"It's probably no surprise, but Elijah has asked me to request that you leave." He laughed at her directness.

"No, it's not a surprise. I'm sure it's equally unsurprising that I'm not leaving."

"No, I know you well enough by now to know there's nothing I could do or say to make you leave." Her comment was met with that damn irresistible smile, and she tried to ignore the way it did funny stuff to her insides. "That wasn't meant to be a compliment."

He shook his head. "I didn't think it was."

"Then why do you look so pleased?"

"I like the idea that you know me so well after such a short period of time." She fought the mortification wanting to surface.

That is not the message I wanted to communicate. Damn it! He is so...
frustrating.

Before she could come up with a witty rebuttal the alarm on her
phone sounded. She rolled her eyes at the irritating object and fought
off the urge to ignore its command. However, given she had gone
well above her limit on her run she shouldn't skip her morning snack.
She walked to the refrigerator and grabbed one of her already
prepared snacks. She retrieved her food journal to log everything in
and pulled herself up on one of the counter stools. Before she could
take her first bite, Marcus rounded the counter to face her.

"What the hell is that?"

"I beg your pardon?"

"That." He pointed to her journal. "Is that a food journal?"

"I'm not sure how that's any of your concern."

What the hell? Why is he so pissed off all of a sudden?

"Damn it, Sarah, answer the question. Is that a food journal?"

"Yes, it's a food journal. What's the big deal?"

"What's the big deal? The big deal is you have no business trying
to lose weight!" The look on his face was one of utter shock and
disappointment.

She was completely confused. "What makes you think I'm trying
to lose weight? And even if I were, again—how is it any of your
concern?"

"Don't be ridiculous, of course it's my concern. Let me see that."
He reached for her journal but she pulled it away from him. He might
have gotten away with that move with her music player, but she
wasn't going to let him see her food journal. "Sarah, let me see it."

"No." Her anger began to build but it stopped as abruptly as it
began. Her voice of reason was loud and clear in her head.

His mom suffered from severe anorexia. Elijah said they believed it caused
damage to her heart, and that's why she died. Marcus is concerned. He sees an
underweight woman, cataloging her food, and it's natural he would fear you have
an eating disorder.

The sobering thoughts caused her to lighten her reaction. "Marcus,
I'm sorry, but my journal is private. But I will tell you I'm not trying
to lose weight; I'm trying to gain it. Based on your reaction I assume
you've noticed I'm... somewhat underweight. When we were
downstairs, I mentioned my running had gotten out of control after

the accident. In addition, I sort of forgot to eat most of the time. I've gained weight since being here, but I still have a long way to go. Elijah insisted I meet with a nutritionist, and that's why I'm journaling my food and workouts. I have to review it with her a few times a week." His stance relaxed, and a touch of embarrassment reached his face. She didn't want him to feel like he needed to explain his actions so she pushed the hummus in his direction. "I won't share my journal, but I'll share my food."

He gave her a half smile and scooped a cracker through the hummus. They ate in silence for a few minutes before Marcus spoke between bites. "So, my father was the one who insisted you see a nutritionist?"

"Yeah, and it annoyed me for about a second and then I realized it was a brilliant idea. Elijah's method of getting me to put on weight was to stuff me full of food. He's a great cook, but I constantly felt like I was going to explode." They returned to silence and he looked more thoughtful than he had a few minutes ago. She couldn't help but wonder what was going through his mind as she got up to clear away the mess. "So, you've not only interrupted the flow of our weekend, but now you've eaten all my hummus. Looks like I'd better make a list of what else we need to accommodate the extra visitors." She tried to ignore the way he watched her take inventory of the food in the kitchen. He answered her questions as to the food he and Leanne's family preferred. When she finished making her notes, she sat in the chair by the fireplace and organized the shopping list.

"So, I have to ask. What's exactly included in your job description? My understanding is you're here to manage my father's personal project endeavor, but from what I've observed you also seem to manage personal aspects of his life. Please don't tell me he went so far as to fire the cleaning staff and is making you clean this beast of a house along with all the shopping and cooking."

She looked up and waited for him to sit down before responding. "First of all, no he has not fired the cleaning staff. Thank God. Elijah actually does most of the cooking." She hesitated, almost blurting out that he didn't do it any longer, but then Marcus would ask why, and she wouldn't be able to tell him. "I help out with the shopping as thanks for him allowing me to stay here, rent free, and use his home."

"I suppose that makes sense." When he started picking at an

invisible piece of lint on his pant leg she had to restrain a laugh. She was certain he had no idea how much he was like Elijah. "Does my father intend to stay in his office all day?"

"Probably."

"What's going on in his office? I noticed most of the stuff was cleared out."

"He's having it remodeled." It technically wasn't a lie. She just wasn't going to tell him the new furniture would consist of a medical bed and toilet.

He nodded his head slowly, but he never looked up from that stubborn piece of invisible lint. "I noticed he has a slight limp. What happened?"

She studied him.

He's definitely fishing for information.

It was time to start piling on the lies and she hoped she could keep them all straight over the weekend. However, with her luck, Elijah would say something to contradict her story and negate her efforts completely.

"He slipped on some ice the other day. The doctor said it was just a slight twist, nothing serious."

He finally looked up at her and his scrutiny made her uncomfortable. She was confident he knew she was lying. "I'm surprised. He's commented several times over the last few years how the company does a remarkable job of not leaving any ice patches behind."

So that's how he's going to play it. He's letting me know the polite way he doesn't buy what I'm selling. I've never been any good at lying.

"I'm not sure." She made a show of checking her watch. "I'm sorry. I need to make a phone call." She grabbed her phone and walked through the dining room to the far side of the great room. She sat down by the fireplace and pulled up Tina's number.

"Hi, Sarah, what's up?"

"Marcus surprised us by showing up today and he's staying until Christmas Eve. Leanne and her family will be here tomorrow and intend to do the same." She tried to lower her voice, but the large house seemed built to carry sound.

"Oh, crap." She heard Tina repeat the information to Miles. "What can we do to help?"

"That's just it. I'm not sure. I was hoping you had some ideas." Sarah saw movement out of the corner of eye. The Christmas tree was obstructing her view, but she had a feeling Marcus was trying to listen. "You might want to consider bringing either an additional dessert or making something different to accommodate everyone."

"Uh...okay. I can do that. But what can we do to help with Elijah's situation?"

"Whatever you think is best."

Tina hesitated. "Oh, Marcus must be there and you can't talk. Sorry, I'm slow sometimes. Okay, I'll try to do this by asking you yes-no questions. Do you need help with this situation?"

"Yes."

"Is Elijah taking this bad?"

"Yes."

"Is Elijah present?" It had become their way of asking if Elijah knew what was going on in the moment or if he was confused.

"For now."

"Is Marcus suspicious?"

"Yes."

"Okay. I'll talk to Miles, and we'll come up with a plan. I'll send you a text and let you know when we can be there. It'll probably be tomorrow, but we can stay the night."

"That would be great. Thanks." After saying good-bye she hung up and pulled up Lisa's number. She decided to send her a text asking if he'd had his medication and what she should do to manage his moods over the weekend. Thankfully Lisa responded quickly saying she would send a medication schedule. With reinforcements secured, her mood lifted. She decided to go and check on Elijah before returning back to Marcus. He was looking at something on the computer but looked up when she walked over to his desk.

"Did Marcus leave?" While it was an unpleasant greeting, she took it as a positive sign because at least it meant he remembered what was going on.

"No, and he doesn't intend to leave until Christmas Eve."

"Then why are you here?"

"I wanted to check on you, see if you needed anything. Are you sure you won't come out and visit?"

"No I don't need anything, and no I won't visit." He turned his attention back to the computer. When she didn't move, he looked back at her. "Why are you still here?" With a sigh she left the room and walked back to Marcus. He was sitting in the same chair as when she left him, but she didn't think he had stayed put the entire time.

"Sorry about that. Tina and Miles are planning to come for dinner tomorrow so I wanted to let them know we would have extra company. I hope you don't mind they will be joining us for dinner?"

"No, not at all. I really am sorry if we messed up your plans for the weekend. I suppose the surprise visit might not have been such a good idea." For as many similarities she noticed between Marcus and Elijah, this was one area in which they were different. She could tell Marcus was genuinely sorry for the impact of his actions.

"There's nothing to worry about. We can all adapt. Well, except for Elijah apparently. He seems intent on acting as though you weren't here at all."

He shrugged his shoulders. "It's what we do." He averted his eyes and walked over to the fireplace to stoke the fire before sitting back down. She detected sadness behind his indifferent front. "So, how come you're here over the holidays and not visiting your family?"

She looked down at her fidgeting hands and stuck them between her tucked in legs. "I've always been close with my brother James, but the sad reality is I haven't been able to spend any time around him since the accident. He has twin boys about two years older than what Danny would have been. James is planning to be home for Christmas and I'm not ready to see them."

"Have you been around any children since the accident?"

"No, not directly. I've gotten to a point where I can handle seeing children out in public but I've not been able to interact with children that remind me of Danny. Until the weekend Oliver stayed here."

"What happened?"

"I had no idea Oliver even existed. When Tina and I got back from shopping, I heard Oliver coming around the corner and passed out cold. Miles carried me up to my room where I had intended to stay the entire weekend. However, Elijah asked me to try because he knew I wanted to see my nephews again. I made some progress each day, and by Sunday I was able to spend time in the same room with him. Later, in the middle of the night, I snuck into Elijah's room knowing they were both asleep. I knelt down by Oliver, and I placed my hand on his chest. I had a breakdown, which woke Elijah, and he comforted me. He talked me through it and helped me realize I missed being able to connect with children, especially those close to me. We talked until we fell asleep. The next morning is when Leanne walked in." She wasn't sure why she felt the need to explain that weekend, but now that she had she felt relieved.

He studied her for a few moments before turning his head and squeezing the back of his neck. Before he looked away, she could see a multitude of emotions fighting to surface through his mesmerizing eyes. Finally, he looked back. The winning emotion was frustration.

"Sorry, I have a hard time reconciling the Elijah you're describing with the father I know. I've never known him to show that kind of compassion to anyone, other than my mother. I'm trying to figure out why he would be that way with you when he has never shown that side of himself to me or Leanne."

She understood his disappointment and hoped her next words offered understanding. "When I first came out to interview for this job, Elijah mentioned he wanted to help me move on with my life. When I asked him why, he told me I reminded him of your mom and that he felt a need to protect me. As I mentioned earlier, I was much more underweight than I am now, and I was equivalent to a walking zombie. He recognized I was in danger of losing myself completely and offered to help me while I managed this project. He's been through the same kind of loss, and he knows he did things wrong, and he wanted to help me avoid those same mistakes."

He analyzed her every word. His face softened, but she knew he hadn't yet completely given in to the idea of Elijah being a compassionate person. "I could see it at the gala. What you said about protecting you. I could see he was genuinely concerned about you and your well-being. Still, I don't understand why he would show it to you and not to his children. Sure, you might remind him of my mother, but so do Leanne and I. I just don't get it."

"Maybe he's tried to show you some level of compassion, in his own way, but you haven't been willing to accept it or recognize it for what it's worth."

"I don't think so."

"Really? Okay, take your dancing. Elijah told me how important dancing was to you and that you hadn't danced since your mom died.

The stunt he pulled at the gala—it was frustrating and it was Elijah making decisions impacting both of us. However, you have to admit he helped. If he hadn't put you in that situation, would you have danced at all that night? Would we have danced downstairs just this morning? While I concur he mostly did it for his own personal needs, I believe he also did it to help you find your way back to dancing. He could have easily asked Leanne and Brad to do a dance in place of what we had planned."

He looked at her for a few moments before finally looking away. He looked uncomfortable and cleared his throat before speaking. "I guess I'm not very good at allowing him to help me. It doesn't happen often, so I don't know how to recognize it when it's right in front of me."

"You know, it's not too late to try to work it out with him. It only takes one person to make the effort. Elijah is a difficult man who's set in his ways, but you don't have to be just like him. You could continue to try until he finally opens up."

"I'm nothing like my father."

She couldn't stifle her chuckle. "Are you serious? You're much more alike than you think." When he raised his eyebrow at her she took it as a challenge. "Okay, well, there's your mutual propensity for thinking you know what's best for others and taking action without consultation. Aside from the dancing example we just talked about, the situation with Oliver is another good example. Sounds a lot like you deciding we all need to spend the weekend together without telling us. There's also your shared stubbornness. Elijah won't come out... you won't leave... Do I need to go on? I could outline your matching facial expressions and nervous tics."

He finally smiled and her stomach did a flip. "No, unfortunately your point has been made thank you very much."

"Are you sure? I—"

"Sarah." She looked at Elijah, surprised he was out of the office.

"Elijah, did you come to join us?"

"You left your—" He looked down at the phone in his hand. He was forgetting the simplest of words. "You left this in my office."

"Thanks." She took her phone from his outstretched hand and started to put it down on the table next to her.

"There's someone on the line. Someone named... Travis?"

"What? You answered my phone?"

"I thought it was mine."

She put the phone to her ear. "Travis?"

"Sarah, hi. Sorry if I'm calling at a bad time. I was surprised when Mr. Kingston answered your phone."

"Yeah, sorry. I left my phone in his office."

"And here I thought you pulled off some sort of Christmas miracle, turning the tables on Kingston and calling all the shots." She smiled at his teasing.

"Right, like that would ever happen. Can you hold on for a moment?" She covered the mouthpiece with her hand. "If you two will excuse me, I'll be right back." She looked at Elijah. "Why don't you have lunch while I'm on the phone? There are sandwiches made up in the fridge." She gave him her best don't challenge me look and he gave his right back. Finally, he sighed and turned toward Marcus.

"Can I get you a sandwich?" Elijah walked in the direction of the kitchen without waiting for an answer.

"Sounds great." Marcus got up and raised his eyebrow at her before following Elijah. She walked in the direction of the office and turned her attention back to Travis.

"Travis? Sorry about that."

"No problem. Did I call at a bad time?"

"No, its fine." Even though they had continued to correspond regularly over email, this was only the second time they had talked on the phone.

"Great." There was a long pause before he spoke again. "So, I hope you're not planning to work straight through Christmas."

"I'm hoping it won't be too bad. How about you? Will you get a chance to see your children?"

"Yes, I'm actually on my way to see them now. I just stopped for a quick break before I got back on the road."

"Well, I'm glad you get to see them. I assume all your Christmas shopping is done?"

Travis laughed. "Yes, as I mentioned in my emails shopping wasn't a fun experience. I had such a hard time shopping for Kate. I mean, ten year old girls are such an enigma to me. Sam was so much easier. Eight year old boys I get. Luckily I got it all worked out. I never did the Christmas shopping before. It was always my ex's thing. It seems like it should be simple—buy your kid a present and wrap it. I never realized it was much more difficult than that."

"I know what you mean. I found it equally difficult to do some of the things Nick had always done. I felt like a fool the first time I tried to start the lawn mower. The neighbor had to come and help—turns out it was out of gas. I gladly accepted Andy's advice after that to hire someone to mow it." Looking back, Sarah wished she would have continued to try and do the things Nick had always done. Relying on others to do everything for her allowed her to retreat into self-pity without distraction. She vowed to do things differently going forward.

Travis laughed and changed topics to things going on around the office. She looked at the clock on Elijah's desk and realized they had been talking for twenty minutes. She was enjoying their conversation, but she didn't want to leave Elijah alone with Marcus for too long. She had a sudden surge of panic.

What if Marcus starts asking him questions, like why he's limping? I need to get out there.

"Well, Travis, I hope you have a safe trip and a wonderful Christmas. I'm glad you called, but I should probably go."

"Oh, sure. I just wanted to wish you a Merry Christmas. I hope you have a peaceful day."

They said good-bye and she turned to leave the office, stopping as her eye caught sight of something on Elijah's desk. She pushed some papers aside and let out a groan. A credit card. She quickly brought his laptop to life, but Elijah had closed all the windows. She pocketed the card and walked out of the office, knowing she would need to address the issue with Miles. She walked into the kitchen to find Elijah sitting alone at the counter.

"Where's Marcus?" She wondered if he finally succeeded in getting him to leave.

Elijah looked up and for a moment she thought he might be lost. Clarity entered his eyes and he got up. "He went to get his bags."

"What did you two talk about?"

"He asked me questions. I told him to mind his own business." That wouldn't help set Marcus and Elijah in a direction of mending their relationship, but at least it meant he didn't contradict anything she had told Marcus earlier. "I'm going to go lie down." With that he left her standing alone in the kitchen.

CHAPTER 17

Sarah rolled over in her bed, listening to the faint sound of a shower. It was time to wake up, but her head hurt and her eye was twitching. Soon the house would be full of people and she prayed it would be as smooth as yesterday. Elijah had held to his threat and remained in his office or bedroom, leaving her to keep an eye on Marcus. They had spent the entire evening talking. He even asked about Nick and Danny. Surprisingly, she didn't mind and actually respected him for the way he'd asked the questions, making her feel comfortable in answering openly. She had been filled with a mixture of emotions. When spending time with Marcus, she didn't feel like someone who was missing two-thirds of her being.

The shower went off and it grew quiet. She felt herself drifting back to sleep when she heard a slam, causing her to bolt upright. At the second slam she was out of bed heading in the direction of Elijah's room. She found him in his bathroom, slamming cabinet drawers and doors.

"Elijah, what's wrong?"

"Where the hell is my... my... Where is it?" She assumed he was talking about his razor. It wasn't the first time he'd forgotten it was gone. Over the course of the previous week she and Lisa had removed things from his reach that could harm him, and he didn't like using the electric razor.

"If you're looking for your razor, you use an electric one now. It's right here." She picked it up, but he knocked it out of her hand.

"That damn thing isn't mine. And what are you doing in my bathroom?"

"You needed help, and that's what I'm here for." She picked up the electric razor again. "Elijah, this is your razor. You—"

"I said that's not mine!" He tried to grab it from her hand, but his coordination was off and he grabbed her wrist instead. He twisted it until she cried out.

"Elijah, stop!" He released her wrist but moved closer, his face just inches from hers.

"You took it, didn't you? What did you do with it?" It was the most aggressive he'd been so far. She reached out to put a hand on his shoulder, hoping the contact would calm him but it did just the opposite. He pushed her out of his way and she tripped over a towel, hitting her head on the opened closet door. The razor fell out of her hand and went scattering across the floor. By the time she struggled back to her feet, Marcus was in the bathroom.

"What the hell is going on in here?" His eyes scanned the mess on the floor and counter and then he looked from Sarah to Elijah, not sure of who to go to first. He settled on Sarah. "Are you okay?"

She rubbed the back of her head. "Yeah, I tripped and hit my head on the door. I'll be fine." Marcus didn't look convinced and turned his attention to Elijah. It was clear he was agitated and Marcus was suddenly on alert. He turned back to Sarah, eyes wide with alarm.

"Did he hit you?"

"No, Marcus, it's not like that. Like I said, I tripped on this—"

"Yes I pushed her! She doesn't belong in my bathroom!" Unfortunately, Elijah cut her off.

"What the *fuck*, Dad?" Marcus grabbed Elijah by the shirt collar. She quickly placed her hands on Marcus' shoulders to pull him off.

"Marcus, please. I can handle this. It's not what you think. *Please*, just wait outside." Marcus relaxed his grip but didn't let Elijah go.

"Get out!" Elijah pulled away and went back to opening and slamming drawers.

"Sarah, what the hell is going on around here?"

"Marcus, please. You need to leave. I can take care of this. Having both of us in here is making him more agitated. *Please*, I need you to trust me." The confused look on his face was enough to break her heart.

"But he pushed you, Sarah. This mess... I don't—"

"Why the hell are you still in my bathroom?"

The confusion on Marcus' face grew exponentially. "Why is he—"

She put her hands on either side of Marcus' face, not sure of what else to do to get his attention. "Leave. *Please.*"

Marcus let out a defeated sigh. "Fine, but I'm going to be right outside the door. If he touches you again, you won't be able to stop me." She walked him out of Elijah's room into the hall. He turned to protest again, but she closed the door and locked it. "Sarah! Why did you lock the door? Sarah!"

"I'll be fine, Marcus. I need you to wait out there. Please." She flinched when he hit the door. He protested a few seconds but finally gave up and grew quiet. She leaned her head against the door and realized she was shaking. She had lied to Marcus. She wasn't sure she could handle this particular outburst.

I need to think. Elijah doesn't know who I am and thinks I took his razor. His meds might calm him down, but how do I get him to take them? I can do this... I can do this...

She took a deep breath and walked back to deal with Elijah. He had his back to her and was rummaging through a drawer, throwing out whatever contents remained. He slammed it shut and looked up to see her through the mirror. "What are you doing in my bathroom?"

"I thought maybe I could help you. What are you looking for?" She watched him look around at the mess in the bathroom.

"My... my..." Even though he was still confused, she noticed most of his agitation had disappeared.

"Do you want to sit while I clean up? Maybe that will help me find what you're looking for." She stepped in his direction and reached to guide him by the arm but he pulled away, looking at her with alarm. She pulled her hands back and motioned toward the door. He walked out of the bathroom and sat down by the fireplace. "I'll bring you a glass of water."

She hurried back into the bathroom, relieved his mood had settled. She cleaned up the mess, hoping the extra time would continue to calm his mood. When the last item was put away, she retrieved his pills from the locked box in the closet and filled a paper cup with water.

"These pills should help make you feel better. Why don't you rest?"

He took the pills and then looked around his room a few times, as if he was trying to remember where he was. "I think I'll lie down." He got up and slowly walked to the bed. She wanted to follow him and tuck him in, but she was afraid she would agitate him again.

"I'll be downstairs if you need anything." She unlocked and opened the door, causing Marcus to almost fall into her arms. She shut the door and walked past him, intending to go to her room to change, but he grabbed her hand.

"We need to talk."

"Yes, I agree. Can I change first?"

"No." He led her down the stairs and to the kitchen. "I want to know what the hell is going on around here, Sarah, and don't tell me nothing."

"Marcus, I know the incident in the bathroom didn't look good. But really, it wasn't a big deal."

He erupted. "Not a big deal? He fucking *pushed* you, Sarah! How is that not a big deal?" He ran a frustrated hand through his hair and paced the floor. "It's clear something is wrong with him. He didn't know what he was looking for and blew up his bathroom in the process. And it's not only what happened upstairs. It's all the other stuff I've noticed. He's forgetting things—words, names, dates. And his behavior! I mean, he's always been an ass, but he's an even bigger one than normal. He's limping and I don't buy that shit about the ice." He stopped pacing in the middle of the kitchen and threw up his arms. "And where are the fucking knives? I came down here to cook breakfast and there's not a goddamn thing in this kitchen sharper than a butter knife! I want some answers and I want them now." She waited a few seconds to ensure his rant was over before responding.

"Elijah has been taking new medication. He has experienced mood changes and confusion. The doctor is trying to find a dosage that helps control the effects he's been experiencing." Her response was full of half truths. Nothing she said was a lie, but she tried to word it so Marcus would assume the medication was the cause of his problems rather than the treatment.

"Why is he taking medication and what is he taking?"

"He's been having difficulty with insomnia." Again, it was only a half truth.

"What is the medication he's taking?"

"I don't know."

"Where is it? I want to see the bottle."

"I can't do that."

"Can't or won't?" He crossed his arms over his chest and stared at her.

"Both, actually. It's not my place to give you information on Elijah's medical treatments. If I felt he was receiving poor medical treatment, I might feel differently. But his doctor is very competent and they're working through the finer points of the issues he's experiencing."

"Why is he limping?"

She looked away. She had already lied on that one and didn't see a way out of it. "I already gave you an explanation for that. I'm sorry if you don't like it. I don't have another answer prepared for you."

He leaned his hands on the counter and groaned in frustration. "You are giving me answers, but you are telling me nothing! Alright, let's try an easier question. Where are the knives?"

She hesitated. Showing him where the knives were would confirm something was wrong. She battled with herself internally for a few moments before finally moving her feet. She would honor the NDA and continue to tell half truths, but she was done with lying. She walked over to where Marcus was standing and stared at him.

"I need you to move if you want to know where the knives are." He slowly pushed off the counter and took a few steps back, eyes locked on her the entire time. She opened the drawer where he had been standing and pulled out a small object. She walked over to the overhead cabinet by the stove and placed the object on the outside of the door, activating the magnetic lock. She pulled open the door and stepped aside allowing Marcus access.

"What the hell?" He pulled things out—knives, slicers, scissors, matches—basically anything that could cause Elijah harm if he handled them in a confused state. She sat down on one of the counter stools and massaged her temples, wishing her headache would go away. She watched him inspect the contents of the cabinet and then shift his attention to the lock. He pulled the magnetic lock away from the outside of the door and put it back again, watching the latch open and close with the wonderment of a child. "I wondered why this cabinet wouldn't open. Sarah, why has my father's kitchen been child-proofed?"

"It's complicated."

"I can deal with complicated." He walked over and stood across the counter from her. The anger had left his voice, and in its place was concern and confusion.

Instead of answering him she got up to put everything back in the cabinet. She felt tears of frustration sting her eyes, and she fought to keep them from falling. After the last item was put away, she locked the cabinet and put the magnet back in the drawer. She leaned on the counter and buried her face in her hands, rubbing out the tears before facing Marcus.

"I decided to put all that stuff behind a locked cabinet for reasons I'm not at liberty to explain. I know it's not the answer you're looking for or one you're likely to accept, but it's all I've got at the moment."

"Does he have dementia?"

She looked away and choked back a sob. She knew she would be questioned on his condition, but she never expected it to be this hard to lie. She heard Marcus sigh and felt his hands on her shoulders, turning her into his chest. She let him hold her while she cried out her frustration before finally pulling away, rubbing at her face with the sleeve of her shirt.

"I'm sorry, Marcus, I can't tell you anything else." She felt him stiffen and he looked down at her.

"He made you sign one of his non-disclosure agreements, didn't he?" She nodded her head in response and looked down. He took her face in his hands, lifting it to look into her eyes, and wiped away her tears with his thumbs. "Hey, you know I would never let him sue you. Besides, it looks like you've become good friends with Tina so I don't think Miles would—wait, Miles must know what's going on." He looked at her for a few seconds in silence before pulling her back into a hug. For once she ignored her fear and instead of pulling away she put her arms around his waist and hugged him back.

"Marcus, can you help Brad with the bags—" Marcus turned and Sarah looked right into the angered eyes of Leanne. "Un-*fucking*-believable! Why is it every time I walk into this house I find you in the arms of either my father or my brother?" Leanne set the bags she was carrying down on the kitchen counter with a loud thump. Sarah tried to pull away but Marcus held on.

"Maybe that's what you get for barging in without knocking."

"Right. Did you knock? Didn't think so." She turned and looked directly at Sarah. "Why don't you just pick one already?"

"Leanne, knock it off. You're being unreasonable."

"I'm being unreasonable? No, what I am is apparently stupid. I actually believed you when you said you wanted to make up for the stuff at the gala. In reality you were looking for a way to get Sarah into your bed before Dad did. Oh wait, he already beat you to it." Sarah shook her head in anger and frustration. She was not in the mood to fight with Leanne, so she made a move to leave the room, but Marcus resisted her movement.

"Leanne, I said knock it off! Why don't you learn to ask questions before being a bitch? Sarah and I—"

"Merry Christmas, everyone. I see the weekend is off to a pleasant start?" Brad entered the kitchen, eyeing everyone with apprehension and holding a squirming Oliver. Fresh tears sprang to Sarah's eyes at the sight of them and the room suddenly became suffocating. She pulled on Marcus' arm.

"Please, I need to go to my room. *Now.*" He let her go in understanding and she quickly rushed up the stairs and shut herself into her room.

Sarah quietly watched Elijah's sleeping face. He looked so peaceful, and she wished it could remain that way for him. She already missed him. He was no longer the same Elijah she had come to know the first few weeks after she'd arrived. She pulled his blanket up and lightly touched the side of his face. She turned to leave and jumped when she saw Marcus standing near the door, watching her. Marcus closed Elijah's door as they left and before she could understand what was happening, he ushered her into her room.

She watched him look around, his eyes eventually settling on the photo she had of Nick and Danny on the desk. He studied it for a few seconds and turned his attention to her. "Are you okay?"

"Not really, but I intend to find a way to get through this. Seeing Brad holding Oliver, on top of everything this morning, was too much. The good news is I didn't pass out. I was able to make it up here all by myself without needing to be carried. That's progress I suppose."

"Well, if you need to be carried—at any time, for any reason—I'm happy to oblige. I understand Miles currently holds the responsibility, but I'll fight him for it." He smiled and she couldn't help but smile in return. He looked at his watch. "I don't think you've eaten anything yet this morning given all the drama followed by my unbecoming interrogation. Do you feel up to going downstairs, or would you rather I bring something to you?" She felt her heart beat faster. Everything he said, everything he did, had an impact on her. He didn't judge her, and more importantly he didn't pity her. He respected her and was trying to understand and support her.

She took a deep, steadying breath. "I'd like to go downstairs. I have to learn to get through these situations without hiding away in my room. But don't be offended if I suddenly run for the hills again."

"I'll only be offended if you don't let me run after you." She felt her face flush and she looked away. While she had reluctantly admitted to herself there was a connection between them, she couldn't understand how he could make such intimate comments after knowing her for only a short amount of time.

Maybe he's like this with all women. This must be his style and I'm reading more into it than necessary. I need to remember it's all just harmless, flirty banter.

"Come on." He opened the door and extended his hand. On impulse she took it and then tried to change her mind, but it was too late. He had locked their fingers together and wouldn't let go. He stopped before descending the stairs. "Seriously though, if it gets too much for you let me know and I'll understand." She nodded in agreement and followed him down the stairs. When they entered the dining room he still had a hold of her hand, and it didn't escape Leanne's notice. She looked at the two of them, rolled her eyes and went back to feeding Oliver. Brad rose from his seat in greeting.

"Hi, Sarah, can I get you a sandwich?"

"That'd be great, thanks." Brad quickly disappeared into the kitchen.

"Would you like to sit in here? My newly reformed sister has promised to be nice."

Sarah couldn't help but smile. "Well, since she's promised to be nice I suppose I can reciprocate." She looked down the table at Oliver before taking the seat Marcus pulled out for her. She was as far away from him as the table allowed, but he was in her direct line of sight.

"So, where's Dad?" Leanne didn't look up from her task of cutting up pieces of hot dog and putting them on Oliver's tray.

"He's upstairs resting."

"Dad doesn't do naps. What's up?"

"He wasn't feeling well this morning."

"I hope he's not contagious. The last thing I need is for Ollie to get sick."

Sarah snuck a glance at Marcus to see if he would keep quiet or resume his third degree questioning in front of Leanne. He was concentrating on his sandwich, slowly chewing the bite in his mouth.

Brad returned with a turkey sandwich and a welcomed but uncomfortable silence fell over the table. Halfway through her sandwich, Sarah looked up and her eyes unwillingly settled on Oliver. She watched him pick up a piece of hot dog and scoop it through the ketchup. He deposited the hot dog in his mouth and ran his hand through his hair, leaving a trail of ketchup along the way. He hit the tray a few times with his hands, laughing in delight, before repeating the messy process. Before she recognized what was happening, her mind was lost in a memory of Danny.

"Sarah?" Marcus' voice was soft, but it startled her just the same. She pulled her eyes away from Oliver and trained them on Marcus. She blinked a few times and realized she was crying. She wiped her face, looking around the table to find everyone but Oliver staring at her—she had the feeling she'd missed something.

"Sorry, flashback." There was no point in hiding the truth. There were enough lies and deception going on in the house. "Did I miss something?"

"Leanne was asking about the Christmas decorations. It looks wonderful, but it's different than the usual flair and we were wondering if Dad hired a new decorator this year."

"Oh, yeah. I actually hired someone recommended by Tina. She told me how the house was usually decorated and given... given how busy we'll be with his project this year I thought we should go with something a little less extravagant. It was my gift to Elijah."

Leanne turned to admire the decorations. "It's lovely. It reminds me a lot of how Mom used to decorate for Christmas before they started having those New Year's parties." Sarah decided to take Leanne's comment as a compliment. She rarely spoke any kind words to Sarah so she would take a compliment in any form they were given. The moment was interrupted by the sharp ring of the doorbell.

Oh thank God.

Sarah quickly jumped to her feet, almost causing her chair to topple backward. "I'll get it. It's probably Miles and Tina." Unfortunately, Marcus was right on her heels.

"I'll go with you." Leanne stared at them, mouth agape. As they left the room, she heard Brad say Leanne's name sharply and then Leanne's hushed but still audible response.

"What? They've known each other for all of five minutes and they're already inseparable. It's nauseating." Sarah shook off the insult and hurried to the door. She yanked open the door and instantly felt relief at the sight of Tina's smiling face.

"Hi, Sarah—" Tina moved forward to hand her one of the casserole dishes and froze, eyes looking past her. "Oh, hi, Marcus."

"Hello, Tina."

Sarah reached out and grabbed the dish from Tina and stepped out of the doorway when Miles walked up holding two small suitcases and an overnight bag. He walked into the foyer and Marcus immediately closed the distance between them.

"Miles. Looks like you'll be staying the night as well. I suppose we can put you in the office since all the rooms upstairs are taken. There's no conference table in there, so there's plenty of room for the air mattress." Marcus grabbed a suitcase and headed in the direction of the office before Miles could even respond. Miles raised his eyebrows in his wake.

"We might be awhile. I have a feeling Marcus has some things he wants to discuss. We'll find time to go over everything later today." He gave Sarah's shoulder a light squeeze and went to the office. Sarah turned to Tina and dropped her voice.

"I can't begin to explain how relieved I am that you're here. Thank you so much for coming early and spending the night. This morning was awful. It probably wouldn't have been so bad if Marcus hadn't been there, but he was and then he had all those questions I couldn't answer. I'm not doing a very good job of helping Elijah hide this."

"You're doing the best you can. It's getting to a point where Miles is going to have to make a decision on if he tells them now or in a few weeks. He's been quiet since you called this morning, contemplating what the right thing to do is given the circumstances. I think he wants to wait and see for himself how Elijah is doing. Where is Elijah by the way?"

"He's been sleeping all morning. I should probably wake him, but I'm afraid he'll still be confused. If he is, then it's best he stay away from everyone. Besides, he didn't sleep well last night. He hasn't had any episodes like the night of the gala, but he was up for awhile around three." Just then they heard Elijah descending the stairs.

"Sounds like he's awake. I'll put these away while you see how he's doing." Sarah handed the casserole dish back to Tina and turned toward the stairs.

Please, God, let him be present.

Elijah clumsily rounded the landing and paused when he saw Sarah. She held her breath, waiting to see if he recognized her.

"Did I hear the doorbell?"

"Yes, Miles and Tina just got here." She looked at him cautiously. She still had no indication of his mood or his state of mind. She wanted to ask him if he remembered who she was or what day it was, but those questions usually set him off into an explosion of frustration. She would have to wait it out.

"Were we expecting them?" She felt some of the tension slip from her shoulders. His response indicated that while he might not remember everything right now, he remembered who she was and that she belonged in his house.

"Yes, tomorrow is Christmas Eve and they're here for dinner. They decided to stay the night since Marcus and Leanne surprised us by doing the same." She watched confusion cross his face as he rubbed at his unshaven chin. "You should probably eat something. Do you want to join us in the dining room?"

"Do I have a choice?" She started to respond but he quieted her with a clumsy wave of his hand. "Lead the way." His walk was slower and his limp was getting more noticeable. She matched her pace to his, hoping to keep the change in his gait from appearing too obvious.

"Elijah. So glad you're feeling well enough to join us." Tina entered the dining room from the kitchen at the same time.

"Dad, what's wrong? You probably shouldn't get too close to Ollie if you don't know what you have. I can't afford for him to get sick right now." Elijah looked at Leanne with a complete lack of emotion.

"Hello to you too." Sarah looked at Leanne and was disappointed that she didn't look remotely embarrassed for her rude greeting. Elijah moved to the side of the table opposite Leanne and took a seat. "What's to eat?"

"There are sandwiches or I can heat up soup if you'd prefer." Sarah watched him in anticipation. Every one of her nerves was standing on end, anxious he would blow up at any moment. His eyes were darting around the length of the table, looking at nothing. They darted up at Sarah for a second before returning to the table.

"Soup." She went into the kitchen and heated a small bowl in the microwave. When she returned to the dining room Elijah was still sitting quietly, looking over every inch of the table. Leanne was distracted with Oliver, but Brad was watching him closely. Elijah's attention was finally in focus when she set the bowl in front of him. "Where's the—" He looked all around the bowl.

Shit, how did I forget the spoon?

It was when he forgot the simplest of words his condition was most vulnerable to recognition.

"Sorry, I forgot the spoon." Sarah spoke as quickly as she could, hoping it would sound like she cut him off rather than him forgetting the word. She returned with the spoon and then moved her plate so she could sit next to him. His movements were slow and occasionally jerky, but he was still capable of feeding himself without incident.

"Dad, you're not looking good. Maybe you should still be resting." Leanne looked over to Brad. "Maybe we shouldn't have come. We could do Christmas later in the week or next weekend when Dad's feeling better." Brad opened his mouth to respond but Elijah cut him off.

"I'm fine. No reason for Ollie to miss school and he'll want his presents." The confusion on Leanne's face was evident.

"Dad, Ollie wouldn't know any different if he got presents this weekend or next. And he doesn't go to school."

"Nonsense. Every kid wants presents. And school or whatever it is you call the place you take him every day."

"We have a nanny, Dad. Ollie has never been to daycare. You're not making any sense."

"Usually you're the one not making any sense." Marcus strode into the room and lightly whacked Leanne on the back of the head. Sarah studied his features, trying to gain any knowledge of how his conversation with Miles went, but they gave nothing away.

"Marcus, aren't we a little too old for that kind of shit?"

"Never." Marcus reached over and ruffled Oliver's head causing him to laugh. He pulled his hand back and made a face. "Jesus, sis. Can't you keep your kid clean?" He swiped Leanne's napkin and wiped away the ketchup from his hand.

"He's a toddler, Marcus. They make messes. You'd know that if you'd grow up and get yourself a family." Leanne suddenly turned her attention to Sarah. "That's not an invitation."

Sarah couldn't stop the involuntary laugh from escaping. "I didn't think it was."

"It's a good thing you're not the one to decide if she ever does get an invitation." Marcus reached his seat and looked over at Sarah. He paused a moment and then sat down to take a bite of his unfinished sandwich.

"What the hell is everyone talking about?" Elijah's voice boomed through the room that had grown quiet after Marcus' comment.

"Nothing." The response came in unison from everyone at the table.

"Hello, everyone. Sorry for my delay." Miles walked into the room and clapped his hands, rubbing them together.

"Miles, darling, your timing is impeccable as always." Tina accepted the kiss Miles planted on her cheek.

"Yes, well, they make you take a course on dramatic and timely entrances before they let you take the bar." He walked over and squeezed Elijah's shoulders. "How you doin' old man? Heard you weren't feeling well this morning."

"I'm fine."

"I see that. I'm glad. Got a few minutes? I wanted to go over some things from a call this morning." Elijah stood up, stumbled and almost fell back into the chair before Miles steadied him. Leanne was engrossed in cleaning up Oliver and didn't notice, however Brad and Marcus did. Miles and Elijah left the room and the only noise that remained was Oliver trying to resist Leanne's ministrations.

"I don't mean to be rude, but I need to make a trip to the store." Sarah stood, anxious to escape the house and tension for awhile.

"I'll go with you." Sarah paused and closed her eyes.

Wait for it...

"Are you two attached at the hip? If Dad weren't in the picture it might actually be endearing. But he is, so it's not. You know nothing about her, Marcus, yet you're acting like a whipped dog. I can't deal with this right now. I'm going up to give Ollie a bath."

...and there it is.

Sarah didn't look back. There was no reason for her to view the disapproval she knew would be on Leanne's face.

"Leanne, you promised." The frustration was growing in Marcus' voice.

"Yeah, well, I lasted through lunch. That's an accomplishment. Besides, if you can't take the criticism then don't act ridiculous." Sarah walked out of the room before she could hear any more of their conversation. She had her coat, hat and one boot on before Marcus caught up with her. He quickly slipped on his coat and shoes.

"Ready? I'm driving." Although he gave her a half smile, she could tell he was still annoyed by Leanne's comments. She didn't see a way out of it, so she resigned to her fate and followed him to his car.

Sarah stood with Miles in the office. Elijah had gone to bed, and everyone else was relaxing in the family room. Luckily the day had turned out to be uneventful with Elijah remaining quiet and detached from the group. His behavior fed the perception that he simply wasn't feeling well.

"I thought we should take this time to go over a few things. First, I'd like to fill you in on what I discovered on that credit card."

"Do you know how he got it?"

Miles shook his head. "No, I thought we had taken them all. It's a business card and he must have had it stashed away somewhere. It hadn't been used for over a year and my clerk either missed it or assumed it was no longer active. Regardless, the damage has already been done. He maxed it out and the limit was set at one hundred thousand dollars."

She let out a gasp. "Holy crap. What did he buy?"

"Random stuff—electronic equipment, appliances, clothes, jewelry." He twisted around to grab a paper off the desk and handed it to her. It was a listing of his purchases. "Most of the items are things he already has. I was able to cancel the items highlighted, which amounts to about half of the purchases. I'll have my assistant try to return what she can."

"What about the rest of it?"

"We'll donate it to charity or something."

"Have you been able to confirm if this was the last card?"

"Yes, but I thought that the last time and was wrong. So, as additional insurance I've locked his computer in the drawer and reset the password." He twisted again and handed her a key along with another piece of paper. "Here's the password and drawer key. I don't think you'll need it, but just in case. He might get frustrated when he can't find the computer. Now, the second thing we need to discuss is Marcus. He's digging pretty hard. Has he asked you any more questions?"

"No."

"Good. I made it clear he needed to address his questions to me from now on. I stuck to the story you gave him, which was good by the way, and blamed everything on insomnia and reactions to medications. I think he wants to believe it but is skeptical." He ran a hand across his face and pinched the bridge of his nose. He took a deep breath before continuing.

"I'm still not sure what I'll do. If there's another incident tomorrow like the one this morning, I'll tell them what's going on. If his behavior is like it was for the majority of the day today, then I want to give it a few days before I decide. I'm trying my best to honor Elijah's wishes. He doesn't want them to know until he's taken to the hospital. And that leads me to the final thing for us to discuss. I received a call from Dr. Holden today, right after I spoke with Marcus. As you know, he had an appointment yesterday morning." He pushed off the desk and walked over to the windows, looking out over the night sky. There was enough of a moon to cast a haunting glow over the snow covered mountains. "It doesn't look good, Sarah. Dr. Holden predicts he will start to decline rapidly over the next couple weeks."

He lowered his head and made a loud sniffing sound. She diverted her gaze to the fire burning low in the fireplace. Suddenly her body felt as if it was made of lead and her knees went weak. She stumbled to one of the chairs and fell into it.

"It's going to get difficult, Sarah. Once I tell Leanne and Marcus, I'm not sure how they'll react. They may be looking for someone to blame and Leanne has her claws intent on you already." She felt his hand on her shoulder. "I need you to know you can tell me if it gets to be too much. My loyalty is to protect Elijah's wishes, but one of those wishes was for me to look out for you. I won't let you bear the brunt of all their pain, but it might be hard for me to redirect it at times, and I want you to be prepared."

She knew she was stronger than she had been since the accident, but she also knew she wasn't fully healed. She would need to lean on God and have faith that He would give her the strength needed to not only get herself through what was to come, but to also help Elijah and his family.

The house was silent and dark with the only light coming from the Christmas tree. Sarah sat staring at the soft glow of the lights, her thoughts an agonizing mixture of emotions on everything from Elijah's condition to her feelings for Marcus to her pain of missing Nick and Danny. She reached out for her tea mug when she heard footsteps coming across the foyer. She wasn't sure of the exact time but knew it was after two in the morning. Leanne stepped into the room with a bag in hand. She got down on her knees and pulled presents out from the bag, placing them under the tree.

"You know Santa doesn't come until tomorrow night? Or I guess I should say tonight since it's after midnight." Leanne jumped at the sound of Sarah's voice and looked in her direction with wide eyes. "Sorry, I didn't mean to startle you but I didn't see a way out of it since you didn't notice I was here."

"Do you often sit in the dark?"

"Only when having difficulty sleeping and usually I'm left alone to my thoughts. I didn't expect anyone else to be up at this time." In reality she was surprised Elijah hadn't woken up, but he was sleeping soundly for the first time in a long time.

Leanne looked down at the present in her hand for a moment before putting it under the tree. She proceeded to do the same for the remaining presents before sitting in the adjacent chair.

"To answer your question, yes I know when Santa comes." Leanne was staring at the tree as she spoke. "My mom loved Christmas. She used to leave us a special gift to open on Christmas Eve. She never took credit for the gifts. She'd tell us a Christmas elf left them when he had come to make sure everything was ready for Santa. I decided to keep the tradition going." She turned her attention to Sarah. "Sorry, I didn't bring a gift for you. I'd like to say it was because I didn't know you'd be here, but we both know that would be a lie."

Despite the harsh meaning in Leanne's words Sarah felt herself smile. "I don't expect any gifts. And, thank you for your honesty. If it makes you feel any better, I didn't get you anything either."

"If you don't mind my asking, what has your mind so occupied?"

"Christmas is always a difficult time for me."

Leanne was quiet for a moment. "I know I've made it clear I don't trust your intentions around my family, and I'm not going to make apologies for that. But... I will say I can't imagine what you've been through. If anything were to ever happen to Brad or Ollie—" Sarah heard the hitch in her voice and understood what she was imagining. It was a phrase she had heard more often than she desired since the accident.

"Well, let's hope you never have to find out." Sarah took a sip of her tea and studied Leanne over the rim of her mug. "You know I'm not in a romantic relationship with your dad, right?"

She heard Leanne let out a deep sigh. "After observing the two of you closely—I would say yes, I know you're not in a romantic relationship. Yet."

"'Yet' doesn't apply to this situation, Leanne. Our relationship is one of friendship—now and in the future."

This time she heard a bitter laugh. "I see the way he looks at you, Sarah. And the way Marcus looks at you. My family is fragile enough without you taking the already too wide gap between my father and Marcus and turning it into the Grand Canyon. I'm not sure what it is about you, but somehow you've managed to bewitch both of them, and in the end one of them will be heartbroken and they will never speak to each other again. I'm not willing to sit by and watch that happen."

Sarah was starting to feel like a broken record. She wasn't able to convince Leanne there would never be more to her relationship with Elijah. The primary reason, the fact that he was dying, was something she couldn't share and every other way she had tried to explain had failed. She heard the words escape her mouth before she had given any thought to what she was about to say.

"You know my family died in a car accident. However, only my best friend and my parents know *why* they died in that accident. I'm not sure why I'm telling you, but I'm hoping it will help you understand the nature of my relationship with Elijah." She paused and took a deep breath. "My family should never have been in that intersection when the truck ran the light. They should have been at the restaurant, halfway through their meal. After the accident, that's all I could think about. Why weren't they at the restaurant? When the personal contents from the car were returned there was a present addressed to me. The accident occurred three days before my birthday. I suddenly knew it was the reason they were late that day. I felt so much guilt at being the cause behind their death. If they hadn't stopped for my present, they wouldn't have been in that exact intersection, at that exact time. I let guilt consume me and almost destroy me.

"I finally opened the box last month. It was a digital camera loaded with pictures of the two of them. That's why they were late, because they were taking pictures. A few months ago that knowledge would have destroyed me. But because of Elijah I'm able to see the gift I have truly been given. Elijah has given me something no one else has been able to even though they've tried. I don't fully understand myself how or why, but I choose to accept it for what it is. Because of this, Elijah will always be one of my dearest friends. He knows that's the extent of our relationship and has never given me any reason to think he wants something more."

Leanne remained quiet for a few minutes before responding. "And what about Marcus?"

Even though she was sure the darkness in the room concealed the blush she felt take over her face, she turned away from Leanne. "Marcus has not given me any indication he views me as anything other than some random female."

"Oh, please. You may not know Marcus as well as you *claim* to know my father, but anyone with eyes can recognize he turns into Pepé le Pew around you. He's going to give you his heart, and if you throw it right back in his face then *he* will be broken. So do us all a favor—if you're not able to reciprocate then don't just tell him but stay away from him as well." With that Leanne stood up. "It's my responsibility to protect my family, and I'm keeping an eye on you. It's been nice talking to you—and I actually mean it this time." Without another word she turned and left the room.

CHAPTER 18

Sarah woke with a sharp pain in her neck. She had fallen asleep in the chair after talking with Leanne. The house was quiet, and she knew it was early based on the soft light drifting into the room. She stood and turned to pick up her tea mug to take to the kitchen, but it was gone. She hadn't remembered taking it to the sink before she fell asleep. Too tired to worry about the mystery of the mug, she wrapped the blanket around her shoulders and shuffled toward the steps. She couldn't have slept more than a couple hours and knew she should resume a more comfortable sleep in her bed. However, by the time she reached her room her mind was racing as fast as it had been the night before.

There was only one thing that could possibly help her. She went to the closet and changed into her running clothes. Remembering there was a house full of people, she put on a tank top and one of her longer pair of shorts. She searched the room for her music player and finally remembered it was in the dance studio.

She quietly made her way to the basement door to discover the light to the stairwell was on, as well as a light from one of the rooms. Descending the stairs, she could hear music and in an instant knew Marcus was in the dance studio. She should have turned and left, but it was as if her body was caught in a gravitational pull in the direction of the music. The doors to the studio were open and she saw him as soon as she rounded the corner.

She recognized the song as one from her playlist. It was the same artist as the song they had playfully danced to, but this one was slow and soft. It was about a man who was in love with someone he didn't know and he needed to find her. It was a song of both desperation and loneliness—the desperation of trying to find her and the loneliness when he can't. The movement Marcus added to the music expressed those feelings perfectly, bringing the music to life. She didn't know what style of dance it was; all she knew was it was one of the most beautiful things she had witnessed. The song ended and he quietly walked around the dance floor, practicing a few of the steps she had just watched him complete.

Without the dancing to hold her attention she quickly became distracted by his appearance. He was wearing only a pair of shorts and he had what she considered the perfect amount of muscle definition. It was obvious he worked out to stay fit, but he wasn't one of those bodybuilder types. She was intrigued by a text tattoo on his left side. She normally wasn't fond of tattoos, but something about it felt right on Marcus. She continued to watch him until her thoughts began to shift to a dangerous direction. She rubbed at her eyes and contemplated what to do. She could easily turn and go back upstairs without him ever knowing she had been there. But something deep inside of her made her feet move in the direction of the studio.

"Sorry, I didn't mean to bother you. I came down for a run and heard the music. I know I should've left but I couldn't take my eyes off you. That was beautiful." She felt her face flush and diverted her gaze. "Anyway, it didn't seem right to not let you know I was here. I just wanted to let you know that was amazing. I'll just go now." She turned to leave, feeling awkward by the end of her rambling.

"Would you mind staying and watching it one more time? I thought about adding a few variations, and I'd like your opinion."

"I'd be happy to, but I don't really know anything about dancing."

He smiled at her. "You know enough." He turned to start the music and she entered the studio, sitting down on the floor to the left of the doorway. She leaned back against the wall and watched him begin the dance all over again. She did catch some of the changes, but she was so mesmerized by his movements that all she could do was feel the emotions of the song. It wasn't until it was over that she realized a tear had escaped her eye. She quickly wiped it away, not wanting Marcus to think she was nothing more than an emotional hazard. He looked over at her and raised his eyebrow in a very Elijah-like manner.

"I thought it was just as amazing as the first one I saw. I told you I don't know enough to help." He smiled and walked over to his shirt lying on the floor. He picked it up and ran it over his sweaty head.

"You could help me in another way. I actually envisioned the dance with two people. You could dance with me."

She felt all the blood drain from her face. "No, no way. I can't dance like that and I would ruin it."

"I'd teach you."

She shook her head quickly and started to rise to her feet. Her emotional state was too unbalanced to be able to survive dancing with him at that moment. The dance was nothing like the innocent playful dancing they had done a couple days ago. If he pulled her into the sensual movements she just watched, she would completely lose herself and that was something she couldn't risk.

"No, I'm sorry. I can't." He must have recognized the near panic in her voice because he quickly reached her side.

"I'm sorry, Sarah. Please, stay. I won't make you dance. Can we just sit and talk? We're both up at this unfortunate hour, so we may as well keep each other company." She nodded her head and sat back down. "So, you really liked the dance?"

She studied his features as he sat across from her. She noticed uncertainty in his eyes, and she knew he either had no idea how talented he was or he didn't trust it.

"Marcus, as I said, I don't know anything about dancing. My exposure to dancing before coming out here was my prom and weddings, and those mostly consisted of people moving in drunken chaotic spasms. I do know how to do the sprinkler and the lawn mower, but beyond that I'm hopeless. At least I now know one formal dance. What I watched you do was breathtaking. The way you made me feel the emotions of the song gave me chills. If you are able to do that, after not dancing at all for twenty years, then the amount of talent you have is staggering." His head was down in what she figured was thoughtful consideration of her words. When he raised his head, the uncertainty was gone and in its place was the playful smile she had begun to adore.

"The sprinkler and the lawn mower? Really—I have to see those. Please, *please* show me." By the end of the sentence he was laughing and she was laughing right along with him.

"No way, those only make an appearance at weddings. Sometimes at the occasional house party if the mood is right." Her eyes grazed over his bare chest and her laughter trailed off. He caught her looking and she quickly averted her eyes in embarrassment.

"I'll have to remember that." She turned her attention back to him as he pulled his shirt over his head. Once his shirt was in place she nodded in the direction of his tattoo.

"If you don't mind my asking, what does your tattoo say?" Instinctively he ran his hand over his shirt where the tattoo was located before pulling it up and shifting so she could read the words.

Everything needed to truly love someone can be learned through dance. Faith, trust, endurance, pain, joy, humility, surrender, commitment, patience. If you want to be able to love someone the way they deserve to be loved, keep dancing.

She took a deep breath and leaned back against the wall. "Is that a quote from something?"

He gave a sad smile and shook his head while lowering his shirt. "It was the last piece of advice my mom gave me before she died."

She contemplated the words forever etched on Marcus' side. "But you stopped dancing."

"I know my mom would have wanted me to keep dancing after she died, but I couldn't. Her words continued to haunt me over the years, and I finally decided to get this tattoo. I had hoped it might get me back on the dance floor, but I never felt ready. And she was right—when I took dancing out of my life I also took away my ability and willingness to love. Eventually it got to a point where getting back out there terrified me. It wasn't until I danced with you at the gala that I knew I could never stop dancing again."

"What about the people who don't dance? How are they supposed to find love?"

"It's not really about dancing. It's about being yourself and embracing every part of who you are. I'm a dancer so I put everything I have into it. That's the point. That's what my mom wanted me to understand about love. That if you want it, you have to give it everything you've got and take everything it gives you back."

"And what if you have nothing left to give?"

"There's always something left to give. It may not be as much as it was before, but there's always something." They grew quiet, both knowing their conversation had taken a turn away from hypothetical situations. "What do you say we help each other learn to dance again?"

"You already know how to dance."

He shook his head and his eyes grew somber. "Not really. It's been twenty years after all." She suddenly wondered if there was more to his story and maybe twenty years ago he had lost more than his mother and dancing. Almost as quickly as the humor left his expression, it returned. "Besides, I've heard the best way to learn something is to teach it to someone else. I can teach you contemporary and you can teach me drunken chaotic dance." She couldn't resist smiling at his jest.

"I don't know. I'm not sure I'm ready for dancing again. I think you've depleted all my reserves."

"Okay, I'll make a deal with you. We will not dance again until our third date." She felt a chill run down her spine, chased by an electrifying heat.

"That would imply we would have a first and second date."

"Yes, it would. That's a perfect segue to something I wanted to ask you. My friends are hosting a New Year's Eve party and I should make an appearance. I was hoping you would go with me. There would be dancing at the party—not the kind of dancing at the gala, but probably closer to the drunken chaotic spasms you mentioned—and so that would have to be our third date. In that case, we could have dinner the Friday before and then on Saturday or Sunday we could have our second date." Everything came out in a rush.

She thought it was possible she was in shock. She opened her mouth to speak but instead of words coming out her world tilted on its axis and the room wobbled. She closed her eyes and took a series of deep breaths. When she opened her eyes again everything was steady. Marcus was watching her with dawning realization she was going to reject him.

"Marcus, I can't—"

"Surely my father would give you the weekend off. He can't make you work through the holidays without a break."

"It's not that. I'm not ready, Marcus. Besides, I haven't been on a date with anyone other than Nick since I was a teenager, so even if I were ready I wouldn't know how to go on a date."

"No dates at all? Not even with that Travis guy?"

What? How does he know about Travis?

She suddenly remembered Elijah answering her phone when Travis called and mentioning who it was in front of Marcus. "No, no dates at all. Not even with Travis." His spirits seemed to pick back up.

"We could start off easy, do lunch instead of dinner. Or we could meet for a drink. Really, it wouldn't be much different than our casual dance studio meetings and our trip to the store. We don't even have to call it a date. I just want to get you away from the negative vibe of my family, enjoy your company in a relaxed environment, and see if I can get you to smile the way you did for that Travis guy. I've given some of my best attempts since I saw it and can only assume I've failed because of the very watchful and critical eye of family."

"You've made me smile. And laugh."

"Not like that. I came close, a few minutes ago when I asked you to teach me your dance moves, but it still wasn't the same."

"Since I can't see my face when I smile, you'll have to give me more information."

"When you were on the phone with that Travis guy, he created a smile that lit up your entire face—especially your eyes. All the smiles I have been able to coax out of you have been more reserved, more guarded."

She understood and knew he was right. She may not be able to see her own smile, but she could feel it. She *was* more relaxed with Travis, but it didn't have anything to do with Elijah or Leanne.

"It's not your family, Marcus. It's because you make me nervous and comfortable at the same time. And that scares me." She knew her directness could be shocking for some, but Marcus seemed encouraged by it.

"Come on, just one date. I won't commit you to all three. We'll take it one at a time."

"I don't know—"

"You could even establish the boundaries for our relationship."

Now it's a relationship?

She took in a deep breath and held it to steady her mind before she allowed it to spin out of control.

Of course it's a relationship. Everything is a relationship, what matters is what kind it is. Boundaries would help me keep control.

"There would have to be a lot of boundaries."

"As long as we can periodically review and reset those boundaries, then I can live with as many as you need."

She almost agreed to lunch when Miles' words from last night came ringing into her head. Things were about to get bad with Elijah. She'd been up most of the night trying to forget them, yet in just a few minutes with Marcus she had forgotten completely. Leanne's warning came close behind reminding her to stay away from Marcus if she wasn't sure she could return his feelings. This wasn't the time for her to experiment with her ability to date.

"I'm not sure it's a good idea, Marcus. When the project is over I go back to Indiana."

"What if you had a reason to stay?"

What? He can't be saying what I think he's saying. We've only known each other a week. I can't uproot my entire life and move for a relationship I'm not even sure I want with a guy I don't even know. Real life doesn't work that way. Not for someone who is whole and certainly not for someone who is as broken as I am.

"It's too much right now, Marcus. I'm sorry. I can't give you anything more than what we have right now." He nodded his head, shoulders sagging in defeat.

"Can I at least get your contact information? We could email and talk on the phone. Become better friends and when you're ready we can have that date. It could be here in Colorado if it's before you leave or out in Indiana if it's after you're gone. There has to be something fun to do in Indiana."

"Marcus—"

"Come on, that's not asking for too much. That Travis guy obviously has your phone number and I assume he has your email information also."

"Okay, let me set the record straight—'that Travis guy' is renting my house and is a close friend of my boss. I have talked to him exactly twice on the phone."

"That smile told me there was more between you two than that."

She shrugged her shoulders and crossed her arms over her chest.

"He emails me, frequently. I don't know, I suppose he's an *almost* friend. I've never met him in person, so I don't think I can even call him a friend. Friends know the color of their friend's hair. So no, he's not even a friend." It wasn't lost on her, or probably Marcus either, that her level of defensiveness grew with each passing word.

"Okay, so I should definitely have your contact information. You know the color of my hair *and* we have danced together four times. That has to at least put us in the friend category, and friends have each other's contact information." The playful smile had returned to his face and she rolled her eyes in response.

"Maybe. I'll think about it."

"I'll remind you." Her stomach let out a loud and embarrassing growl. Her reaction turned quickly from embarrassment to admiration when Marcus patted his own stomach. "But right now I'm hungry. Want to help me make breakfast?" He stood and extended his hand to help her. He held on to her hand a few seconds, looking into her eyes, before letting go to get her music player. He handed it back to her and slowly ran his thumb down the length of her finger, causing her to lose clarity. "As we discussed in the car yesterday, you should use your phone when you run outside."

"And, as I mentioned in the car yesterday, my phone is rather dumb based on today's standards. It only has extra intellect for taking pictures and checking email, but not for playing music. You see what I run in." She made a sweeping motion down the front of her clothes. "Where in the world would I put a phone *and* a music player?"

"I liked what you wore the last time you ran." He winked at her and left the studio, leaving her at a loss for rebuttal.

If I'm going to have any chance at successfully staying away from this man, I need to find a way to stop the touching and the flirting.

Lost in thought, she followed Marcus up the stairs. Once in the kitchen, they realized it was just before seven and the house was still asleep. Out of habit, she went directly for the coffee maker.

"Do you drink coffee?" She wasn't sure how she could have been in the same house with him for almost forty-eight hours and not know if he drank coffee.

"No, I never could acquire a taste for it." She smiled internally at his response.

Good, now he has two negatives—he can't sing and he doesn't drink coffee. I knew he couldn't be as perfect as my starving female hormones were leading me to believe.

When the coffee was done she took a long sip, letting it burn her mouth slightly. Just as she was about to ask Marcus what he would like for breakfast Tina entered the kitchen, stifling a yawn.

"Good morning, Tina. Miles still asleep?"

"Morning. No, Elijah needed to talk with him so they booted me out." Sarah tried to read her features for any clue as to why Elijah and Miles were talking, but she gave nothing away.

"Would you like me to make you a cup of coffee?"

"I'll get it. You rave so much about this contraption, and I'm dying to get my hands on it." They froze for a fraction of a second at Tina's casual reference to death, feeling the impact of Elijah's rapidly progressing illness. Tina regained her momentum quickly and Sarah was convinced Marcus hadn't noticed a thing. Tina made her way over to Sarah's side and stopped before grabbing a coffee mug. "You look like shit."

"Tina! That's an awful thing to say and completely false." Tina turned her scrutiny on Marcus.

"She might look like a ray of angelic sunshine to you at all times, but I call it like I see it. She looks like shit. So do you by the way. Were you two up all night or something?" Her eyes suddenly grew wide, darting back and forth between Sarah and Marcus. "*Were* you two up all night?"

"Tina!" This time the scolding came from both in unison.

"What? As I said, I call it like I see it and you can't blame me for asking."

"I was up most of the night, but not for reasons you're insinuating. I can't speak for Marcus."

"I was up most of the night as well. I wish for the reasons you're insinuating." Sarah choked on her coffee, causing her eyes to water with pain.

"I'm going to take a shower." She gave Tina the evil eye at her traitorous laughter and strode out of the room. It wasn't until she got into the shower that she realized she had forgotten about her run. She also realized that after spending time with Marcus she no longer felt the need. Her head was telling her to add this to her growing list of reasons to stay away from him. She didn't want to depend on someone to provide her with a sense of comfort. She knew it was dangerous to place her happiness in the hands of a person who could at any moment be ripped from her life. As she stood under the hot water, letting it wash away what remained of her fatigue, she wasn't sure if her head would be able to convince what remained of her heart.

Sarah put the last dish away in the cabinet. The events of the day flashed across her mind and she smiled wider. She turned to Tina, who was smiling as well. It had turned out to be a great day. Not only had Elijah been more present than he'd been for weeks, but he was in a decent mood. It was truly a Christmas miracle. She was grateful his family would have fond memories of their last Christmas together and that she had her friend back, even if only for the one day. They jumped when a sudden profanity erupted from the other room.

"Everything okay in there, dear?" Tina's voice didn't hold an ounce of concern.

"Yep, didn't need that toe anyway." Miles' response was a half groan half yell. Miles, Brad and Marcus were in the great room rearranging furniture around the Christmas tree under the command of Elijah. Based on all the bickering they heard during the process, Sarah was surprised there weren't any other mishaps. The pair turned to join the men and encountered Marcus walking in their direction. He scrutinized Sarah and stopped her as she walked past, leaning to whisper in her ear.

"There's that smile again. Should I be jealous of Tina now too?"

Despite her best attempt to resist, she leaned in to whisper back. "I'm just feeling very happy at the moment. It's not because of anything Tina said or did, but because I have enjoyed this day." Before she could step away he put his hands on her hips and pulled her closer.

"Well then, I'm very glad to have been a part of it. Hopefully, it will continue to get better." She closed her eyes and breathed in the scent of him.

I really need to stop allowing myself to be put in these situations.

She reluctantly pulled away and went to join the others. Elijah was standing in the entryway and she put her hand on his arm.

"Sarah. Ready to open gifts?"

"I'm ready to watch all of you." Sarah didn't expect anything. She and Tina had exchanged gifts before the gala, and she planned to give Elijah his after everyone left. He gave her a smile and placed a hand on her back, guiding her to a couch.

"Have a seat." She sat down and expected him to sit next to her, but he continued to stand. "Are we about ready?"

"Let me see if Leanne is almost done." Brad bounded out of the room in the direction of the stairs as Marcus entered the room and stood next to Elijah.

"Have a seat, Marcus. We'll start when your sister gets back." Elijah was pointing to the space on the couch next to Sarah. Marcus and Sarah looked at each other in surprise and then over at Elijah. Marcus sat down without hesitation. Elijah gave Sarah's shoulder a gentle squeeze and then sat on the couch adjacent to her. She couldn't shake the feeling Elijah had given her and Marcus some sort of acknowledgement.

Tina and Miles sat down on the same couch as Elijah, and Brad sat on the remaining couch while Leanne took to the floor with Oliver. Oliver had finally lost his shyness after spending so much time in everyone's company. He squirmed away from Leanne and ran to Marcus, grabbing his legs. He reached over and tugged on Sarah's pant leg with his chubby hand and she tensed considerably at the contact. It took every ounce of strength she had not to jerk her leg away. Marcus sensed her anxiety and quickly scooped Oliver up to take him back to Leanne. He grabbed a present from under the tree to keep him occupied.

"Marcus, don't give him that." Leanne tried to retrieve it from Oliver's hands, but he proved to be surprisingly strong.

"Leanne, it's one of the gifts from me. He can open it."

"But we have a process—"

"Leanne. Let him open it." Everyone turned their attention to Elijah. His face held his classic 'don't argue with me' look. Elijah turned his attention to Marcus and gave him a slight nod. Sarah could tell the acknowledgement was significant for Marcus. He stood straighter and squared his shoulders with confidence while returning to his seat. Leanne let go of the present and Oliver began tearing into the wrapping paper. It was a truck, and he immediately started pushing it around the floor while it was still in the box. He got frustrated and took it to Brad.

"Uk, uk." He pounded impatiently on the box while Brad opened it. Once it was out of the box, he was back on the floor pushing it around and pressing all the buttons he could find. A lump formed in Sarah's throat and her vision clouded as she watched him play. Before a single tear could escape, she felt Marcus grab her hand and she instinctively leaned into him. The contact helped soothe her anxiety and her clarity returned.

Leanne pulled out the presents she had put under the tree the night before. She handed one each to Brad, Elijah, and Marcus before sitting down to hand one to Oliver. They opened the gifts in turn and sounded like a normal family. Marcus let go of her hand to open his and reached for her again once he was done. Brad got up and handed a present to Leanne, which she accepted with feigned surprise. Once the gift was opened and gushed over, Leanne pulled out the remainder of the presents and placed them in front of Oliver, except for four which she looked over critically. Sarah recognized one of them as her gift for Elijah. Before she could tell her to leave it under the tree, Leanne handed it to Elijah and the remaining three to her. Sarah couldn't hide her surprise and turned to Elijah who was whispering with Miles. Elijah cleared his throat and focused his attention on Sarah.

"The top two are from me."

"You didn't have to get me anything. We can open them tomorrow—"

"No, I'd like you to open them now." He picked up the present Leanne handed him and held it up to his face. He pulled it closer and then pushed it farther away, trying to read the label. "Looks like this one is from you."

"What's the matter, Elijah, refusing to get reading glasses in your old age?" Brad laughed in playful jest. Only half the room understood his vision was failing as a result of CJD rather than old age.

"Something like that." Elijah rubbed his eyes. "Sarah, why don't you open the small square one first?"

She pulled her hand from Marcus and unwrapped the present. The box within looked like a jewelry box and she felt Marcus stiffen next to her. She opened the lid and let out a small gasp. Inside was a circular pendant with a smooth aquamarine stone in the center. She lifted it and noticed the stone rotated freely around a post. She disentangled the chain from the holder and brought the necklace out for closer inspection. It was beautiful.

"You had mentioned it was your favorite color. Also, you're always fidgeting with things. Thought this might be better than your scarves and napkins." Already her fingers were spinning the stone in slow back and forth motions.

"Here, let me." Marcus took the necklace from her hands and opened the clasp. It was the perfect length for her to wear under most of her shirts. The thoughtfulness of the gift caused unshed tears to sting her eyes.

"Thank you. It's perfect." She wanted to go over and give him a hug but felt it might make everyone uncomfortable.

Screw it.

She got up and not only gave him a hug, but a peck on the cheek. "Thank you, really." She sat back down while staring at the pendant. Her trance was broken by the sound of Leanne's bitter voice.

"Open yours, Dad."

Sarah watched with anticipation as Elijah opened his gift. He pulled out the small album and opened it to the first page, which displayed a close-up image of Elijah holding Oliver. He studied each page in detail, and when he reached the last page she could see tears in his eyes. He blinked them back and cleared his throat. He opened his mouth to speak but instead just nodded his head.

"Do you mind sharing with the rest of us? Based on your reaction it seems like Sarah was able to find you the perfect gift." Elijah handed the album to Leanne without hesitation. Leanne's expression changed from one of annoyance to one of confusion to one of appreciation. "I assume these were taken the weekend Ollie was here." She closed the book and handed it to Brad. "Can I get a copy of the photos?"

When Elijah dies you will have that whole album.

It wasn't something she could voice out loud so she simply told her yes.

"Sarah, before you open the other gift from me, why don't you open the mystery gift. Who's it from?" Sarah looked over the present but the tag only had her name in handwriting she didn't recognize.

"It doesn't say." She felt Marcus shift next to her.

"It's from me." The unexpectedness of Marcus' response caused her heart to beat a little faster. She held onto the package, not daring to open it. "Go ahead. It's not going to bite you."

"But I didn't get you anything."

"By opening and accepting this gift you will be giving me something in return." The confusion must have been clear on her face because Marcus laughed. "Just open it. You'll understand."

Sarah removed the wrapping paper and the image on the outside of the box caused her mouth to drop open in a very unflattering way. Still in disbelief, she opened the box to see if the contents matched the image.

"You bought me a phone?"

"Well, an intelligent woman can't go around with such a dumb phone. Besides, like I said, you should run with a phone." He took the phone from her hands and turned it on. "See, look, you can sync your playlist. I loaded some additional songs I thought you might like. And I downloaded a running app that uses GPS—it tracks how far you run, how fast, all that stuff. You can access your email; you just need to set it up. I wasn't sure if you liked to read, but I downloaded a reading app anyway. I didn't load any games, but you can do that if you want. I put the number under my plan. I already have unlimited talk and text so there wasn't much of an incremental charge. I wrote the number down and it's in the box, along with my password in case you want to download any other apps." He stopped talking abruptly when he realized everyone was watching him closely. A slight blush rose up his neck and she felt a sudden urge to rescue him.

"If you really wanted me to run with my phone, a new armband would have been sufficient. So that can only mean you bought this as a means to have my phone number, which I was probably going to give you anyway. You didn't have to buy me an entire phone." A slow smile spread across his face.

"Well, then I should just take this back." His playful tone matched hers and he halfheartedly reached for the phone.

"No way. This is very cool, and I'm already attached to it. But I'm not letting you carry me on your plan."

"Sarah, I already told you, there's no real incremental cost."

"No real incremental cost means there's still a cost." Realizing they didn't need to argue about it in front of everyone, she let it go for the moment. "Did you get this when we went to the store?" He had left her for about thirty minutes when they'd arrived at the store, stating he needed to find something. He nodded his head. "Thank you, Marcus. This was incredibly thoughtful of you." She leaned into him in a form of a hug, and he put his arm around her. He took hold of the phone with his free hand and touched a few icons to access the contact list. There was one name listed and her heart skipped about five beats before resuming normal function. She looked back at him, and he gave her a wink.

"As touching as this little display is, why don't you open your last gift? We need to be taking off soon so we can get Ollie home and in bed at a decent time."

Sarah refused to let Leanne's return to bitterness spoil her good mood. She set down the phone and picked up the last gift. She opened it to discover an envelope. The contents, on top of the two gifts she'd already received, was enough to send her emotions out of control. She felt the tears escape her eyes and she let them fall freely.

"Elijah, I can't—"

"Yes you can, and you will. You have about an hour to pack before Thompson picks you up."

"No, you don't understand. I don't think I can do this." Suddenly Elijah was in front of her. With his limp and coordination issues she wasn't sure how he managed to get to her and down on his knees so quickly. He took her face in his hands and forced her to look at him.

"Yes you can. Sarah, look over there." He nodded in the direction of Oliver. "You've spent the entire weekend in the same room with Ollie. You can do this. You want to see your brother and nephews and this is the time to do it." Sarah took her eyes from Oliver and landed them back on Elijah.

"You continue to be the only one who believes I can do these things."

"And I'm always right, aren't I?" Sarah laughed between sobs and nodded her head. He was always right. It was her fear that held her back and it was time to face that fear head on. If she couldn't go home and face her family, she didn't know how she would be able to face watching Elijah die. She had to try. "Don't be like me, Sarah. Don't hide away from your family until it's too late. The flight leaves tonight and you return the day after Christmas. It's a short trip. You *can* do this." She looked over to Miles and Tina who both nodded their head in approval, letting her know they would be there to take care of Elijah while she was gone. She set everything she was holding down and leaned in to give Elijah a monstrous hug.

"Thank you." She pulled back and wiped the tears from her face. "One hour? I'd better get packing."

"I'll help you." Tina stood and extended her hand.

Sarah switched off her phone per the instructions of the flight attendant. She pulled out her new phone and confirmed it was also turned off. It looked so fragile compared to her dinosaur phone. She searched out a safe place for it then tucked her purse under the seat in front of her. She leaned her head back, closing her eyes. She was so tired she felt dizzy. Her mind drifted to the hour before she left the house with Thompson. Thinking back to the emotional good-byes, she felt like she was leaving forever rather than a two-day trip. Tina had remained quiet through most of their packing. When the final bag had been zipped closed, Tina had taken Sarah's hands and sat down on the bed with her. Tina's words continued to haunt her.

"Miles wanted me to tell you this is not just a trip home to see your family. This is also your escape clause. If you feel like it would be too much for you to return and see this thing through, no one will fault you for it. You have to think of your health first, Sarah. We all love you and want what's best for you. If you need to stay home, it's more than okay."

After saying those words, Tina had pulled her into a hug and left the room without waiting for any kind of response. Seconds later Elijah had entered without knocking. He'd told her Miles had reminded him of everything they had planned and that it was all Elijah's idea. They had made all the arrangements in early November. He confirmed everything Tina had said, telling her she was free to stay home if she felt she couldn't return. However, the look he gave her told her he believed she had the strength to face it all. She'd pulled him into a hug and told him she was scared. He hugged her back and his response caused a fresh round of tears.

"So am I, Sarah."

Their embrace had been broken up by a light knock on the door.

Elijah left the room and Marcus entered. He paced for a few seconds before he finally turned to her, holding out the new phone she'd left downstairs. He'd asked if he could call her. She'd given his request thoughtful consideration and told him he could. They had stood in her room, both clearly feeling a mountain of emotions, yet not sure of what they should do. He had suddenly closed the distance between them and took her into a hug that spoke of desperation. His words had been whispered and full of emotion.

"When will I see you again?"

His question still caused shivers to run down her spine. Not because she feared seeing him again but because the next time would be when he found out about Elijah, and she wasn't sure how he would feel about her keeping something so important from him.

She was pulled from her thoughts when the man sitting behind her let out a loud snort. She opened her eyes and tried to adjust to the dim cabin lighting.

Will I go back?

She hadn't thought about leaving since the day she'd overheard Elijah and Lisa talking. Now she couldn't stop thinking about it. A part of her wanted desperately to return to her home and be surrounded by all the familiar things she'd shared with Nick and Danny. Another part of her was terrified of going back to the way things were before she'd started this journey with Elijah. The final part of her knew she would feel an extreme amount of guilt for leaving Elijah before the end. She hoped the time away would give her the clarity she needed.

The man behind her continued to snore loudly but she was so tired, both physically and emotionally, it didn't stop her from drifting off to sleep.

CHAPTER 19

"Mommy, Daddy, hurrrry uuuup!"

Sarah was pulled from her fitful sleep at the sound of her nephews barreling down the stairs. Everyone had been asleep when she arrived, so she'd quietly let herself into the house and crashed on the sofa. Now it was Christmas morning and she was about to see her family, some of them for the first time in two years.

"Josh, look, Santa came!"

"Look at that BIG one, Jack! That one's for me."

"No way, it's—" The boys halted their frantic movements toward the presents when Sarah sat up. They both stared at her with wide eyes and open mouths. A lump formed in the back of her throat at how much they had grown in two years.

"Boys, wait for Gram and Gramps. You know you can't open anything until we're all down..." Juliet stopped behind the boys and her words trailed off. "Sarah?"

"Hi Juliet, Merry Christmas."

"Oh, God, Sarah! James! James!" Juliet rushed her, nearly knocking her boys over in the process. Sarah rose just as she crashed into her. "You're here, you're really here."

She was nearly a foot shorter than Sarah but she was solid and the force of her hug almost caused Sarah to fall back onto the couch. When Juliet pulled away, it was obvious that the toll of raising two rambunctious boys had taken a few years off her usually youthful features.

"Juliet, what's wrong?" The sound of James' voice floating down the stairs caused Sarah to tremble. She knew she missed her brother desperately, but she didn't realize how much staying away from him had affected her until she'd heard his voice. "Boys, what's going on?"

"Daddy, who's Mommy hugging and why are they crying?" Sarah looked over Juliet's shoulder to see James enter the room and turn his attention to the pointing finger of Jack.

"Sarah?" It came out as a whispered croak. The only response Sarah could manage was a nod of her head. He quickly closed the distance between them, his hug even more crushing than his wife's. He kissed her forehead and pulled her into a more manageable hug. "Oh, Sarah, I swear if I didn't miss you so much I would be mad at you right now." They held each other silently, trying to make up for the lost years.

"What's all the commotion about?" James continued to hug her, neither addressing their mother's question. "James?" Finally James moved to the side, keeping one arm around Sarah and wiping the tears from his eyes with his free hand.

"Look who Santa left under the tree." Their mother shrieked in delight and clasped her hands to her mouth.

"Sarah! You didn't tell me you were coming." She made her way across the room and looked her over. "Oh, honey. You look great. Really, really great."

"Um, can we all stop crying now and open presents?"

"Joshua Thomas. If you're going to start acting like presents are the most important part of Christmas, then we're going to return all of your gifts. Your Aunt Sarah is here, and right now that's more important than any present under the tree." Josh mumbled something in Jack's ear in response to Juliet's scolding.

"You boys remember your Aunt Sarah?" James walked back over to the twins and put an arm around each of their shoulders. The boys looked from James to Sarah.

"Sort of. Is she still sad?"

"I'm still a little sad, but not as much as I was before. I'm working on being happy again."

"Is Uncle Nick and Danny still in Heaven?"

Sarah felt her throat tighten but she was able to croak out a response. "Yeah, they're still in Heaven."

Jack looked thoughtful for a moment. "Presents make me happy. Maybe Santa left something to make you happy too."

"But not that big one though, that's for me."

"No it's not, Josh, it's for me!"

"Alright boys, that's enough. You'll find out soon who that big one's for. Besides, I think it's for me." The boys turned and tackled James to the floor, all three arguing over who was going to claim the present. Sarah's dad walked in at that moment and the whole process of hugs and tears repeated once more. Sarah wasn't sure if it was everything going on with Elijah's condition or if it was seeing the strained relationship he had with his children, but something made her hug her dad harder and longer than usual.

She finally pulled away and her mom nodded in the direction of the kitchen. Knowing their destination was coffee, she gladly followed. She pulled out mugs while her mom went to work on the coffee maker. She turned around and found her mom staring at her.

"You really do look good, Sarah. You've gained weight, I can tell. You've got some color back in your cheeks, and those damn circles are almost gone. But mostly, your eyes, they—" Her mom stopped short and buried her face in her hands. Sarah walked over and hugged her again, pulling away once the sobs had subsided.

"Thanks, Mom. I am better. Taking this project was really good for me. You were right. I needed to get away for awhile." Sarah couldn't help but wonder if she would look just as good in a few weeks or if she would return back to the shell that was her former self after Elijah's death.

"Well, I'm glad. I wasn't sure if this project was going to be a good idea. That Mr. Kingston fellow seems to work his employees rather strenuously. I remember all those stories you used to share about him at your office. I only hope that once the distraction of the work is over you can keep making progress."

"I hope so too."

"So, what made you decide to come?"

"It was Elijah's idea actually. He—"

"Elijah?"

"Um, Mr. Kingston. We've been spending so much time together on the project we dropped the formalities soon after I got there. Anyway, Elijah bought me the plane tickets as a Christmas bonus. I didn't know I was coming until late yesterday when we opened presents with his family."

"You spent Christmas Eve with his family?" Sarah noticed her mom's features were starting to cloud with scrutiny.

"Yeah, well, it was casual. They didn't want me to spend the holiday alone. Besides, Elijah's lawyer and his wife were there also. They're all friends."

Her mom's scrutiny became more targeted and Sarah felt a sudden urge to tell her everything. Some outside perspective might help her determine what to do. However, her instincts told her to keep quiet, knowing her mom wasn't the one to talk to about her situation.

She wouldn't be objective and she'd just worry about me even more.

Finally, her mom nodded and turned back to the task of making coffee.

"Well, that was very nice of them. And I'm grateful he sent you home. How long are you staying?"

"My return flight leaves tomorrow afternoon."

Her mom turned back to face her with disappointment in her eyes. "So soon? It seems such a waste to come all this way for just one day."

"I know, but we're at a critical point in the project and I really should get back as soon as possible."

Her mom nodded and turned back to the coffee. "Well, at least you're here today. And thankfully Tom and Peter are planning to come by later. It will be so wonderful to have all you kids here together. It's been far too long." Sarah could hear the pain in her mom's voice and she suddenly acknowledged how much her suffering had affected more than herself. While she was ostracizing herself from the world, her family was suffering from a loss as well. Sure they also missed Nick and Danny, but Sarah's actions had caused them to lose her as well.

"I'm sorry it took me so long to come home."

"Oh, it's no worry. You made it home in time for—" Suddenly her mom understood what Sarah was actually saying. Her words and her movements stopped for a few beats and when she spoke again her words were quiet and heavy with emotion. "You made it home. That's what's important."

Once the coffee and presents had been distributed, Sarah settled on the couch next to James. He instantly put his arm around her shoulders, pulling her closer to him, and she was happy to enjoy the comfort and safety of being near her brother. Jack and Josh were staring anxiously at Juliet, waiting for the cue to begin the process of shredding wrapping paper. The instant she gave her approval paper went flying.

Sarah watched and smiled at their exclamations of excitement over toys and even managed a giggle when they quickly tossed any clothes off to the side. She closed her eyes and pictured Danny sitting right alongside his cousins. She wondered if he would have been like a gentle breeze, taking his time opening and observing each gift before moving on to the next, or if he would have been like a tornado, ripping everything open and then going back to sort through the damage. She settled on the former, deciding he was such a carbon copy of his father he would have made an enjoyable process out of gift giving and receiving.

"You okay?" The sound of James' voice pulled her back to reality.

"Yeah, just dreaming about how things might have been."

James nodded and looked out at the boys before turning his attention back to her. "That's cool." She felt James lift her necklace, not even realizing her hands had found it.

"Thanks. It was a gift from my boss. He noticed I was always fidgeting with things. It's quite addictive."

"That was thoughtful of Andy."

"Andy? Oh, no, I meant Elijah. The guy I'm managing a project for out in Colorado." Sarah looked past James and noticed she hadn't kept her response quiet enough to keep her mom from overhearing. Her expression turned hard and Sarah looked away, uncomfortable under her mom's magnifying glass.

"Hum. That's a pretty nice gift from some guy you barely know. Typically a guy doesn't buy a woman a rock of any kind unless he knows her pretty well, or unless he wants to get to know her better."

Ugh, not James too.

Sarah was about to respond when the boys hurtled the mound of toys on the floor and landed on James' legs.

"Time for the big one, time for the big one!"

"Alright, let's see who this big monster is for." James made a production over checking for the tag. "Ah, here it is. It's for... Josh." The room laughed at Josh pumping his arm up and down in triumph while Jack dropped into a pouting heap on the floor. "Oh, wait. It's also for Jack." The laughter grew when the boys traded reactions, almost exactly. "Clear a spot on the floor for it boys, it's getting heavy and I need to put it down." The twins bulldozed toys and boxes and paper in all directions, clearing an adequate space in the middle of the floor. The boys tore at the paper as though they hadn't just spent the previous thirty minutes doing the same thing. A plain brown box lay beneath, and they worked together to find a way to open it. They dove into the packing peanuts, arms flying fast and furious. After about ten seconds of frantic digging, they sat back with confusion and disappointment.

"Dad, is this another one of your jokes?" Josh looked like he was near tears.

"There's something in there, I promise. Keep digging." They let out a synchronized sigh and began digging again, albeit at a much slower pace. Finally, Jack pulled out a single sheet of paper.

"It's a picture of a play set."

"Congratulations. You found it."

"Are we getting a new play set?"

"No, the one you already have is fine. Instead of putting a gift in there your mom and I decided to spend the money on a new play set for the shelter in town. And as a reward for your generosity of forfeiting your gift, we'll take you out for a pizza and movie night."

"But, I thought—" Josh's lip started to quiver and he was unable to finish his sentence.

"You thought you were going to have a gigantic new toy?" Both boys nodded their head in agreement. "Look around you boys." James paused long enough for the twins to survey all the presents they had already opened. "I think you've been very blessed indeed. It's appropriate for you to give back to others who don't have as much as you do. Now—" James stood and clapped his hands. "Let's get this room cleaned up before Gram gets my hide." Once the room was cleared of the mess and the boys were back to being satisfied with the gifts they'd received, James sat back down next to Sarah.

"That was kind of mean. You could've handed them the paper rather than making them think they had a present in the box." Sarah expected her brother's playful banter in return. Instead his features grew serious.

"Then the lesson would have been lost. I've learned these last two years it's important to know how to recover from life's many disappointments. I think it's important I start teaching them this now. Hopefully, they will never have any significant loss to deal with in their lifetime, but we both know that's not how it works. If they start learning the lesson now, hopefully they will be prepared later." Sarah hadn't anticipated his words. All she could do in response was lean into him for support.

Sarah opened the door to her childhood bedroom and stepped inside for the first time in over a year. Nothing in the room resembled her childhood life. One of the many side effects of living in a family of architects—the house was always changing. She scanned the room, taking in the recent changes, and realized it was the room where the twins were sleeping. She walked slowly to one of the beds and ran her hand over the Batman pajamas. She picked up the shirt and held it to her nose, taking in the little boy scent. She felt her control start to unravel so she folded the pajamas and placed them on the end of the bed. She turned to the other bed and her eyes fell on something that pulled the pins right out of her knees. She picked it up and curled into a ball, rocking slowly back and forth. She remained that way for an indeterminate amount of time, thinking about all she lost and all she wanted back. Eventually, there was a soft knock on the door. Instinctively she knew it was James.

"Sarah?" He waited and when she didn't respond he sat down on the opposite bed. "You want to talk about it?"

"I'd forgotten we got the twins each one of these the same Christmas we got one for Danny." Sarah looked down at the stuffed dog identical to Danny's Max. "This is how I had spent the entire day on Christmas in the past. Also on Halloween...and Danny's birthday... Just like this—curled up in a ball on the bed or on the floor of Danny's room while clinging to Max. I thought I had finally gotten past this point, but when I saw this dog it all came flooding back." The sobs started all over again and James sat there, not saying a word. "I... th-thought... I was... p-past... this. How... how... am I... e-ever... going... to... to m-make it?" Sarah felt the bed shift and James pulled her into a hug. He held her until her sobs subsided, gently rocking her back and forth and stroking her hair.

"You know, just because you slipped doesn't mean you've completely fallen down. You've made significant progress, Sarah. You have to know that. Even though we haven't had a chance to talk about it, I can tell. I mean, you're here, right? You haven't talked to me, in any capacity, since a few days after the funeral. But here you are—here *we* are. This is significant. So you came in here and had the wind knocked out of you by a toy that reminded you of Danny. That's not failure. It's a natural and understandable bump in the course of your healing." Sarah tilted her head back so she could see his face.

"I know you're my wise older brother, but how do you know so much about recovery?"

"Do you remember when I quit smoking? I'm trying to compare the loss of your family to my loss of a bad addiction, but recovery is recovery. The challenges are the same—they're just more difficult in situations such as yours. Anyway, when I was going through the process of quitting I encountered lots of bumps. Some days I would buy a pack just to throw it in the trash on the way out the door. Other times I would make it to the car and put one in my mouth before getting back out and throwing them away. A few times I even lit up and took a drag before I tossed them. Each time I thought I had wasted all the progress I'd made and it was just a matter of time before I was back to a pack a day. It was Juliet who helped me realize a bump didn't have to be a mountain if I didn't want it to be. Eventually the bumps got fewer and less severe. That was fifteen years ago, and I still get cravings. It will never fully go away, I just had to learn how to make it over the bumps, even recognize when they were coming, and make it through the best I could without turning it into failure. Just as you will never stop missing Nick and Danny. You just have to learn how to manage the bumps."

Manage the bumps.

She liked the logic of that.

"So, I'm curious—if you don't mind my asking—what prompted you to come home? How did you make it past this particular bump?"

Before she could even think to stop herself, she had told him everything. The only details she left out were her private interactions with Marcus. She wasn't ready to fully acknowledge the situation to herself let alone talk to someone else about it. When she was done talking, she was amazed at how she could physically feel the weight of the burden being lifted from her shoulders.

"I believe in my heart I've done the right thing by going out there, but I'm not sure if it's healthy for me to go back."

James remained so quiet and still she had to shift to make sure she hadn't put him to sleep. He was awake, staring straight ahead—his gaze burning a hole in the wall across the room. He stood and paced the room.

"You know, this is the kind of thing you should have talked to me about *before* you accepted the job." There wasn't anger in his voice, only concern.

"Had I been talking to you, I probably would have."

"I have to admit it all sounds suspicious. Some man you barely know presents you with a job offer, at twice your salary, and requires you to live with him for an indeterminate amount of time while helping him through his death—all because you remind him of his late wife and he wants to help you?"

"Why does it matter what his motives are? He's dying. *Very* soon. He's significantly richer than me and I don't have a cure for his disease, so unless you can think of another reason he would deceive me, I don't see why there's a need to be concerned over his motives."

"There's reason to be concerned if those motives involve him having feelings for you that go beyond platonic."

She studied him closely as he continued to pace the floor. "James, first of all, he has never made a pass at me or given me any reason to suspect he wants more. And again, he's *dying*." She put heavy emphasis on the last word, trying to make her point.

"That's my concern exactly. He's created an environment in which you have come to depend on him entirely. By the sounds of it, it's an environment mostly isolated from the outside world and full of intimacies between the two of you. It might not be romantic in an obvious way, but it seems to me it's the perfect way to get someone who's vulnerable and starving for affection to become dangerously attached. What happens when he dies?"

He had a point and she understood the danger of her situation. "I know it sounds like he's forcing me to rely on only him, but really he's teaching me to rely on myself. Through the process, I realized I also need to rely on God. That's where I'm putting my faith, not on Elijah. He's giving me the tools and the courage to use them. That's all. I've come to understand even if the people I care about leave my life, I still have God and myself. I let go of both before and now I know that's not an option for survival."

He gave her an encouraging smile. "Then I suppose you have your answer. If you know you have to hold strong to God and yourself, then you'll be fine regardless of your decision. However, I know you, and if you don't go back I'm not sure you'll get over the guilt of leaving him in his darkest hour."

It was what she'd needed to hear. She knew she would go back. She just needed some form of validation from someone she trusted. It was one of the things she missed most now that Nick was gone—the simple act of voicing out her thoughts with someone she trusted.

"I want you to promise me something though. When the time comes, when Elijah's about to die, you'll call me. I'm coming out to support you through it."

"James, that's not necessary—"

"It's not up for debate, Sarah. You need someone you can lean on through this. It sounds like his children might not take it well when they learn you've kept this a secret. While you've become friends with the lawyer guy and his wife, I don't know them and so I don't trust them. And if you don't keep me informed I'll tell Mom the entire story. She already thinks Elijah is taking advantage of her baby. Giving you tickets home is understandable, but that expensive looking rock hanging around your neck set off her alarm. You keep me informed, and I'll keep Mom at bay. Besides, I just got you back so I'm hell bent on making up for the last couple years. Let me be your big brother again."

There was really only one choice so she nodded in agreement.

"Good. Now that we have that all settled I'll let you finish getting ready. Tom and Peter should be here soon." He walked over to pull her up from the bed and gave her another hug, the Max look-alike squished between them. He pulled it out of her hands. "Can I put this back down or do I need to take it with me?"

"You can put it back on the bed. I'm feeling much better now." He flashed a proud smile then suddenly turned serious again.

"I'm sorry I gave up on you, kid."

"You didn't—"

"Yes, I did. When you wouldn't respond to my emails or calls, I thought what you needed was space and time. I should have known while you did need those things, you also needed to know I was still there. I should have kept trying and I'm sorry I didn't. I won't make that mistake again." He left her with a kiss on her head that warmed her heart. She entered the bathroom and studied her reflection in the mirror, feeling proud of her accomplishments. She had crossed off two more things on her list.

Spend one of the holidays outside of bed
See my brother and nephews

CHAPTER 20

Sarah's head snapped up at the abrupt stop of the car. She was exhausted and couldn't remain awake for the duration of the ride back to Elijah's house. Thompson put the car into park and got out, going straight to the trunk to retrieve her bags.

"Thank you, Mr. Thompson. I can take it from here." Thompson handed over her bags with a slight nod before returning to the driver's seat. She walked toward the house and wondered what she would walk into. The trip had been quick and full of emotions and as a result she had forgotten to turn on her phone. She had a short text correspondence with Tina at the airport but there was no hint as to how things were going with Elijah. She punched in the house code to open the door, but nothing happened. She took off her glove, thinking she had entered it incorrectly, and punched in the code a second time. Still the door didn't unlock. Confused, she rang the doorbell and waited for someone to let her in.

"Sarah! You're back. We weren't sure what time you'd be here with the delay." Tina grabbed her bag off the porch and stepped aside.

"Sorry to ring the bell, but the code wouldn't work."

"Oh, right. We forgot to tell you. Elijah changed it."

"When did he do that?"

"We're not exactly sure, either sometime late on Christmas Eve, after everyone left, or early the next morning. The good news is he wrote down the new code." Tina ran her free hand across her forehead. Sarah couldn't help but notice how disjointed she seemed. Looking at her closely, Sarah thought it was possible she hadn't slept at all in the time she was gone.

"Tina, what's happened?"

Tina hesitated and looked around the foyer. "I'll let Miles and Ms. Reynolds fill you in."

"Ms. Reynolds is here?"

"She moved in yesterday."

"I thought she wasn't going to move in for another week or two?"

Tina shifted the bag she was holding from one hand to the other. "Well, things got complicated and we all thought it would be best for her to move in now." She turned at the sound of footsteps coming from the great room. "There's Miles. I'll let him tell you what's been going on. I'll take your bags to your room." Before Sarah could protest, she had grabbed the bags and hurried off in the direction of the stairs.

"Sarah, I'm so glad you decided to come back. I hope you had a pleasant visit with your family." Miles gave her a welcoming hug.

"It was a very nice visit and long overdue." Sarah noticed he looked as bad as Tina. She felt her concern grow rapidly. "Miles, what's going on with Elijah? Is he okay?"

"Take off your coat and boots and we'll talk in the kitchen." She complied and followed him through the house. She glanced around as they went, looking for Elijah or any clue as to what had happened while she was gone.

"Miles, please, I'm starting to worry. What's going on and where's Elijah?"

"Elijah's in the office, or I should say his new bedroom, with Ms. Reynolds." She waited for him to continue and when he didn't she grew impatient.

"Miles, tell me what happened while I was gone."

He let out a defeated sigh and sat down on one of the counter stools. "It started early on Christmas morning, around three. It was awful, Sarah. I know we need to expect this and it will keep happening and he will keep getting worse, but we weren't ready."

She walked over and stood across the counter from him. "I need to know what happened, Miles."

"Tina heard him first and woke me up. He was yelling and screaming. The only thing we could make out was your name. I told Tina to stay in the room and I went to try and calm him. He didn't recognize me and thought I was a monster. It was the kind of moment that should have been funny, but it was terrifying. When I entered his room he screamed and threw a lamp at me. I went over to him and he recoiled, yelling over and over 'where's Sarah, what did you do with Sarah' and calling me a monster. I couldn't do anything to calm him, not even the music worked. Tina eventually came down but I sent her away and told her to call Ms. Reynolds and find out what we should do. We didn't have what we needed in the house so she came and gave him a shot to calm him down."

She instantly regretted her decision to leave.

The trip was good for me and helped me heal, but it caused nothing but trauma and confusion for Elijah.

As if reading her thoughts, Miles reached out and covered her hand with his.

"It wasn't your fault, Sarah. Your leaving didn't cause the delusion. He may have reacted the same way even if you were here." He gave her hand a final squeeze before letting go. "As a result of the episode, Ms. Reynolds decided to move in early. She also called to expedite the medical bed and it arrived this morning, so as of today Elijah is officially moved into the office."

"What else are you not telling me?"

He let out a deep sigh. "He wouldn't eat yesterday or let us do anything to help him. Not even with his... personal needs. Every time we tried to help he did something to prevent it. Ms. Reynolds had to keep him sedated, and he spent most of the day in a near comatose state. I hated it, but it was the only way we could help him."

"How is he today?"

"Still delusional, but the medication is keeping him sedated so the aggression is manageable."

"Is he still asking for me?"

"He—"

"Mrs. Mitchell. Welcome back." Sarah looked up to see Lisa enter the kitchen.

"Hello, Ms. Reynolds. I'd like to see Elijah now." Lisa looked her over with a critical eye.

"I'm not sure that's a good idea, Mrs. Mitchell. It looks like you should sleep for the next forty-eight hours first."

"I appreciate your concern, Ms. Reynolds, but I'll be fine."

Sarah could tell Lisa wasn't happy about it, but she relented just the same. "We need to go over a few things first. He's still in a delusional state, but I have him sedated with medication. If he doesn't know who you are, don't push him. I know you've handled his confusions well in the past, but a delusion is more extreme. Be calm and make sure you keep a soothing tone. He doesn't like having multiple people in the room at one time, so I'll stay by the door."

Sarah nodded in understanding and walked to the office with Lisa and Miles. She hesitated for only a moment before opening the door and quietly stepping inside. Although she mentally pictured the scene, she couldn't help but be gripped with emotion at the sight of Elijah in the medical bed. She took a deep breath and cleared her mind. When he saw her, he reached out a shaky hand and struggled to sit up.

"You're back." Sarah's heart lifted.

He remembers.

She walked over and took his hand. He clumsily covered it with his other hand and brought it up to his face.

"Hello, Elijah."

"You're back. I was worried."

"There's nothing to be worried about. I'm safe and I'm here."

He held her clasped hand to his mouth. It was when he planted the first kiss on her knuckles that her happiness started to slip. He kissed her hand again and turned it to rest his cheek against her palm. Her heart beat faster as dread filled within her.

"Lena. It took you. It was hurting you." His voice cracked with emotion and she felt a tear fall on her palm.

Why is he calling me Lena?

She looked back at Lisa and Miles, unsure of what to do next. Miles was staring with clear astonishment and Lisa looked like she wanted to shake her and give her a resounding 'I told you so.' She quickly thought back to everything she had learned about CJD patient suffering from a delusion. The important thing was to not make him more confused or agitated.

"No one hurt me. I'm fine." Sarah shifted, intending to sit in the chair next to the bed but Elijah gripped her hand tighter.

"Don't leave, Lena. Don't leave. It's out there."

"I'm not going anywhere. I'm just going to sit here." He looked at the chair she pointed to and shook his head frantically. "Okay, okay. How about I sit at the end of the bed?"

He pulled on her hand. "Lay down. Need you close. Gone... It had you." His words were strained and disjointed. He shifted in the bed in attempt to make room. Her first instinct was to resist, feeling that lying down with him would be playing out the delusion too far. But one look in his terrified eyes convinced her that the right thing to do was lie down and let him believe his Lena was safe. She didn't seek approval or reproach from Lisa. Instead, she got in the bed so her head rested on his chest and allowed him to wrap his arms around her. His tremors had gotten worse so she couldn't be certain if the movements in his hands were involuntary or if they were deliberate. She felt the beat of his heart slow and eventually his breathing settled into a steady rhythm indicating he had found sleep. She thought to get up, but her own fatigue took over and she gladly gave into it.

Soft light fell on Sarah's closed lids and she opened her eyes onto Elijah's sleeping face. She gently eased out of bed and paused to make sure she hadn't woken him. Once she was confident he was still sleeping, she slipped out of the room and quickly made her way to the bathroom. After finishing with her morning needs, she went to the kitchen to make a cup of coffee and encountered Miles.

"Good morning, Miles." He looked up at her with a tired smile.

"Good morning, Sarah. Taking advantage of Elijah sleeping?" They all knew when Elijah was experiencing his delusions he was fine as long as Sarah was with him. They didn't know when the delusions would occur or how long they would last, and as a result she rarely left his side. Lisa had lowered his medication since he'd grown calmer after Sarah's return, allowing him to be more lucid even though he was often in the firm grasp of his delusions.

"Yes, I thought I would take the opportunity to stretch and get some coffee." Miles nodded and looked down into the cup sitting before him. They jumped at the sound of the phone ringing. Sarah walked over and looked at the display. "It's Marcus."

"Don't answer it." They waited for the ringing to stop. A few seconds later Elijah's cell phone rang. They knew it would be Marcus so they let it ring. Sarah wondered why he was calling so early in the morning and hoped it wasn't anything serious.

When Elijah's cell phone went quiet Sarah asked Miles the

question that had been on her mind since she returned. "Do you think it's time to tell Marcus and Leanne?"

He looked at her sharply. "No, I don't. He's in the middle of a string of delusions, Sarah. He thinks you're his dead wife and that a monster has taken you every time you're out of his sight. I don't think it would be good for them to witness it. Tina hasn't stopped crying since yesterday. How do you think his children will react?"

She ran her hands over her face. "You're right. I'm tired and not thinking clearly. But what if the delusions stop today? Shouldn't they know what's going on now?"

"I don't know. I'm Elijah's friend, but I am also his lawyer. He explained exactly when he wanted them to know, and we're not there yet. I need you to promise me you won't tell them."

"You know I won't. And not just because I signed a NDA. I promised Elijah I wouldn't tell them, and now I'm promising you. As much as I don't understand it or agree with it, I won't tell. But I won't lie anymore, Miles."

"Then I guess as long as you don't answer any of his calls we won't have an issue. Has Marcus—" His question was cut off by Elijah's scream and they both took off for the office.

"Elijah, we've talked through this. Ms. Reynolds is here to help. She's trained to help you where I can't. Miles will be here and I'll be outside the door."

"No! You can't go out there. The monster!" Elijah clung to her hand as Lisa tried to pry her away.

"Just go. He will scream and fight but Mr. Morgan and I will take care of it. We'll bathe him quickly and get him into some fresh clothes. Wait outside until we're done." Sarah looked over Lisa's shoulder to where Miles was trying desperately to restrain Elijah. She backed out of the office, never taking her eyes from Elijah until Lisa closed the door. She felt Tina's arms wrap around her.

"It'll be all right. It—"

"LENA! Please, LENA! Let me go, the monster... Please!" Elijah's screams turned into gut wrenching sobs.

It had been two full days since Sarah returned. The delusions came without warning but were always the same, and he became terrified when she left him. During the delusions, she tried to keep her own personal needs to times when he was asleep. When he was awake she read to him, or he talked of a past he'd shared with Marlena. She had no idea if his memories were real, but she thought they must be because he told her the same ones over and over again. Some of the details would change—such as what Marlena was wearing—but the important details were the same, convincing her they were real.

Now it was time for Lisa and Miles to attend to Elijah's personal needs and, just as the day before, Sarah found herself on the other side of the closed door cringing every time he cried out in terror. Finally, Sarah couldn't take any more and opened the door.

"Mrs. M—" Lisa stopped herself, remembering that in Elijah's mind Sarah was Marlena. Sarah didn't wait for her to finish and went quickly to Elijah's side. He instantly calmed and pulled Sarah into a hug, burying his face in her shoulder.

"I can't. I can't stand out there and listen to this. I will remain in here and hold his hand while you do what you need to do."

"But it's not proper—"

Sarah turned her sharp glare to Lisa. "I think we're well beyond proper now, don't you? I can handle seeing you clean him up much better than I can handle standing on the other side of the door letting him scream in terror when I know I can do something about it." She squeezed Elijah once more and then inched back so she could see his face. "It's all right, I'm right here. I'll stay right here as long as you let them help you." He nodded his head in agreement. Miles and Lisa went to work removing his clothing, the whole time he never took his eyes off of hers.

"Lena?" Sarah turned her head in the direction of Elijah's whispered voice. Even though it was the middle of the night, the room was well lit by a full moon and clear sky. He was looking down at her, stroking her hair.

"Shouldn't you be sleeping?"

He pulled his arms tighter around her waist. "I was thinking about when Marcus was born. Do you remember?"

"You tell it so much better than I do." It was the same response she gave for each memory he wanted to discuss.

He ran a shaky hand down her arm. "He came quickly. We thought we would have time but we barely made it to the... the..."

"Hospital." Even though she hadn't been there to share his memories, she was often able to fill in the simple words his mind forgot.

"Yes, the hospital. You wanted the... the..."

"Epidural."

"Yes. They told you it was too late. You were mad." It was a new memory, one he hadn't shared before. Suddenly she felt him tense around her. "Where's Marcus?"

She quickly sat up on her elbow and looked at him, seeing the terror start to grow in his eyes.

No, no, no. Please don't extend your delusion to Marcus. I can't produce a young Marcus.

She wasn't even sure how old Marcus should be in Elijah's current state of mind. She put her hand to his face, forcing him to focus on her.

"Marcus is fine." She needed to distract him before the terror set in. "Do you remember the day you asked me to marry you?" It was the memory Elijah had shared with her on their hike months ago. "Remember you came to pick me up for a hike but I was wearing heels?" She felt his tension ease and saw his eyes clear.

"Yes, heels. The lake was beautiful. But not more beautiful than you. You're still so beautiful." She rested her head back on his chest and felt a single tear slip down her cheek. She could handle talking to him about memories that weren't her own. She could handle him calling her Lena. But she had a difficult time when he spoke to her with endearments he would have shared only with his wife. Those were the moments she felt guilty for playing into his delusions.

"We should rest now." She was relieved when he remained quiet but it was a long time before she fell asleep.

It had been five days since Sarah returned and Elijah's delusions still occurred frequently. Miles and Tina used vacation time so they could stay and help. A few days ago, they'd tried to bring in another nurse to assist but Elijah's response to the unknown person was nothing short of terrified.

It was New Year's Eve, but there wouldn't be any celebrating at the Kingston house. They had all found a routine that kept Elijah's mood stable and they didn't intend to shift from it just because it was a holiday. It was early in the morning and Elijah was sleeping. Miles was in the shower and Sarah was eating breakfast with Lisa and Tina. Just as Sarah was about to take the last bite of her yogurt there was a loud banging on the front door, followed by the sharp shrill of the door bell. The three ladies stared at each other in surprise for a second before leaping into action. They all hurried in the direction of the door, but weren't quick enough as the bell sounded again. Just as Sarah reached the door Miles came down the stairs wearing only a towel around his waist and dripping from his shower.

"Get it, quick! Who is it?" Miles looked frantically from the door to the direction of the office. Sarah looked out the glass panel to the side of the door and felt her heart surge.

"It's Marcus." She jumped as there was another round of pounding on the door.

"Damn it! He can't come in." Miles looked down at his towel wrapped waist and cursed under his breath. "Go out and talk to him. But don't tell him anything!"

Sarah shot Miles an annoyed look. "I won't, but as I said before, I won't lie either."

"Sarah! I can see you through the glass. Open the door." Sarah turned and motioned for Lisa and Tina to lock the door behind her. She opened the door to find Marcus with his arm raised, ready to bang on the door again. She took the opportunity of catching him off guard to push him out onto the porch. It was snowing but they were protected by the portico.

"LENA!" Unfortunately Elijah's scream escaped before Lisa and Tina had shut the door. Marcus looked at Sarah, clearly confused, and then pushed past her to bang on the door again. He turned to her in frustration when it wouldn't budge.

"Did he just scream my mom's name?"

"Marcus—"

"Don't! Just don't, Sarah. Give me the code to the door."

"I don't know what it is. Elijah changed it while I was gone."

"What? Why?"

"I don't know."

"Damn it, Sarah! What in the hell is going on? And don't tell me nothing because it's obvious there is!" She noted not only anger in his voice but desperation as well.

"Marcus, please don't do this. Elijah doesn't want to see anyone. I can't change his mind and your banging isn't helping."

He closed the distance between them and grabbed her by the arms. She instantly felt electricity flash its way through her at his touch. His momentary hesitation told her he felt it too, but he remained focused. "Please, Sarah. He's my father. I know something's not right. I need to know what's going on."

If it were Leanne standing before her she might have been able to turn her back and walk away. But it was Marcus. She was learning she didn't have the strength to deny him much. She wanted to pull him close and take away his pain. But she wouldn't. Right now there was only one thing stronger than her connection to Marcus, and that was the promise she'd made to Elijah. He'd given her so much; the least she could do was honor his one request. She felt guilty for not telling Marcus the truth, but she knew if she broke her promise to Elijah her guilt would be greater. It hit her in an instant.

Elijah played on my guilt. He knew it's the one thing I can't shake. That's what's keeping me from telling his children, and he knew all along that it would.

The realization sent a flash of anger surging through her entire body. The anger was displaced when another muffled cry came from inside the house. She needed to get Marcus away from the door.

"Fuck! It's cold out here." She pulled away and ran through the snow to his car.

"Did you just curse?" She shut out his astonishment as she closed herself into the passenger side of his car, waiting for him to join her.

"Do you mind turning on the heat?"

He slid the key in the ignition, turned over the engine, and quickly cranked up the heat to full blast. They sat in silence until she stopped shivering.

"Sarah, please, why was he screaming my mom's name?"

She weighed her words carefully. "He's experiencing a delusion and is confused as to where your mom is."

He pounded his fist against the steering wheel. "Is this from the same medication? Who the hell is his doctor and why is he still taking that shit? It's clearly not doing him any good!"

"I'm sorry, Marcus, I can't tell you."

"No, you *won't* tell me! We've been through this, Sarah, that damn NDA doesn't mean anything."

"You're right, I won't tell you. It's not about the NDA. It's because I made a promise to Elijah and I keep my promises. Marcus, you know how he is. He's the most stubborn person I've ever met and once he sets his mind to something there's no changing his course. No matter how much I don't agree with his decision, I cannot change his mind." There was understanding in his eyes, but also pain. He turned toward her and took both of her hands in his. He rubbed them, trying to pull out the cold. The gesture, as well as the contact, instantly generated warmth within her. She tried to pull her hands away, but he held on tighter.

"Marcus, I really am sorry. I want to tell you but I owe Elijah so much. He helped me live again, to feel again. I can't deny him this one request." He finally let go of her hands and squeezed the bridge of his nose in frustration. He was silent for several seconds, clearly trying to regain his composure.

"Alright, let's try another question for the moment. Why didn't you answer any of my calls or messages? I was worried about you."

She looked at him in confusion.

Crap! My new phone.

She had forgotten all about it with the trip home and then being thrown into the midst of Elijah's delusion when she returned.

"I mean, if you didn't want to see or talk to me again you could have at least responded with that rather than nothing at all."

"No, you don't understand. I turned the phone off on my flight out and put it in my purse pocket and forgot to turn it back on. I didn't even have a moment to think on the trip and then with... I'm sorry, I didn't get your messages."

A slight smile touched his lips. "While the fact that you could completely forget about me in less than a week is disturbing, I suppose I can work with that better than you not wanting to ever speak to me again."

"I never said I forgot about you, I just forgot I had another phone." They looked at each other in silence and she felt her emotions start to rise. She looked back toward the house to break the spell and suddenly remembered Elijah was inside screaming for Lena.

Somehow she always managed to forget everything else when she was with Marcus. "I need to get back inside." She reached for the door handle but he grabbed her arm.

"Sarah, wait." His eyes shifted from her to the other car in the driveway. "I know Miles is here. I want to speak to him."

"He won't tell you anything. You should just go home."

"I can't, don't you understand that? What if it were your father in there?" His words gripped her, and she felt the thin chords holding her pieces together stretch to capacity.

"If it were my dad... I would be doing exactly what you're doing." She paused, trying to control her emotions. "You need to understand something about me. I hold guilt for everything. It's my main weakness in this life and I know it but I can't seem to do anything about it. If I told you, I would be consumed with guilt for betraying Elijah who has done nothing to deserve my betrayal. However, if you keep asking me I will be consumed with guilt over not telling you and hurting you in the process. I couldn't take knowing I caused you that kind of pain." Tears threatened her eyes and a lump formed in her throat but she pushed through.

"I can't keep being pulled in both directions. I'll snap, Marcus. I need you to stop asking me, please." Just then a section of the cloud cover broke and the sun cast a strong ray of light on the car. It felt like she was being sent strength from above and she seized the opportunity. For once she was going to choose something for herself—something that would allow her to feel like she was keeping her promise to Elijah, yet helping Marcus at the same time.

"However, I'll give you my opinion. You should follow your instincts. What Elijah is trying to protect you from has plagued your family before. You were too young to remember, but if you look deep enough you'll be able to find answers." She opened the door and got out before he could stop her. She looked back, and the pain mixed with confusion that she saw on his face was enough to make her tears spill over. "I'm so sorry, Marcus." She shut the door and ran back to the house before he could utter another word. Tina was watching for her and opened the door as she ran up the steps. She could hear Elijah still struggling in the office and turned in that direction until Miles stopped her.

"Did you tell him?"

She glared at him through her tears. "No, I didn't. And you know that! I'm furious with Elijah! And you too for that matter! I just figured it all out. You both know I won't tell Marcus or anyone else because I would feel too guilty about breaking my promise. He knows it's the one thing that still holds me back." She let out an involuntary laugh that was way too sarcastic to be mistaken for humor. "Come to think of it, in all our 'therapy' sessions that's the one thing he *never* tried to cure or even discuss. It was all about how to be happy, how to live, but never about how to let go of the guilt on my own. That wouldn't have served his purposes. He needed me to feel guilty so I wouldn't tell anyone. That's my kill button and he's been pushing it from day one, and now the button's been passed to you!" She was yelling so loudly by the end of her rant that Miles actually flinched.

"Sarah—"

"NO! No." She took a few deep breaths to calm herself down as best she could. "I have already forgiven Elijah. He knows how to get what he wants and I can't fault him for it. But I have every right to be mad right now." She walked toward the office, placed her hand on the handle and then stopped. She kept her back to Miles, but she knew he was still listening. "His children are smart. And they are *his* children after all so they won't give up. You have to at least acknowledge that they might figure out he's dying before Elijah wants them to know. Nothing will keep them away if that happens." She opened the door to the office and hurried past Lisa to Elijah's side. He immediately buried his face in her shoulder and mumbled incoherent words. She sat down on the bed, prepared for another day of being Lena. Her anger was still there, just below the surface, but it was fading fast with every sob that escaped from Elijah.

It was almost midnight and everyone was asleep, not able to stay up for the New Year. Sarah had tried to rest, but her mind was racing from her encounter with Marcus earlier that morning. She sat quietly in one of the office chairs while Elijah slept, new phone in hand. She checked to make sure all sounds were off before retrieving her messages. She was shocked to see she had seven text messages and three missed calls from Marcus. He had sent the first one before her plane had landed in Chicago. The remainder had been sent periodically over the last few days.

Sarah, I hope you had an uneventful flight into Chicago. Enjoy your visit with your family and I hope to see you again soon.

I just wanted to wish you a Merry Christmas.

I know you're busy with your family, so I'm trying to not be offended that I haven't received a message in return. I hope you had a wonderful day. I'll try to call tomorrow before your flight.

I tried to call but it went straight to voice mail. I'll need to show you how to set it up. Anyway, I'm sorry I missed you. I hope you have a safe flight back.

I'm hoping you've had a chance to rest after your whirlwind trip. I hope my father isn't working you too hard and is giving you a chance to recover. I'm hoping your silence is due to the fact that you don't know how to work your new phone. I'll give you a call tomorrow. I miss hearing your voice.

OK, I'm hoping to not come across as a stalker, but I'm starting to worry. I know I shouldn't—I didn't see any reports of a plane crash so I assume you've returned in one piece. I tried to call your phone and then my father's house and his cell... I can't seem to connect with anyone. Please respond and let me know you're safe (and that you're not avoiding me).

New Year's Eve is a couple days away and I was hoping you'd changed your mind about going to the party with me. The offer is still open and I'd like nothing more than to have you join me. Please respond, Sarah, even if it's to tell me to go to hell. The silence is killing me.

I tried to call again with no luck. This will be my last message, but if I don't hear back from you I'll drive up there to see you in person. I can't let it end this way. I at least need a good-bye. So, I'll give you until tomorrow morning to determine if you want to tell me good-bye over a text or in person.

Sarah let out a defeated sigh. If she had only remembered her new phone, the whole incident could have been avoided. She watched the clock tick closer to midnight as she contemplated her response. He didn't say the words exactly, but Marcus' messages had made his feelings for her clear. As she thought about a possible relationship with him, Nick's image jumped to the forefront of her mind. She wasn't ready to move forward with any type of romantic relationship. However, the thought of letting Marcus go created a knot in her chest that felt very similar to how she felt when missing Nick.

Marcus, I finally read your messages. I'm sorry to have caused you worry. Let me set your mind at ease on one account—I don't want to tell you good-bye through text or in person. However, I'm also not ready for that first date. I hope we can remain friends as I sort through my feelings. Also, Happy New Year and I hope you're enjoying your party. Contrary to what you say, I'm sure you're familiar with drunken chaotic dancing and are in the midst of it right now. I'm not sure when I'll be able to see or talk to you again, so don't lose hope if I don't respond right away. Thanks for this very cool phone. I promise not to forget about it again.

She pushed the send button and then investigated the other features of her phone. Less than a minute after sending her message she received notice of a response and her heart leapt into a rapid and nervous pace.

It's almost midnight, and I wish you were here next to me to celebrate properly.

She smiled at his response. He was back to his flirty behavior, and she took it as a sign that he accepted her proposal to remain friends.

I'm sure Heather is there and would be happy to fill in for me.

You can be certain that Heather is NOT here and she could never fill in for you. To clarify, I decided to skip the party and am currently at home, which is a very Heather-free zone.

She couldn't temper her enjoyment from his response. She might not be ready to move forward with him, but that didn't mean she wanted to think about him with anyone else.

If you're home then you should be sleeping.

I'm doing research and couldn't sleep.

She knew he must have taken her earlier words to heart and was trying to figure out what was going on with Elijah. She felt her guilt resurface.

I'm sorry again about this morning.

His response took longer and she felt a sense of dread creep into her core. However, it quickly disappeared when she realized the delay was simply because his longer response took more time to type.

Sarah, I don't want you to apologize again for not telling me what's going on. There's no need. There's nothing for you to feel guilty about. I know how my father is and I place any blame for this situation squarely in his lap. In truth, I hold you in greater respect for being loyal to your word. I understand the reasons for your loyalty and I will not ask you again to betray that.

She was amazed at how quickly her guilt disappeared.

Thank you, Marcus.

You're welcome. Now, as much as I don't want to, considering the time I should let you get some rest. Can I call you later this week?

Her mind quickly went back and forth on how she should answer his question. She typed her response and hit send before she could change her mind.

Yes, I'd like that.

CHAPTER 21

Sarah sat in silence, watching Elijah look out the windows. His delusions had finally stopped a few days ago. In total, they had come and gone over a period of ten days. Since then, he had remained somber and detached from the people and the world around him. He stopped speaking but every once in awhile he would let out some sort of unrecognizable sound. Sometimes he would look when his name was called, but usually he stared at nothing.

She had spent the last twenty minutes trying to get him to eat. After another failed attempt, she placed everything back on the tray and returned to the kitchen where Lisa sat working on her computer.

"Did he eat?"

"More than he did this morning."

Lisa nodded and typed something into her computer. "What time is Mr. Morgan planning to come by?" Tina and Miles returned home the day after Elijah's delusions ended, but Miles still stopped by daily.

"I'm not sure, probably not until close to dinner. He's behind at work from taking so much time off." Lisa finally stopped typing and focused her attention on Sarah.

"Do you need a break? I could sit with him for awhile."

"I've got it. I plan on reading to him. We're getting to a particularly exciting part in the book." Sarah managed a smile and turned to leave. She paused at the entryway of the kitchen, looking at the Christmas tree they had not yet taken down. "Actually, do you think we could get him into the wheelchair? It might lift his spirits to get out of the room." Elijah's movements had become extremely cumbersome and they had finally gotten him to use a wheelchair.

Lisa contemplated the request for a moment before nodding and standing to help. When Miles came by he helped Lisa transfer Elijah to the wheelchair for a few hours, but Sarah didn't want to wait. She needed a change before she went crazy. To her relief Elijah was cooperative and they had no difficulty getting him into the chair.

Sarah pushed him into the great room and positioned him so he could either look out the windows or at the Christmas tree. Maybe it was her imagination, but she thought she saw a flash of life enter his eyes when his gaze fell upon the tree. She pulled an armchair over next to him and settled in to read. She had no idea if he paid the slightest bit of attention to her voice, but at least it made her feel like she was doing something to entertain him.

She was so engrossed in the story that the sound of the front door opening startled her. She glanced over at the clock and was surprised to see more than two hours had passed. She didn't turn to face Miles, but called out to let him know they were in the great room.

"Miles, you're early today. We're in the great room and I'm almost done with this chapter, so you'll have to give us a moment."

She had only narrated four words when the hairs on the back of her neck stood to attention. She felt a hand on her shoulder, sending a ripple of panic down her spine. She could feel his pain through the tight grip of his hand. She looked up at Marcus and saw the pain in his eyes as he looked at Elijah. She allowed herself to imagine what it must be like to see his father looking so different, so fragile, after only a few weeks. Elijah's transformation since Christmas was startling. Not only was he sitting in a wheelchair, but he had lost a significant amount of weight. But worst of all was the lifeless stare from his eyes. The emptiness conveyed he was already gone.

Sarah looked back up at Marcus, her eyes welling with tears. She turned to see Miles, who stood a few feet behind Marcus, looking as if he'd completely failed Elijah, yet at the same time relieved of his burden. Sarah put the book on the table next to her and started to stand.

"I'll let you have some time alone with him." Marcus' grip on her shoulder tightened, anchoring her firmly to the chair. He never took his eyes off Elijah.

"Please, stay." His voice was barely above a whisper.

"Mr. Morgan, you're—" Lisa rounded the corner from the kitchen and stopped in her tracks when she saw Marcus. She looked frantically from Marcus to Sarah to Miles and back again. Miles cleared his throat and walked over to Lisa.

"Ms. Reynolds, this is Elijah's son, Marcus. Why don't we go into the kitchen?" Miles led Lisa out of the room. It felt like a long time had passed before Marcus spoke again.

"Will he know who I am?"

Sarah didn't want to answer, knowing she didn't have anything she could say to ease his pain. "I don't know. He hasn't spoken for two days. Sometimes he acknowledges us when we talk to him or ask him to do something, but usually he just stares as he's doing now."

He slowly let go of her shoulder and walked to Elijah, crouching down in front of him. "Dad? It's me, Marcus." She watched as he hesitantly placed a hand on Elijah's knee. Her heart lifted as Elijah settled his eyes on him. In general it wouldn't seem like much, but in Elijah's current condition they couldn't have asked for a better response. Elijah darted his gaze back to the tree, and Marcus sank down on the floor, burying his face in his hands.

She wasn't sure what to do so she remained in her chair, trying not to feel the mountain of pain settling in her chest—yet at the same time wishing she could shoulder Marcus' pain for him. They all three sat there, each alone and consumed by their own misery, yet somehow supporting each other through their physical proximity. She wasn't sure how much time had passed before Lisa came back into the room.

"I'm sorry to interrupt, but it's time to attend to Mr. Kingston's needs. Mr. Morgan and I will take him into the office and we'll let you know when we're done. Mrs. Mitchell, could you prepare his dinner as usual?"

Sarah stood abruptly. "Of course. Marcus, would you like to help?" Marcus discreetly wiped his eyes before standing. He sat down at one of the counter stools while she prepared dinner. She pulled a casserole out of the freezer and set the oven to the appropriate time. Tina couldn't return to the house after experiencing Elijah's delusions, so she helped by preparing meals.

She stood opposite Marcus as the oven warmed. It took all her willpower to remain silent, knowing he would speak when he was ready. She thought over their phone conversation earlier in the week.

He had kept to his word and hadn't asked her any more questions about Elijah. Instead, they talked of everything else they could think to ask each other. During their conversation she had marveled at his ability to almost read her thoughts. Just at the point when she began to feel a sense of betrayal to Nick's memory, Marcus asked about him. It had made her feel better talking openly. Everything seemed easy with Marcus, and she found with each passing day she wanted to know more about him. It was terrifying.

Marcus cleared his throat and brought Sarah out of her reverie. "Did you know he had CJD all along? Did he tell you before you came out here?"

"He told me on the first day I came out to meet with him. He made it clear his illness was the reason for my being here."

"Did you have past experience with this illness before? Is that why he wanted you to come?"

"No, I had never heard of it before." The look on his face told her he wanted to say or ask more, but he refrained. The oven beeped and she went to put the casserole in. When she turned back, he opened his mouth to speak but was interrupted by his phone. He retrieved it and mumbled something incoherent before answering.

"Hi, Joan."

Who's Joan?

Sarah didn't like that she instantly ruffled at the thought of him talking to another woman.

"Yes, sorry, I forgot to take care of it before I left. I would appreciate it if you could do it for me. Also, how's Sophie doing?"

And who's Sophie?

Sarah turned and went to work on Elijah's dinner, hoping Marcus wouldn't notice her rising irritation.

"That's great. I agree one more day of antibiotics should be enough and then she can go home." Sarah's movements paused as she suddenly realized he must be talking to his partner at his veterinary practice. She didn't want to acknowledge the sense of relief that washed over her. "I'm sorry about all this. I don't know how long I'll be up here, but Dr. Griffith said he would fill in if needed."

Yes, he's talking to his partner.

Sarah smiled internally as she listened to him conclude the conversation.

After Elijah's tray had been prepared she turned back to Marcus. He studied her for a moment before speaking. "Sorry, I left town unexpectedly and there were a few things I apparently overlooked."

"I understand. I assume you will want to stay here at the house?" When he nodded she did the same. "Well, Ms. Reynolds is in the room next to me but the other room, the one you stayed in over Christmas, is open. I suppose Elijah's room is also available since he's now staying in the office. Whatever will make you the most comfortable will be fine."

For crying out loud, stop talking. This is more his house than yours so the notion of you playing the host is absurd.

She diverted her attention to setting the dinner table. She turned from pulling a stack of plates and found Marcus had planted himself between her and the dining room. He took the plates from her hands with a small smile and left the room. They set the table in silence and returned to the kitchen, Marcus sitting at the counter and Sarah standing across from him.

"So, did you figure out he has CJD or did Miles finally tell you?"

He shifted uncomfortably in his seat. "I figured it out. After the advice you gave me the other day, I dug into the past. I don't have a large family, and the hint that I was too young to remember gave me a time frame to work with. I got suspicious when there wasn't a lot of information on how my grandfather died. When my grandmother passed, she named me the executor of her estate and I have most of her belongings in storage. I spent yesterday rummaging through her papers and finally found the answers I was looking for. I didn't want to think it was possible at first, but when I looked up the symptoms of CJD last night I..." He ran a hand through his hair. "I decided to confront Miles today. He confirmed it and then brought me here."

"Does Leanne know?"

"Not yet." Just then Lisa and Miles returned to the kitchen.

"Mrs. Mitchell, would you like for me to feed Mr. Kingston tonight so you can visit with Mr. Kingston?" There was a slight hesitation as she referred to Marcus, realizing the confusing nature of including both of the Mr. Kingstons in the same sentence.

"I'll feed him since Marcus might have some questions for you. I'll join you in the dining room once Elijah's finished eating." Sarah excused herself and took Elijah his dinner.

He was back in the medical bed, and she pulled a chair next to him. Unfortunately he was more reluctant than usual and she had a difficult time getting him to take the first bite. Each time she tried to help him eat, he clamped his mouth shut and turned his head. He was probably upset Marcus found out, and it was the only way his body would allow him to express his feelings. She racked her brain for ideas and then walked over to the music player. Usually music was enough to soothe him, but it wasn't working.

"Come on, Elijah. You need to eat. Are you angry?" He didn't give her any form of acknowledgement. In frustration she walked out to get the book she'd been reading to him, hoping a few minutes of reading would get him to cooperate. Miles came out to meet her.

"Is everything okay?"

"He's refusing to eat. I tried the music but it didn't work so I thought I would try reading. If this doesn't work, I'm not sure what else to do other than pry his mouth open and cram it in."

Miles thought for a moment. "You could try the video. I've had success using it to calm him. Given there's a chance he's refusing to eat because Marcus is here, it might actually be the best remedy."

"What video?"

"It's already in the DVD player. If it doesn't work, let me know and I'll help you pry open his stubborn mouth." He gave her shoulder a squeeze and walked to the other side of the room to make a call.

She returned to the office and stood by the chair, staring at the DVD player. She had no clue what video Miles was talking about and her curiosity was getting the best of her. She put the book down and walked over to play the video.

If this calms him down, why didn't Miles tell me about it before?

She turned on the TV and hit play. The image on the screen caused her to sink into her chair. She watched the video in astonishment until the very end and then played it again. When it completed the second time, she regained her senses and turned to Elijah. His eyes were fixed on the TV screen, and she pressed play a third time. She watched in amazement as his eyes followed every movement. She tried to get him to eat again while it was playing and was grateful when he opened his mouth. By the fifth play he had finished half his dinner, and Miles entered the room.

"Is it working?"

"Like a charm. Why didn't you tell me about this video before?"

He shrugged his shoulders. "I don't know, I guess I thought you knew about it. I suppose with all that's been going on I never thought to mention it. I didn't even attempt to play it until his delusions ended, but since then I play the video when I sit with him."

"What video are we talking about?" Miles shifted and made room for Marcus to enter. She noted Marcus' hesitation when he looked at Elijah and remembered the first time she experienced seeing him in the bed.

Miles clapped Marcus on the shoulder before turning to leave. "Why don't you join them and find out." She suddenly felt a blush creep up her neck. She tried to push it down and when she failed she turned her attention back to feeding Elijah, handing Marcus the remote. She kept her gaze focused on Elijah, but out of the corner of her eye she could see Marcus had the same initial reaction she'd had.

"It's our dance from the gala." His voice was just a whisper. She still couldn't look at him. The image of the two of them dancing sent a flurry of emotions through her that were hard enough to contain without him sitting right next to her. "Did you know he had it recorded?"

"Not until just now."

"I don't understand..."

She had to force herself to look at Marcus. She couldn't allow this to be about her fears. This moment was important for him and he needed to understand what she knew this meant to Elijah.

"Remember when Elijah interrupted us on the balcony after the dance? I confronted him after you left—I told him I knew he'd intended all along to pull out of the dance and have you step in. He confessed and cited two reasons for doing so. The first was because he didn't think he would be feeling well. But the second, and what I think is the real reason, was because he wanted to see you dance one more time. It makes sense he would have had it recorded, knowing there was a high probability he would forget." She watched as a tidal wave of emotions crossed over Marcus' face. He stood abruptly and paced the room a few times before turning toward the door.

"This is all too much." He bolted through the door and she had to fight the urge to go after him. She wasn't sure if he needed her, but she knew for certain Elijah did. She summoned all her focus and played the video again while she attempted to finish helping Elijah with his dinner.

Sarah stretched her arms above her head as she descended the stairs. It had been Lisa's turn to respond to Elijah's needs overnight, and she'd been grateful for the opportunity to get a full night's rest. At the bottom of the stairs she automatically turned in the direction of the office to check on Elijah, stopping outside the door when she heard Marcus' soft voice.

"Come on, Dad, hold still a moment. You need a shave. Didn't you always tell me a real man kept his face smooth?" Sarah smiled at Marcus' comment. In the short time she'd known him she knew he'd rather have low stubble on his face than be clean shaven. She was usually more attracted to men with no facial hair, and it was another example of how Marcus made her want to redefine 'normal'. She heard the sound of the electric shaver and then Marcus curse a few times before it went off again.

"Are you opposed to the shave in general or to me doing it? Would you rather have Sarah do it? I know I would if I were you, but she's not here and I am. Just hold still, *please*." She could hear the frustration in his voice and decided it was time to help him out.

"Actually he's opposed to the electric shaver. Remember the incident in the bathroom the last time you were here? It was because he didn't want 'that damn thing.'" Marcus looked up at her when she entered the room.

"So what's your secret to getting him to cooperate?"

"I let Ms. Reynolds do it after she's attended to his other needs. Usually, he's so tired from fighting her on everything else he relents by the time she gets to the shaver. She must have skipped it yesterday given the circumstances." Marcus shook his head and tossed the shaver onto the table. She scanned the room and noticed Elijah's breakfast. "Did he eat?"

"About half. I thought I would try again after the shave, but so much for that idea." She nodded, unsure of what to do next. She suddenly felt like she was in the way and didn't know how much control she had now that Marcus was involved.

"Well... it seems you have everything under control, so I'll just be in the kitchen if you need anything." She turned to leave but Marcus called out to stop her.

"Would you mind joining us?"

"Sure, I'll get my coffee and breakfast and be right back." When she returned from the kitchen, she noticed Marcus had pulled a chair next to his. She settled into the chair and took a bite of her cereal. They sat in silence while she ate and Marcus continued to try to feed Elijah. He finally gave up and ran his hands over his face.

"He doesn't stop moving, yet he won't talk and his eyes look so lifeless. It's a frightening contrast." She thought about Marcus' description. In reality, Elijah's movements were less frequent but Marcus hadn't been there to witness them at their peak. While for him the movements were disturbing, it was the slowing of the movements that bothered Sarah. She knew it meant his illness was progressing.

"Have you talked to Leanne yet?" She regretted her words as soon as she saw Marcus' eyes well up with unshed tears.

"No. My plan was to see him myself first. I had intended to call her last night, and waiting that long felt wrong. But I wanted to be able to tell her what to expect. Now, the ironic thing is I completely understand why he didn't want us to know. After spending a day here, there's a large part of me that doesn't want to tell her. I don't want her to see him like this." He stood and walked over to look out the windows, folding his arms across his chest. "Christmas was the best one we'd had in a long time, and I want her to be able to remember him that way—not like this. But if I don't tell her she might feel like she missed her opportunity to say good-bye in a way that would last forever. I can't take that away from her either." He finally turned to look at her. "What should I do?"

Sarah released a heavy sigh and took a moment to think about her words. They came to her from somewhere deep within. Words she had long forgotten.

"I told you how I hold onto guilt. Nick was always the one to help me let go. He once told me to remember life wasn't strictly black and white, and most of the time there was no one right answer. Instead of worrying about what to do I should quickly consider the facts before me, make a decision, and then spend my energy figuring out how to live with that decision going forward. If I've learned anything over the years, it's that we can spend our whole lives second guessing the decisions we've made. Regrets only hold us back. To grow we need to support our past decisions, knowing that we did our best with what we had been given at the time."

He remained quiet for several seconds before speaking in a low voice. "It sounds like Nick was a pretty amazing guy."

She looked down at her fingers, rotating her pendant, and pushed through the lump forming in the back of her throat. "Yes, he was amazing."

"Well, I guess I have a phone call to make."

"Do you want me to call Miles and see if he can be here?"

"Yes, that would probably be best."

"Marcus, I don't understand why we had to come over here so early. I had to cancel several important meetings, one with a potential client that could bring us a significant amount of revenue. What's so urgent it couldn't wait until later?" She shot an irritated look at Sarah. "If this is for some sort of 'announcement' you two want to make, I'm not going to be happy. And where's Dad?" Sarah never thought it was possible for someone to be so high-strung they couldn't recognize a critical situation when they were right in the middle of one.

I wonder if she would pay closer attention to what's going on if this was all happening in the middle of the Kingston boardroom.

"Leanne, Marcus said this was important and urgent. I'm sure it must be or else we wouldn't be here. Let's give him a chance to explain." Sarah was grateful for Brad's level head.

Leanne checked her watch. "Fine. What did you need to tell us?"

"Let's go in the other room." Marcus held out his arm in the direction of the family room. Before Leanne could protest further, Brad gently led her away. Leanne looked over her shoulder and stopped suddenly.

"You aren't joining us?" Her features finally shifted from annoyed to curious.

"No, not right now." Sarah watched them leave the room and turned to stand by the patio doors. She was too full of nervous energy to sit. A minute or so after they left the room, the front door opened and Miles entered. Lisa exited the office at the same time.

"I see Leanne and Brad are here."

"Marcus is talking with them in the family room." The three of them stood or paced anxiously about the room as they waited. The sudden eruption of Leanne's voice caused them all to jump.

"No! This is bullshit!" Leanne entered the room and headed straight in Sarah's direction. "You knew about this all along and didn't say a damn word! You BITCH!" Sarah felt the impact of Leanne's fist on her face before she even saw it coming. She stumbled backward, putting her hands to her face.

"Leanne!" Marcus ran to Sarah while Brad grabbed on to Leanne. For some reason Sarah had the irrational urge to laugh at the entire situation. Luckily for the other side of her face she'd resisted.

"Don't you dare protect her! She's been lying and deceiving us the entire time. She—"

"Leanne, this isn't Sarah's fault. Elijah made her sign a non-disclosure agreement that prevented her from telling anyone, especially you and Marcus. It was Elijah's decision not to tell you." Miles stepped forward and planted himself between Sarah and Leanne. The idea that it took three grown men to keep such a tiny woman from pummeling Sarah to the ground almost caused her to lose her battle against the laughter.

I really must be losing my mind to want to laugh right now.

"Don't pull your lawyer shit on me, Miles! You are just as much at fault as she is. NDA or not you both chose to lie."

"Technically, Sarah never lied. Dad did hire her for a project. We just didn't know the project was to help him through his illness."

"Well, I did tell the one lie—about the ice." Sarah looked up at Marcus through her uninjured eye and was relieved to see a half smile on his face.

"Okay, she told one lie and in reality it was a pretty bad lie. Every other question I asked her about Dad she told me what she could without giving away his condition or simply said she couldn't tell me."

"She lied to *me*!"

"You never asked me any questions regarding Elijah's health, Leanne. All your questions centered on my relationship with him and I told you the truth every time." Leanne lunged at Sarah again, but she was no match for Brad. He hauled her to the other side of the room and after a few seconds it looked like she was ready to give up her attack on Sarah, at least for the moment.

"Where is he? I want to see him."

"He's in the office but—" She stomped in the direction of the office not waiting for Miles to finish. Lisa blocked her path.

"Who the hell are you?"

"Ms. Reynolds, Mr. Kingston's private nurse. And you're not going anywhere near him until you calm down."

"Excuse me?" Brad grabbed a hold of her again, clearly thinking she might strike out at Lisa as well.

"Mrs. Troupe, I understand you've just had quite a shock and you have every right to be upset. However, Mr. Kingston's condition is delicate and he can be easily agitated. For his health, which is my *only* concern, you will not be permitted to see him until you calm down." Leanne looked like she might explode at any moment. Brad wrapped his arms around her, whispering into her ear. Finally most of the tension left Leanne's face and she nodded her head. Lisa led them in the direction of the office, explaining what they were about to see. Once they were out of the room, Sarah sank back against Marcus who still had his arms wrapped around her. He tilted her face to inspect the damage from Leanne's punch.

"We should get you some ice." He gently guided her to the couch in the family room and went into the kitchen for ice. He sat down next to her and she flinched when he put the bag of ice to the injured side of her face. "You've got a cut. We should doctor that as well."

"It's too bad she's left handed like your dad. It's also too bad Brad had to buy her such a large rock." Now that the excitement had ended, she could feel a sharp ache where Leanne had punched her. She put her hand up to the ice bag, intending to take over holding it, but Marcus didn't drop his hand. Instead, he pulled her over so she was resting on his chest while he held it in place.

"I'm sorry. I never thought she would hit you. If I had, I would've stopped her."

"There's no need to apologize. Hell, I don't even expect *her* to apologize. Sometimes we act a little crazy and lose control when we learn someone we love is dying. Now, if she hits me again once the shock wears off I might be forced to hit her back." She felt him chuckle slightly. "Do you find this amusing?"

"No, you just always seem to say something I don't expect. It's refreshing." They sat in silence while her face numbed. She felt so comfortable in Marcus' arms she silently thanked Leanne for decking her. She closed her eyes and lost herself in the feel of his arms until she felt the ice bag lift from her face.

"Yep, that's going to be one heck of a shiner. Come with me Mrs. Mitchell and we'll take care of it." She could feel Marcus reluctantly shift behind her as she stood to follow Lisa.

"Are they still in with my father?"

"Yes, Mr. Kingston. Mr. Morgan is in there and you might want to join them. Also, your sister has requested a meeting with Dr. Holden and I'll try to set that up for tomorrow. I assume you'll want to be in the meeting as well."

"You assume correctly. I trust you'll take good care of Sarah, so I'll leave her in your capable hands." He looked down at Sarah. "Will you join us after you're done?"

"Marcus, I'm not sure that's a good idea."

"Nonsense. Leanne's going to have to get used to the idea of having you around. It's that simple." He lowered his head and planted a soft kiss where Leanne hit her before walking out of the room. She watched her vision falter and knew it had nothing to do with her injury. Lisa took her by the arm and held her up.

"Come along, Mrs. Mitchell, before you pass out." She allowed Lisa to lead her to a stool and waited for her to return with a first aid kit that could make MacGyver envious. Sarah winced with each task she performed on her face. After she placed the last of the butterfly strips to her cut, she held Sarah's gaze. "Are you doing okay?"

Sarah touched her sore cheek. "It hurts, but some basic pain pills should do the trick."

"I'm not talking about your shiner, Mrs. Mitchell." Lisa gave her a stern look, indicating she thought Sarah should know full well what she was talking about. Lisa let out a sigh and started packing up her kit. "I know you're aware Mr. Kingston asked me to look after you as well during this whole situation. I don't like the way Mrs. Troupe is blaming you for his actions. However, I'm happy to see that the younger Mr. Kingston is willing to support you. Mr. Morgan as well. All this has to be difficult on you, and I want to make sure you're feeling strong enough to continue."

"Thank you for asking, Ms. Reynolds. I'd be lying if I didn't admit my emotions fluctuate rapidly from sad to angry to tired to frustrated.

But I expected all of it so I've been preparing myself. It's helpful to have the support of Marcus and Miles. And of course there's Tina and yourself. I'll make it through the best I can, just like everyone else."

"Fair enough." Lisa snapped the kit closed and looked at Sarah for a moment before speaking again. "Normally I wouldn't put my nose where it doesn't belong, but since I've started down this path I may as well let you know what I think. That young Mr. Kingston is the real deal. I can tell by the way he looks at you. It's okay to start another relationship with someone, if that's what you want. Even though I don't know him, I'm sure your late husband would approve of the match. Now, I'm going to go give Dr. Holden a call about that meeting tomorrow." She smiled at Sarah and walked out of the room.

Sarah sat for a moment and thought about Lisa's words. Everyone, with the exception of Leanne, seemed intent on encouraging her into a relationship with Marcus. She knew they had good intentions, but she wasn't ready to go down that path.

Although, I'm not doing such a good job putting distance between us either. And I don't think I want to any more.

Knowing there was no immediate answer to her torment, Sarah pushed the thoughts away and went in search of medication for the throbbing in her cheek before joining the others. Elijah was awake and staring out the windows as usual. Leanne was sitting in front of him, eyes and nose red from crying, with Brad by her side. Marcus and Miles were talking by the fireplace and glanced over when she entered the room. Marcus immediately walked over to inspect Sarah's face.

"I'm afraid it's going to look worse before it looks better." He poked gently around her cut. "Ms. Reynolds did a nice job patching you up."

"Leave." Sarah looked from Marcus to Leanne as she uttered her one word command.

"Leanne, let it go. I asked Sarah to join us and she'll stay if she wants to."

"You need to choose, Marcus. It's either her or—"

"Stop right there, Leanne. If you force me into an ultimatum you won't like the outcome. You're angry, and I get that. Well, so am I! But Dad's the one you should be angry at, not Sarah. I think we have enough to worry about and we don't need you constantly attacking her. You need to accept the fact that she was Dad's choice as a companion through this whole thing and that she's the—" Marcus was cut off by the unexpected sound of Elijah laughing. It was labored and haunting, but it was unmistakably a laugh. Everyone stared at him, captivated by the sound, not knowing what to do or say. Leanne eventually spoke first.

"Dad?" His only response was continued laughter. "Dad, are you hurting? Do you need something?" Leanne's voice broke slightly making it obvious Elijah's behavior was affecting her.

"Sarah, has he done this before?"

Sarah tore her eyes away from Elijah and looked at Marcus. "Not exactly—"

"What? Now she's the expert here? I think—"

"Leanne! Cut the shit! Yes, right now she's the expert. She has spent the last few months with him, dealing with all his episodes, talking to the doctors, doing the research—I'd say she knows more about CJD and Dad's behavior than all of us combined at the moment. If you would just get your head out of your ass—"

"OUT! Now. All of you—out! From now on this room is going to be run with strict visiting hours. No more than two people at a time unless I give the okay for it to be otherwise." Everyone turned to face a fuming Lisa who was standing in the doorway, feet wide and hands on hips. "I want you all to go into the dining room and you're not to leave until you've worked out your issues like the adults you're supposed to be. We have a very difficult road ahead of us, and all this arguing is going to make everything worse." Everyone was rooted to the spot, humbled by Lisa's scolding and haunted by the continued sound of Elijah's laughter. "NOW!"

Miles was the first to move and everyone followed along obediently. They walked into the dining room as ordered and stood looking at anything but each other. Sarah knew there was only one way to resolve the situation.

"If you gentlemen don't mind, Leanne and I need to speak alone." They all looked at her as if she'd sprouted another head. "Please. The only issue here seems to be between Leanne and me so we're the only ones that need to work it out. If you would all go downstairs for awhile, we would appreciate the privacy." Miles led a reluctant Marcus and Brad out of the room. When they were gone, Leanne huffed and sat down dramatically at the table. Sarah took the seat across from her and waited for Leanne to speak first. It took some time and when she did her irritation was still elevated.

"Well? This was your idea so what do you have to say?"

"Let's start with why you don't like me."

Leanne crossed her arms and pierced her with a glare that could penetrate steel. "You know why."

"No, actually I don't. At first I thought it was because you were under the impression I was involved in a romantic relationship with your dad and then one with Marcus. You seemed content to freely call me a whore, if not in those exact words, and tell me I was to blame for causing a larger wedge between them. I've told you, more than once, you were incorrect, yet you still hold a grudge. Now you claim I've been lying to you and you're angry about that. The bottom line is you don't like me and you will continue to find reasons to blame something on me. So, the question is—why don't you like me? Until you're honest about it I don't think we'll be able to get anywhere."

"You think by opening up we will suddenly become best pals?"

"No, I don't expect you will ever like me. But I want you to be honest so we can at least respect our differences and at the very least not argue at inappropriate times." Leanne's face hardened and her mouth drew to a fine line. Sarah sighed and leaned forward on the table. "I'm trying to be patient and understanding here, Leanne. You just found out your dad is dying from a horrible disease. This is going to be a very difficult time for you and I don't want to make it worse. I'm here to support Elijah through this as well as you and Marcus. I'm not asking for us to become friends, just to put our differences aside."

Leanne leaned forward and slammed her fist against the table.

"And what happens when it's all over? You leave and I get left with trying to mourn my father and help my brother heal from a broken heart all at the same time? You ask why I don't like you—it's because I can see you're only looking out for yourself. Normally I would encourage someone to do just that, put their own wellbeing first, but when those actions negatively impact my family I have a problem with it. Have you told Marcus you don't want a relationship with him?"

"I told him I'm not ready for anything more than friendship right now."

"Yet you allow him to hug you and hold your hand and hell, maybe more I don't know about—you continue to give him hope for something more. When you walk away from here, you will leave him holding that hope while it drags him into the ground like quicksand."

Sarah felt her tears threaten. "I understand your point, and I wish I were strong enough to resist. But do you know what it feels like to not have anyone other than your parents or your best friend hug you for more than two years? There's no accurate way to articulate the void that's created by a lack of physical contact. To be touched only out of sympathy or pity or obligation. I'd forgotten what it felt like to be touched simply because the other person wanted to and was comforted by my touch in return. I've tried to resist, but I can't. I need it. Maybe that makes me selfish but I already made it clear how broken I am. All I can do is be honest with Marcus about my feelings. It's up to him to decide how much he's willing to risk. I don't want to hurt him, and I'm trying my best not to. I might fail, but that's what forgiveness is supposed to be for." Sarah wiped away her fallen tears. It was the first time Leanne had looked at her with something close to compassion.

"Fine, I'll back off and trust that you and Marcus can work it out." Leanne suddenly pushed away from the table and stood. "Also, I'm sorry I hit you."

Reeling from the unexpected cooperation, Sarah had to work hard to focus enough to form a coherent response. "Apology accepted. Just promise me you won't do it again."

"You know I can do no such thing. I might understand you better after this little talk and have agreed to call a truce for the moment, but we're still not friends. I'll reserve the right to hit you in the future should you deserve it."

"I figured as much, but you can't blame me for asking. Just know that next time I'll hit you back." Leanne actually smiled as she turned away.

"I'll call up the men. We need to work out sleeping arrangements and schedules if we're going to make it through this." Leanne was back in business mode and ready to take over. For the sake of everyone involved, Sarah had full intention of handing over the reins.

CHAPTER 22

Sarah sat in the office, alone with Elijah, answering emails on her tablet. A week had passed since Marcus and Leanne discovered the truth, and somehow they had all managed to survive living in the same house together. Elijah was getting worse each day and Dr. Holden had cautioned them he was nearing the point when he wanted to be admitted to the hospital. His movements had almost completely stopped, but he continued to make random and incoherent sounds. Today it sounded like he was trying to imitate a chicken.

Sarah tried to drown out the sound and focus on her emails. She was behind and suspicions were starting to rise. She had just finished her message to James, letting him know the time for him to come was quickly approaching, when Marcus entered the room fresh from a shower. Her pulse still quickened every time she saw him.

"Good morning, Sarah. How was your run?" Sarah ran each morning around the time Marcus found his way to the dance studio. It took all of her willpower to not join him after she finished her run. Not that she wanted to dance, she wanted to watch. The way he moved—and the shape of his body if she was being completely honest with herself—was simply intoxicating. She was trying her best to put distance between them, and the hour after her run was the only time she was able to be alone with Elijah. So every morning she reluctantly pushed herself past the studio and up the stairs, but not without at least one glance.

"Invigorating. How was your dance... workout... practice? I'm still not sure what I'm supposed to call it."

Marcus laughed. "Workout would be fine and it was also

invigorating." He watched her for a moment before turning to Elijah. "Good morning, Dad. How are you feeling?" Even though they knew he wouldn't answer, they couldn't keep from asking him questions hoping a miracle would happen, and he would respond. Marcus let out a soft sigh before he turned to sit in the chair next to her. "Did he eat anything?"

"No." They sat silently looking at Elijah, knowing if he didn't start eating again he would be in the hospital by the end of the week. After a few silent minutes, interrupted only by Elijah's occasional clucking, Marcus rubbed his face and shifted in his seat to face her.

"What are you working on?"

"Emails. I was afraid if I let them sit any longer the investigators would be sent out to make sure all my limbs were still intact."

He narrowed his eyes. "That Travis guy?"

She couldn't stop the smile from spreading across her face. "Yes, Travis is one of the people I need to respond to." He suddenly got up and went to Elijah's bed. He raised it slightly and then started fidgeting with the blanket. He turned and looked at her and then turned back to Elijah. She found his obvious frustration over Travis both entertaining and endearing. Choosing to let him squirm, she read through the latest email from Maggie and typed a response. He sat back down and even though he didn't speak she could tell he was watching her. She finally looked back at him when he cleared his throat.

"Sarah, I—" Elijah made another one of his clucking sounds and Marcus stopped. He ran a hand through his already tousled hair and stood to walk over to the windows. He let out a quick sigh and turned to face her. "Sarah—" Again Elijah made one of his clucking sounds. If she didn't know better, she would think Elijah was timing his sounds purposefully. "Damn it, doesn't he ever stop doing that?" He ran a hand back through his hair. "There's something I want to say, but I can't do it when he's making that stupid clucking sound. It's as if he's mocking me."

"Marcus, you know he can't control those sounds. They bother me as well, but you can't let it get to you."

"I know—I'll try to ignore it. Anyway, I've been struggling with something for a few days and if I don't say it soon I'm afraid it'll be too late once he's in the hospital." He took a deep breath and looked at the clock. They had about an hour before they would be interrupted and the flurry of activities for the day would begin. Elijah clucked again in rapid repetition.

"Do you want to talk in the other room? I'm sure Elijah would be fine alone for a few—"

"I don't want you to go back to Indiana." His face showed a mixture of relief at saying the words and uncertainty over her reaction. He held up his hand, silently asking her to not say anything until he was finished, and walked over to her. Instead of sitting in his chair, he squatted down in front of her and took her hands in his.

"I've struggled with whether or not I should tell you how I feel but then I remembered what you said the other day about making decisions. I decided that either way I run the risk of losing you. If I tell you how I feel, you might get frightened and never speak to me again. If I don't tell you, then you leave and I might never see you again. The risk is the same either way, so I figured it was best I at least tell you how I feel to help you make your own decision. I know you said you weren't ready for anything more in our relationship right now and I understand. I can wait, and we can take it slow—just don't leave." He paused and studied her face for a reaction. Her mind was whirling and she couldn't find her voice or the words she needed to say. Although she knew Marcus had feelings for her, it was still overwhelming to hear him speak the words out loud.

"Sarah, I know we haven't known each other very long but it doesn't matter to me. I know what I feel. I need you in my life. I'm afraid that if you get on a plane when this is all over that life and time zones will get in the way and you won't be able to find your way back to me." He fell silent again and she knew he wouldn't speak until she responded in some way. Words formed slowly in her mind and when she spoke they came out just as slowly.

"I admit there's a strong attraction between us. I felt it from the first moment you rescued me at the gala. But I don't know how I pick up my life and move for something that might just be a temporary attraction."

"I can assure you there is nothing temporary about my feelings for you and it's more than just an attraction." He spoke with such intensity she could only believe him. She was finding it very difficult to breathe.

"How can you be so sure after only a few weeks?"

He squeezed her hands. "You know the story of how my parents met. How could I not believe that when you know you just know? After my mom died I promised myself I wouldn't give my heart to anyone, because someday I would meet the woman who already owned it. I finally met her, thirty-four days ago, in the least likely way I thought imaginable—on the arm of my father."

She blinked rapidly, trying to stay focused.

Leanne was right, he's giving me his heart and I'm going to stomp all over it, causing him nothing but pain. I can't do that, but I don't think I can let go either.

She squeezed her eyes shut and tried to still her mind. The rampant thoughts were not helping.

"Marcus, you deserve so much more than what I can offer you. I'm not able to give you all of my heart and you deserve someone who can." He released her hands to gently cup her face, forcing her to look into his eyes.

"You need to accept that you no longer have all of you to give. A part of you will *always* belong to Nick and I don't want you to sacrifice that for me. I don't need all of your heart, Sarah. I just need the rest of it. And if the part that's left only has the capacity for friendship, then I'll take it. Just don't leave. I think I can survive anything except never seeing you again."

She had no words and her emotions finally broke past her hastily built defenses. Instead of offering him words she didn't have, she leaned forward and buried her sobs into his shoulder. He wrapped his arms around her and held her until they subsided. When she felt like she could breathe again, she lifted her head and saw Elijah over Marcus' shoulder. He was looking at her. His eyes weren't just settled on her, he was *looking* at her.

"Marcus, your dad..." Marcus instantly pulled away and turned to Elijah. When Marcus rose and walked to the bed, Elijah shifted his focus from Sarah to Marcus. She watched as Marcus pulled his dad into an embrace. He whispered into Elijah's ear, but she couldn't make out any of the words. She watched the two of them, thanking God for giving Marcus this moment. It wasn't much, but it was more than they could have hoped for under the circumstances.

How can I possibly push him away? He's offering to be anything I need, which is more than I deserve.

She continued to watch the two men before her. Two men she didn't know a few months ago, yet now she wouldn't know what her life would be like without either of them. One would be gone from this world very shortly, and the other she would leave behind. Feeling her emotions unravel she closed her eyes and thought of the other men who had held importance in her life. Certainly there was Nick, and she missed him with every fiber of her being, but he could never be anything more in her life again than a memory. Then there was her brother James. She had let him go and didn't fully understand the pain she had caused herself by doing so until she saw him at Christmas. She would never let him go again. Her dad was the other man in her life that had somehow slipped through her fingers. Somewhere she had stopped being daddy's little girl and they drifted apart, even if ever so slightly it was too much. She opened her eyes and looked back at Marcus holding Elijah.

No, I can't do anything to keep Elijah in my life, but I can certainly hold on to Marcus.

The thought hit her with a surprising amount of resolve. She didn't yet know what it meant, didn't know what she would be able to offer him, but at the very least she could fight to keep him in her life. She'd had enough loss and pain for more than one lifetime, and she was determined to hold on to as much happiness as she possibly could from that moment forward.

"Damn it." It was the second time Sarah had knocked over the lamp. Her hands were shaking from emotions she didn't want to acknowledge. She tried to stand the lamp back up, but it fell over again. In frustration she threw it across the floor. The sound of it clattering against Elijah's now unused bed caused her to jump. She put her face into her hands and sat down in a chair by the fireplace.

Elijah's in the hospital. He will never set foot in this house again. He will be gone from my life so very soon.

Her breathing became shallow and a familiar tightness formed in her chest. She shook away the tears and stood up to resume her task. She didn't know what she was looking for, but it didn't stop her hypnotic search through Elijah's room. She walked back to his desk and pulled out the top drawer and rummaged through the contents before slamming it shut and repeating the process with the remaining two drawers. A stray tear escaped down her cheek and she swatted it away. She walked to the left side nightstand by the bed, pulling open the drawer and blindly rummaging the contents. Suddenly, things came into focus as she looked upon a small notebook. It was the notebook she'd seen Elijah with during those last few months. She knew instantly it was what she was subconsciously looking for.

He had created himself a memory book. The pages were filled with notes in Elijah's handwriting on facts he didn't want to forget once CJD started taking his memories away. The first page was a message to himself, explaining the nature of his disease. Several pages were dedicated to Marlena and his children. Next she saw pages for Miles and Tina. She stopped when she got to a page with her name written across the top. He had jotted down facts about her—how she had lost Nick and Danny, why she was there, her favorite food and favorite color. She flipped through more pages and noticed where he had written down things he needed to do. These included changing the house code and watching the DVD of her and Marcus dancing. She continued looking over the rest of his notes and then flipped past blank pages, hoping there would be more. She wanted to absorb as much of his final thoughts as she could. She was rewarded near the end of the notebook, the corner of the page folded over as a marker. It was his bucket list.

Hike to the lake
Go to the ballet
See Marcus dance
Tell Sarah the truth

The last item caused her to drop to the ground. She had helped Elijah complete all the other items on his list but the last one took her by complete surprise.

Tell me the truth about what? Did he already tell me and I didn't realize it was some sort of confession, or did he never get to it? What could he have possibly lied about that he would add confessing the truth to me to his bucket list? I have no idea, and now it's too late to find out.

Her entire body shook as the enormity of her loss hit her like a brick. She could no longer ignore Elijah would die any day, and in reality he was already gone. She curled up in a ball on the floor and allowed herself to start grieving.

Sarah had been sitting next to Elijah's bed for over ten minutes. It was her time alone with him to say good-bye, but she couldn't form a single word. She closed her eyes and tried to picture the man she met that first day at his house in October. He had been so full of life, and it was impossible for her to merge the memory of that man with the fragile one who lay in the bed before her. She wished she knew if he was in pain. If he was aware of his surroundings and what was happening to him. If he wanted to communicate, but was unable to because he was trapped in a mental straight jacket. She prayed he was at peace and was sleeping through the torment of his illness. She opened her eyes and looked at him again, knowing it was time to start talking before her time was up.

"Elijah, it's me—Sarah. I don't know if you can hear me, but I'm going to talk anyway." She paused and gently took his hand in hers. "I'm not sure what I have to say is a surprise since you always seem to know everything, but I need to tell you anyway. I want to say thank you, but that doesn't seem to be enough for what you've done for me. In such a short time you've not only become one of my dearest friends, but you truly were the catalyst I needed to live again. You saved me, Elijah. How do I properly thank you, especially since you will be gone? I wish you could be here so I could continuously find ways to repay this priceless gift you have given me. All I can do is promise you I won't go back to the way it was before. I promise I will continue to find ways to live out my life—to be happy again and find the beauty in everything around me. I suppose I'll start with right now.

"On the surface there is nothing about this situation that contains any sort of beauty. But I found one. It's your strength and courage. Not many people would have been able to face this wretched disease through to the end. But you did, and you did it with your head held high the entire way. You fought it to the best of your ability, and instead of reducing yourself to self pity you chose to cherish every day you had left, and lived it to the fullest. You remained true to yourself, even on decisions some may not have agreed with. I admire you for

how you faced down this monster and I find it absolutely beautiful."
She had to pause to find her voice before continuing.

"I will miss you so much, Mighty Mr. Kingston. I pray you soon
find the peace you have rightfully earned." She stood to place a kiss
on his forehead. She pulled back and wiped away her tears that had
fallen onto his face. She felt the sobs come in gut wrenching force as
she sat down on the bed and laid her head on his chest. She remained
that way, even after the sobs had reduced to quiet tears. Several
minutes later she heard the door to his room open, but she remained
where she was. She still didn't look when she felt a familiar set of
hands settle upon her shoulders.

"Sarah, I'm sorry but your time is up. I might be able to get you a
few more minutes later, but Leanne has made it clear that the rest of
this time is to be reserved for family only." She finally opened her
eyes and looked at Miles. His eyes were red and there were deep
circles beneath them.

"No, it's okay. I said what I needed to say. I'm ready." She slowly
stood and looked down at Elijah. She bent to place a final kiss on his
cheek and whispered in his ear. "Good-bye, Elijah. I won't forget my
promise, you have my word." She leaned into Miles as he walked her
out of the room.

Sarah sat in the hospital waiting room, feeling numb and empty.
Marcus and Leanne had been in Elijah's room ever since Miles
escorted her out. Marcus came out every few hours to check on her.
His concern for her in the midst of his grief was almost enough to
make her agree to stay in Colorado. The first few times he came to
check on her he'd asked her to go back with him into Elijah's room,
but she'd convinced him it wasn't a good idea.

Now they were all just waiting for Elijah's torment to be over.
Elijah's wishes made it clear he didn't want to be put on a feeding
tube or any other form of life support. There was no defeating his
illness, so prolonging things would only make it more painful for
everyone. She turned her attention to the door when it opened.

"Mrs. Mitchell? There's someone here to see you." Sarah's brow
furrowed for a moment before she realized who it must be. She leapt
up and crushed into James as he walked through the door. His

presence brought forth a new round of tears. He guided her to one of the sofa seats where he held her and stroked her hair while she cried. She'd felt so alone in her waiting, and it would be good to have someone by her side for the remainder of the ordeal.

"James, I'm so glad you're here. Thank you for coming."

"I wouldn't be anywhere but here right now." He tried to shift her, but she refused to move from the comfort of his arms. He gave up and settled back in the sofa seat. "What's the status of Mr. Kingston? The nurse wouldn't tell me anything even though I'm on the approved list of visitors."

"I haven't heard anything for a couple hours, but last I knew he was still holding on. It won't be long though." Just then the door opened again, and she lifted her head from James' shoulder when Marcus stepped into the room, stopping with a hard look on his face as he looked at James. He stood there for a few seconds, staring at James, before finally walking over. She noticed he was shaking.

"Marcus, is Elijah... has anything changed?"

"No, he's still the same." He never took his eyes off James. She looked at her brother, his expression clearly displaying his confusion at Marcus' scrutiny. She stood, allowing James to do the same.

"Marcus, I'd like you to meet my brother James. James, this is Elijah's son, Marcus." Marcus' features instantly softened as he let out a sharp breath. He extended his hand to James in greeting.

"I'm happy to meet you Mr.— er, James. Sorry, I don't know your last name and I know it's not Mitchell."

James shook Marcus' hand and studied him carefully. "Polanski. However, please call me James. It's nice to meet you as well. Sarah's mentioned you and it's good to put a face with the name. I'm just sorry we have to meet under these circumstances." Marcus looked at her and she blushed. James gave her a questioning look until he noticed her eye. His features quickly turned to anger as he pulled her face closer to inspect the black eye that was still visible. "What the hell happened to your eye?"

She pulled away. "It's nothing. I ran into a door. A short but very stubborn and surprisingly strong door." She glanced at Marcus and noticed he was trying to contain a smile. She decided to change subjects before James asked more questions. "Why don't we go to the cafeteria? I need coffee."

"Do you mind if I join you?" She was surprised at the request. Even though Marcus came out regularly to check on her, he only stayed a few minutes before going back to Elijah's side. He must have read her mind. "The nurse needs time alone with Dad. We can go back in there in about thirty minutes."

"Sure, that'd be great." She blushed again when Marcus put his hand on the small of her back and led her out of the waiting room. She knew James would be scrutinizing every detail of their interaction, and he would insist on answers. Once in the hall, Marcus dropped his hand and the three walked alongside each other until they were approached by Leanne. She looked at James with almost as much disapproval as Marcus had before he learned who he was.

"Who's this? I thought we were keeping things quiet until it was over." She pointed her glare at Sarah.

"This is James Polanski, Sarah's brother. Miles and I agreed it would be good for him to be here for Sarah." She shouldn't have been surprised at how quickly Marcus stepped up to defend her and take responsibility for something he didn't even know about, but she was just the same. Marcus turned to James. "James, this is my sister, Leanne Troupe. Also known as the door." Sarah couldn't stop her surprised laughter from erupting and she tried to cover it up with a fake cough.

"The door? What's that supposed to mean?"

"Don't worry about it, sis. You can think of it as a term of endearment."

Leanne shook her head in frustration. "You know what, I'm too exhausted to play your games today. If you're going down to the cafeteria, bring me back a diet-soda." With that she turned on her heel and walked off. Sarah held her breath in anticipation of James' reaction. To her relief, and surprise, he laughed.

"Short, stubborn and strong. Yes, I believe I can see the accurateness of that description." They all laughed, releasing some of the tension that had been building. They continued in silence to the cafeteria where they separated long enough to get their drinks and then joined Miles and Tina at a table. Sarah made the additional introductions and they quickly fell into casual conversation. After a few minutes, the group fell into an uncomfortable silence until Marcus cleared his throat.

"So, we should probably address the elephant in the room and acknowledge that tomorrow is Dad's birthday." Sarah looked up at Marcus in surprise.

How had I not known Elijah's birthday was tomorrow?

"Tomorrow's Elijah's birthday?" She couldn't manage anything beyond a whisper as she looked from Marcus to Miles to Tina for confirmation. All three hung their heads and nodded. She fell back into her seat in dismay. "Oh."

"I wouldn't put it past Dad to be holding on so he could kick it tomorrow, waiting for that last opportunity to throw something in our face. We always do something special to honor my mom's memory on her birthday. But not Dad, no, he needs to forever link his birthday with the day he dies so we can't even have one day to honor him without the sting of him being gone." There was sarcasm in Marcus' voice, but mostly Sarah heard pain. She instinctively reached over to squeeze his hand which he turned so he could lace his fingers with hers.

"Yes, that does sound like Elijah. However, he's also one for finishing everything he starts. Could you imagine the torment he would put the after-life through if he'd started another year without the opportunity to finish it? Maybe we could appreciate his thoroughness, and respect that he didn't leave a new year unfinished." She held Marcus' gaze and gave his hand another squeeze. "And it's still possible he won't die tomorrow." Marcus responded with a small smile before lifting her hand to plant a soft kiss on her knuckles and then dropping their still joined hands into his lap. She felt her face flush and refused to look over at James. Miles finally broke the silence by standing up.

"We should probably get back." Feeling the need to escape, Sarah excused herself from the group.

"I need to use the bathroom, so I'll just meet you in the waiting room." She disentangled her fingers from Marcus and quickly left for the bathroom before anyone could stop her. Once in the bathroom, she locked herself in a stall for several minutes in attempt to regain her composure. She knew once she was alone with James the inquisition would start, and she needed to be prepared. By the time she made it back to the waiting room, James was alone and talking quietly on the phone. She sat down and waited for him to finish.

"Juliet says to tell you hello." He walked over and sat down across from her.

"Did you tell her what was going on?"

"Yes, but she knows not to say anything to Mom." James sat back in the chair, resting one foot on a knee and folding his hands across his chest. He studied her and she waited, knowing what was coming. "Speaking of what's going on around here I noticed you left a few things out when we last talked."

"What do you mean?" She knew what he was talking about but didn't want to make it easy on him.

"You know exactly what I mean." She raised her eyebrows to him in question. "Marcus? You two seem... close."

"Oh? I hadn't noticed." She wasn't sure why she was playing this game. It would only frustrate James further and make him ask more questions.

"Sarah, quit being difficult. Why didn't you tell me about... whatever it is that's going on between you two, and why aren't you telling me now?"

She took out her ponytail and ran her fingers through her hair before pulling it into a sloppy bun. "I don't know, James. I guess I'm not ready to acknowledge... whatever it is."

"It's obvious he has feelings for you. Has he said anything?"

"He wants me to stay out here." She looked down at the pendant Elijah gave her as it twirled from her nervous fingers.

"What do you want?"

"That's just it—I don't know. I'm not ready for any type of relationship, yet the thought of never seeing him again... I don't know." He was silent for so long she reluctantly looked up to find him watching her.

"Well, you know I will have an opinion, but I'll wait until you're ready to talk about it." She narrowed her eyes in suspicion.

"That's it?"

"Yep, that's it. For now." She breathed a sigh of relief.

Sarah stretched and attempted to crack her neck. She had refused to let James take her to the hotel the night before and the waiting room sofa was not made for someone her size to sleep on. She sat up, looked around the room, and saw James sitting nearby working on his computer.

"What time did you get here?" She yawned halfway through her question and James handed her a cup of coffee.

"About an hour ago. I got the coffee about five minutes ago though, so it should still be fairly warm." She took a big gulp.

"It's perfect." She blinked several times trying to clear the sleep from her eyes and looked at the clock. It was a few minutes after six in the morning. "Did you see anyone else out there?"

"I ran into Leanne's husband, is it Brad? Right, Brad—I ran into him in the cafeteria. Tina drove over with me from the hotel and stayed to help Brad with drinks. I saw Miles talking to the doctor and that private nurse lady down the hall and I assume Marcus and Leanne are in Elijah's room." Brad had returned home last night to be with Oliver while Leanne and Marcus remained by Elijah's side. Miles had attempted to sleep in the waiting room with Sarah while Tina and James had gone to a nearby hotel. "How much sleep did you get?"

"I feel like I didn't sleep at all, but I think in total I slept about three hours. Marcus and Miles were in here talking until well past midnight, and I fell asleep at some point during their conversation, but woke up several times between then and now."

"I wish you would have gone to the hotel. You need sleep."

"I'll sleep when this is over. Until then, coffee is my friend."

She watched the minutes click past on the clock while he continued to work. She was wound up with nervous energy, and when she wasn't pacing the floor she was sitting on the sofa chair bouncing her knee. At one point James placed a gentle hand on her knee to try and keep it still, but it was only effective for about thirty seconds. Twenty minutes had passed since she woke up when the door opened, causing her to jump. It was Miles and Tina. Sarah looked at them expectantly. Miles frowned and shook his head. They sat down near James but everyone remained silent. It was as if something was hanging in the air, sucking out all ability to speak.

Another half an hour passed before the door opened again and everyone watched as Marcus stepped in, eyes red and tears falling. He walked straight for Sarah where he dropped to his knees in front of her and buried his face in her lap. She cradled his head in her arms and wept with him over the loss of his father and her friend.

CHAPTER 23

Sarah zipped her suitcase closed and pulled it out of the closet. She stood for a moment, looking around the room.

It's almost time to go. After the meeting it's off to the airport.

The thought caused a complex mixture of emotions to run through her.

The funeral had taken place two days ago. True to Elijah's word, he had been the most prepared person on his deathbed and he had seen to every last detail. He had chosen to be cremated and had arranged for a private service for family and close friends. A memorial reception had been held in downtown Denver, and a staggering amount of people attended. Sarah had been filled with an overwhelming sense of relief when Maggie and Andy showed up at the reception. At the sight of her best friend, she had been struck with an intense urge to pull Maggie off to the side of the room and tell her everything. Somehow she had found the strength to resist, knowing it wasn't the time or the place.

The whole experience had been difficult for Sarah but Maggie and James had helped ease the pain. One of them had remained by her side the entire time, except for those moments when Marcus found a way to extricate himself from others to be with her. Sometimes they would sit and he would talk about memories. Other times he would simply stand next to her, holding her hand or putting his arm around her waist. Even consumed with grief, Sarah noticed several people shot curious glances their way. Maggie included.

As Sarah looked around the room that had been hers for the past few months, her eyes settled on the bed and she felt heat rise up her cheeks. It had started the night Elijah died. She had been lying awake when her door opened without warning. Marcus quietly made his way over, where he stood silently asking to be welcomed into her bed. She hesitated, but quickly shifted to the side. He immediately crawled under the covers, taking her in his arms. He held her to his chest and there she remained, wrapped in his arms, for the rest of the night. When she woke the next morning, Marcus was still there. He was awake but didn't appear to have any intentions of moving. He looked down at her for a few minutes before planting a kiss on the top of her head. Then he started talking. He opened himself up whole and shared all his personal feelings where Elijah was concerned. It was a moment she would cherish always.

He had come to her bed every night since, always after he had spent several hours in his own bed and always just to hold her. He hadn't even kissed her—aside from the soft kisses he'd planted on her hands, her cheek, her forehead or the top of her head. And she could finally admit to herself that she wanted him to kiss her. But she had respected him so much more for *not* kissing her. Both were in such a raw state of vulnerability that if he had, it would have likely led to things they weren't ready to share.

There was a light knock on the door before it swung open. Marcus walked in and looked from Sarah to her bags and back again. The sadness in his eyes tugged at her heart.

"So, you haven't changed your mind? You're still leaving?"

"Yes, I'm still leaving. I need to go home. You understand, right? There are things I need to address before I can move on with my life and I have to be home to do them." He closed the door and leaned against it, putting his hands in his pockets.

"I know you tried to talk to me about this yesterday, and I wasn't being very receptive. I'm sorry, but you know what I want. However, I respect and understand your decision." He looked down at his feet, suddenly appearing very shy. "Can I call you while you're gone?"

She took a deep breath. This was the moment she had been dreading. She'd tried to tell him what she needed last night, but he had stormed off after she told him she was leaving. Now, it seemed impossible to say the words.

"I need some time alone first." His head shot up and the pain she saw almost made her change her mind. She closed her eyes and reminded herself why it was important. "I only ask for a month where we don't talk. I know you're certain in your feelings but I'm coming from a different place and I need to be sure before making any life changing decisions. I can't think straight when you're around. Even virtually I believe you will have the capacity to strip away all logic and rattle my senses."

He looked away from her but nodded his head. "One month. I can do that if it's what you really need."

"Thank you. It won't be easy for me. I don't like the idea of not talking to you, Marcus. I need you to believe that. I also need you to know I don't intend to cut you from my life. I don't know what I want out of our relationship, and I need to figure it out. That's all."

He looked back at her and studied her a few seconds before walking over to her. He placed his hands on her hips, drawing her closer.

This is it. Oh, God, he's going to kiss me.

He leaned his head down and she closed her eyes in anticipation. Instead of feeling his lips, she felt his forehead rest on hers. They stood there, forehead to forehead, breathing slightly erratically for what felt like hours. The sensation of being so close to him, of anticipating a kiss that wasn't coming, caused her head to swim. She placed her hands on his arms for support which caused him to take in a sharp breath and pull her closer. Finally, he pulled away and planted a lingering kiss on her forehead. She dropped her head to his chest and wrapped her arms around his waist, not wanting to let him go. They remained that way until there was a soft knock on the door. Reluctantly, she lifted her head. Marcus gently wiped away her tears before finally opening the door when there was another knock.

"Sorry to interrupt, but the car is here. It's time to go." James looked at Marcus suspiciously.

Always the protective older brother.

Sarah couldn't help but smile at the thought, causing James to soften his stance. "Let me help with your bags." Marcus handed him one of the suitcases and picked up the other one. Sarah followed them out of the room, but paused for one last look around before leaving. She felt like she should feel more closure than she did, but for some reason she had the sensation it wouldn't be the last time she would see this room.

Sarah, Marcus, Leanne and Brad sat in a conference room, waiting for Miles to retrieve some papers from his office. Sarah still wasn't sure why Miles had insisted she be at the reading of Elijah's will. Deep down she knew there was only one reason she legally needed to be there, but she refused to acknowledge the possibility. Miles finally entered the room and sat down across from everyone.

"Thank you for making the time to be here today. This will be difficult for all of us, so I intend to stick to the reading of the will and we can conclude the meeting."

"Miles, why is Sarah here? We all know the details of the will and there's no reason she needs to be here."

"Leanne, don't start." The warning was clear in Marcus' voice.

"For once I actually agree with your sister. I don't understand why I'm here."

Miles let out an exasperated breath. "If you would all be quiet, I can read the blasted thing and then it will become clear." He looked over at Leanne with a somewhat apologetic look. "Besides, Elijah revised the will a few months before he died."

"He did what? Miles, you can't be serious. You know he wasn't in his right mind most of the time!" Leanne sat forward in her chair and slapped a hand against the table.

"He was when he made the changes. I was aware of his condition from the time we started working together, so I never would have let him make any changes if I didn't feel he knew what he was doing." Sarah was suddenly on alert, knowing Elijah's changes must have included her. She didn't look, but she could feel Leanne's burning gaze on her. As if trying to shield her from it, Marcus shifted in his seat to block Leanne's line of sight and took hold of Sarah's hand. Miles cleared his throat and started reading. Sarah felt uncomfortable listening in on the details of Elijah's assets, but she remained attentive.

I can't believe Elijah did this. He'd better not have left me anything substantial.

Miles explained how all of Elijah's holdings in Kingston Enterprises would go to Leanne. A sizeable amount of his funds were set aside in a trust for Oliver and the remaining amount was divided among Leanne and Marcus. Miles continued to describe what Elijah had wanted donated to charities, at the final decision of Marcus and Leanne. Marcus tensed next to her when one of those charities was for animal rescue. She looked at him and could see the impact of Elijah's intention. Miles continued reading and eventually paused to shoot a quick glance at Sarah.

"I wish to leave my coffee machine to Sarah Mitchell to which she has become extremely attached." She sighed in relief and smiled at Elijah's humor.

If that's it, Miles could have sent me the damn thing rather than make me sit through this.

Her relief ended when Miles continued. "Since the coffee machine is extremely attached to the house, I also leave her full ownership of my home and all contents within, except those pertaining to Kingston Enterprises." Miles paused again as his words sunk into her like weight. Suddenly everything in the room became quiet and her vision blurred. She felt Marcus squeeze her hand, bringing her back from the fog.

"Sarah, are you all right?" She could only manage a slight nod in response to Miles' question.

"Shall I continue?" Miles waited until she nodded her head again. "Mrs. Mitchell has the right to retain or sell the home and all its contents as she sees fit. However, my hope is that she chooses to live there and make it her home for the next phase of her life." Miles stopped talking and looked at everyone. The tension in the room was thick. Sarah wasn't surprised when Leanne was the first to speak.

"This is unbelievable! He left her the house and everything in it? Damn it, the house belongs in the family! What was he thinking Miles, and why did you let him give the house to her? You're going to give it back." Sarah could barely hear Brad whispering calming words to Leanne.

"Leanne, I'm warning you. Not another word. Dad made his choice, and it's Sarah's right to do with the house as she wishes." Leanne started to protest again but Brad silenced her. Miles opened a folder sitting in front of him and pulled out a stack of envelopes. He handed one to Leanne and Sarah and two to Marcus.

"Elijah left all three of you a letter. You are free to read them whenever you like. Marcus, you have two and I've numbered them in the order he wants you to read them." Everyone sat looking at the envelopes in their hands. Suddenly, Marcus pushed away from the table and walked out of the room. Sarah wasn't sure what to do and was about to get up and follow when Leanne walked out. She remained in her seat, deciding it was best to give them privacy.

Brad asked Miles questions about the trust for Oliver and Sarah's mind drifted down to the letter in her hands.

When had he written this?

She dropped it on the table, as if burned. She looked away and her mind drifted to the house. Her anger rose slowly as she thought about what he had done. He had to have known Leanne would blow a head gasket.

Why did he do it? I never indicated a desire to live here. Miles said he made these changes months ago, and he couldn't have possibly anticipated Marcus and I would have a connection and that he would ask me to move out here. I—

"Sarah?" She looked up to Miles.

"I'm sorry?" She had missed what he'd said. He was pushing a large yellow envelope across the table at her.

"This contains the information and documents you need for the house. There are some keys in there, but as you know the primary door uses a code which you already have. You also already have the security code. Tina and I can help with any maintenance and any decisions you make with regard to the house." Just then the doors to the room opened and Leanne walked in. Sarah turned and caught the fury in her glare.

"Miles, you know I'm leaving today. I'm not sure when I'll be able to make it back. In the meantime I would like for you to walk Leanne and Marcus through the house. They have my permission to take anything they want."

Miles studied her carefully. "Sure, I'd be happy to. Should I catalogue what's removed and the presumed value of each item?"

"No, that won't be necessary. Regardless of what Elijah has said, the items in the house belong to his children, not me. Except for the coffee maker, which I intend to keep." She looked at Leanne and watched her visibly soften as a result of the offer. Feeling suddenly uncomfortable, she stood and picked up her envelopes.

"Miles, I'll talk to you soon. Give my best to Tina and tell her I'll call her when I get home." Miles walked around the table and gave her a hug.

"Take care, Sarah. You know you're welcome out here any time, and Tina and I both hope you decide to come back. Have a safe trip."

He gave her a kiss on the cheek before releasing her. Brad was next to wish her good-bye and she was surprised when he also hugged her. She turned to face Leanne and was struck with uncertainty for what to say. Leanne spoke first and surprised her even more than the hug she'd received from her husband.

"Good-bye, Sarah. I hope at some point in the future we'll be able to be on better terms with each other. I know I'm a difficult person, but I am my father's daughter after all. If you remain at Jacobs Management Firm, maybe I can persuade you to work on a project for me in the future." She stuck out her hand and Sarah shook it mutely. "Marcus is out there waiting with your brother. I think he intends to go to the airport with you." With that she turned and walked over to Brad's side.

Sarah hugged the envelopes to her chest and walked out of the conference room to join James and Marcus. They both stood when she entered the lobby and stepped in her direction, stopping to look at each other. Marcus stepped back and extended his arm, yielding to James.

"You okay, kid?"

"Yeah, no... I don't know. Elijah left me his house."

James nodded his head. "Marcus told me. He said you might be in shock."

"Yes, I think that's a very definite possibility." She glanced at Marcus. "Are you okay?"

He smiled. "I'll be fine. Come, we'd better get you two to the airport before you miss your flights. I've already called Thompson and he should be outside waiting."

"Thanks again for coming." Sarah gave James a light, affectionate punch on the shoulder.

"It's what big brothers are for, right?" He returned the playful push before pulling her into a hug. As he pulled away, he nodded his head in the direction over her shoulder. "He seems like a really good guy and I think he cares an awful lot about you. It pains me to say that, being your protective older brother and all. It also seems strange for me to accept given you haven't known him long, but I thought I should tell you what I think. I know you're not ready to talk about it, but I'm here when you are." He planted a quick kiss on her forehead. "Take care of yourself."

"I will. Tell Juliet and the boys I said hello and thanks for letting me borrow you. Text me when you get home." He winked at her and then raised his hand in a good-bye salute to Marcus before turning and walking to the security check. She felt Marcus come up next to her and they watched until James passed through security.

"Why don't we find some place to sit?" Marcus placed his arm around her back and rested his hand on her hip, giving her a little squeeze. She had about an hour before needing to get to her departing gate. She nodded and allowed him to lead her to a restaurant. Instead of sitting across the table from her, he took the chair directly to her left and pulled his chair close to hers. They ordered drinks and fell into a comfortable silence. The waiter returned with Marcus' beer and Sarah's water. Marcus took a large swig from the bottle before finally speaking.

"I can see why you and James are close. I'm glad he was able to be here for you."

"It felt good to see him again. It wasn't until I saw him at Christmas that I realized how much I really missed him."

"I'm going to miss you." He reached over and took her free hand.

"I'm going to miss you too. But we will talk again, in one month. And I meant what I said, I don't intend to cut you from my life so once I figure all this out we'll go from there."

His gaze was concentrated on their joined hands, his thumb tracing small circles on the back of her hand. "I know, but it doesn't make it any easier." He looked up and a playful smile touched his lips. "I do feel better knowing my father left you our house. You at least have to come back to deal with that, and if you decide to move out here you'll have a place to live."

She shook her head and took another drink of her water. "I still can't believe he did that." The thought ran through her mind that if he were still alive she would strangle him, and it caused a pang of emptiness deep in her core. She opened her mouth to speak, but the words died off before they even formalized on her tongue.

"What is it?"

She took a deep breath. "Do you intend to get tested for CJD?" He shifted his eyes to the label on his beer bottle.

"I don't know. I want to live my life for now, not what will happen twenty to thirty years from now, and I may not have a choice once I know the truth." He shifted in his seat and cleared his throat. "Do you think it will make a difference in your decision? Do you need to know if I have CJD before you decide if you'll move out here and start a life with me?"

"I'd like to think it wouldn't matter." He focused on her again and his look was intensely serious.

"I'll get tested if not knowing is a deal breaker for you."

Her heart surged at his declaration. "No, I only want you to do it if you feel you need to for your own piece of mind. I'll make my decision based on the fact that I know it's a possibility."

They finished their drinks in silence. Marcus paid the bill and took her hand again, holding it the entire way to the security gate. They stood looking at each other, not sure of how to say good-bye. She felt like her heart might burst through her chest. Before she had time to register what was happening, she felt his lips on hers in a gentle but passionate kiss. He let go of her hand and wrapped his arms around her waist, pulling her closer and deepening the kiss. Her knees went weak from the sensations but his arms tightened, keeping her upright. When he finally broke away, she was lightheaded and was having difficulty breathing. She looked up at him and he wiped the tears away from her cheeks. A small frown formed between his brows.

"I'm sorry, I shouldn't have done that. I've wanted to kiss you since I first laid eyes on you." She realized he mistook her tears for those of sadness rather than joy. To convince him otherwise she pulled his head back to hers and kissed him again. They broke apart when someone accidentally bumped them; reminding her they were standing in the middle of a busy airport. She buried her face in his neck for a final hug, not wanting to let go.

"Promise me something?" His whispered voice on her ear stirred all sorts of physical reactions that were long forgotten.

"Not fair. Right now I think I might promise you anything." His arms tightened around her and she felt him chuckle.

"As tempting as that sounds, I would never take the advantage. No, my request is pretty simple. I'll give you the one month with no contact if you promise you won't see or talk to that Travis guy either." She looked up into his beautiful face.

"Are you really that worried about him?"

"More than I care to admit."

"Okay, I promise I won't see or talk to Travis either. I'm going into a month of solitude with my only contact being with my family, Maggie and Tina. And my therapist. Sound fair?" She watched his face relax with relief.

"Yes, that sounds acceptable."

"Will you promise me something?"

"Anything."

"Will you promise to keep dancing?"

She felt his whispered 'yes' on her mouth right before his lips touched hers again. Somehow they managed to keep it brief and when she pulled away he handed over her carry-on. She felt her chest tighten and her throat clench at the thought of saying good-bye.

"One month, starting now, and not a second longer. With the exception of one text from you letting me know you got home safely." Sarah nodded and walked away before she lost all her resolve. She looked back only once before turning the final corner that led to her terminal. He was standing in the same spot, eyes locked on her. She raised her hand in farewell and he did the same. Taking a deep breath she walked on unsteady legs to her gate.

She spent the entire flight home in a surreal state, replaying the moment in the airport with Marcus over and over in her mind. If she'd had any lingering doubts about the connection between them, they were effectively dissolved the instant his lips touched hers. It had taken every ounce of her strength to walk away. When the pain of leaving him started to creep back up, she reminded herself of all the reasons why she needed to do this.

I need to learn how to survive on my own—to trust I can rely on myself to be happy. I need to know if I'm in love with Marcus or simply attracted to him.

Although it was late when Sarah's flight arrived, Andy had been waiting at the airport as promised. He greeted her with a hug and silently led her to baggage claim. They made casual conversation on the walk to the car but she could tell he wanted to talk about more important things. As he was paying the parking attendant, she pulled out her phone and sent off a quick text to Marcus.

I'm in Indy. Andy picked me up and is driving me home. Thanks for providing me with some pleasant thoughts for the flight home.

Marcus' response was almost instantaneous.

It was my intention to provide us both with enough pleasant thoughts to last a month. I'm already counting down.

She smiled and tucked the phone back into her purse before glancing at Andy. His jaw was set into a hard line.

"Andy, you can say whatever is on your mind. We've known each other long enough to skip past the bullshit."

"I promised Maggie I wouldn't give you a hard time on the ride home."

"Well, I promise I won't tell Maggie I forced you to do so. Out with it, what's on your mind?"

"Why didn't you tell me, Sarah? Christ! Kingston is our biggest client. A little heads up would have been appreciated."

"Elijah had me sign a NDA the day I started, and he specifically included you on the list of people not to tell. Now that it's over I'll answer any questions you have, but you'll have to get over being angry about me not telling you. If his children can let it go, so can you."

He stole a glance at her and there were enough street lights to see the confusion on his face. "His children didn't know about his condition?"

"No one knew except me, his lawyer and his doctors." She heard him let out a harsh breath.

"So you knew what was going to happen, yet you accepted the assignment anyway?"

"Yes. I know it might be difficult for people to understand my reasons, but it turned out to be the best decision I've ever made."

"Because of Marcus? Don't give me that look. At the memorial reception I could tell something was going on between you two."

"Yes, I suppose meeting Marcus was one of the reasons I'm glad I took the assignment. However, mostly it's because Elijah saved me. Someday I'll be able to explain to you how much he helped me, but right now it's too painful to talk about." She crossed her arms over her chest to try and counter the tightening grip forming around her ribs.

"You two became pretty close?"

"Yes." He must have heard the pain in her voice because he stopped asking questions.

When he finally pulled into her driveway, she wasn't prepared for the flood of memories that came rushing back to her. Nick and Danny consumed a majority of her thoughts while she was gone, but being back where she shared a life with them brought the memories back in a crushing force.

This is how it was. This is what I did for two years. I suffocated through the pain and memories until I had no more strength in me to fight against it.

She closed her eyes as her vision faded and a pounding formed between her temples.

"Sarah? Are you all right?" Andy's voice came from far away and slowly became closer. "Sarah, please answer me." Finally she was back in the present.

"Yes... no... I'm not really sure. The house... I didn't expect it to hit me so fast." She felt the car moving again. "What are you doing?"

"I'm taking you to our house. You can stay as long as you need, and Maggie can come with you when you feel up to coming back here." She didn't have the strength or the desire to argue with him. She closed her eyes and leaned her head against the cool window.

I have to figure this out. I have to figure out if I can let this pain go and move on with a new life. I promised Elijah I wouldn't go back to the way it was before. I have to figure this out.

Sarah spent the first two weeks at Maggie and Andy's house. In that time she reconnected with one of her previous therapists, Dr. Cole, and each day she felt her strength growing. Dr. Cole helped her realize she needed to grieve for Elijah before she pushed herself back into the emotional turbulence of her former life. Andy had agreed to an indefinite leave from work and she spent her days helping Maggie.

Each day that passed she knew Maggie was itching with need to ask her questions about Elijah and Marcus, but she somehow restrained until toward the end of the second week. They were sitting alone in the sun room while Andy had taken the kids to a movie.

"I'm really glad you're here, Sarah. Your transformation has been amazing. You look great. And I'm still astonished you're able to be around Nathan."

"It's hard, but I'm learning to separate him from Danny."

"I know Dr. Cole has been a tremendous help to you this time around, but I also have the feeling a lot of this has to do with your time with Elijah. Are you ready to talk about it?"

She smiled at Maggie's look of anxious anticipation. "I'm surprised you were able to hold off this long without asking." Maggie groaned in frustration.

"You know me, it's been killing me. But I called and asked Dr. Cole what I should do, and she told me I should give you two weeks. I almost made it."

Sarah leaned over and patted her knee. "You did good. How about we get some wine first?" Maggie jumped up and in no time returned with two glasses of sparkling white wine.

Sarah took a sip and started talking. She told Maggie everything that had happened from the moment she had arrived at Elijah's house to the parting kiss from Marcus. Unlike her conversation with James over Christmas, she included everything about Marcus. They were two weeks into her requested month of no contact and she still thought about him every day. She also acknowledged that her feelings for him were just as strong, maybe even stronger. She also told Maggie about her correspondence with Travis since the context of Marcus' jealousy over him would be lost without it. When she finished, she sat back with her half finished glass of wine and waited for the questions to start.

"Wow. I can't believe you went through all of that over the course of four months. It doesn't seem possible." Maggie gulped down the rest of her wine and left the room, returning with her glass refilled and the bottle. She topped off Sarah's glass before sitting back down. "I have so many questions and comments I'm not really sure where to start. I think, as your best friend, I need to start with Tina. I have to admit some natural jealousy that she got to be there for you through this and I didn't, but having met her at the memorial reception I can quickly forgive you. She's a doll, and I think I might be in love with her myself."

"She's always reminded me of you. I wished so many times I could tell you everything. I hated not telling you. I found myself often asking, 'What would Maggie say?' Your voice always came through loud and clear, even though you weren't there." Maggie rewarded her with a warm smile and took another sip from her wine glass before resuming her inquisition.

"Why do you think Elijah did all this? You mentioned others felt there was more behind his motives but what do you believe?"

"To tell you the truth, I don't know. If I dug deep enough I could probably come up with an answer, but I don't know what good it would do. He's gone so why stress out over something I will never fully have the answer to?"

"Have you opened his letter yet? It might have an explanation."

"No I haven't, and it's because I think you're right. I'm not ready to read what he has to say."

"What are you feeling about Marcus?"

"I miss him."

"Do you want what he wants?"

"A part of me thinks yes. But another part of me thinks that's crazy after only spending the equivalent of one month with him. I mean, there is an obvious attraction—"

"Ya' think? Girl, the chemistry between you two was shockingly obvious at the memorial. I mean he's almost painfully hot so an attraction is understandable, but what I saw was so much more. From both of you."

"But what if that's only because he's the first man to express interest in me since Nick?"

"Are you being serious with me right now?"

Sarah furrowed her brow at Maggie. "What's that supposed to mean?"

"Okay, so you've *always* been oblivious to the attraction you have on men. Half the men at the firm fell at your feet when you walked by, even when you were grossly underweight and took no attempt at your appearance. So other men *have* expressed interest but you didn't care enough to notice. And you can't sit there and tell me you seriously think you only feel the way you do about Marcus because you haven't dated anyone since Nick. I understand the need to be certain about your feelings, but don't lie to yourself."

Sarah ran a hand over her face.

Maggie's right. I'm just trying to talk myself out of my feelings because it's easier than facing the truth.

"Has he told you that he's in love with you?"

"No, not in direct words at least. However I don't think you ask someone to move for them unless you are. And it was kind of implied when he told me I already owned his heart."

"Do you love him?"

Sarah looked passed Maggie out the window. "Ask me again in a month." By then she will have talked to him again, and she would know more about her own heart as well as his.

"Are you sure you're ready for this?" Maggie held onto Sarah's elbow as they approached the house.

"Yes, it's time."

Sarah took a deep breath and unlocked the door to her home. She braced herself for the impact and was surprised when the force was barely a tremor down her spine. In the time she had been gone the house had taken on a different feel. It still looked like her home, but it didn't feel the same as it had before she left. She wasn't sure if it was because Travis living there had somehow altered the atmosphere, or if it was because of the progress she'd made. She looked around and memories of her past came floating back to her, but they weren't painful or suffocating.

She walked slowly through the house, barely registering Maggie following a few steps behind. She hesitated only when she approached Danny's closed door. She reached out a shaking hand and turned the handle, swinging the door open. She took a sharp intake of breath and tears stung her eyes. Her knees went weak, but she forced herself to remain standing.

I need to find a way to get past this. I promised Elijah and I owe him that much.

She stepped inside and then turned to motion Maggie forward.

"Are you sure?"

"Yes, it's time I stopped treating this room as a shrine." She turned and made her way over to Danny's bed and picked up Max. She closed her eyes, hugged him to her nose and took a deep breath, searching for any trace of Danny. It was gone. Her heart lurched and she finally sank to the bed. "I don't feel him in here as much as I used to."

"Are you okay with that?"

"Not really, but I know it's for the best." She closed her eyes and tried harder to feel his presence. They sat there for almost an hour before she finally stood, wiping her eyes. She walked with Maggie back to the door and turned for one last look before walking out. Next they headed to her old bedroom. She stood staring at the closed door for several minutes before finally putting her hand on the handle. Maggie spoke softly before Sarah opened the door.

"I'll let you do this one alone. I'll be downstairs and I'll check on you in a little while if I don't see you." Maggie gave her a hug from behind before she descended the stairs.

It's time to go in this room and cross another thing off your list.

She swung the door open before she could change her mind. The shock of entering the room after having avoided it for over two years was more acute. She barely made it two feet into the room before she dropped to her knees. The memories of her life with Nick came at her like a tsunami, crashing over her and pulling her in. She finally allowed herself to feel the pain of missing him for reasons more than needing him to help her through Danny's death. She grieved him for the man he was—her husband, her lover, her best friend, her confidant, her strength. It was time to fully acknowledge what she had lost and let go of the pain.

It was time to start saying good-bye.

CHAPTER 24

Sarah's phone rang almost exactly one month from the time she had kissed Marcus good-bye at the airport. "Hello."

"God, it's good to hear your voice." She felt a flush creep up her neck and cheeks at the sound of Marcus' voice.

"It's good to hear your voice as well."

"How are you?" She was surprised at how quickly she started telling him all about the month since she'd been home. She told him about her sessions with Dr. Cole and how she felt she was getting stronger each day.

"I'm really happy to hear that. I've wondered how you were doing. Actually, I've thought about you practically every second of every day for the last month. That's not so convenient when doing surgery, so I convinced my partner to let me only perform spays and neuters. I can do those in my sleep, so the distraction wasn't an issue." He hesitated. "I hope that doesn't come across as too pathetic."

"Maybe just a little, but would it make you feel better if I told you I experienced the same thing? Except for the whole spay and neuter part of course."

"It makes me feel like I'm on top of the world." She could practically hear his smile through the phone.

"Tell me what you've been doing in the last month."

"Besides thinking about you? Well, let's see. I worked of course. I took in another dog and two cats. All three have now made their way to new homes. Leanne and I went through the house." He paused again. "Thank you by the way. It meant a lot to Leanne, and I think it's possible you're off of her shit list as a result."

"I'm going to have to put that on my year end list of accomplishments. I never thought I would see the day that would happen." He laughed and it was a beautiful sound to her ears. She settled into the couch and they continued with easy conversation over the next two hours. The way they kept asking each other questions made it clear neither wanted to end the conversation. A month without talking had been difficult for both of them. Unfortunately Sarah's fatigue won out and she was unsuccessful at stifling a yawn.

"I should let you sleep. I forgot about the time difference. Can I call you tomorrow?" She liked the way he kept asking for her permission before calling. It showed he understood her need to go slow in their relationship.

"Yes, I'd like that." They arranged a time to talk the next day and said good night.

Sarah jumped at the sound of the doorbell.

He's here.

As she walked past the mirror in the foyer she stopped to check her appearance and internally scolded herself for the butterflies in her stomach. She took a deep, cleansing breath before opening the door. The man standing before her broke into a wide grin making her smile in return.

"Hi, Sarah, it's nice to finally meet you in person."

"Travis, hi, please come in." He stepped inside and they looked at each other awkwardly. He was about her height, light blonde hair cropped short and light blue eyes. He wasn't as striking as Marcus, but he was handsome in his own right.

Great, he's only been here for two seconds and already I'm comparing him to Marcus.

She shook her head to focus her thoughts. "Here, let me take your coat."

"I know I only lived here for a few months, but it felt strange to ring the doorbell. I had to stop myself from using the key out of habit."

She laughed. "I know what you mean. I caught myself a few times thinking of Elijah's home as my own."

And now it really is my home.

The reminder made her stumble for half a step. "Can I get you anything to drink?"

"Sure, what have you got?"

"Um, water of course. I made tea and I think I found a couple of your bottles of beer."

I've got wine too, but that would make this feel more intimate than I'd like.

Sarah was starting to get irritated with her already irrational thoughts. She blamed it on nerves. It was the first time she'd entertained a man alone in the house that wasn't Nick. Even though it wasn't a date, it felt weird.

"One of my own beers would hit the spot nicely." Sarah opened the refrigerator and retrieved a beer and a bottle of water.

"Shall we sit?"

Travis took a swig of his beer and it reminded her of sitting with Marcus at the restaurant in the airport.

Stop it, Sarah. Focus on Travis.

She turned abruptly, feeling like he would be able to read her thoughts, and sat down at the table. He walked over and took the chair adjacent to her.

"So, I heard about the situation with Kingston. It's pretty unbelievable. I assume you knew what was going on before you went out there?" Sarah settled back in her chair. It was a question she was getting used to hearing.

"Not before I left, but on the first day I met with Elijah he told me all about it. I had to sign a NDA though so I couldn't tell anyone about it, including Andy."

"It sounds like it was a pretty intense experience."

"Yes, it was. Elijah and I became good friends in the process. It was very hard. I miss him." She recognized the look on Travis' face and smiled. "I know it's hard to believe that he had a good side, but he did. I owe him a lot."

"Well, I'm glad it worked out okay for you. The whole office is still in a whirl with his passing. Some of the Kingston projects were put on hold for awhile, but now they're back in full swing and it seems as if they're determined to load us up past capacity. Kingston's daughter, Mrs. Troupe, visited the firm last week. I never had the opportunity to meet Kingston, but the unanimous conclusion around the office is that she's scarier than he was." Sarah smiled at the thought.

"Can you keep a secret?" He sat forward in eager anticipation.
"Absolutely."

"See this little scar here?" She pointed at a spot just under her eye.
"That's from Leanne's ring when she punched me."

"No freakin' way! She hit you?"

"When she found out about Elijah. She never really liked me from
the start and blamed me for keeping the truth about his condition
from her. She packs quite the punch so you don't want to provoke
her."

"Did you hit her back?"

"No, but I told her if she ever hit me again I would." He laughed
again and shook his head while taking a swig of his beer.

For the next several minutes they talked casually about things
going on at the firm. She had been home for seven weeks and still
hadn't been back to the office. As he talked, she stole glances at him
and found his appeal grew the more she was around him. He actually
reminded her a lot of Nick, and that was both comforting and
unsettling. The conversation shifted to his excitement over his
children's upcoming visit over the weekend.

"They're looking forward to coming, although I think they're
bummed I'm not still living here. The apartment's small in
comparison."

"I'm sorry—"

"No, no, don't. I didn't mean to make you feel bad. I knew from
the start the living arrangements were temporary. I just mentioned it
to let you know they really liked your house." He paused for a
moment and looked around. His eyes settled on the boxes stacked
near the garage door. "Are you planning to move again?"

She took a deep breath. "I'm actually packing up some of Nick
and Danny's things." Unspoken words hung over them like a heavy
weight. Travis gracefully checked his watch.

"Well, I hate to leave, but I need to get a few things done before
my kids show up tomorrow. Here are your keys and here's the
paperwork for some maintenance I had done on your SUV. Andy
took care of the payments, but I wanted you to have the papers for
your records." Sarah knew he could have easily given all this to Andy
at the office or dropped it by the door. However, she was glad he had
used it as an excuse for them to meet. Having a reason helped remove

the awkwardness of meeting in person for the first time. They stood and she walked him to the door, retrieving his coat from the closet. He stepped outside but turned to her before leaving.

"Well, it was nice talking with you. Maybe we'll see each other around sometime." He looked like he wanted to say more, but instead he waved before turning toward his car.

"Thanks for coming over to help me. I was determined to learn it all on my own, but I got stumped with this thing." Sarah kicked at one of the pieces of lawn equipment sprawled out on the driveway. It was a warm spring day and she had decided to address her lack of lawn care knowledge.

Travis laughed as he crouched down to pick up the object she'd kicked. "It's my pleasure. You should know you can call me any time for anything."

She had hesitated to call Travis. Even though they talked either via phone or email regularly, she didn't want to start a pattern of dependency on someone. She had pleased herself by figuring out how to start the lawn mower, followed by a successful mowing of the grass, but then got tripped up when she came across all the other lawn equipment. She had no idea how or when Nick used any of them. She researched on the Internet and was able to identify most of the items that currently occupied her driveway. But the Internet couldn't give her the confidence to use it. After attempting for an hour to start the trimmer, she'd decided it was best to sacrifice her pride rather than one of her fingers. Her original intent was to call Andy, but they were out of town for the weekend. Nearly twenty minutes of internal debate later, she finally called Travis and he came right over to help.

"Okay, so I know that thing is used to trim around things, like the landscaping walls, but I can't get it to start. I put gas in it."

"That's a good start. Has Andy been taking care of the lawn or have you hired it out over the last couple years?"

"Sometimes Andy would come by and check things, but he hired a service to do most of the work."

Travis stood while nodding. "It's my guess this thing has been sitting for awhile. It might need a new spark plug and the oil probably needs to be changed."

"Right, okay. Well, let's get to it."

He analyzed her for a moment, a smile on his lips that fluctuated between amusement and understanding. He picked up the trimmer, and she followed him back into the garage. He spent the next few hours patiently showing her all the ins and outs of the lawn equipment. It was knowledge overload, but at least she finally felt like she could hold her own. They worked together to get everything in working order and then he took her out to show her how to use the trimmer and edger. She was thrilled at how empowered she felt by the end of the day.

It was almost dinner time when they finished putting everything back in its proper place. She felt like she should invite Travis in after helping her all afternoon, but the thought made her feel anxious. It would feel too much like a date being alone with him in the house. However, they certainly were in no physical condition to go anywhere. She debated with herself for awhile and finally decided proper etiquette would need to win out over her fears.

"Thanks again, Travis. This has been extremely helpful. Are you hungry? I could make up some sandwiches."

That works. It sounded casual enough, not like I was asking him out on a date or anything.

He finished washing his hands in the garage sink and she took his spot to do the same. By the time she had finished he still hadn't answered.

Crap. Maybe I was wrong and he does think I'm asking him on a date.

He was looking down at the towel in his hands, folding it and unfolding it. He finally gave her his attention and handed her the towel.

"Actually, I have something else I need to do tonight. However, I was wondering if you'd like to go out to dinner with me on Friday?"

She swallowed the instant lump that formed in the back of her throat.

Now that sounded like a date.

"Like a date or something?"

He gave her a warm smile, settling her nerves. "Yes, but not *like* a date—I was thinking of an actual date. I understand if you're not ready or if you're not interested."

"Can I think about it?"

"Sure, okay, well... I'll talk to you later then." She walked with him out of the garage and he paused to look around the lawn. "You did a good job today, Sarah."

"Thanks." They said good-bye and she stood in the drive as he pulled away. She remained there for a few more minutes trying to figure out what she was going to do.

Sarah sat in bed staring at her phone. She had talked to Marcus for a few minutes earlier in the day since he had plans with some friends that night. She had been on edge since Travis asked her on a date and Marcus noticed something was bothering her. She could tell he was becoming worried that she was pulling away, so she decided to tell him about the date. Chewing on her bottom lip, she picked up her phone and typed out a message.

Travis asked me out on a date.

She held her breath and hit send. She knew he wouldn't get it for hours since he was out, and by then she would be sleeping so it would give them both time to process the situation. Her phone was ringing before she even set it down on her nightstand. Heart pounding wildly, she answered.

"Did you say yes?" Even over the loud noise of the restaurant behind him, she could hear a clear edge in his voice.

"I told him I would think about it."

"What's to think about, Sarah? You won't go on a date with me, but you'll consider going on one with him?" She could hear his heavy but controlled breathing on the other end of the phone. "Do you want to go on a date with him?"

"Not really, but I feel like I need to."

"Why?" His growing irritation was clear.

"Because I think it might help me understand my feelings for you. Help me figure out what I can offer you in our relationship. If what we have now is all I have to give or if I can, and want, to give more."

"Why can't you go on a date with me to figure that out?"

"Well, first of all, you're in Colorado. It's not like you can just drop everything and fly here for dinner."

"The hell if I can't." The edge in his voice was growing rapidly. "I'll book the first flight out on Saturday. What's your second excuse?"

Her list of reasons for why she couldn't figure out her feelings by spending time with him was rapidly dwindling, so she grabbed on to the one that scared her the most.

"I can't seem to think straight when you're around. My hormones start firing on all cylinders and I can't determine if my reaction is just physical or if it's something more. I'm envious that you're so sure of your feelings. But I'm not the kind of person who can be definitive on something as important as this after spending only a few weeks with you. I need time to confirm, validate, and test. I can't change my entire life if it's just a physical attraction." She felt near tears. Her words were more honest than she had intended, and she didn't want to hurt him.

"No, you need to have faith. You more than anyone should understand you can't predict the future. You have to leap into it with your arms open, and trust that I'll be there to catch you. It's that simple, Sarah. As to your question about whether or not this is just a physical attraction—we haven't seen each other in over nine weeks. You should be able to tell by now if it's just physical." He paused to let out a deep breath. "Please, go on a date with me before you agree to one with that Travis guy. If you feel you still need to go out with him after to confirm your feelings, then I'll find a way to deal with it."

She paused for a few seconds before finally pushing past her fear. "So I guess I'm seeing you on Saturday?" After they said good-bye she spent the evening thinking about what Marcus had said. She thought about how she felt with Travis compared to how she felt when she was around Marcus.

Marcus made her feel alive on so many different levels. She felt compelled to give him everything, even her darkest corners no matter how painful.

That was the root of it all. She didn't know if she could risk everything to pursue a life with a man that made her feel alive and scared in the same breath. A man she knew she loved and would be terrified of losing. A man who might have to face a horrible death at the hands of CJD. She didn't know if she could take the risk, or if she could only accept the comfort of something familiar. If she could only be with a man like Travis—a man she respected, but couldn't lose everything to because she couldn't give him everything to start with.

Sarah paced across the hotel lobby, her body racing with nervous anticipation. She shifted the overnight bag on her shoulder. Marcus had told her to bring at least three sets of clothes, and she smiled at what she thought he had planned for the day. She turned and all her thoughts disappeared. The sight of Marcus watching her from across the lobby quickly confirmed the spark was still very much alive. She smiled as he walked toward her, and she took the time to mentally debate how she should greet him. He ended her debate by swiftly pulling her into a hug. He released a deep breath as he pulled away.

"I've missed you."

"We talk every day."

"It's not enough." He looked her up and down and then settled his gaze on the pendant Elijah had given her. He picked it up and spun the stone with his thumb. "It still bothers me he knew you better than I did. I watched you toying with this while you paced the lobby. It really was the perfect gift. I just wish I would have thought of it first."

"You know there was never a competition between the two of you, right? His gift was thoughtful but so was yours. I love my phone and everything you took the time to put on it." He smiled and planted a lingering kiss on her temple.

"You look wonderful by the way. I didn't think it was possible, but you look more beautiful than the last time I saw you." She smiled and tried to fight the blush. She was almost back in the healthy range for her weight. She wasn't sure what to wear so she'd opted for dark jeans and a fitted top.

"You're pretty good looking yourself." She reached up and ran a thumb across his smooth chin. "You shaved." Her pulse fluttered when he rewarded her with his dimple induced smile.

"You like?"

"I like either way actually." She held his gaze.

If he keeps staring at me like that I'm going to lose it right here in the middle of the lobby.

"So, what's the plan for today?" Her question did the trick and he pulled away.

"Well, I had the whole day planned, but it's pouring outside so it's all about being flexible and going with the flow. Come, let me take you to your room."

"Wait, my room?"

"I booked the room next to mine so you can change between dates. I figured you would be more comfortable if you had your own room rather than using mine. It will also come in handy if you don't feel like driving home later tonight." He winked at her, taking her bags and her hand, before leading her in the direction of the elevators. Even though there was only one other couple in the elevator, he pulled her close until the doors opened on their floor. He tapped on a door as they walked but didn't stop.

"This is my room." They stopped at the next door and he pulled out a key card. "Here's your key. Just knock on my door when you're ready. What you have on is perfect for the first date I have planned." He handed over her bags and walked to his room before she could produce a single word.

She opened the door and stepped into a large suite. There was a huge bouquet of red roses on the coffee table in the sitting area. She walked over and picked up the card leaning against the vase.

I'm looking forward to spending the day with you—Marcus

She leaned down and held one of the roses to her nose before hanging up her garment bag. She searched her other bag for her make-up case and went to the bathroom. She touched up her powder and lip gloss and then ran a brush through her hair. She grabbed her purse and key card and went to knock on Marcus' door. He opened the door quickly and stepped aside, waving a hand to usher her in.

"Welcome to our first date." She hesitated and gave him a questioning look. "Don't furrow those pretty little brows at me. I told you we had to make some alterations for the weather." She stepped inside his room, which was the mirrored opposite of her own. He closed the door and took her hand, leading her into the sitting area.

"So, for our first date I had intended for us to walk around downtown but now that's not a possibility. I researched alternatives, but ultimately I decided what I really wanted to do was have an opportunity to be alone with you. I've popped popcorn and you get to pick the movie." It was all so simple, yet perfect at the same time. She felt her nerves melt away. She put her purse down on the small kitchen table and turned to face Marcus. The way he was looking at her caused a warm, tingling sensation.

"What?"

"I'm happy I've finally gotten the smile I've been waiting for." Her smile widened.

"I guess now you know all it takes is you, a movie, and some popcorn."

He tapped his forehead. "Yes, and now it's firmly locked away for future reference. Have a seat and pick a movie." After selecting a movie she kicked off her shoes, grabbed the bowl of popcorn, and settled into his side.

A movie and a change of clothes later, Sarah was ready for what Marcus called date number two. She was told to change into something nice but casual for an early dinner. She'd decided on the black slacks and silk blouse. She had a feeling she knew what he was up to and wanted to save the little black dress for the last part of their date. He was due to knock on her door any moment, and she paced the room in anticipation. She stopped again by the roses and ran a hand across the blooms. She felt her purse vibrate and retrieved her phone to find a text from Maggie asking how it was going. She responded and Marcus knocked on her door as she tucked the phone back in her purse. He had changed from jeans and a T-shirt into a darker pair of jeans, a white button down that hung loose, and a black jacket. Her eyes swept the length of him and when they settled on his face she saw his amusement at how she was checking him out.

She returned his smile. "You look really nice."

"I'm just trying to keep up with you. I like the way that color brings out the green in your eyes." Since the accident she had avoided wearing colors that accentuated the green in her eyes. It was the physical part of her Nick had loved most, and she wanted to hide it away from the rest of the world. Dr. Cole had helped her learn to accept that Nick would have wanted her to continue to show off the parts of her he loved most—both physically and internally.

He took her hand and led her to the elevators. The elevator doors opened to reveal a group of people laughing loudly. Marcus stepped back, intending to wait for the next elevator, but one of the occupants held the doors open.

"Come on in, there's plenty of room for both of you."

It was clear the group had decided to get a jump on happy hour. As the doors closed, she noticed the women in the group casually checking out Marcus. Her smile widened, thinking she couldn't blame them. She felt Marcus' arm tighten around her and she looked up at him when his thumb brushed her cheek. The way he was looking at her made her want to hit the button to return back to her room. Instead she looked away and noticed one of the guys looking at her. Leering was probably a more accurate way to describe it. The man's smile faded when he glanced at Marcus and he shifted uncomfortably, looking away. She turned her attention to Marcus and saw he was giving him the Kingston look of death, causing her to laugh. Marcus tightened his arm around her, and she noticed the corners of his mouth struggling to hold the firm line of the patented look—which made her laugh harder. Marcus finally released the poor man from his death glare and leaned down to whisper in her ear.

"How am I supposed to scare off the wolves if you distract me from being intimidating?" In that moment, filled with so much joy, she felt it. She finally knew what her heart wanted. The realization sent a tingling sensation down her spine and her heart racing. The scrutiny in Marcus' eyes told her he sensed a shift in her, but he remained quiet.

The elevator reached the lobby and Marcus led her out before the others, taking her in the direction of the hotel restaurant. The rain had slowed, but they'd decided staying in was their best option. They were seated quickly and since it was early the dining room was quiet, allowing them the opportunity to talk easily. When the dinner plates were cleared, they remained seated, finishing their drinks.

As Marcus settled the bill, Sarah stared into her wine glass. After her revelation in the elevator, she felt like every part of her senses had been heightened. With every look into his eyes, every whiff of his soap, every brush of his hand she felt like she was going to explode. He reached across the table and held her hand.

"Is everything all right?" She wanted to say it. She wanted to blurt it out right there, but it wasn't the right time or place. She wanted it to be special, not rushed. He deserved that much. She smiled, trying to shake her jitters and ease his anxiety.

"Yes, everything is perfect. I'm lost in thought that's all."

"Do you want to share?"

"Yes, but not right now." He gave her a curious look but didn't push her. He took a drink and settled back in his chair, still holding her hand across the table.

"Have you opened the letter my father left you?" She studied his face.

"No, not yet. I'm scared to hear what he has to say. I know I will at some point but I haven't been ready. Besides, I'm still mad at him for dying and leaving me the house. How about you?" He smiled and squeezed her hand.

"Same as you. I'm not ready yet." He downed the rest of his drink in one gulp and stood. "I need to get you back so you can get ready for our third date." Before turning to leave he looked at her empty wine glass. "If you have a few more of those, I'll look forward to carrying you up to your room later tonight." She could only blush in response, making him laugh.

As anticipated, Marcus had taken Sarah dancing for what he called their third date. The club had been busy with no open space to dance the way he was made to dance, but she was more than content to be held close as they let the music move them. He had held onto her the entire evening, letting go only once when she had to go to the bathroom.

Now they stood before her hotel room door. Not able to find a way to speak the words, she opened the door and stepped aside to let him walk past. He walked into the sitting room and stood with his hands in his pockets, his back straight as a rod. He looked nervous. She walked to the small refrigerator and took out two bottles of water, handing one to him. He took it, eyes locked with hers the entire time.

"I never thanked you for the flowers. They're beautiful." A playful smile touched his lips, loosening some of his tension.

"One dozen for each date." He took a drink of his water and trained his eyes on the bottle. "Sarah, I can't help but feel like you've been holding something back since dinner." She wanted to look away, but she forced herself to keep her eyes on his downturned face. This was an important moment and she wanted to remember every detail.

"In the elevator I finally realized what it is I want. What I need." She paused and waited for him to meet her gaze. She could see the uncertainty in his eyes and noticed he was twisting the water bottle in his hands. "It's you, Marcus. I need you. I love you and I—"

She couldn't finish because he was suddenly kissing her. Both water bottles had been absently dropped on the floor and he had her backed up against the wall. The kiss was much more desperate and passionate than what they'd shared at the airport. He pulled away and held her face in his hands.

"Oh, Sarah, I love you so much. I have wanted to tell you so many times but I was afraid you would have slapped me with a restraining order. I mean I've danced around it a few times and tried to make you understand how I felt without saying the exact words, but... oh who cares. Say it again?"

"I love you, Marcus." His eyes closed at her words as if they had taken all the air right out of him. He bent to kiss her again. The kiss was much softer than the last but just as passionate. She felt on the verge of losing control, and out of self-preservation she reluctantly broke the kiss.

"Marcus, I need to take this slow." He instantly put some distance between them, but still held her in his arms.

"Right, I'm sorry." He pulled her into a hug and she could feel his rapidly beating heart. "Does this mean you'll move out to Colorado? I could always move here if you needed to stay close to your family. Or we could move someplace new and both make a fresh start. I'll do anything so long as we're together." He slowly ran his hand up and down the length of her spine.

"I'd like to move to Colorado. I enjoyed it there. I just need to take this slow. I don't know when I'll be ready to move, but I will."

"It's going to be difficult to maintain a long distance relationship. Now that I know where we're headed I don't want to spend another day away from you."

"It won't be long, I promise. I need to let go of one more thing before I can fully move on." He didn't ask her to articulate. She'd already shared with him the things she felt she needed to let go of before she could move on with her life. Over dinner she had told him there was one more thing on her list.

"We'll make it work. I'm not going anywhere, and I want you to do what you need to do. We'll figure it out together." He kissed the top of her head before looking down at her, running his fingers down the side of her face. "Can I stay with you tonight? I promise to not even kiss you again if that's what you need. I just want to hold you and wake up with you in my arms." She nodded, finally accepting the love and happiness he was offering.

"Are you sure this is a good idea?"

"Andy, quit antagonizing her."

"I'm trying to save my arm hair, that's all." Andy ran his hands up and down his arms as if trying to rub out the memory of the last time Sarah tried to manage a grill. Just then, Travis stepped out on the back patio with the plate of steaks. He registered the laughing faces and paused.

"Did I miss something?"

"No, Andy was just being an ass as usual." Sarah took the steaks from Travis and hesitated before opening the lid to the grill. She refused to flinch, believing in her newly discovered self-confidence. Her friends settled around the patio table in conversation while she cooked the steaks. After a few minutes the conversation died away.

"Everything going okay over there?"

"Yes, Andy. You can put the fire extinguisher away now."

"Not until the very end darlin'. I still don't know how I got stuck with the last disaster while Nick was 'conveniently' in the bathroom."

"Is anyone ever going to tell me the grill story?" Sarah turned to face Travis at his question. Both Andy and Maggie were looking at her, acknowledging it was her story to tell if she wished to share.

"Nope." She turned back to the steaks.

Nick, you may be gone but I can still keep some secrets with you, right?

She felt warmth settle into her chest and she knew it was Nick telling her he was happy to keep her secrets.

"Alright, fine. Have I mentioned that's a really nice grill you bought?"

"Consider it a house warming gift."

"I can't believe you're moving to Colorado. I'm happy I get to buy your house, but I think we all wish you were staying." Sarah had told them of her plans at the start of dinner. Travis had looked like he'd gotten the wind knocked out of him. He wasn't aware of Marcus, just that Sarah needed to make a fresh start and she was choosing to do that in the home Elijah had left her. She had told Maggie the day after her date with Marcus. Maggie had cried, but she was excited for her just the same.

Sarah pulled the steaks off the grill and smiled in triumph. She turned to find her three friends on their feet, applauding to her success. She gave a mock curtsy and sat down to the best meal she had ever made.

CHAPTER 25

The doorbell rang and Sarah opened the door to a flushed Maggie.

"Okay, where is he? And you do know I've met Marcus before, right? Although, I admit we didn't really get a chance to talk. The memorial reception wasn't the right place for me to interrogate him and ensure he's worthy of my best friend. I warn you, today I'm not holding back." Sarah smiled. She had called Maggie and told her she needed to come over and meet the new man in her life. Maggie had dropped everything and rushed over.

"I have a feeling he's going to have you so smitten within the first two seconds you will have forgotten everything else."

Maggie waved her hand in the air. "He may be gorgeous, but I can handle him. Where is he?" Sarah led Maggie through the house and out to the back patio. Maggie looked at the patio table and back at Sarah in confusion. "Where is he?"

Maggie jumped as Sarah suddenly whistled. She barely had time to recover before she was playfully attacked by a bounding ball of fur.

"Maggie, this is Max. He's the newest man in my life." As if on cue Max enthusiastically licked Maggie's face. Maggie burst into laughter.

"You are so mean! I thought Marcus was here!"

"I know, sorry, I couldn't resist. However, I promise to invite you out to Colorado where you can spend as much time as you like giving him the third degree."

"Deal." Maggie crouched down and nuzzled Max's neck. "When did you get this big fellow?" She scratched him behind the ears, earning his eternal love.

"I've been searching for awhile and found him last week. I picked him up yesterday, on Danny's birthday."

Maggie nodded in understanding. "So this is it huh? You finally crossed off the last item on your list?"

Sarah looked at Max and crouched down next to Maggie. Max instantly tried to climb in her lap. Even as a puppy he was too big to accomplish such a task and almost knocked her down.

"It's finally done. I finally found a way to let go of Max."

"He looks just like Danny's Max."

"He does, doesn't he? Except this Max is full of life and adventure." Maggie pulled Sarah to her and kissed her cheek. This earned them both a sound face licking from Max, and they fell onto their butts in a fit of laughter.

Sarah looked out the window, spinning the stone of her pendant between her fingers. She was worried about Max in the pet hold area of the plane. However, Marcus had assured her that with the sedation he would only remember having a really good nap. Thinking of Marcus helped ease her anxiety. His fortieth birthday was a week away and she had made a rush of the moving process to get there in time. Deciding to sell her house to Travis had made things a lot easier than trying to put it on the market. She also sold him her SUV since it turned out Elijah had included his vehicles when he said she was to own everything in the house.

Even though she was primarily moving to Colorado to be with Marcus, she was planning to live in the house Elijah had left her. Marcus would be over an hour away, but he assured her they would work it out once she got there. She had taken Tina up on her offer of a job. Leanne connected with Tina to start a regional foundation to support CJD research and families of CJD victims. They both agreed Sarah would be the best person to lead the efforts.

Thinking about Elijah, she pulled his letter from her computer bag. She had finally read the letter for the first time the day after her date with Marcus. Since then, she'd read through it several times. She unfolded the letter and began again at the top.

* * *

My Dearest Sarah,

First let me mention that this is being typed by Miles. He knows all of this, so he can fill in any blanks my memory serves up. I've given him permission to edit my speech errors so you can understand what I'm trying to say. I'm actually having a good day today, I can feel it. It seems that for some reason God has decided to give me a Christmas miracle.

I know it will bother you that I instructed Miles not to give this to you until after I've died, but you know me—I like to have the last word. Don't be too hard on Miles for this (or the other surprises I left you)—he's just honoring my requests. I wish I could have explained this to you in person, but you haven't been ready. At the time of this letter you've made so much progress, but you're still so fragile. Don't scowl at the paper—you know I'm right. I've run out of time, so I'll have to be satisfied with a letter you will receive after I'm good and gone.

The main reason for writing you this letter is to complete the final item on my bucket list:
    Tell Sarah the truth

I have certainly stoked your curiosity, and I wish I were there to see your face. I love how your eyebrows come together when you're confused. Anyway, I'm sure you want me to get on with it—I know Miles does. I lied to you on the first day you arrived to meet with me about the project. It's one of the few things I remember from recent events. You asked me if there was really a project or if you were the project. I believe you also referred to yourself as a pathetic charity case. I'm sure I told you that you were neither pathetic, nor a charity case—that part was true. But I also told you there was a real project. That was the lie. You were the project.

Everything else I told you that day was true. I didn't want anyone to know about my illness, but it would have been easy to be a hermit with a private nurse and the help of Miles until I ended up in the hospital. As you surely know by now, I don't have much of a personal life so it wouldn't have been difficult. The gala would have been the only event I wouldn't have wanted to miss. Yet I don't remember it.

Sorry, I digress. Back to that first day.

I'd also told you that you reminded me of Lena and that I felt a fierce need to protect you. That was also true. It was the driving force for me to come up with the fake project to get you here. I'm sorry for lying, but I knew you wouldn't stay if you knew the truth. I'm sure you're wondering why.

It all started on one of my last trips to visit your firm, I don't remember exactly when. I don't even think you knew I was there. I remember walking by your desk on my way to Andy's office, and you were staring at your computer screen. The most startling thing about it was what I saw in your eyes, or more accurately what I didn't. They were completely void of expression and emotion, as if you were nothing but a shell sitting in the chair. That image of you haunted me all the way home and for the following weeks. In my dreams my mind transposed you and Lena, and I would wake up with an intense need to help you. My subconscious had merged you into Lena and Lena into you to a point where I could no longer separate the two of you in my mind. I would do anything to free Lena from the kind of pain you were suffering, and due to my mind merging the two of you into one it meant I had to help you as well.

That's what was in my heart. However, my mind was trying to be more logical. Sure I knew who you were and had kept track of your progress over the years, but I didn't really know you. I kept telling myself it wasn't my place to interfere and even if it was, what could I do? You would think I was a crazy person if I came up to you and started giving you advice on how to move on with your life. Then the idea of the project came to me. I figured the distractions would be good for you, but also the fact that I would become dependent on you to function was going to give you a reason to live. Again, I was hesitant to interfere and was afraid exposing you to the fate of my condition would make things worse for you. As I think you already know, even Miles tried to talk me out of it. In the weeks before my final visit to your firm, I think it was in October, I received several signs I needed to do this—for both of us. I'm not usually one to believe in signs, but these were obvious all I had to do was stop being stubborn and take a leap of faith. Once I finally allowed myself to see the signs for what they were, I knew the project idea was the right thing.

Some say we all have a purpose in life. I never felt strongly one way or the other on the subject until the day I saw you sitting at your desk, and the need to help you consumed me whole. Looking back, I recognize it as the day I discovered my purpose.

Here's where I have to stop letting you think this was a completely selfless act on my part. I'm no saint and I saw something in this for me as well. Staring at death's door really does make one think about their actions in life. After the colossal mess up with my children when Lena died, I felt I needed to make up for it somehow. I couldn't fix things for them and I was hoping to make up for it by helping you regain your life. My life for yours, so to speak.

So there's the truth. You were the project, my project, but you were not a charity case. You were my purpose. And even though I don't remember it all, I know you have made my final days some of the best of my life. That was an unexpected gift I will never be able to properly thank you for.

Now, I have something else I want to say. If I were in my right mind I probably wouldn't say anything, but I'm not so I have an excuse.

I heard you and Marcus in the dance studio this morning. I woke up early and heard you going downstairs. I figured you were going to run and I could already feel I was going to have a good day so I followed you hoping we could talk. By the time I got downstairs, I heard Marcus invite you in to watch him dance. I had to watch as well, and I'm so thankful for that gift. I know there's a chance I won't remember it tomorrow, but I will replay it over and over in my mind today and that will be enough. I should have left when he finished dancing, but I stayed to listen to most of your conversation. I'm sorry. Well, no I'm not—Miles don't write that last part. Miles, stop typing everything I say. Damn it.

Anyway, I should have gone upstairs but I was frozen in place, and I'm not sorry—I'm glad I eavesdropped. You see, there's my selfish nature again. And yes, there go your eyebrows again (I'm certain of it).

So, why am I glad? Because I never thought I would have lived to see the day when Marcus fell in love. When I watch the video of the two of you dancing at the gala, the connection between you is obvious. Based on how I fell in love with Lena it must not surprise you I believe in the kind of love that can happen in an instant—or really before you even meet. I see that between you and Marcus. I didn't believe Marcus was capable of loving someone in that way, and my first instinct this morning was to barge into the studio and protect you from getting hurt. I thought what I heard was Marcus being Marcus and he would try to make you a conquest and move on. I couldn't let that happen. But something made me stop and listen, and I couldn't deny the truth.

Marcus loves you the way I loved Lena. You're his perfect match.

Again, I don't think you should know this until you're ready and from what I heard you say to Marcus you're not ready. I hope you are by the time you receive this letter. However, before you can determine if Marcus is your perfect match, you need to make sure you're happy with living life—on your own. Take the time to go back home and see the beauty that surrounds you once again. When you can do that, then determine if you can love Marcus the way he loves you. I hope you can see what I see now, that you already do.

Just remember experiencing a new, different love doesn't mean the old one was inferior. Loving Marcus will not take away the love you held for Nick. The two types of love will enhance each other and will enable you to be happier than you have ever been before. I won't tell you how I know this, just trust that I do.

If you decide you want to be with Marcus, you have my full and enthusiastic blessing. I felt this was important for me to make sure you knew since I've shared some less than favorable details about him. I can see he has met his match and will be forever changed because of you.

Finally, the house. You should know by now I've left you the house. It's yours to do with as you wish, however I certainly hope you decide to move in and start the next phase of your life here. I know you're probably mad, but get over it. It's just a house and I like the idea of you living in it.

Thank you so much for all you have given me in my last few months of life. You're a remarkable woman and deserve the best life has to offer. Don't feel guilty about living, and being happy doing it.

I'll be sure to find Nick and Danny in Heaven and say hello, but after I find Lena first.

Elijah
(I can't think of an appropriate closing and I don't want to say good-bye)

ABOUT CJD
From Deana Simpson

I would like to take this opportunity to thank Carrie for helping to bring awareness to this real, fatal, devastating disease – Creutzfeldt-Jacob Disease (CJD). I appreciate her courageous spirit in following her dream (literally) and reaching out to ensure that she presents CJD in a factual light.

I am all too familiar with the devastation that this disease leaves in its wake for the person afflicted with CJD and the loved ones left behind. I have lost 13 family members over five generations to CJD (the genetic form), including my mother and my brother, and more are to come unless a treatment or cure is found.

CJD is a rare, fatal, neurodegenerative disorder with a peak plateau age of approximately 62 years of age and a life expectancy of less than one year. The CJD incidence rate is one case per million, per population, worldwide which equates to approximately 300+ new cases each year in the United States.

We all have proteins in our brain. CJD occurs when the normal proteins in our brain spontaneously convert to an abnormal 3-dimentional shape or configuration known as a 'prion' protein. Once a protein takes on the abnormal shape, it begins to convert other normal proteins to the abnormal shape and the disease process begins.

There are three types of CJD; (1) sporadic, (2) genetic, and (3) acquired.

(1) Sporadic CJD represents 85% of cases and what causes the disease to present itself is unknown

(2) Genetic CJD represents 10% of cases and individuals carry a mutation inherited from a parent. The mutation is a 'dominant' gene meaning it does not skip a generation. If a parent carries the mutation then the children of that parent are at risk of also carrying the mutation (the percentages varying based on type of mutation). The genetic form includes Fatal Familial Insomnia (FFI) and Gerstmann-Straussler-Scheinker Syndrome (GSS)

(3) Acquired CJD represents less than 1% of cases and can be acquired through contaminated neurosurgical equipment, dura matter transplants, corneal transplants, human growth hormones, and human gonadotropins. This category also includes variant CJD (vCJD) which is acquired through consumption of contaminated beef. Note that there have been no incidences of vCJD in the United States.

Symptoms start subtly and include memory loss, personality changes, unsteady gate and visual disturbances. Memory loss progresses to dementia, visual disturbances may progress to blindness, and the unsteady gate progresses causing the patient to fall. Other symptoms include involuntary movements (tremors, myoclonus, and seizure like activity), social withdrawal, depression, delusions and hallucinations. Eventually the disease takes over the body and leaves the patient completely dependent and unable to, move, talk, communicate, or carry out any activities of daily living. The inevitable outcome is death.

CJD is very difficult to diagnose because the symptoms resemble so many other diseases/disorders including Alzheimers, Parkinsons, Huntingtons, stroke and psychosis. Diagnostic tests are available and can be used, in conjunction with other parameters, to indicate the presence of CJD and include CSF Spinal Tap for the presence of 14-3-3 protein or tau protein in the cerebral spinal fluid, EEG, and MRI. Because the symptoms resemble other diseases/disorders, CJD cannot be diagnosed by the symptoms alone or one single test but rather one must look at the total picture and the progression of the illness. The one distinguishing feature of CJD is how rapidly it progresses. The only confirmatory diagnostic test is an autopsy.

Due to the rareness of CJD many physicians have never heard of CJD or have never seen a case. When they are presented with a patient that may have CJD they may not know to even consider CJD as a diagnosis. Due to how fast the disease progresses, having a diagnosis is extremely important so that (1) the patient can know and understand what is happening to them, (2) the patient can receive the care they deserve and (3) the family can spend as much quality time with their loved one before their memory loss progresses to the point they may not remember them. This disease brings with it a horrible stigma due to a lack of awareness and education that results in horrific responses from some physicians, clinicians, funeral home directors and the community leaving the patient and the family feeling alone and abandoned. We can stop this with awareness and continued education.

CJD is hardest on the family as there is absolutely nothing that can be done – there is no treatment and no cure. We are left to watch as life is drained from our loved one. CJD is a rare disease but I ask you; how rare is a mother, a father, a grandparent, a sibling, a wife, a husband, an aunt, an uncle or a friend?

For more information please visit the CJD Foundation website at www.cjdfoundation.org. I would like to acknowledge and thank all the researchers, across the globe, that are working very hard to find a treatment and/or cure for this devastating disease.

Deana M. Simpson, RN
Deana Simpson received her associate degree in nursing from Ferris State University, her BA Magna Cum Laude from Oakland University and is currently pursuing her Masters in Nursing. She started her nursing career at William Beaumont Hospital in Royal Oak, Michigan caring for patients on a medical unit. As computer technology became

more prevalent in the healthcare arena, she became involved in Healthcare Informatics. She currently works at St. John Providence Health System as the Chief Clinical Transformation Officer which involves setting the vision and strategic plan for integrating computer technology into clinical practice across the care continuum in order to reach optimal patient outcomes.

Ms. Simpson's involvement with CJD is one of a personal nature. Her mother died of familial CJD at the young age of 64 (1998), a brother at 57 (2012) and her family has lost 13 family members spanning five generations to the disease. Following her mother's death, she was compelled to provide support to other families afflicted with familial CJD by becoming the founder and director of CJD Insight.

Ms. Simpson partnered with Dr. Paul Brown to create CJD Insight. The objective of CJD Insight is to provide information about familial CJD and support to families impacted by familial CJD. She has corresponded with numerous families throughout the U.S. and other countries across the world. She wants to use CJD Insight to assure people that they do not have to feel helpless and alone when facing the realities of this horrible disease. As the CJD Insight logo indicates, we are "In this together."

Ms. Simpson is a member of the CJD Foundation Board, an active member of the CJD International Support Alliance, participates in fundraising activities for CJD research, and provides education to healthcare professionals and physicians through educational presentations and hospital grand rounds. She also co-authored an article with Florence Kranitz, "Using non-pharmacological approaches for CJD patient and family support as provided by the CJD foundation and CJD insight." CNS Neurol Disord Drug Targets. 2009 Nov;8(5):372-9.

SPECIAL ACKNOWLEDGMENTS
For Mom-II and Angie

I want to take a moment to give special acknowledgement to my stepmom, Merry, and my sister Angie.

Merry, you are one of the strongest women I know. While no child wants to experience the divorce of their parents, I was at least blessed in that it brought you into my life. You have taught me many things over the years, but mostly about strength. My only wish is that the circumstances under which you taught me these lessons could have been different. When we lost April and Bryhan, it was my first experience at losing someone so close to me. As I watched you overcome the pain of losing your daughter and grandson, I was inspired by not only your strength but also your faith.

Angie, my sweet 'baby' sis. I have wanted to protect you ever since I was a teenager and held you for the first time. As I watched you grow, I could tell the kind of woman you would turn out to be— funny, loving, caring, stubborn and strong. You were very young when April and Bryhan died. I held you and Jess in my arms, clinging to my two remaining sisters and wishing you didn't have to go through that kind of pain. Years later, I had to watch you go through something even more devastating. But like your mom, you have proven to have the strength to overcome the loss of your four month old baby—Kassi. I know you hurt every day and will continue to hurt for the rest of your life. I wish I could take that away from you.

You have both lost a part of your light, but you never gave up on hope or faith. Thank you for showing me the strength of a mother's heart.

ACKNOWLEDGMENTS

I never thought I wanted to write a book until a friend told me I could. A few weeks later, a dream presented me with a possibility. I took a leap and ventured into unknown territory to find a passion and purpose that will forever be a part of my DNA. I want to thank everyone who has helped me make this book a reality.

Thank you, Jaime Lewis, for telling me I could do this before I even knew I wanted to. Also thanks to the rest of my M&M girls who encouraged and helped me down this path—Phuong-Linh Nguyen-Fay, Melinda Patrick, Jennifer Sanders and Melanie Sandlin. You are more than friends—you are my family.

Special thanks to Deana Simpson. I feel fate has connected us through this book. Your willingness to provide comments based on your personal and professional knowledge means more to me than I can properly express.

Many thanks to friends and family who read the book and provided their compliments and criticisms: Kelly Babb, Tanya and Shawn Bauman, Kari Desnoyers, Eric Fay, Robin Gray, Linda Kozlowski, Steve Kozlowski, Emily McKeon, Lisa Pairitz, Allie Bringle-Posey, Beth Ramsey, Lara VanValkenburg, Brian Walters, and Amanda Williams.

Thank you to my daughter, Julia. You patiently put up with Mommy's writing and offered your creative mind from time to time. Thank you for also teaching me that the most enjoyable parts of a story are the cliffhangers and outtakes.

Finally, and most importantly, thanks to my husband, Jason, for supporting me through this journey—and for not laughing (too hard) when I first told you I was writing a book.

ABOUT THE AUTHOR

Carrie Beckort has a degree in Mechanical Engineering from Purdue University and a MBA from Ball State University. She spent seventeen years in the corporate industry before writing her first novel. She lives in Indiana with her husband and daughter.

For more information, visit my website at www.carriebeckort.com or my Facebook page at www.facebook.com/carrie.beckort

Made in the USA
Charleston, SC
19 March 2016